W. *A Novel*

STEVE SEM-SANDBERG

Translated from the Swedish by SASKIA VOGEL

THE OVERLOOK PRESS, NEW YORK

WOYZECK. Have you ever seen nature inside out, Doctor? When the sun stands still at midday and it's 's if the world was going up in flames. That's when the terrible voice spoke to me.

DOCTOR. You've an aberration, Woyzeck.

WOYZECK. The toadstools, Doctor, it's all in the toadstools. Have you noticed how they grow in patterns on the ground? If only someb'dy could read them.

Georg Büchner: *Woyzeck*

I.

At the Inquest of the Detainee

If we were to make a detailed study of the past life of the patient,
prior to the complete derangement of his psyche, we would perhaps
find that the key to the organic degeneration of the brain and of
the vessels lies in this life itself, in its wrong conduction, its excesses
and debauches.

Johann Christian August Heinroth, *Textbook of Disturbances of
Mental Life or Disturbances of the Soul and Their Treatment* (1818)

(Stab 'er stab 'er stab that Woost woman stab 'er dead . . . !)

she hadn't given her word, after all. But she wasn't there when he arrived. Neither was she at Warneck's or on Sandgasse where she rented a room from Frau Wognitz. She must have set off quite early that morning, if she'd even been home at night; and this was why he, for the first time, had decided to go there. Go where? the constable asked. To Funkenburg. To the garden restaurant. Perhaps she had wanted to get there early, to secure a table by the bandstand. But he'd heard from some acquaintances loitering at the old brewery that she had been seen earlier that morning on the Brühl, strolling arm-in-arm with a soldier named Böttcher, and he was already acquainted with this Böttcher, a tall and handsome fellow with a ruddy complexion, a bristled mustache, and whiskers. He had already seen the two of them together several times. Once in Bosens Garten. He had passed them at close range and decided against saying hello. But what would those two have cared anyway? They were walking arm-in-arm and Johanna only had eyes for this other man, was strolling and smiling at him, but not like she smiled at him, Woyzeck, the smile one offers a child or someone of lesser mind, no, her smile was frank, he might go so far as to call it forward, and there had indeed been something about her smile that made him seethe, because afterwards he wasn't sure if it was that same night or another or weeks later, he'd been so upset and despondent that he couldn't help but seek her out on Sandgasse despite her expressly forbidding him to do so, and then of course he didn't know whether or not she had been with that Böttcher fellow again or another man and neither did he have a chance to find out because her landlady Frau Wognitz had intervened with a broom and shooed him down the stairs, after which she appeared in a window and screamed for the whole neighborhood to hear *Get on home, Woyzeck, get on home: farewell, farewell . . . !* The constable has finally lost his patience with him. He wants to know how this relates to the murder weapon. Did Woyzeck have it in hand the first time he set out for Funkenburg, that is to say, in the morning? Or was it only once he realized that Widow Woost had instead chosen to be involved with this soldier what's-his-name? What was his name? He directs these last words to his subordinate, who quickly skims his notes and mutters his reply. Blöttcher, the man says, wetting the corners of his mouth with his tongue. Or did he acquire the weapon earlier? If so, how had he come by it? W. wipes his face with both hands. For the life of him he can't understand why they are so preoccupied with the weapon itself. He is trying to get them to understand that the blade from the saber had long been in his possession, it wasn't whole, more than half of it was missing and he had kept it in a leather-lined cloth bag but it was missing a hilt. Is this to say he had decided to carry out the act the moment he realized that Widow Woost was not going to keep her word and instead chose the company of that soldier, what was his name again . . . Blechner? No, that wasn't the case at all. I didn't decide anything, he says as calmly and quietly as he can. Everything had already been decided, you see, constable. It was like a giant's hand had grabbed me by the chest and afterwards it was like nothing had happened. I felt lighthearted, he says, staring down at his hands, which he is clasping in his lap. They've started shaking again. The constable also notes his hands. Let's return to the day in question, he says after casting a knowing glance at his colleague. And after you found out that Widow Woost was in the company of that soldier Böttcher, what happened next? Woyzeck runs his hands from his hairline over his forehead and eyes, then down his chin and neck. They're shaking even harder now, his whole body is shaking. He's trying to remember. The days blur. Actually in recent weeks he hasn't had a fixed abode, he's mostly been drifting, borrowing a few groschen when possible, sleeping indoors when he'd been granted lodging and outside on the days he'd found none. The nights *had* been warm and dry. Now the constable has definitely run out of patience. Did he have it with him during this time as well? he asks, meaning the saber blade. Woyzeck doesn't know what to say. Surely the constable must understand, one amasses things, it was only half a saber blade but he might have been able to barter it for something, like food. Never for an instant did he imagine it would be put to such use. And anyway after the fact he had forgotten it all. I had run into a few acquaintances down at the inn. The pharmacist and Bon, the butcher's shop assistant, and both of Warneck's apprentice boys. I sat with them a while because they were in the shade and were buying. So you were drunk at the time? No, not drunk! How could he explain this to them? It was like he had found himself in a place beyond thought. He remembers the wind high up in the linden trees, the light sweeping leaf-shadows across the still-empty tables, and on the ground below: the pattern made by those trembling leaves, and how he suddenly feels free of all that otherwise burdens and stifles him so. Empty, and almost weightless. The pressure of other bodies in motion that otherwise follows him wherever he goes, the voices, the screams, all this no longer concerns him. It is as though he were drifting between sleep and wakefulness, body as if sunk in torpor, and yet he is so bright and clear of mind that everything squeezes into him with the full force of perception; and at times he has thought that this is the only true state. Once his surroundings no longer concern him he is able to focus his attention on what he actually wants to remember, to think about Johanna's skin, where it is at its most naked and defenseless, behind her ear and down along the neck, the dip of her throat or between her shoulder blades. Her deep, dark laughter as she slowly guides him into her. Into the sweetness, hot and wet. But this he can't explain to them. He takes his eyes off the constable who keeps staring at him with an enjoining but nonetheless unsympathetic gaze and looks down at the hands in his lap, palms facing up. Murderer's hands. They've stopped shaking now. He remembers how the evening light lingered long after the church bells had chimed, like a greenish copper glow across the sky, protected by church spires and rooftops. Many people are out and about, all of them walking as though they could not possibly be separated from their shadows. Only she is shadowless. He sees her crossing Rossplatz, her gray-streaked hair gleaming in the last of the evening light. She is not walking with her usual brisk, determined steps, rather she seems to be encountering obstacle upon invisible obstacle and must veer aside, one arm flailing in the air. But she is alone. Her cavalier has apparently walked out on her or he has already had his way with her. She walks with her eyes on the ground and her mouth is large and crooked, lips parted on one side, as they so often are when she has been drinking, as though they had frozen in an aspect of tedium and scorn. Johann, she says when she catches sight of him and staggers sideways, but unvexed, unsurprised, too, as though she thinks it perfectly natural to find him here. And he wants to impress upon the constable that in this moment the saber in its sheath is forgotten. In this moment he could just as well have been standing before her stark naked, as he was when he emerged from his mother's wails, utterly pure and innocent. He says that he will escort her home and gently takes her elbow. And she does not protest, but neither does she yield to him nor allow herself to be led. Still he imagines that they are walking together as they once had walked, as they should walk, as he had imagined all day during his search that they would walk, arms linked and slightly inclined towards each other. Even though people had laughed at him. Are you out chasing your bangtail again? Where's your Woostie got to now? And he does not say he spent the whole day searching for her, he says nothing in fact; and all is as it was before between them, until they arrive at Sandgasse and enter her building, where she tears her arm free with a sudden, furious movement, as though he had been trying to steal it from her, and with her face close to his she screams *Stop following me everywhere!* Only then does he remind her of what she said, that she had promised to accompany him, not Böttcher, to the dance pavilion. He is calm and levelheaded, he doesn't even raise his voice. But she keeps shouting right in his face. He wants to grab her by the arm again, this time to calm her—they are standing inside the gateway and out on the street people have stopped to see what the commotion is—but she turns around and starts hitting him with her fists. He's standing in her way. She's screaming. He better get out of the way. Screaming. Still with that shrill senseless voice he doesn't recognize. And if now his hand reaches for the saber blade, then it is still without the slightest intention of using it. He wishes only to quieten her. But she keeps hitting him, hard now, and in the face, while trying to beckon one of the people who have stopped on the street, as though for succor (from him, he who has never wished harm upon her), and this is when he loses control of himself. He tightens his grip on the hilt and turns the blade so it is pointing up and when she leans forward as if to steady herself on his shoulders he drives it straight up with a mighty thrust. And if he then happens to keep thrusting, it is only to free the blade and push her away. And her eyes grow large and wide and open in surprise, and with a careful, almost trusting gesture she turns her torso, chest, and throat towards his, places both her hands on his shoulders and rests her head in the hollow of his neck. It makes him want to support her, tenderly support and carry her, but when he tries to catch her slowly sinking body, the mouth she turns to his is no longer a mouth but a great gorge from which dark black blood is welling. There is blood on his chest and on his hands. And out on the street every onlooker's face mirrors his own, evincing the same astonishment, the same dismay that the body in his embrace doesn't have the strength to stay upright and is falling to the ground. And with this, the saber blade can no longer be concealed. He looks at it, the others look at it; and he throws his arms in the air and staggers towards them with urgency, as though he wants to explain himself. But all they see is her blood on his arms and chest, and his grip on the saber blade, and they shrink back in horror. And in the distance someone shouts *catch him* and then he starts running, his strides long and lumbering, then faster, down Sandgasse and onto Rossplatz. Even though most people move out of the way others run at him, he sees them out of the corner of his eye, he hears a policeman's whistle blow, and he knows he must dispose of the saber blade, and then he sees the pond before him and he hurls the blade away without seeing where it lands, and they catch hold of him and at long last it is over, Frau Woost, his Johanna, is dead, the woman he loves above all else is dead and it was his doing and now she is dead.

HE IS ALONE IN HIS appointed cell. Light filters through the barred windows high up on the wall and during the day the hot air is so thick and suffocating he instinctively retreats to the shadow of a far corner. There he crouches for hours, legs drawn into his chest, scratching the cell walls until his nails are thick with dirt and mortar. The walls bear the mark of all who have sat there before him, obscene words and drawings he can't make out carved into the stone. It occurs to him that the bare cell wall is like slowly corroding skin, the prisoners' own skin. Many voices cram in here, as they do farther down the corridor where the other inmates are kept but his head is empty and remarkably lacking in resonance. He can hear buckets tipping over in the yard, and horse-drawn carriages being guided in under the arches, the wagoner's calls, the jangle of halters and chains as the horse is unharnessed and led to the stable. The sound dampens in the afternoon when the light in the cell fades and with the darkness he falls asleep without realizing it and sleeps the sleep of the exhausted the whole night through, empty and absent of thought.

At dawn when the light in the cell is still but a feeble gray grit the guard arrives with breakfast and replenishes the water and empties the latrine bucket. Breakfast consists of bread soaked in a ladle of milk and coffee. He eats and drinks without thinking, relieves himself in the stinking bucket in the corner and then falls asleep again, as the light wanders like a cupping glass across the riven skin of the cell. Once the light has passed the bunk on which he lies the guard returns with the midday meal, a bowl of watery soup with a few chunks of stringy meat and more bread. Though there are other guards, mostly there are these two. One is called Wolf and is a lanky, round-backed older man with a pointed nose and sunken temples who goes about his daily tasks in W.'s cell with his eyes to the ground and sure but somnambulant movements. The second is called Conrad and has a sizely, stark, candid face with round staring eyes below his arched eyebrows. His face seems to have been carved from wood. Conrad makes various attempts to engage him in conversation. When he has the morning watch, he can be heard whistling and humming and talking to himself long before he brings the morning meal with heavy, shuffling steps. This is the first time I've broken bread with a murderer, he says as he unlocks the cell door. He wants to know everything, every last detail. Did the murder victim resist during the deed? And if so, how violently? Did anything in particular cross her lips *as the death blow was being dealt*—they say that people can be very lucid in their final moments. And what type of woman was he, Woyzeck, actually dealing with; everyone knows what women are like, their lips say one thing and their hearts another, if they even have hearts, that is, and aren't all but wet sexes and sinful thoughts. But Woyzeck doesn't respond, he sits on his bunk staring at his hands. Murderer's hands. She was the gentlest, most angelic being I've ever known, he whispers. She had the noblest heart, always ready with a gift or a good word for the poor. Conrad looks at him with his expressionless wooden mask of a face. Whatever his thoughts or opinions on the matter, he does not betray them, just picks up the latrine bucket and leaves.

On his second or third visit Conrad is accompanied by his, Woyzeck's, lawyer and his confessor. Goodwill and Anguish, as he will henceforth call them.

His lawyer and his priest are brothers, but they are each other's opposite in almost every way. Mr. Hänsel, the lawyer, is a nimble and restless man. Unable to stand still, he paces forward-stooped as though the weight of his long torso were drawing the rest of the body to the ground, thus giving his head with its inquiring eyes a lizard-like aspect. His brother, Pastor Hänsel, is not a tall man by nature, but cuts an imposing figure, as though his calling had caused his body and soul to leaven.

While his brother, the lawyer, takes the floor, loses his thread, paces restlessly between the cell walls, Pastor Hänsel lingers in the doorway, as though stuck. His face is also stuck: in fact only his gaze expresses the discomfort he feels as it wanders between the prisoner (W.) and the cell door, where Conrad's face can still be seen through the hatch.

However, Mr. Hänsel, the lawyer, is full of confidence. Now he is saying that W.'s one-time landlord, the newspaper distributor Haase, has personally intervened on his behalf. At his urging, articles have run in newspapers and petitions have been drafted. In of his unfathomable goodwill Haase has also affirmed that not just he, but also several of his acquaintances and friends can be called upon to testify that W. is fundamentally of a calm and peaceful nature and could not possibly have committed such an atrocity other than in a state of extreme befuddlement.

As long as W.'s case is soberly examined, he can be assured the best possible outcome!

But even as the lawyer offers these reassurances his sights are already set elsewhere. He bangs the cell door with one arm to draw the guard's attention. But Conrad's face is already in the hatch, as though he and the hatch were a painting that had been hanging there for decades.

So Goodwill leaves, but Anguish remains.

Pastor Hänsel looks at him smiling widely, but not enough to hide his distaste.

Hänsel (the pastor). I can do nothing about the misfortune that You have brought upon Yourself, but perhaps I can advise You in Your great aberration.

W. is holding his hands in his lap. When he opens them he feels that they are two open wounds. What to do with hands that have become wounds? They are good for nothing, but neither can you be free of them. He looks to Pastor Hänsel, and his gaze must have harbored an appeal, for the priest's stiff airs seem to soften, if but for a moment.

Hänsel (the pastor). I have come to advise You in your great aberration and unease, Woyzeck. And if possible, minister to Your pains.

(Johanna, Johanna . . . !)

Hänsel (the pastor). Have You ever asked Yourself *what did God intend with me?*

Days, weeks pass in this way.

One morning Conrad arrives with two other prison guards, and Conrad tells Woyzeck that it's time to pull himself together because he has a distinguished visitor.

Conrad speaks with his lips stretched into a wide grin, as if he in fact meant something quite different, and it strikes him that there will be no judicial investigation, he won't even receive a verdict, they will do away with him as they do unserviceable animals, a slit throat or a shot to the back of the neck. And for the first time since he was brought here, he feels something of his old resentment growing inside him again, the shame of those forever treated unjustly who are never given a voice of their own, never given pen and paper to write to their nearest and dearest or even a chance to set things right before leaving this earthly life, and God knows he has debts to repay.

But when he tries to say this, to Conrad who in the first instance is nearest to him, the guard hits him hard on the head and wrenches his elbows behind his back. Thus joined, prisoner and guard stumble through a long corridor, up a flight of stairs, and into an interrogation room. After a moment he realizes this is the very same room to which he was taken a few weeks prior. But this time it is filled with divers gentlemen. Mr. Richter, the prison commandant, is in the room, as are the two constables who first interrogated him. Behind his lectern a clerk stands frozen, as if frightened to death. There to the prison doctor, an elderly corpulent man with bristly eyebrows who the others address as Dr. Stöhrer. The lawyer Hänsel is present, too, tall body bent by angst, smile fleeting.

The center of this congregation, however, is not made up of any of these gentlemen, but an elderly man who, because of his modest size, is hard to discern in this crowd of uniformed guards and policemen.

Herr Hofrat Clarus, the court councillor, is here to examine You, says Prison Commandant Richter after the tumult unleashed upon his arrival has subsided somewhat and he has been pushed towards this diminutive personage. You are asked to remove Your prison clothes.

Two guards step forward to take off his clothes. Instinctively, he cringes at their touch. It's his old instinct roused, the one that befalls him when he is in the midst of too much movement and fears blows or reprimands. Suddenly he loses his sense of everyone in the room, they tumble into each other like skittles. His whole body is shaking, but the guards are resolute. One of them restrains his hands, the other pulls down his stained trousers and draws his smock over his shoulders and head.

They have now formed a circle around him, and he is in the middle: naked, trembling. Like an animal. Some are laughing out loud, others stare shamelessly at his crotch, over which he is pressing both hands. Others avert their eyes as though the sight of him in all his animal misery has now become overpowering.

The only man from whom he, and everyone else, seems to fall out of sight is the diminutive councillor. As W. was being undressed, Clarus opened a large black bag with a brass lock, which he placed on the middle of the desk and from which he, with no apparent haste, is now unpacking various instruments. Clarus grabs hold of his arm, takes his pulse at his wrist and the side of his neck, looks into both his eyes, listens to his breathing with a tube pressed to his chest and back, squeezes and presses wherever he can, including his head.

There. Now can Woyzeck describe the voices he claims to have heard? And with which ear?

Laughter in the room.

And what sort of sound did these voices produce?

More laughter, excited conversation.

Was it a rumbling, or—how was it put?—"wetter" . . . ?

And when he looks confused, Clarus repeats every word, very slowly and with exaggerated arm gestures, as though he were in fact hard of hearing.

Was it with *this* ear? Or could it all have been up here?

Clarus knocks on W.'s skull above the left ear and when W. defensively wraps both arms around his head, several people in the room start laughing. A grin, if a bit strained, tugs at the corners of even the councillor's mouth, as if to reveal that he does understand their amusement but his sense of duty and professional honor prevents him from openly partaking in it. Once the laughter has waned, he stretches to his full insignificant height and clears his throat with a serious expression.

You may all leave the room now so that the delinquent and I may speak in private. The clerk may stay.

Amidst continued mirth, the interrogation room crowd departs, while the clerk remains at his lectern, hesitant and afeared. With certain ceremony, the councillor installs himself behind the desk and puts the examination instruments back in his large bag. Within reach of his seat at the desk is a small bell linked by a cord that runs along the ceiling to a similar bell in the adjacent guard room so that he can call for help should the delinquent become violent. But the councillor appears to fear no such eventuality. He regards W. with scrutiny, not curiosity, at once insistent and indifferent. Finally, something like a smile appears on Clarus's dry face. It is not a smile exactly, rather more like the skin of his face is cracking open to bare a smooth row of teeth.

The detainee may take his seat, the councillor says, and directs W. to the chair that has been placed by the desk, and the second W. sits down, the clerk readies himself behind the lectern.

Clarus. Your lawyer Mr. Hänsel has had the good sense to apprise me in advance that the detainee is of a calm and peaceful nature. Fundamentally. Is this observation consistent with the truth?

Woyzeck. I don't dare comment, Herr Hofrat. It's for others to—

Clarus. The act You have committed must thus have taken place in a state of sudden unconsciousness. In brief: You must have lost Your mind. To commit a deed of such bestiality and with no sign of remorse, and moreover for all to see, cannot be explained otherwise, or what says the detainee?, provided You were not intoxicated at the time, and the two constables who arrested You assert that You were not, at least no more than usual? Is this correct? Were You under the influence of intoxicants?

Woyzeck. No.

Clarus. Can we then commit this to the record: the criminal has no idea how or why he committed this act and intoxicants have no bearing on the matter at hand?

Woyzeck. (. . .)

Clarus. Does the delinquent feel any shame at all or rue the heinous act he has committed?

Woyzeck. (. . .)

Clarus. Would the delinquent please look at me when he answers.

Had there been a smile on his face it is now gone. He dips his pen in the inkwell and writes. Then he rings the bell without looking up from his papers.

The guard is quick to arrive.

Clarus. That is all. The delinquent is dismissed for today.

BUT PERHAPS THERE IS SOME truth in what Clarus has surmised. Guilt refuses to settle in. He feels empty, almost weightless. Not having to keep her in his thoughts day in and day out comes as a relief. But before long the relief gives way to a feeling of unreality. After all, this could have taken a different course. He starts thinking about how it might have been had he not set out to find her that day and instead had waited at Funkenburg, like he said he would. And why did he *have* to procure a hilt for that broken blade? Not to mention running around with it like a fool, mocked by those watching him come and go and asking for her again and again, without having the slightest idea of where he was going or why. Had he simply settled down and stayed put, what then? Would she have come to him, as she had done before, once he stopped trying to steer and command her? She did always come, sooner or later. The more he thinks of this, the greater his distress. It was only to escape the stranglehold of anguish that he was charging around like a madman, as if he were one of the animals inside the baiting cage being driven on by the master of the hunt. The master of the hunt had a long staff with a crook at one end so that the desperate and hungering animals couldn't get close enough to bite him, and in this manner Henze toured kingdom and country with his wild-beast baiting show and people everywhere were persuaded to stake their last coins for a chance to see the miserable animals trampling around inside their cages, even though everyone knew that they were far too lost and starved to go after the prey that had been placed out so enticingly for them. Surely they must have placed bets on him too, up at Funkenburg, while he was running around with his pathetic half saber blade. *Will the panting fool drive out his trollop in time?*

He scrapes at the wall in an attempt to conjure her face one last time. But the image of her is tarnished, lacerated, and it is he who cut it to pieces, bit by bit, and he screams out in agony as the emaciated vixen had shrieked when the trapdoor opened beneath her, foremost among Henze's hunting beasts, and she got stuck, caught by the neck, while the spectators, roaring with rage, thrust poles and cudgels between the bars to incite the poor animal into motion again.

Always in motion, never at rest.

Then the lock rattles and someone says his name out loud. It is spoken so clearly that at first he does not recognize it and when he opens his eyes neither does he recognize the cell, familiar only are the guard Wolf's chiseled face lowering itself over his and the hands pinning his flailing arms to the bunk.

Can we have a light? a surprisingly deep and mild male voice says from elsewhere in the cell.

The prison chaplain is paying you a visit, Wolf says and releases his grip.

But W. has already recognized the priest by his soutane and rounded hat.

Doesn't he have a candle? the priest asks and steps forward. Well, then get him one right away!

Wolf opens then locks the cell door behind him and his heavy, shuffling steps disappear down the corridor. W. doesn't know what time of day it is, if it is late in the evening or early in the morning, and not knowing fills him with unease. Who has called the prison chaplain? What did he say or do to prompt this visit? He can't recall, and what's remarkable is that neither can he remember what he was doing before he fell asleep or even how long he's been sitting here, it could be days, weeks, or months: time has no hold on him. All he knows is that it's cold and his skin feels almost numb as he rubs his fingers over his face.

The shadows on the wall part like a curtain being pulled open, and Wolf appears with a candle. He hears the voices of the other prisoners in custody, the clatter of bowls and cutlery. So it must be early morning. But not yet light outside.

My name is Pastor Oldrich, says the prison chaplain in a mild yet penetratingly deep voice. Presumably you don't remember, but you called for me.

In the light of the candle that Wolf set down on the edge of the bunk, he can see that the prison chaplain is very young, the skin on his clean-shaven cheeks shiny and red with cold. He can't be more than aught and twenty years old, but he is tall and towering, standing more than a head above W.

Pastor Oldrich. I understand that you are in agony over what you have done.

W. (. . .)

Pastor Oldrich. No one becomes a murderer of their own free will. God would never allow it.

W. And yet it came to pass.

Pastor Oldrich. So perhaps you did not act of your own will, you were beside yourself, in the hands of something you could not control.

W. I have done wrong, I have broken the law, I know it.

Pastor Oldrich. I do not speak of the law, Woyzeck.

W. It was as though a giant's hand grabbed me by the chest.

Pastor Oldrich. You acted against your own will, Woyzeck, and in this sense against God's higher reason, too. Why would God want anything for the beings he himself has created but what is wise and decent and right, what even poor people like you harbor a yearning for . . . ? Try to bear this in mind, Woyzeck.

W. (. . .)

Pastor Oldrich. God receives and forgives even those who have strayed from the path of reason, as long as you feel sufficient remorse and regret for your actions there is no shame in admitting to it. You *are* a literate man?

He plucks a Bible from the wide soutane, neatly parts the skirt and kneels in front of the bunk and signals for W. to do the same. Read along with me, he says and puts his finger to the top of one of the pages he has opened. The candle's flickering flame leafs through the room as if it too were a book.

Pastor Oldrich. "I sought the Lord, and he heard me, and delivered me from all my fears."

W. . . . and delivered me from all my fears.

Pastor Oldrich. "This poor man cried, and the Lord heard him, and saved him out of all his troubles."

W. . . . and saved him out of all his troubles.

Pastor Oldrich. "The Lord is nigh unto them that are of a broken heart; and saveth such as be of a contrite spirit."

W. . . . and saveth such as be of a contrite spirit.

Pastor Oldrich. "The Lord redeemeth the soul of his servants: and none of them that trust in him shall be desolate."

W. . . . and none of them that trust in him shall be desolate.

He looks up because he thinks prayer time is over. But the priest is still kneeling, forehead to the bunk, and in the flickering light he looks down on the priest's exposed neck. The back of his neck is oddly white below the hairline and far too vulnerable now that he has removed the rounded hat. I too will one day be in this position, as exposed as he is before God's sword, he thinks.

Amen, the priest says and rises.

W. tries to rise as well. But his legs buckle and he stays on his knees by the young priest's side as though he were begging him for something. The priest smiles as one smiles at a child's prank, grabs him by the shoulders and helps him to his feet.

Pastor Oldrich. Now, Woyzeck. Perhaps we were not meant to crawl around in the dirt like harmless animals! You too were probably destined for greater things, in spite of this unfortunate turn.

Then he makes the sign of the cross and W. keeps his head bowed and receives the blessing. All the while Wolf has been in the cell, waiting; now he locks the cell back up and disappears down the corridor with Pastor Oldrich. In the meantime it has become brighter, bright enough for the cell walls and their carved and gutted faces to close in again.

A FEW DAYS LATER HE is brought back to the interrogation room. Doctor Stöhrer and Councillor Clarus are already inside when the guard admits him. This time it's Stöhrer who is conducting the examination, while the councillor sits motionless behind the desk. Stöhrer measures his pulse and heartbeat, listens with the long tube in his ear and palpating around and on top of his pate. He then walks over and whispers something in the councillor's ear. Clarus makes one or more hasty annotations, then gestures for the doctor and guard to leave the room and for Woyzeck to take a seat in the chair that the guard, under Clarus's supervision, has placed a few arm's lengths from the desk. Still having offered no greeting, Clarus uses his quill pen to point to a cord that runs from the desk along the wall of the room and the cornice to the bell on the other side of the door.

In case the detainee causes any mischief, he says. Or decides not to answer my questions politely and correctly.

Clarus has a way of craning his neck and jutting his head out of his collar that makes him look like a little turtle. That wizened face even attempts what must be meant as a smile but most resembles the sharp rim of a wound inside which a row of small teeth, as gray as his face, are revealed. With a surprisingly gentle, almost intimate tone, he explains that their conversation now and hereafter should not be regarded as an interrogation in the proper sense, but has the purpose of clarifying the state of mind the detainee was in at the time of the act. The detainee should therefore feel that he can speak freely and from the heart, without risking reprimand or punishment. It is in the interest of both parties that he account for the details of the case with as much economy and clarity as possible.

Clarus. Now about these voices that the detainee said he heard during both police interrogations on the fourth and seventh of June, did he hear them directly in conjunction with the crime, or at an earlier or later time?

The councillor looks at him with his head tilted and his brow set in furrows as though meeting each word with disbelief, which elicits a desire to comply and make amends. Therefore he begins by saying that he had neither heard voices on the day in question, nor earlier. All this must be due to a misunderstanding, Herr Hofrat. There were so many people around, and there was a band playing, perhaps not right away but later in the day. And besides it was a hot day and it's common knowledge that on a hot summer's day voices can easily be carried far and wide. Furthermore, he knew many of the people who had spoken to him, he says and expounds on this theme. This, even though he notices the furrows on the councillor's forehead deepening with each word he speaks until finally the man holds up one hand as though to ward off all this volubility.

Clarus. The detainee need not be prolix, simply give a brief and direct account of the immediate circumstances surrounding this alien voice.

Woyzeck. I'm not sure I can.

Clarus. You stated at the police interrogation that You heard a voice that said *[reads]*: stab 'er, stab 'er good and dead . . .

Woyzeck. That may be. I can't recall.

Clarus. On what occasion were these words spoken?

Woyzeck. I do not recall, Herr Hofrat.

Clarus. Can You at least try and recall when You last heard these voices?

Woyzeck. It must have been when I was staying with Haase, the newspaper distributor. He put me up in his attic. A chimney divided the attic in the middle, and then it was like rustling on the other side of the chimney wall.

Clarus. Like rustling?

Woyzeck. Yes.

Clarus. And can the detainee elaborate on this rustling?

Woyzeck. Like the sound of twigs and branches in the wind.

Clarus. You mean here, by the ear?

Woyzeck. I cannot go into further detail, Herr Hofrat. It came a bit from every direction all at once.

Clarus. Perchance You thought that this bit of muslin, the surgeon's widow, was on her way to You as You related earlier in the course of the interrogation.

Woyzeck. No.

Clarus. These sounds, voices, or rustling You say You heard, were they always in conjunction with Your thoughts of the widow Woost or did You perceive them in other contexts as well? If so, can You state in which context it was?

Woyzeck. I remember clearly, once a voice said *come on then* and *your time has come.*

Clarus. And how does the detainee suggest these words be inter-preted? As an exhortation to commit the act?

Woyzeck. No. Not at all.

Clarus. As an exhortation to take Your own life?

Woyzeck. I do not know how the words were meant to be interpreted. That is the God's honest truth, Herr Hofrat.

Clarus. Now now, calm down. Can You as concisely as possible account for when and under which circumstances this occurred?

Woyzeck. I don't quite remember, Herr Hofrat. It could have been a few months prior.

Clarus. Prior to what?

Woyzeck. Prior to what happened, Herr Hofrat. What—

Clarus. Did You enter into conversation with this rustling voice?

Woyzeck. No, they were statements plain and clear, Herr Hofrat.

Clarus. In Your left ear as well?

Woyzeck. Yes.

Clarus. Would You say it was exclusively through Your hearing that You perceived this, or were Your other senses also involved. Sight, sense of taste, or smell.

Woyzeck. I don't understand, Herr Hofrat.

Clarus. Did You see anything as You were hearing these voices?

Woyzeck. Yes, there ... I don't know ... I suppose one always sees things.

Clarus. I'm referring to this specific occasion.

Woyzeck. I don't know if You've ever noticed, Herr Hofrat, but on certain days the sky is full of light even though there is no sun in the sky.

Clarus. [making notes] Is this what the detainee observed on this occasion?

Woyzeck. Someone told me it was the Freemasons, that they have the power to take the sun from the sky and still it will be as bright as in broad daylight.

Clarus. Now where are these ideas about the Freemasons coming from?

Woyzeck. I suppose it's the kind of thing one hears, from the people one meets. Someone I was in the service of, a nobleman by the way, said that their powers are so great all they have to do is put a needle to your heart and you drop dead. My father said so, too.

Clarus. Your father?

Woyzeck. My father was a God-fearing man, make no mistake, Herr Hofrat, honest and upright in all things; but he always believed there was more to fear from the servants of the faith than from those who only have eyes for money and credits.

Clarus. The priesthood? Was he opposed to the priesthood?

Woyzeck. My father believed that our world is created in such a way that there are those whose lot it is to toil and those who possess higher knowledge and power, but that these men join together in secret societies to ensure that nothing of what they know reaches anyone who is undeserving of this knowledge.

Clarus. In truth?

Woyzeck. When you see black angels crossing the sky, it's a sign, he always said. One day I dreamt it. I was out on a large barren field, it was evening and the sky was still bright; but suddenly there came a great roar and two black wings beat across the sky, and it was like when you pull a curtain over a window because it went dark like in the darkest night and in the sky were three glowing lines. The one in the middle was a bit bigger than the other two. That was the sign.

Clarus. What kind of sign?

Woyzeck. The Masonic sign: God our Father, with Jesus Christ and the Holy Ghost sitting on either side of Him. It's how they greet each other.

Clarus. So this is supposed to be a greeting? Would he care to show me how it is performed?

Woyzeck. I dare not, Herr Hofrat.

Clarus. But You have before. You've done so in secret. Don't force me to convict You of perjury.

Woyzeck. Yes, once, and it came to a terribly unhappy end, Herr Hofrat. It was in Stralsund, after I levied with the Swedes. I had been ordered to bring a captured soldier to the adjutant's quarters, then I was to stand guard at the door in anticipation of the adjutant's arrival. It then occurred to me that instead of the required military salute I might make the Masonic sign to see if the adjutant was a Freemason, and when he appeared . . . I assure Herr Hofrat: it was not in earnest and not premeditated. The adjutant walked past me, and as if by its own force my hand flew up, and thus I made the sign. For a moment it seemed as if the adjutant was about to give me a hiding. I can assure Herr Hofrat that never in my life have I been so afraid. But then the adjutant invited me in, poured me a glass of red wine and said that if you know something, you must well say it. That's exactly how he put it. And then he said I should go . . . Afternoons were for drills and as the drill was about to begin, the adjutant arrived and I heard him tell the field usher to let him know if he started coughing up blood. He meant me, Herr Hofrat; I could tell by the way he was staring at me. And we had barely resumed the drill when I felt something like a needle prick my heart and it felt like my blood was being shaken around my body like in a bottle, and then I felt what I thought was a blow to the neck and that's all I remember, all I know is that my comrades carried me away unconscious. That's what happened, I swear, Herr Hofrat, I do not exaggerate.

But Clarus isn't listening. He has reached across his desk and is tugging at the cord that runs into the guard room. Outside a bell jangles and soon a guard appears in the door.

Clarus. Would You ask Doctor Stöhrer to come in?

The doctor is there in an instant, as though he had been waiting behind the door. Again a large black bag is opened and instruments of various sizes are taken out. W. stands on command and undresses, though without understanding what all the fuss is about. Silence. Doctor Stöhrer listens through his tube. The councillor makes notes.

Doctor Stöhrer. There is nothing wrong with this man, Herr Hofrat.

Clarus. [without looking up] Well then. In that case, the delinquent is dismissed for the day.

At the Inquest of the Detainee (1)
Regarding his external and physical health:

Gaze, countenance, posture, movement, and speech entirely unchanged, complexion somewhat more pallid for want of fresh air and exercise; no remark on respiration, skin temperature, and tongue.

In addition the detainee affirms that his sleep is calm and peaceful and free from troubling dreams, that he has a good appetite and his bowel movements are regular. The two latter conditions have been confirmed by Prison Commandant Richter who adds that W., during his stay in his cell, has not once complained of indisposition.

In contrast hereto I noted that the tremors running through his body which I'd observed during the first minutes were protracted, in particular when my visit was unanticipated, and though pulse and heartbeat were indeed steady and regular, they were harder and faster, and the pulse, when examined over the course of our conversation, remained somewhat agitated and the heartbeats were more intense and palpable and more vigorous than in a natural state. Though when he, as once occurred, was apprised of my arrival half an hour in advance, I observed such changes to a far lesser extent.

ALL THAT CAN BE HEARD in the room is the rasping of Clarus's quill as it moves across the page, him dipping it in the ink pot, and continuing to write. Then he rests his pen in its stand, knots his fingers under his chin, and looks at him, which unsettles W. What is happening? Is he meant to confess his want of reason to the councillor now or is there a different aim?

But on this day Clarus seems to have taken an interest in W.'s person and wishes to question him about his apprenticeship. According to the record You are to have spent some time with a wigmaker by the name of Stein. Is this correct?

It was after Mother's death, he says, and as if by way of apology: not much came of that apprenticeship, I mostly kept an eye on the children.

And Your father?, the councillor says and rakes the table as if his fingertips were claws, the one who rebelled against the priesthood, a ne'er-do-well like yourself, one may assume!

Yes, what is there to say about this father? Stephan Majorewsky *Woyzeck*, or *Woyetz* as he preferred to be called. It sounded more French. And as fine-limbed as the French he was, but clumsy of gesture and forward stooped, the incline steeper the faster he walked. He had small, slender, sensitive hands, the same as his son's. And something about him, an abiding zeal, a desire to please, roused the trust of customers and appealed to those with whom he caroused. He was called the Polack and could sometimes, his face flushed with intoxication, launch into dreadful harangues in his childhood tongue, of which the son had only learned fragments, single words or expressions, such as *proszę państwa, co u pana słychać*, and *kurwa*. (The latter was but one of many profanities that he tossed out when unobserved. When he knew others were watching or listening nary an ungodly word crossed his lips, then it was all smiles and a wet ingratiating gleam in the eye.)

It was the father who insisted that the children go to school; for the mother was indifferent to all but the most concrete things. Through the mediation of an influential customer, Majorewsky had managed to get his oldest children into the Ratsfreischule school at the foot of Pleissenburg, the old fortress barracks. They accompany each other to school each day, he and his sister. One morning as they are crossing Marktplatz snow begins to fall straight down from the sky so that a portico seems to take shape around them. He is almost always afraid. His sister Lotte isn't afraid, even though she is two years younger. For this fearlessness he bestows upon her a crown. He sees it floating a mere arm's length above her head. A crown of snow interspun with silver.

They all sit in the same chilly classroom, at least thirty children of various ages, including Lotte and her crown. Their teacher is a young man, a poor theology student from the university, with stiff, frozen fingers and a hoarse, half-choked voice that sounds like a door creaking on its hinges and which the children love to mimic. Their teacher often stands with his back to them as he speaks, as if he despised them or was ashamed of himself or both. The children are taught catechism and Bible study. Their knowledge of reading and writing will at least be serviceable.

But his relationship to words and letters is unusual: for him they are like living things. Like living things, words must be coaxed to open up before disclosing their meaning, and once they have, they lay waxen on the page, like empty houses, shells of what once was but isn't anymore. He would often spend time rearranging the empty word-shells in his mind, unsure of what to do with them. This also applied to the few Polish words he learned from his father and that would be of help to him later, when as a soldier he crossed the endless mire on the far side of the Memel where there was nothing to eat and the only water there was to drink was poisoned by rotting cadavers and the only way to keep your wits about you was to *sing* the Polish words right out into the vast emptiness.

Childhood, he recalls, was the first time with these secret signs. Not those of the alphabet, the other ones. One of the first is the crown he bestows on his sister. There are others, too: the chimney sweep's black hat, a sign of danger; the window cross, its shadow stretching over the yard and becoming God's pale name; the hands of the clock on the town hall tower that measure time, both the time that runs in line with the hours of the day and the *dangerous* time that runs backwards; a rooster's red comb, the ominously sharpened fork of the wooden peg stuck in front of the privy door, the pale-veined floral patterns on the hearth's tiles: thin fibrous stems and leafstalks and their interwoven path which he can't help tracing with his finger, especially when his mother lights a fire inside and the flowers' silver threads heat up against his fingertips. Fingerflowers. He has those, too. A flower for each finger. He carves signs into the wall, he scores wood with a knife, or uses his heel to scratch patterns into the gravel and mud in the yard. He fences in, he pushes shut, he hooks tight and builds up. Sometimes he thinks his whole life can be read as a succession of signs. The people around him, or the events that occur, don't become real until he can place them in a context he is able to survey. If they move ever so slightly outside of his own perimeter of thought he can't understand them. Of course his sister is indifferent to all this. You forgot your crown, he shouts after her, aghast, and Lotte throws the crown to the ground and stomps on it and screams, her voice loud and shrill, *idiot, good-for-nothing, cretin!* as she's heard the schoolmaster say. But it doesn't matter how much scolding comes his way: the signs are more robust than that, they are even more robust than what bears them, and they linger in the air long after the final blow has been dealt.

We were poor, he explains to Clarus, my mother didn't have it easy with five children to provide for. Neither did my father, he wants to add, whose hands with the years were given to shaking from the alcohol and so could no longer hold his razor and scissors steady.

Maria Rosina once took in laundry but in later years had to enter the employ of one Herr Rossner who also ran a dye-works at Grimmaische Tor. Where the father is soft and acquiescent with his customers or any form of authority, the mother is hard and stern but hollowed out inside, with a will that never used words or external gestures, but was still inviolable. Most clearly he remembers her hands: discolored by lye and hard and chapped from years of scrubbing against rough washboards. Rossner's laundry wasn't large, but there was always a hurry to tend to the linens they took in from the upper class and bourgeoisie in the city, and everywhere is a flurry of people, packers and deliverymen and laundresses sorting the washing or stirring the tubs with long poles and around them rises a thick vapor of armpit sweat and sour laundry fumes.

One day he and Lotte were allowed to accompany their mother to the laundry, he can't remember why. They play tag among the washing tubs and women's legs and hide in laundry baskets, the sister in one, he in another. The baskets are as tall as men; afterwards he can't understand how they managed to climb into them in the first place. Their stomachs tingle because they both know that someone will soon fetch the still-damp sheets for mangling. He has no memory of Rossner's rage when they are finally hauled out of the baskets, nor of the thrashing they must have received (Lotte too), no memory of their mother's dry-eyed despair when Rossner dressed her down and then dismissed her in front of all the other women (*imagine bringing the children along only to make a mess for the old man*); all of this was only made clear to him afterwards by his foster mother, her tone triumphant: as if to prove his mother had never been any good. All that remains of that day is what the child in him remembers: the prickle of pleasure he felt as he lay with his skin and breath bared in the darkness of the sheets, a glimmer of light leaking in between the basket's laths; shielded from everything, but still vulnerable, because he knew that at any moment he could be discovered. But what protected him most was the knowledge that Lotte lay in another identical basket, impossible to reach but still there, right beside him, as silent as he was, and in his imagination the laundry baskets became Moses baskets made of braided reeds that slipped out of Herod's hands and across a dark river above which the laundry vapors ripple like long dark blue veils. The sister's basket had a red lantern in the form of a crown, that's why he was able to follow her. As always: she first, he after. And he fell asleep and dreamed that long black hooks, like boat hooks, reached out over the water and hauled them towards an invisible shore.

Shortly thereafter Maria Rosina died. Maybe she was already sick then, maybe she, ever more feverish and frail, had long borne a cough in her tight chest. She had been so thin that when the illness really began to eat away at her hardly anyone noticed a difference. She never complained. She became but drier, more terse, and so hollowed out inside that you could hear the cough heaving itself through her body like a restless animal, and finally she lay there, embraced from within by her own immobility, and the rooms they lived in were filled with mourners: people he had never seen before; and all of them stretched out their long arm-hooks and pulled him to them to mumble meaningless admonitions or to simply embrace their own future misfortunes.

He doesn't remember much of the funeral itself, only that it was an icy winter day, sharp grains of snow beat his face, and walking hurt as much as standing still and seeing and hearing all these strange people, as though daylight itself were shining in a language unknown to him. They had hardly been aware of her existence, and then she existed no more. She was the only one in his world that hadn't had a sign, maybe because the sign that she was encompassed all others.

The doctor couldn't explain her death with anything but consumption. She was twenty-six years old. She'd had enough of life. Or had life had enough of her?

BUT HOW COULD HE TELL the councillor about a mother's death, or about a father who could not stand the sight of his children afterwards so he sits in taverns playing dice and bickering with old acquaintances who think they have debts to collect from him, a father who, when he finally does come home, is often so drunk that the eldest son, under threats and curses, must help him into bed?

In the mother's stead a strange woman is called in to run the household. The woman, Josephina Geier, daughter of an armourer from Delitzsch, asserts that she is related to the mother, that is to say she is an Irmisch. She is large and sweeping both in word and gesture, has a violent temper, and moreover is besotted with everything to do with money. No sooner has the father remarried than does she turn into a scold over an inheritance that Maria Rosina should have laid claim to before her death and which she believes is up to her new husband to claim on behalf of his dead wife.

Even though he is barely ten years old he is considered old enough to contribute to the family's upkeep and because wigmaking is all the father knows, it's into a wigmaking apprenticeship he goes. First he lands at a wigmaker named Stein, whose wife feels sorry for him because he has just lost his mother, and because he is a nice and well-behaved lad he's allowed to stay among the children, which enrages Josephina because she wants the boy to learn a trade and not drag his feet and after only a few months with Stein he is sent to Master Knobloch instead, an acquaintance of Majorewsky's who in addition to a wigmaking workshop runs a shaving parlor and hairdressing salon with two employees in the adjacent apartment.

He studies under Knobloch for four years, then spends another two in *Condition* (in conditional employment). By then his father has also been lost to consumption, the strange illness that only seems to strike those who have nothing in this life, as he puts it to Clarus, and which begins with a rattling, stubborn cough and ends with wan sunken cheeks and empty staring eyes. Master Knobloch keeps only two apprentices. In addition to Woyzeck, whom Knobloch feels he owes it to old Majorewsky to look after, there is also a younger apprentice who is then replaced one by one. The apprentice who stays the longest is named Isidor Horvath but is simply called Isa. Both apprentices take at least one meal together with the master and his family. Woyzeck shares a room and sometimes a bed with Isa. In this room also sleeps the master's younger brother whose name is Karl but is called Li'l Scoop. Li'l Scoop is around twenty but is as frail as a ten-year-old and has the mind of a child. His ill will is that of a fully grown man, and he is contrary about even the smallest particulars and fights and bites and shouts imprecations as soon as you try to touch him. Even such a man has his quiet moments, whereupon he crouches in a corner, intensely preoccupied with his arms and hands, raising them up to the light and twisting and turning them around as if they were foreign objects that belonged to a different person entirely.

He was nicknamed Scoop because the bed he sleeps in looks like a spice scoop. The bed is two cubits long, as long as Scoop himself, has a high headboard and high sides so that this little handful can't tumble out and crash to the ground, but it's open at the foot so that Scoop can crawl in and out on his own. Tasked to both apprentices, it's not explicitly stated but is somehow understood, is also the minding of Scoop, to avert or at least divert his worst outbursts and to make sure he washes himself and makes it to the toilet in time. But sometimes he is so intractable that nothing can be done. On such an occasion he lays in his scoop and screams the house down, rousing Master Knobloch's ire, and not seldom are they beaten or made to go to bed without dinner. Then one morning we wake up, he tells Clarus, to a silence in the room that is so uncanny you could hear a feather drop; and when we get up, we see the poor boy in bed with one arm reaching over its edge. But dead, he adds. It was as if he had wanted to touch the Angel of God with this outstretched arm. At least that was the explanation Frau Knobloch gave: one of the Lord God's angels had come to spirit him away to the heaven of the poor and simple. And after that we weren't beaten anymore, and it was as if a gentle, solemn mood spread throughout the wigmaker's abode.

Clarus has been listening to this digression with an expression of patient suffering. Now he sighs and fidgets. Who else in addition to simpleminded apprentices and idiots were to be found in the Knobloch household? he asks, and when W.'s reply doesn't come immediately (perhaps W.'s thoughts are still with the slight soul in his spice scoop bed), he clears his throat more loudly. I am of course speaking of the widow Woost, he clarifies and that's when W. finally lifts his gaze and looks at the councillor with his clear, blue, wide-open eyes, a look that must have roused a certain unease in Clarus for he dips his pen in the ink pot and energetically begins making notes while with an absent expression he commands: Can You without interruption and as concisely as possible account for when and under which circumstances You made this woman's acquaintance? For it must have been there that You first made her acquaintance, or am I misinformed?

W. continues to be silent, then says what the councillor and everyone else already knows. That Frau Woost lived together with her surgeon husband Woost in a room that he rented close to the hospital, and if she, the wife, visited her mother and stepfather, it was rare that she deigned to speak with any of the apprentices hunching over their wig stands. Mr. Knobloch issued strict instructions to refrain from looking up each time they pull the strand of hair through the tulle. Pull up the strand and pull it through the mesh and tighten. Pull up, pull through, tighten. Each strand should be firmly laced to the cap. So that you can do it in your sleep, do it even when other things are going on around you and without looking like you're doing anything but concentrating on the movements of your hands.

And so this is what he does each time Frau Woost walks by.

He hooks and pulls the strand through and tightens, listening to her trilling banter with the customers in the shaving parlor.

Her standing around and joking is the surest sign that she is not accompanied by her husband: otherwise she wouldn't dare. Personally, he has only seen the surgeon once: a short man of a stout build and very hairy, with a resolute, sloping gait and a face that seems to stare invitingly at you each time he looks up. In spite of his modest height he dominates each room he enters with his gruff voice and brazen manner. Sometimes his wife treats him with great kindness and sometimes with an irritable contempt. When an insolent voice from inside the shaving parlor requests his wife's services, presumably absent the knowledge that the surgeon himself is near, the man's screams of *trollop* and *Satan's whore* can be heard from inside the room they occupy when visiting their parents-in-law, whereafter the furniture can be heard scraping against the floor along with heavy blows being dealt. The surgeon's blether appears to have little effect on Frau Woost, and presently dreadful old Woost is as tame and charming as before.

Though Master Knobloch knows well to appreciate his winsome stepdaughter and not rarely does he treat his shaving parlor customers to a drink when she's present, so a giddy mood always prevails when she comes to visit. Doors are slammed; windows are opened so a fresh breeze can blow through the room, setting the stale dust in the wigmaking workshop in motion, and even though he never lifts his burning eyes from the wig stand he can tell by the particular smell of her skin and clothing how far or near from him she is. It's like he is endowed with a sixth sense specific to her. He doesn't even need to see or hear her, and so continues tying loops and threading the strands through the mesh. All the same it feels as though he only need reach out a hand to touch her in the most sensitive of places.

Incidentally Knobloch has let it be known that he is satisfied with him as an apprentice. For a year now he has been allowed to be present when the master takes the head measurements of new customers, and it is as he is counting up the measurements that Knobloch calls out to him that he catches sight of her in the door of the shaving parlor, her gaze intent on his. He has fine hands, that Woyzeck, she says, like a child's, or a young girl's. These are the first words she directs to him and him alone. But as soon as they are spoken it's as if the pale smile that for a moment so brightly lit up her face—that vague triangular smile that he will later come to know well: the one that begins as a tremble in one corner of the mouth, then stretches and lays claim to the rest of her face—snuffs out and her face falls into indifference. She responds to a shout for her from out in the yard and where she once was standing now only hovers a smudge of light.

But he will forever remember this smile and these words. And from that moment on even his hands are transformed. When he draws the loops through the tulle it is her hair he is threading through. It is her slightly blotchy skin that his fingertips are touching. It is to her neck and the dip in her throat that he presses his cheeks and his mouth and his lips, so as to catch anew that which he so clearly perceives as her special scent.

Until one morning when he hears her voice resounding through the house.

Though her voice is normally deep and slightly muffled, almost veiled (later, when she speaks tenderly to him, he thinks of her voice as a small animal curled up beside him), it becomes remarkably loud and resonant when raised. She calls to her mother for more water. There is a small gap at the edge of the landing, where the stairs lead into the cramped passage on the top floor that in turn leads to the apprentices' attic room. Through that gap he sees the front of the wigmaking work-shop and down into the kitchen on the ground floor. Bodice around her waist, she is bending her head over a tub in the middle of the floor. From above he sees her broad torso, those round shoulders, her neck and two strong arms reaching up and lowering a black tangle of hair into the tub, then her fingers begin to scrub her scalp. At the same time her breasts appear from under raised arms and start swaying back and forth over the rim of the tub. Her mother arrives with the requested kettle of hot water, and when Johanna leans forward to receive the shower over her head she stretches her upper body so far that her full back is bared. He sees her spine writhing like a supple glossy eel under her skin, from the soapy hairline at her neck all the way down to where her wide hips splay and become a quick and silvery undulation. And suddenly his knees are trembling with pleasure. He reaches inside his waistband and

starts kneading his member with the same restrained yet tense movements as the female hands kneading the thick mass of hair down below,
and the pleasure that surfaces in him is much deeper and hotter than
the next kettle of water that the mother brings and pours over her, and
much smoother and firmer and glossier than the skin on her back and
across her arms and her mighty breasts. And so filled, or rather flushed,
by this pleasure-water is he that he does not hear Knobloch coming up
behind him until the man is howling in his ear: *What in the . . . stop this
at once, you rascal . . . !* And gripping him firmly by the back of the neck,
Knobloch hurls him down the stairs headfirst, and he tumbles all the
way into the wigmaking workshop with a terrible racket.

Worse than the sprained arm is the shame: lying there at the foot
of the stairs with his sex exposed to all, servants and customers alike.
This he can't tell Clarus, but it is from this painful ordeal that he dates
the agonizing desire with which he was often overcome later, clandes-
tinely spying on other people, watching without anyone knowing that
he is watching. After being caught red-handed follows fourteen days of
unbearable torment. He sits as though nailed to his wig stand and waits
for the sound of that voice, to catch that fleeting scent again, and when
after a long time she still has not come he is convinced it is because of
him, it is because she *knows* he was spying on her.

He falls silent.

Clarus clears his throat. So it was after this episode that your employment was terminated? His otherwise strict lizard face has cracked into a
scornful and expectant smile, as if he can hardly wait to hear the answer
that he believes will come. No, W. responds, it just fell out of fashion. The
crease between Clarus's eyebrows deepens. *What* fell? he asks. It was no
longer customary to wear a wig, W. says, among the gentlemen, at least.
Clarus stares at his detainee as though the man has said something highly
improper. I suppose they followed the French Emperor, the detainee feels
obliged to add and brings both index fingers towards each other until
they create a cross in the eyeline of a startled Clarus.

Emperor *Napoleon*? Clarus asks. But surely You were *punished* for
your misdeed?

The subject of the interrogation claims in all seriousness that there was no question of punishment. What he had come to understand was that Frau Woost never suffered any distress, for she had not seen it with her own eyes; and it was Master Knobloch himself who was probably the most eager to get the now-feral youth out of the house.

And perhaps this could be construed as a punishment: instead of continuing to assist in the measuring of living customers he was instead sent off to measure, dress, and paint the faces of the dead, as well as fit the often bald corpses with suitable head coverings.

You *what?*

Clarus still cannot comprehend it.

Please understand, Herr Hofrat, because the demand at this time was waning, Knobloch had cabinets full of unused, unsold, or returned wigs, and what could be better, and pay more, than to fit them on one or another bald corpse? It pleased their surviving relatives in any case; they could see their deceased dressed up and adorned as if they were still alive and well. A number of the corpses looked and smelled as if they had lain around for weeks, others had only recently crossed the threshold to the hereafter.

He remembers one stiff particularly clearly: which man had complained of stomach cramps a mere day before, a doctor had been called who had him swallow four leeches and then he had gotten cramps and was coughing blood and had died early in the morning. The deceased's father asked him to immediately do something about the emaciated face frozen in fear, whereafter he, according to the rules of the art, powdered the cheeks with zinc and applied color on the blanched lips. Then he fitted a wig, which he had first powdered with stove ash and crushed broad beans, and afterwards the bloodless man looked like a small innocent child, born again.

Clarus looks disgusted.

But then there was an end to that business as well, W. says. Even the dead were to be coiffured according to the new French mode.

BUT HE COULD JUST AS well have recounted this instead:

That even though he was only pulling wigs over dead skin his hands remained as alive as ever. He would wake up with a hot weight in his body, as though the impression of her skin were still there, of her neck, her firm shoulders, the round of her breasts.

Remarkable, he could have said, that a man who'd never touched a woman could so clearly imagine all of this.

He knew he had to write a letter. Not to her; this he never would have dared. The letter would be addressed to her husband, the good surgeon Julius Friedrich Woost, and to this man he would apologize for the lewd thoughts that had taken hold of him, would explain that they constituted but a passing moment for a young man who God had not yet had the wisdom to admonish, and surely Woost himself remembers what it is to be young and not yet quite right of mind? And for the first and only time in his life W. enters the lofty colonnade of words where one can stand in reverent silence but never quite find a foothold:

> Highly Esteemed Herr Chirurgicus,
> Kindly receive this letter as the ultimate proof of submission from a Young Man who in a moment of error allowed himself to not be guided by Reason but who, through God's gracious intervention, has gained insight into his grave Transgressions and now wishes to confess his Repentance and humbly begs Forgiveness for the sinful Thoughts that have penetrated his Spirit. In the Holy Scriptures it is written that thou shalt not Covet thy neighbor's wife and that every such Storm of Lust

must be nipped in the Bud. In another Scripture that fell into the hands of the undersigned, authored by Pastor Pförter, it is written that a Holy man had a Clock cast and blessed that was so resounding and powerful it could still the ocean's every Storm. Now too my own Oceans of Desire have of this Clock's Holy Clangor been penetrated and now there blows, I can happily impart, no more than a gentle Breeze. I am therefore writing to Herr Chirurgicus in hopes of securing His Forgiveness and Pardon, as he too must have been Young once and tossed 'round by the Waves of Fornication.

Respectfully,
your humble servant
J C Woyzeck

If his efforts up until that day had been in service of getting as close to the surgeon's wife as possible, now he does all he can to avoid her. As soon as he hears her laughter or clamor in the kitchen, he finds some excuse to slip away, as though the desire that set him aflame were a disease that could blight the entire household. When after the war and his long years as a soldier he finds out that the surgeon Woost passed away only a short time after he himself had left his post with Knobloch, he is at first convinced his letter is what killed him, that each word was like a poison that had eaten into the surgeon's body and finally caused him to die in excruciating agony.

The voices plagued him greatly during this time.

You're sick, Woyzeck, only you don't know it, they whisper, and:

Just do it, go on, go on . . .

And more than once the voices are accompanied by visions in which the surgeon's claw-like hand reaches for him or appears severed on the ground, black and stiffened into a crucifix.

But when he finally sees Johanna Woost again, the anxious look of her slanting eyes is unchanged. Her smile, too, is the same, as tender as when she said that he had beautiful hands. Like a child's, a young girl's hands, she says. And she takes them in hers. And he wants to cry because he knows he isn't worthy of these loving gestures because the desire it awakens in him once killed her husband. But when he dares mention the Letter after his return, she says she has no memory of it. Quite the opposite, she bemoans that in all the years he was absent he never wrote a single word to *her*. And then he dares say no more for fear of bringing his past misdeed to life.

WHEN HE ATTEMPTS TO CALL to mind the subsequent years, his *journeyman years* as Clarus calls them, rarely do specific events come to mind.

The world has no color. It is made of distances, not places.

Neither does time have meaning other than the hungry must be fed, the weary must rest. So days exist, daylight exists, and darkness. Seasons. Rain and cold. The trees that reach for the stars in the dark of night but freeze in fear when the sun rises up to complete its thunderous round across the sky.

He spends hours waiting by staging posts and outside coaching inns to beg a ride somewhere, anywhere, so long as he doesn't have to walk another stretch on his tired legs. Still he mostly travels by foot, and for he who travels by foot there is only mud and clay, and the same unending colorless sky.

Almost everywhere he goes people turn their backs on him. From a distance it is obvious what sort he is. A *Condition* is out of the question. He must accept the odd jobs that are on offer. First he works only for his lodging as a groom, then with a cobbler, and thirdly with a Jew in Dessau who runs a pawnbroking but also sews and mends clothing. Schwalbe is the Jew's name, a hermetic character who in spite of the splendor with which he surrounds himself in his large apartment—room after room full of chaise longues and credenzas, taken in pawn but never redeemed—only cares for a wooden chest that he keeps under his single bed and contains his prayer shawl and phylacteries.

Several times a day he wraps himself in the prayer shawl and prays in a voice so thin and toneless that the words would be indiscernible even if a good Christian could have understood them.

During prayer study, or when the Jew drives around in his one-horse carriage doing his business in the area, it is W. who is left with the sewing work behind the threadbare drapery that divides the shop from the rest of Schwalbe's large apartment. He is used to this kind of task, and can sink into a thoughtless slumber for hours while all that can be heard is the pendulum clock chiming in the next room. The clockface is also visible in a standing mirror that has been placed just inside the door (presumably so that Schwalbe can see which customers are arriving without needing to peer out from behind the drapery), and in that reflection time seems to be crawling backwards.

One day, as he sits there following the retreat of time, a great commotion can be heard on the street outside and shortly thereafter in the mirror W. sees a young man running into the shop. An accident, an accident! he screams and runs out again before W. has had a chance to put down his needle and thread and follow after.

It turns out that a carriage has become stuck near the tollhouse down by the Elbe Bridge and all hands are needed to get it back on the road. Around a blacksmith who with lever and hammer is trying to pry loose one of the carriage wheels that has wedged itself between two curbstones, a group of curious onlookers has gathered. The gentleman who was traveling in the carriage, a short young man with bushy blond hair and a peculiarly open, clear, blue gaze, walks around the bystanders offering his regrets, as though he were not only seeking help but also some form of forgiveness. It is obvious that the cause of this predicament is some unwieldy piece of furniture that hadn't been properly lashed and so slid to the edge of the loading platform until the entire carriage was in danger of toppling over. The young gentleman must have tried to stay the carriage himself because his clothing is soiled with mud and a slit up to the elbow has been torn into the sleeve of his overcoat. Because W. doesn't have the physical strength to help the other men on site he walks with reverent obeisance up to the indignant man and offers to take care of his clothes while he waits. Curiously the young gentleman halts his restless roving, fixes his blue eyes on him, and accepts his offer with a smile that reveals a long, even, and surprisingly white row of teeth.

W. sews behind the curtain while the young man paces in and out of the mirror's reflection. Perhaps it is because a wall of cloth separates them that he dares be so revealing. He is a student of anatomy in Wittenberg, he explains to W. He was on his way back from his family's estate in Waldenburg, where to his father (*the miserly devil!*) he had lamented his meager purse, when this unfortunate incident occurred. Had he a proper servant staff this would never have happened. Hereafter it is revealed that he does not possess a staff of any kind, except for a coachman, who is clearly unfit for his work, and a housekeeper. The manservant he once had has "run off," he explains as W. strides out from behind the drapery and hands over the mended coat, and the young man regards him as though for the first time, turns and twists the garment, expresses his satisfaction, and even asks his name. *Woyetz*, Woyzeck replies because he thinks it sounds better, more distinguished, so to speak. Splendid, the young man replies. Why doesn't someone like You seek my employ? And W. answers that he doesn't know, he must first speak with Schwalbe, but he has yet to secure a proper *Condition*, which the young man interprets as his offer having been accepted and so writes down his address in Wittenberg on the back of the bill W. has presented him with and tells him to be at hand posthaste. It is then that he will be paid for his sewing.

W.'S NEW MASTER IS A student of physiology and anatomy, but has yet to earn a degree. Nonetheless, in the household he goes by "the young doctor," as though the fact of his noble birth confers on him an academic rank he has not yet earned. The family in Waldenburg is of a late branch of the noble house Schönberg-Hohenlohe, a fact that the young doctor in his capacity as a Republican does not attach the least bit of importance. For being of this higher class he pays little attention to his appearance and doesn't seem to mind his reputation. Not that he carries himself in a way that is beneath his dignity, but the rooms he rents from the widow of a Wittenberger professor that his father, formerly a doctor in Prince-elector Friedrich August's court, knows from his own student days, are if not directly impoverished then at least quite humble. They consist of a salon to which the widow also has access, but in practice it is only the housekeeper, Frau Pförtner, for the widow is bedridden. There are two other rooms, one of which is used as a bedchamber and the other as a library. The young doctor spends the better part of his time in the latter. It is here that he eats his simple meals, which Frau Pförtner carries in to him and here that he pursues his studies, most often standing or pacing with characteristic awkwardness, a book held up to his face, as though he were not reading it so much as scrutinizing it. Now and then he is heard spouting lengthy monologues, as though he were speaking to an invisible or imminent auditorium.

W. has been allotted a place to sleep in an old maid's chamber next to the kitchen, where the housekeeper used to sleep before she moved into a room next to the widow's. In the maid's chamber is enough room for a table at which he can tend to the young doctor's clothes, which he lays out each morning. His daily tasks aren't particularly taxing. The young doctor often spends his evening hours at one of the student unions to which he belongs, and W. rarely needs do more than heat the wine he imbibes each night before bed and that he says is the best cure for the chronic sleeplessness from which he claims to suffer.

In what spare time he has, W. folds small paper figures of cardboard or crêpe. Or, when Frau Pförtner is out on some errand and he is as close to alone as he can be in the apartment, the widow silent and half blind in her room, he prowls around the writing cabinet, which the young doctor keeps in the library.

It was this considerable piece that had been insufficiently secured to the platform when the doctor's equipage slid off the road at the foot of the Elbe Bridge. The young doctor is namely so enchanted by his writing cabinet that he refuses to part from it even when traveling. Several men are needed to carry it down from the apartment, lift it onto the platform, and strap it down. Then at least one must sit beside it for the entirety of the journey to ensure that the cabinet does not rattle itself loose. What's worrisome, the coachman Metzger explains to W., is that the young doctor can't afford to have people lift and carry his cabinet here and there. He can barely afford his coachman, and how should one go about keeping an eye on everything so that nothing gets nicked or scratched or comes loose and slides around, does the doctor think he has eyes in the back of his head?

The writing cabinet itself, which Metzger points out in vain to W. is *Chinese*, is comprised of a desk with an abattant made of cherrywood with a pen tray and a built-in inkwell and an inner cabinet with two folding panels adorned with a floral motif. If both panels are folded out, something W. has seen the young doctor do only once, a long row of shelves is revealed, each one with a number of drawers with mother-of-pearl and enamel fittings. The inside of the panels, like the exterior of the cabinet, is painstakingly decorated. Whereas the exterior is ornamented only with plant-like coils, the interior opens onto unusual landscapes with peaked mountains and buildings and fields of grain with kneeling ladies and men with slanted eyes and long queues.

W. has never in his life seen anything like it. It's as though the world has suddenly acquired an *interior*.

The young doctor is often at home in the mornings. W. draws him a modest breakfast table. Afterwards he can be seen pacing in front of his cabinet as though he were beseeching it to stay put, and if W. happens to be in the room the young doctor might even address him. Herr Woyetz, he might say, cupping a brooding hand around his chin, have You ever been struck by the knowledge that You bear something great and terrible inside, something You've long borne with you? And that what You are carrying around is like a great scream, yes, even greater, because You know that screaming alone would not be enough to rid Yourself of it?

W. doesn't know if he should listen attentively or politely turn a deaf ear. Therefore he continues vigorously brushing one of the young doctor's boots. And the young doctor continues pacing back and forth with tripping steps in front of the cabinet.

Which certainty, You might ask? Well, the certainty that we live in a world we lack the correct measures and proportions to comprehend!

When he turns to Woyzeck it is with a blue gaze so intense that W. feels impaled by it.

The young doctor smiles his white-toothed smile, affected but friendly:

And if I show myself to be polite or kind with You, Woyetz . . . yes, even if I speak to You as if You had the slightest prerequisite for understanding what I'm saying, it is but a mask I don . . . *a frightful mask . . . !*

The mask continues to smile, the white row of teeth, even the bright blue eyes are smiling, small V-shaped wrinkles at their corners; but from within the gaze becomes ever more rigid and unseeing, and the doctor himself ever stiffer, as though the abrupt way in which he had been circling the cabinet had now moved into his body.

He raises both arms overhead and exclaims:

YOU ARE A SERVANT, YOUR MANDATE IS TO SERVE; SO SERVE FOR GOD'S SAKE, MAN, SERVE!

W. doesn't understand if it is to him these sudden words are directed or to the cabinet, for the young doctor turns his back as soon as he has spoken them, and with a dismissive gesture, as when casually tossing something over the shoulder, he takes a wide step forward as if to exit the room. But no sooner has he begun the step than he drops to the floor, as though by his own force, and begins twisting and writhing in violent convulsions. Frau Pförtner comes rushing with a ladle. With a practiced movement she tears a cushion from the chaise longue, shoves it under the head of the young doctor, still flailing around on the floor, then shamelessly straddles him, lifts his head with one hand and with the other drives the kitchen ladle between his jaws. In the corners of his mouth a strange fermenting froth has appeared and the recently matte, staring eyes are wide-open and as white as hens' eggs.

Without changing her position atop the young doctor Frau Pförtner turns to W. who is still standing there, the boot pulled over one hand, the brush in the other:

Naturally Herr Woyetz is now imagining that the devil himself has flown into the young master. But I can assure Herr Woyetz that his master is a good man who has never wished ill on anyone nor has he harbored a cruel thought about anyone or anything. Just so Herr Woyetz knows, she adds, and isn't under any illusions.

SO YOUR BENEFACTOR SUFFERED FROM the falling sickness! Clarus says, as though only now has he fully understood what the detainee was trying to tell him. Did he ever speak with you about his—he draws a circle with one arm—temptation?

The young doctor spoke of many a thing, W. says, but only once did he mention his sickness, and by then it had already been decided that his services were no longer required. Of every other possibly curiosity the young doctor spoke more. Of the tiny nerves and muscle fibers that allow the human eye to see; of fish and why they swim in schools and why a school of fish behaves as if it were a single body; and might Herr Hofrat ever have given a thought to how birds manage to stay in the air for so long and how they find their way with such ease from their nesting grounds to far-off places in Africa or wherever they winter?

I imagine politics was the main topic of conversation, Clarus says dryly and with a watchful gleam in the corner of his eye intimating that he would not exactly listen unwillingly if W. were to elaborate on this point.

But what can a servant know of such things? The young doctor may be a man of meager means, but is nonetheless generous with invitations. Several nights a week his library salon is full of student friends and research assistants and W. must assist Frau Pförtner in serving and attending to the guests, a job for which, in his constant slumber of thought, he is perhaps even less suited to than brushing shoes, ironing clothes, or crimping the linens. But even though a hint of displeasure occasionally crosses the young doctor's face, his bumbling seems to be tolerated. W. almost gets the feeling that the two of them are engaging in some sort of game. As if there were a silent agreement that if W. does not mention the young doctor's maladies, then in turn the young doctor will overlook that W. is absent the tact and sense required of a true valet. Sometimes he even catches the young doctor giving him a strange look, at once pitiful and pitying, as though the man were suffering on behalf of them both.

W. soon understands that the young doctor is an esteemed person, esteemed not only in the sense of being held in high esteem but also as you esteem something frail and rare that one has learned to regard with embarrassed indulgence. In conversation he becomes hot-tempered and strained and speaks in a way that makes all present fall silent and look away. He has a reputation as an atheist and Republican, and incidentally W. finds out that he once was arrested by the police after having been overheard slandering the Saxon king and mocking which man's craven neutrality treaty with France, and only at the last second, thanks to his father's intervention, was saved from imprisonment.

Once or more than once each semester the medical students make local excursions and W. is allowed to be among the other young gentlemen's servants. They travel in several equipages to Dübener Heide or the nearby lakeland. One day when the autumn is in its fullest glory they drive as far as to Weddersleben in the Harz by the high Devil's Wall, a row of towering sandstone cliffs, the jagged contours of which burn darkly against the slanting but still saturated sunlight. W. has retreated to a small hillside away from the rest of the servants and is busying himself with cleaning and greasing tack for coachman Metzger. When the work is done and the students have yet to show signs of parting he scrapes up a fistful of scree from the ground and engages in target practice with some boulders downslope. In the low-lying sun, each stone casts a sharp shadow until they all, shadow as well as stone, slice into each other in sibylline patterns. So engrossed is he in the stones that he hardly notices the much larger shadow now leaning over him. But the young doctor's voice is surprisingly gentle:

He is a child of nature, that Woyetz. This is why I have always found him so charming.

One of the young doctor's legs slips down the slope and he allows the unplanned movement to advance into a studied pose, elbow propped on knee.

Pray tell, has he ever had occasion to read Rousseau?

W. doesn't know how respond, or if he is meant to respond at all. Pardon? What now . . . ? *Roo-so?*

The young doctor also realizes that the addressed can hardly offer a comprehensible reply and turns his gaze to the slope where the party in pairs or groups is slowly making its way to the carriages. The servants have already begun loading the luggage and picnic baskets. Voices and laughter rise up from below as through a bottleneck.

Tell me instead what he, Woyetz, sees when he looks out over this landscape? Or what he imagines? For images are what we make of them, not a thing that arises from nature itself.

This last part is uttered with a measure of bitterness, W. thinks. He says nothing because he is almost sure that a thoughtful silence is what the young doctor is expecting of him. And as if this were correct the young doctor resolutely withdraws all that he has exposed—hand, smile, and gaze—as when he shuts the doors of his writing cabinet. Then he sets off downslope. Halfway to his destination he waves, an effusive greeting, at the rest of the party, who at the sound of his voice stop mid-step, just like the stones in arrest at the edges of their own shadows.

A FEW WEEKS AFTER THE excursion to the Harz, the young doctor announces that he must travel home to his family for a time and orders the cabinet be carried down. Since the excursion, the light has left the clear autumn sky and a misty haze has been drawn over the world like a gray woolen sock. Day after day, a sour steady rain pushes through the knit of the sock. Now W. too is called upon to help carry down from the professor-widow's apartment the writing cabinet, wrapped in thick rugs and curtains, and lash it to the carriage to which Metzger has harnessed the horse.

It is clear that the young doctor is not in his usual mood. He spends the whole journey up on the coach box lost in thought beside Metzger, while W., farther back on the platform, tries to shoulder the worst of the careening. It is draining work. The shaking of the coach forces him to constantly seek new positions so that the cabinet won't glide in this way or that, and after only half-a-day's travel he is so ricked it feels as though the wood of the cabinet and platform have dug into his marrow.

The journey to Waldenburg grows long and arduous. They are forced to overnight more than once because parts of the road have been washed away by mudslides and in one place a bridge has collapsed and they must take a long detour. After four days of near-constant rain the sky slowly clears, and when in the early morning they turn onto the paved path to Waldenburg Castle long rifts of clear blue light open in the sky, across which lingering wisps of white fog are speeding, so close it seems one could reach out and touch them. In the long shadows on the castle park's avenue, weird vivid birds are fleeing the carriage wheels on either side of the road.

Those are peacocks, Metzger explains, leaning down from the coach box as if to chase them away with his whip. One of the birds stops and fans out its plumage like a bold card player who of a sudden wishes to show his full hand, then strides off with the haughty steps of a head waiter. A strange invention of Our Lord, creating a bird unable to fly, W. says as they free the young doctor's writing cabinet from the platform. Oh, but they can, Metzger says. Only it seems to be beneath them. At night when no one is looking they fly into the trees.

The young doctor's father, the city physician and medical advisor Günther Schönberg, lives with his second wife (the first, the young doctor's mother, died in childbirth when the young doctor was a mere ten years of age) and their two children in a stately home at the far end of the castle park. And it is clear that the eldest son is expected. The servants are already in place to receive the writing cabinet, unload it, and carry it in. W., it has already been decided, shall sleep with Metzger in the stables; but the young doctor insists on having him in the house among the other domestics, wherefore he is assigned a room that faces the rear court-yard, near to the kitchen. The housekeeper and all the kitchen maids are rushing around and preparing the evening meal without taking much notice of him as he sits idly in one corner of the sideboard room, trying to draw the peacocks from memory, how they advance with the small short steps of young noblewomen, lifting and lowering their feet with deliberate leisure. One of the maids passes by and wants to see what he's "drawing on," but is chased away by the housekeeper, who sternly bids him to absent himself from the kitchen and wait in his room until it is time for him to serve.

The subsequent evening meal bears every mark of a ritual that has been performed in exactly the same way for many years. The father, the medical officer, a still-imposing man of more than sixty years with thick white hair and the sharp, sculpted nose passed down to his son, sits at the head of the table. Arranged beside him is a long row of periodicals and books that he leafs through or reads aloud from while chewing and drinking. And so consumed is he with his pursuit, the eating and reading aloud, that he does not look up from the pages of his books even when one plate is carried off and another dish takes its place, he but slows the turn of the page.

Across from him sits his smiling young wife, her gaze fixed in the distance, and on either side of the table the two children: the elder, a boy, with a timid look, and a young girl. All three, including the little girl, sit stiffly and attentively, so as not to betray with a look their inattention to the father who continues to go between eating and mumbling with a book or pamphlet raised before his face.

And to the right of the father sits the young doctor, but his eyes are not on his reading father, but on W., who has assumed his post by the door should the young doctor think to call upon him.

Then comes the moment it seems all have been waiting for. The father startles in the midst of his reading, wipes his mouth with the serviette that was on his lap and then exclaims *Now here's something for you* . . . , it concerns a man who is born with a fistula so large you can see right into his stomach, and of course this unfortunate man ends up in the hands of a menagerie exhibitor who travels around with him like a circus animal. Give him something, anything, a bite of apple, and if you've paid a groschen you may in full glare watch the apple dissolve in his stomach cavity and slide down into his intestines.

Which reminds me, surely Johann, you recall . . . !

From his place at the door W. sees the father look up, and his smile is almost identical to his son's: the same shiny white row of teeth.

Johann, you recall that woman who came to my practice one day saying she had swallowed a full bundle of needles. Tried to take her own life, the poor woman. But however many needles she consumed she could not succeed in her venture. She'd swallow a needle only for it to reappear without having caused any apparent damage. Do explain to me, Johann, I'm sure you know, how the swallowed needle, regardless of size and regardless of position, always exited the body headfirst and without occasioning damage on its way through the body? Pray tell to what does this owe, Johann? Is it the influence of magnetism, or a peculiarity of the female organism?

All eyes around the table turn to the young doctor; both children curious, the stepmother with a smile that doesn't quite have the energy to be full of confidence. But Johann does not respond. He remains in the same contorted pose, his body against the edge of the table, head turned to one side and his eyes on the door. In this studied three-quarter view, he seems to W. like a proud and timid bird who has taken refuge in one of the darkened trees because something on the ground has frightened him out of his wits.

Then a long shiver seems to run through the young doctor. He crumples up his napkin and abruptly tosses it aside, rises and walks with his characteristic quick and casting steps towards the door. W. is sure he is about to fall and has already moved to catch him under the arms. But the young doctor pauses at the last moment, twitchily moves past him, and even manages to toss a few words over his shoulder:

You're no longer needed, Woyetz. You may return to Your quarters.

But in a while, when W. is still fully dressed and lying awake on his bed in the small room assigned to him, the bell rings anew and soon one of the kitchen maids knocks on the door. She says that he has been called to serve the wine. She has, however, already heated and poured the wine into a pitcher, apparently well-acquainted with the young doctor's habits. She hands him the wine on a tray and accompanies him through the servant's passage until once again they are in the rooms occupied by the family Schönberg. The dining room which had been so festively lit is empty now, the cleared dining table white as a marble slab in the night's cold gleam falling through the windows. Through the doorways the rooms appear in succession as though they were nesting boxes. The light that guides them is coming from the room-box furthest in, the book-filled library, where the young doctor has put his writing cabinet. He sits there now, in the same pose as at the dining table, his lower body pressed to the abattant and a book open in front of him. Though the floorboards groan loudly, at first he seems to pay no mind to W. when which man arrives with the wine, but then he spins around and reveals his white row of teeth, frightening in this light: as though you could see right into his skull.

My sincerest apologies, Woyetz. Such a spectacle You were made to witness today! My father loves to test me, he would so very much like me to take up his mantle. But how is one such as I meant to hold a scalpel? Can Woyetz tell me how? He has seen everything, he knows.

W. wants to say that he doesn't know anything about anything. He hasn't seen anyone take a fall. Or anything else.

But the young doctor has already moved on:

Say, Woyetz, he says. Does he believe in God? He does, of course; but is he truly *enlightened* in spirit? Does he know anything *about* his faith?

And before W. can interject or deflect the question:

In the lower classes it is common to feel wonder over God's (what shall we call it) being, but also rage against what he does with us humans, that he intentionally, it seems, elevates some to angels and turns others into beasts.

Haven't I seen Woyetz hovering around this piece of furniture, he says and swiftly stands up and flings open the wing doors wide.

There's that row of teeth again and something in the gaze that should already have frightened him then. But W. only has eyes for the cabinet.

In retrospect, he would have a hard time explaining, not least to Clarus, what he actually saw in there. As if the memory of what he'd seen disappeared the second it was revealed. Or as if what he saw was not intended to be seen at all. That which dwells in the interior of the world is perhaps not meant for human eyes. Such things belong to the realm of the soul, and if one lacks the right words, and if one knows nothing of the order in which the objects are to be placed, and does not have the tools to place them there, neither do they, it seems, want to be perceived.

Angelic materia, he could have said. Even if each single thing he saw was concrete enough, comfortably resting in itself as a shadow rests in its light.

While he was presenting all this, the young doctor recounted that it had been a relation of his, one Prince von Schönberg-Waldenburg, who had begun collecting natural history specimens at a modest scale towards the end of the previous century. Later he had received help from an apothecary in Leipzig called Reichel and a baker named Oberländer, who donated a large number of bird's eggs to the collection. Here are a few of them, says the young doctor and holds out three small quail eggs in a woven basket. He holds one between his fingertips. Look how small it is, and yet its top is large enough to house a whole continent.

The young doctor holds out a piece of dried seaweed: a wave made stiff, halted mid-swell with what once were veils of pearly foam dried into tiny blisters. He also brings out reeds in meticulously bound bundles; each brittle reed wrapped in a knuckle-like girdle.

The young doctor pulls out yet another numbered drawer in which apothecary bottles are kept, brown and bulbous. Even the salt he sprinkles in his palm is varicolored: red, brown, ocher. There is also a jar with a pure white salt, a salt he says comes from the shores of a dead sea, thin and brittle as chalk.

And all the while, as he opens compartments and pulls out drawers, he is explaining to W. why it is unthinkable for him to be parted from his cabinet:

It's a kind of magnetism. Is Woyetz familiar with this phenomenon? Just as the Earth's axis draws us to it and keeps us upright by the force of its infinite gravity alone. It is as if I am bound to this cabinet by the same force. If I fall beyond reach of this axis even by an arm's length, a stupefaction passes through me, I lose all sense and fall. It's remarkable that one can be created in such a sorry way, and yet so sensitive.

Ah well, Woyetz, he then says to W. as though immediately regretting his open-hearted confession. Step closer so that he may see!

The young doctor takes a key from his vest pocket and holds it up for a while as if to present it, then sticks it in the lock of one of the drawers, it too with mother-of-pearl fittings but unlike the others elongated in shape. From the bottom of the drawer he lifts up what W. first takes to be a collection of letters, rolled up and girded with a silk band. The doctor loosens the band and unfurls the pages, each and every one curled into the one before. He hands one to W. while saying:

Do not allow your spirit to be shocked, Woyetz, it is but how God has created us.

The page is made up of an engraving or etching of some sort. Set in a frame in the middle a group made up of two half-dressed women and one man pose by a piece of furniture that resembles the writing cabinet.

The man is sitting on a chair next to the abattant, or rather half-sitting because he is stretching and twisting his body so as to reach his face to the high bosom that the woman on his right is offering him. On his left is the other woman, one hand around his stiff sex, the other cupped around her own, thumb and index finger placed as one does the fingers around an eye, the other three fingers—middle finger, ring finger, little finger—spread as though to give the viewer a sign.

W. has a lump in his throat but doesn't dare swallow.

He immediately wants to hand the picture back, but the young doctor doesn't extend a hand to receive it. Instead he has taken out another key for another drawer and is presently handing him another picture. At first he thinks these are the same figures, but fully dressed. In fact this one is about two, not three, figures; and their positions are reversed. This time it is the woman who is sitting by the abattant and next to her is a boy of five or six with long blonde hair done up in beautiful curls spilling over an old-fashioned ruff.

Come closer, says the young doctor when he sees that W. isn't withdrawing. Do You see the locket around the boy's neck?

W. says he sees it. The young doctor then opens a box and takes out the very locket threaded on a small chain. He opens the locket.

Do You see the picture framed in the locket?

He holds the locket out to W. Inside the locket is the same image that the young doctor just showed him, and here too sits a boy with the locket around his neck. Which is of course extremely odd. W. bends over to study the picture more closely. In the medallion worn by the boy in the picture in the locket is there a picture of a woman with a boy who is also wearing a locket? If so, it could go on like that for all eternity. The thought is dizzying.

That's my mother and me in the picture, the young doctor says, and hardly has W. begun to grasp this fact before the young doctor has taken out yet another box, this time scarcely larger than a collar button box. From it he takes a ring.

And this, he says, is her wedding ring.

The young doctor holds the ring up in the light. W. catches a glimpse of the small stone set in the middle.

It was once my father's. He pulled it off her finger when she lay dead in the room above. I've taken it back.

With a sudden gesture he wraps his hand around the ring and joylessly smiles his strange toothy smile.

I'm going to take everything back. All that is mine. And You shall assist me.

That was all, he adds, as if this revelation had been an irrelevant afterthought.

You may go now, Woyetz.

W. goes. But before he leaves the gentleman's apartment he turns around one last time. Furthest in, at the edge of the slit of light falling through the doorway, he sees the young doctor sitting at his writing cabinet. But now with his back to him again, with all the doors and boxes pulled out, like an organist at his great church organ.

AFTER A BRIEF EASING, THE downpour continues, days-long, impenetrable, and the young doctor continues his restless wandering through the bare unheated rooms: face leaden, as though he were no more than a spirit image in the windows dissolved by rain.

He is waiting on the father, on a crucial conversation or decision from the man. But the father appears at odd times of day, impossible to predict, and if the son dines with him at one of the tables hastily drawn by the servants the father scarcely makes time to speak with him and instead reads from or leafs through the stack of books and periodicals as usual, then rises in haste, saying he must be off.

Sometimes the father's arrival draws out long into the night, or even into the small hours of the morning. It is on one such occasion that W. hears their voices booming, first from the courtyard, then up the stairs into the parlor. W. glimpses them in one of the dining room mirrors as they walk by, and never before has the contrast between the two, one all-powerful and the other powerless, been so stark. The father stands in full riding costume in front of the escritoire while the young doctor is still in his nightclothes. Pale and raddled he stands there, as though he has not slept for days, steadying himself against the walls and the doorways as he searchingly and cautiously approaches his father, who does not even pretend to have seen him.

The conversation is about money. Hence the son's ever louder, more pointed formulations, about him not possibly being able to continue his studies and his intention to enlist in the military, which only makes the father snort derisively. What, a weakling like yourself? No one will have you. Wherewith the son says that he can't stand it anymore. Because he is not in possession of the requisite strength, he must subordinate himself to some external order. On whose side, may I ask? the father asks as though he had heard nothing. There is only one side, says the son; the side that takes up arms against tyrants and autocrats, those you have served for all your years. And what of being slaughtered like a dog? the father asks sarcastically. Is that what you want? What would your mother have said to that?

When the mother's name is mentioned it is as though something in the son goes slack. He gasps after breath and with both his hands leans heavily against the doorpost.

Weakling, says the father storming by in his boots.

No more than a few minutes pass before the servant's bell rings, and when W. comes running the young doctor is already in full swing packing up his belongings. He orders his carriage to be hitched up and driven out and the cabinet be carried out and loaded at once. A moment later the coachman Metzger is holding the coach at the front doors, and never has the cabinet seemed so cumbrous and hulking as then. It takes six men to carry it out, and W. is already dreading what it will take to get it up to the professor-widow's apartment since only he and Metzger will be left to support it on their feeble shoulders.

The stepmother has come out with both of the young children to bid him farewell.

The servants are there too, as silent as statues. The father is not present.

Nevertheless the young doctor is anxious to get on his way. The writing cabinet has barely been set on platform when he calls to Metzger to take up the reins. But they get no further than the entrance gate before another carriage passes them at high speed causing the horses to shrink back, curtsy, and almost rear up. Then the platform tips over, and before anyone can intervene, least of all W. who has his hands full just holding on, the cabinet begins to slip and soon the whole monstrosity falls to the ground with an awful crash. From atop the platform W. watches as the panel doors, which he would have secured had they not been in such a rush, fly open and the young doctor's entire collection tumbles out. The bird's eggs, the mussel shells, the mother-of-pearl box case, the peacock feathers. From the crack that has upon impact split right through the cabinet a heap of glass and silverware falls out, which W. last saw arranged on the table in the parlor. As well as wall ornaments, a tablecloth, a small silver pitcher, and a hand mirror inlaid with mother-of-pearl.

At once, several things become clear to W. He realizes that the stop in Dessau was no coincidence: Schwalbe had presumably bought things off the young doctor before; this is why, during the journey to Waldenburg, the young doctor had ceaselessly complained of the Jewish pawnbroker's unpaid bill, which by law, with regard to the sewing services W. provided, should have been the selfsame man whose bill was paid. (He personally had not received a single groschen.) He also thinks he understands why the previous valets in the young doctor's employ had all "run off." There's no mystery to it if one is forced to assist one's master in the removal of stolen goods.

Even the servant folk can't manage to suppress their dismay. The housekeeper drags a chambermaid with her out into the courtyard and tries to gather up divers scattered movables in her apron folds. But the stepmother stops them with a commanding sweep of her arm as though the gateway and entire courtyard had instantly become poisoned ground.

Upon the coach box the young doctor looks as though he had just been hit in the face. He tries to smile, but the smile that can otherwise seem so inviting is but a grimace of teeth. He orders W. and Coachman Metzger to load the cabinet onto the coach, which they manage to do, with considerable fuss and before the servants' silent gazes, and without even feigning to pack and bind it properly they drive away along the castle hill. Then they turn off at Kirchplatz and onto the large country road in the direction of Chemnitz.

BUT THEY DO NOT GO to Chemnitz. A short distance beyond Waldenburg the young doctor orders the coachman to turn southeast instead, towards Stollberg. W. is sitting furthest back on the platform and trying to cling to a cabinet not worth clinging on to anymore. Up on the coach box he sees Metzger turn around in surprise.

Why are we taking this road, milord? I don't understand.

But the young doctor is huddled, stiffly wrapped in his own arms, and isn't to be spoken to.

They travel through the places where brown coal lignite once was mined. The open cast mines widen into unreal hollows in the landscape, lakes of rainwater lay between the savaged crests, some of which appear to have been cut right through by a giant pair of shears. After a few hours of travel, the landscape grows mountainous, then the path winds steeply up a long slope. Now the road is lined on both sides with a spruce forest. The higher they go the brighter the sky seems. But this brightening is treacherous. The rain increases in strength and when the forest thins out they are batted around like a sail in the wind, which is capricious up here; a mighty swelling rain, heavy with its own moisture, icy sharp when it ricochets from below into W.'s face, as he hunches under his collar, blinded, his hands numb with cold.

Gradually the road ends and becomes a pitted mess of granite and mud and he and Metzger have to go out and push the coach from behind. When horse as well as carriage still do not move, the young doctor turns to the baggage strapped at the back of the coach box, takes out a rifle, and instructs W. to follow him.

He doesn't look at him as he says it.

Where are we going? W. asks, but the young doctor doesn't reply.

They walk without a word, the young doctor half a dozen steps ahead, as though he had a specific destination in sight even though no such destination can be discerned. All that can be heard is the sound of pouring rain being driven by the wind across the barren earth where hardly a blade of grass is to be seen. A cluster of trees appears through the haze and as he is thinking that they will finally have a moment of respite from the wind and rain, a murder of crows rises shrieking into the sky and all the trees vanish. As though the crows had only pretended to be trees.

Everything is in this way but gloss and dissolution. The muddy ground beneath his feet no longer supports his steps. He stumbles, gropes around so as not to fall over. The young doctor, however, does not seem troubled in the least. With an affected drawling gloom, he speaks of the livestock plague that made its way through these mountains several years ago and took a grave toll on the local shepherds. Every animal had to be slaughtered, the meat was inedible, the young doctor says, and it is as though the rain has quite hollowed out his thin face so that only bare bones protrude, this and his thin smile. Mask and skull in one.

Tell me, Woyetz, You who draws; how would You depict this?

They're standing atop something that in the darkness of the rain he has first taken for a slope but upon closer inspection seems to be a long crack or dip in the ground. It is as though the landscape had let go of itself in one fell swoop: fragments of boulder are scattered across an area that could be as large as one field or several fields, in the haze there is no end in sight, the rocks overgrown with a coating like wounds from leprosy or another disease. Here and there remnants of white bone can be seen, strangely luminous in the flat, gray rainlight.

W.'s whole body is shaking, as though the harsh cold emanating from this place has squeezed into his marrow. Beside him the young doctor continues to hold forth about how the shepherds put their animals down. Not only those beset by the plague had to give their lives. All the other useless creatures too, ewes unable to give birth, their udders swollen, were brought here, their throats slit, and left to bleed out.

The poison comes to light here, You can see for Yourself, Woyetz.

But W. isn't listening anymore, he only sees the young doctor gesticulating with his rifle. What is he going to do with it? They are hardly in an area suited for hunting. Has the young doctor once and for all lost his patience with his absentminded and negligent valet? Does he perhaps think his valet has seen too much of what shouldn't have been shown and now intends to get rid of him as one gets rid of a dog? And who would ever find him up here? Of course the young doctor could tell Metzger that W. has simply run off. Like all the other valets ran off.

What place is this? he asks in a whisper.

Up here they call it the raptor's trap, the young doctor says. Don't you see the birds, Woyetz, how they circle up high? They are forever on the lookout. For them, there is no difference between the living and dead. Nor between animal and man, for that matter.

W. doesn't dare look to the sky, or anywhere else.

This place is like my sickness, Woyetz, he hears the doctor say beside him. Such am I on the inside. Nothing is what I can become with my affliction, not an officer, not a doctor. And all of us must serve, is that not so, Woyetz? Serve some purpose at least. And those no longer fit to serve, those are brought here.

Right then. Let's get this out of the way, he says and W. hears him raise the already loaded rifle. I hope the gunpowder hasn't spoiled in the damp.

With those words it is as if W.'s legs give out underneath him, but instead of the icy mouth of a rifle at the back of his neck he feels something being pressed into his arms. When he opens his eyes he sees the young doctor on all fours beside him. W.'s first thought is that he is suffering another attack. So he flings the rifle aside, which for some reason has ended up between them, and tries to get him back on his feet by taking hold under his arms, only for the young doctor to angrily push him away.

LET GO OF ME YOU WRETCHED MOLLUSC, YOU'RE SUPPOSED TO SHOOT ME!

W. lets go. For a moment the only sound is that of the rain seeping through the moss and the already sodden grass. The doctor remains on all fours; then he straightens up and his breath clouds around his contorted mouth:

YOU ARE A SERVANT, DO AS YOU ARE TOLD. GO AHEAD AND SHOOT!

With unrestrained movements he picks the rifle up from the place where W. has thrown it, grabs the barrel with both hands and swings it like a bludgeon at W.'s head and shoulders. W. feels the blow land right behind his ear, then nothing more. He only knows that he is on his back, his hands against the boulder's wet, ravaged rock.

The rain seems to have eased. This is his last thought before the pain in the back of his head swells and draws him down as though into a deep, dirty maw.

Eternities seem to pass, but perhaps it is only a matter of minutes. From far away the young doctor's voice can be heard: *Metzger, you have to hurry, I'm not sure what I've done,* and the coachman shouts an indistinct reply. Still maybe Metzger is on his way. He wants to raise his arm and wave to those rushing over, as though even in this downcast state he still has a duty to point out his situation. But he is unable to lift a limb. Instead he stares up at the sky as it opens above him like a deep well, and now the rain has in fact eased because highest up he sees two birds of prey circling, wings spread as though crucified.

Patiently, back and forth, they circle beneath the sky.

EXACTLY HOW LONG THEREAFTER HE can't explain to Clarus, but at some later time W. returned to Leipzig and found a post as a driver with Councillor Hornig in Barneck. At the councillor's, stable hands and carters aren't allowed to mix with the other servants. Nevertheless W. cannot rid himself of the memory of what it was like to live in a manor house, of waiting on the young doctor and listening to his unusual expositions, and he can't stop thinking about the wondrous writing cabinet that cracked in two and how all was seen that should not have been seen and how the rich too can harbor shameful secrets.

W. now has a place to sleep with wadding maker Richter and the man's son in a small house right across from Hornig's splendid residence, but he spends most of his time in the loft above the stall where the councillor's carter Anton Heuss has made a simple dwelling for himself.

Heuss is a widower, having recently lost his wife and child in childbirth, a touch reserved but a hale and honorable fellow, orderly and liked by all. W. helps Anton clean the stalls and repair the tack in the evenings and in return they share a bottle if Anton has one to hand. He has acquaintances in the places around the area to where he drives the councillor and his family, and whenever he returns from an errand he has a humorous anecdote. But he is not intrusive. They can spend hours in silence, each one consumed to their own end. There's something about the alcohol and about the animals in the stable, about the smell and heat of the hay and the horses' bodies, that allows his slumber of thought to spread through him almost like pleasure. Occasionally they get to talking in the evening, and then he might tell Anton Heuss about his *Condition* with the old wigmaker Knobloch, about the

Jewish pawnbroker in Dessau, and other masters he has had in Berlin, in Breslau, in Teplitz.

Heuss asks what he thinks of being in the councillor's service, and if there is anyone in service of this house, if there is anyone in Barneck who might find themselves in his good graces, he who is so worldly, and perhaps W. is incautious in this moment, perhaps it is just the alcohol and well-being emanating from Anton Heuss himself, whatever it is he can't help but mention the name of young Fräulein Schindel.

Luise Schindel is wadding maker Richter's stepdaughter and works as a housemaid for the councillor. She is not beautiful, rather thickly built and blowzy skinned. She has a beautiful smile that she lets bloom like a flower. As soon as his gaze falls upon her she smiles: without a thought, it seems, without shyness either. It is as though him setting foot in the same room is enough to light up her face from within with this smile. He thinks of her often and imagines that she only smiles for him and so he becomes clumsier in her company, which makes her laugh.

One day she asks him why he stays in the stables and not with her stepfather, where he has his bed?

Now everyone knows that Richter treats people badly, not just his lodgers but also his own son, his wife as well as her daughter. Richter was quite simply born disobliging; he is a person who forfeits no opportunity to complain about everything and everyone, is always contrary and never pleased. His complaints about his son Joseph are unending, even though the man is diligent and capable. But Joseph too has withdrawn; he works as a carpenter's apprentice in a neighboring village and is never at home more than necessary.

Surely he isn't ashamed to be in her company? Luise asks and lets her beautiful smile bloom, and what can he say, but that he sees her far too seldom because she stays mostly indoors and the councillor has forbidden people like him to cross the house's threshold?

One day as winter is nearing it is agreed that Luise shall go to Burschendorf to help with the slaughter and W. nags his way to an invitation. Heuss drives the two-horse carriage, and the two of them sit at the back, legs dangling over the edge. Pheasant shooting is underway in the forests, they can hear the sharp muffled cracks of the rifle shots in the trees. This makes him think of the young doctor. Once, he says, I was in the service of a young nobleman who kept eggs from a thousand different birds in a cabinet he had. He also had a collection of tail feathers, he says. And also of peacocks: the most beautiful birds on earth. She tells him that she has only seen them in books. And then he says that the young nobleman would travel to an estate that was full of such birds. The males would fan out their full train of feathers behind them and each and every tail feather seemed to have its own eye, but the colors were so beautiful, like mother-of-pearl and turquoise and another shade of blue that was unlike anything he had ever seen before.

She becomes animated as he recounts this. She grabs hold of his hand, but perhaps it is only to support herself during the jolting ride, and says: he who is so handy, can't he make one for me?

A peacock? he asks.

Yes, after all he has such beautiful hands, that Woyzeck. Surely he can make something fine.

And so it begins—a story of love and shame and borrowed finery.

Through Joseph Richter he comes by a lovely piece of aspen wood that he cuts and carves until it resembles the body of a bird. The aspen wood is smooth and pliable, it does not seep resin. Moreover it is easy to work with. He devotes the entire winter to carving the body, so immersed in labor's respite is he that the tree's smooth grain flows along with his movements all the way down to his fingertips. The tail feathers, which are to number eighteen, are also made from aspen wood and he joins them together like a fan. And so these tail feathers can fan out too: first he fashions a model made of stiff paper, which can be expanded and retracted with the help of a string fixed to the underside of the bird's body. More than once he shows Heuss how the whole device is meant to work, and Heuss pensively chews his wad of tobacco but doesn't say a word. Most difficult to get right are the colors. The colors can't be too shiny, nor too bright, for then they would be frivolous. Nor can they be left to crack as they dry, for then the bird will lose its luster.

All of this could have progressed in a natural way and would have been perfectly in order had he not kept running to the house to ask for this or that essential thing for the making of the bird. For this he is given a nickname. He becomes the Loon. The Loon seems to think that woodwork is enough of a prelude for an offer of marriage, it is said. From the windows of the house one can look onto the stable where the Loon has set up his workbench. Young boys cluster around the bench each morning and Heuss shoos them off only to see them standing a score of yards away, still gawping.

Of course it is clear who the intended recipient is. Young Fräulein Schindel laughs when she is asked about the courtship, but it is as if her smile has suddenly become as thin and brittle as glass.

During the winter and the long spring that follows, the two of them, thus far considered practically engaged, scarcely meet at all. The bird-creature seems to take their place. At night it wakes and struts back and forth with high ducal steps, sweeping the stable floor with its velvety train. Even Heuss who had once regarded the spectacle with certain indifference now enters his workplace with trepidation and shines his hand lantern over the countless tail- and wing feathers spread out on the floor, wave upon wave of slim, pliant plumes, each tailored to fit its special place on the bird. He tries to divert his young charge's thoughts. All women love trinkets and trifles, he tells W.; but how will this be received?

Even Joseph Richter, the wadding maker's son, appears in the stables one morning vacillating over something he wants to have said. *I am to relay on behalf of my sister that she declines.* But by then the bird is as good as ready, what is there to be declined? It is already standing there: a gruesome likeness, its beak open in one of the cries these birds emit that are like death cries, the train fanned out to its full span, a peacock heaven full of intrusive eyes, staring out from their own impenetrable turquoise-blue expanse.

On the day the gift is to be presented the entire neighborhood is on its feet, word has gone from house to house, and everywhere, behind trees and outbuildings, in windows, on front steps and in doorways, people have their eyes fixed on Councillor Hornig's residence.

Woyzeck appears on the stable yard, his gift covered with a small cloth.

It is like when an orchestra is playing, then suddenly stops.

Look here comes the Loon, someone says, and in that initially reverent silence laughter is heard, soft at first, then (as others join in) ever louder.

And at once all shyness and veneration are blown away, people are pushing each other aside and cramming in and soon the lookers-on have cohered into a moving mass of spectators who follow the lone W. who with his gift has already climbed Richter's front steps.

He manages no more than a knock and an apprehensive backwards step before the door is flung open and wadding maker Richter emerges in full fury.

He's about to get what's coming to him for running around and making a mockery of decent people! he says and slaps the bird out of the suitor's arms, then follows after him swatting and pushing W. back into the yard until the man stumbles and falls and crawls away from the swift kicks of the boot towards the place where the peacock has landed. A pale Luise peers out from behind her furious stepfather. At the sight of her, W. climbs to his feet and grabs hold of the maltreated bird with both hands. Don't be frightened, Fräulein Schindel, he says, see how pretty it is. But the young Fräulein puts her hand over her mouth and rushes back inside the Richter home. Richter himself interprets his stepdaughter's sortie is the end of the courtship, turns to the crowd and shouts *Off with you, you devils!*, then strides into the vestibule and slams the door behind him.

The following week Luise goes to Burschendorf. She has been given a *Condition* there and is no longer to be seen at Hornig's in Barneck. And now he must drop this matter of the bird. Everyone says so. Even Heuss, whose advice he otherwise tends to heed. But nothing is dropped. Quite the opposite. It's as though he is stuck in a vise, the jaws of which are clamping down on him ever harder. On the stable floor the bird of shame sits beneath its cloth, but he spends his nights roaming the forest. He walks along the road to Burschendorf in hopes of encountering her. He lurks in bushes, his eyes on the servant's wing. If while he was making the Bird of Shame he thought he was invisible to all, now it seems he is ever in view.

And so it begins again: that which will make a laughingstock of him for the rest of his life. The sneaking around. The spying on of people and things from great distances. The desire to hide. But also the cabinet dreams: he wishes the world were like a cabinet and that he might decide for himself how everything in there should be made. He'd keep a bed in it, he thinks. A table and two chairs. One for him, one for her. A withy basket full of dreams. Luise's face behind a screen of leaves. The smile that blooms in her face, like a bird who blooms from the foliage, then spreads across the sky.

He and Joseph Richter dream of fleeing and enlisting. From the young doctor he believes he has learned everything there is to know about Napoleon Bonaparte and his brave generals. Joseph Richter may be young, but his face is already furrowed. With an old man's import, he arranges it in worried folds as W. confesses his love for his sister. One day he arrives with a key that he claims fits the door of the side wing in Burschendorf. His sister has by no means turned her back on him, he says. On the contrary, she still holds him dear and would gladly see him again. She was merely frightened after all the fuss about the Bird. And because her stepfather beat her. He beat her so senselessly, yellow and blue, thus she had to move away. So Hornig and all the others in Barneck wouldn't see how badly the father had abused her. And so he tells him to go visit Luise in Burschendorf, and if it starts to go awry he should say hello from him, her brother: him she trusts. And from this conversation a mad, dizzy dream emerges in W. about running away, the three of them, Joseph and he and the sister, who then would become his wife forevermore.

One Saturday night there's a dance at a tavern a half hour's ride outside of Burschendorf. From the roadside he can already hear the strings of a violin being stretched, a rosined bow testing its glide across the bridge: a shrill sound that soon grows softer, more amenable. True to his habit he hides behind some bushes a short distance from the dance floor and watches her swinging around in the low, flat evening light. That smile is on her face the whole time. By that smile he recognizes her, but because it is not to him that the smile is directed it feels as though she were wearing a mask.

Those with whom she dances are from Burschendorf or the surrounding farms. But there are also people from Barneck. He hears the two camps laughing and trying to call each other out, to challenge each other. And the girls are passed from one pair of arms to the next and there is much brawling but largely concord prevails. Only when the musicians have packed up and set off do the two groups part. But instead of stepping forward and making himself known to his people, those from Barneck, W. follows the still boisterous and laughing bunch who are on their way to Burschendorf. He keeps to the forest, walking along ditches, sometimes sunk to his knees in the mire left behind by the rain. He lingers at the forest's edge when they turn onto the long avenue that leads up to the farm. Patiently he waits until the ruckus from the servant's wing has died down and he is sure that everyone has gone to bed.

Then he takes out the key that he has been squeezing in his trouser pocket all night and tries to stick it in the lock, just like Joseph said. However hard he tries, he cannot get it to fit. Enraged, he beats and pounds the door and then the dogs wake up in the main house and much more quickly than he expected, unfamiliar men arrive. They have their lanterns in hand and their dogs leashed, and they begin to beat him with cudgels and do not let up until they've pushed him into a corner of the yard, and surely they would have beaten him to death had she not broken through the dense wall of men and barking dogs.

She: Luise.

He sees her bosom heaving in anger. The smile has left her blowzy face. He doesn't know how to rewaken it.

People are standing around in a circle, even the older domestic servants.

It is like when he was going to give her the peacock and everyone crowded around him, staring. And this he cannot stand. It can by no means happen *again*. Is this perchance your key, he then says, stepping forward and holding it up in front of her face. And up for everyone else: gloating.

Might this be her key, you think? How else do you all think I came by it?

Still it seems to be happening again. He stands there and makes a mockery of her, laying her out for public view and shame. Again he sees her bosom heave. But the embarrassment is gone from her face, there is only disdain, and then they come, the words, like an angry snort:

it's not . . . it's not that You . . . lack all measure . . .

You are sick, Woyzeck, but You don't know it

Then he steps forward and hits her in the face with the key in his clenched fist and she flies backwards with a shriek. She covers her face with her hands and blood drips between her fingers. When the others rush to her aid, a gap appears in the crowd and he seizes the opportunity to tear himself free and escape, but in the avenue he can still her awful screams and the barking of dogs.

The news travels faster than he can run. Halfway to Barneck he is intercepted by young Richter who informs him that her father is raving because he disgraced his stepdaughter and he has sent the police after him. If you hold your life dear, never come back to Hornig's, Joseph says. I can bring you your things tomorrow. So he sleeps under a few spruce branches that night. It's not cold because it is the middle of summer, but his dread is such that he is run through with shivers. Again and again young Fräulein Luise's smile is split bloody by his pounding fists. At dawn he watches from a safe distance as Heuss hitches up the Berlin carriage and helps Frau Hornig up, and soon thereafter Joseph comes running with a backpack in one hand, in the other his scuffed boots.

I'm coming with you, he says, and W. who hasn't even considered having to flee, realizes that this is his only way out. A few hours later they are out on the country road without having left word with or bidden anyone farewell.

JOSEPH KNOWS HOW TO SET bird traps. Mostly they catch small birds, sparrows darting across freshly plowed fields in swift knots. They empty the traps and build a fire, threading the birds on long willow skewers and polishing them off bones, gristle, and all. They then continue their hike along the lakes that carry the dawning light upon their mirrored waters. In the hours before the light gains enough strength to lift the day, it is as if they are walking along the edge of the celestial round as the globe, still swept in misty darkness, vaults heavily below.

For ten days and ten nights he and Joseph Richter are underway, mostly by foot and through rugged forest terrain. Finally they cross the border into Prussia.

Above the Havel River the sky is full of birds.

W. stands with one hand outstretched, down feathers in his hair and on the back of his hand and between his fingers. He carefully blows the down off his fingertips and watches it sail away. In spite of it all, there are objects in the world more transient than air. Just when you think you've made contact with the wonder of love, the promise of self-transformation, it has already fled and passed by.

A few months after the two young men's escape, in October 1806, Napoleon annihilates the Austrian emperor's and Prince-elector Friedrich August's Saxon troops in Jena. On the stroke there follows in the middle of November, as is written in the Books of Chronicles, an unusually rich shower of falling stars, as though the sky itself had been dealt a dizzying blow by the French emperor's victories.

THE DUTCH ARMY'S RECRUITMENT OFFICE consists of a few rough-hewn planks laid over two wooden trestles in a courtyard surrounded by half-timbered houses on Grosse Strasse in Grabow. About twenty young recruits, Mecklenburgers mostly, are freezing in the line leading up to the plank table. Behind the table Assessor of War Grebstock sits next to a recruitment officer and behind them stands a French soldier. He is there to ensure the line does not become disorderly but he seems more interested in hollering at his comrades who are gorging themselves at a nearby tavern. The language the French speak consists of long incomprehensibly muttered words snared into long tirades and neither he nor Joseph understand one iota from where they are in the crowd, except perhaps for the curse words which seem to sound alike in most languages.

The town is swarming with Frenchmen. They're guarding the troop- and ammunition transports that are advancing down the city's main road. Moreover the soldiers are generous customers of the tobacco peddlers who sweep past the rows of officers, or of the junk sellers who have pushed out their shop carts or of the farmers who traveled to the city with bread, vegetables, and fruit, wares that are being advertised in loud, shrill voices from every street corner the troops pass by. War seems to give rise to a special order where everything gets mixed up and where excess is the only measure of things: an excitement that can only be stilled by further excess, like a fever that refuses to leave the body though the body itself is being consumed by it.

Even Assessor Grebstock, who is charged with keeping the enlistment process on the straight and narrow, allows himself to be persuaded to taste what the tavern has to offer and doesn't decline the offer of yet another tall dram of schnapps in a tall dram glass. Now and then, perhaps mostly for appearance's sake, he bends over the enormous ledger that the recruitment officer holds open in front of him and makes a notation, but only after carefully setting aside fork and knife and wiping his mouth with a napkin. The recruitment officer doesn't seem to be in a hurry either; everyone who is accepted shall be entered into the books with their baptismal name and their hometown and the names of their father and mother. Or perhaps the war creates its own measure of time, in which the distance between life and death lacks all meaning. The only time that counts is the time that passes between the recruit taking his place at the end of the line and, after much shoving and swearing, getting to the front where he can finally give his name, accurately translated by Grebstock if the recruitment officer doesn't understand, and then see it be inscribed beneath all the other names that are already there and so have his fate sealed with ink and sigil.

Assessor Grebstock is a wrinkled man, gaunt by nature with a sharp aquiline profile but gentle eyes. When he bends over his plate and glass, the crown of his head shines porcelain white beneath the thin strands of hair he has combed over his pate. Now and then a word or two escape him when his gaze happens to glide over the names that the recruitment officer is struggling to spell correctly.

So he wishes to be a soldier, Wojtschek. What merits does he have? Can he handle a rifle?

But he doesn't look up when he says this, for what he is saying is not a question of conscience but for the register or for eternity. Then he takes fresh hold of the tall dram glass and signals to the waiter for more schnapps.

One week later he and young Richter have installed themselves at a provisional commissariat supply service next to the staging post on the other side of the newly built stone bridge. They are given uniforms and instructed by a Dutch field usher in how to wear the cap and fold the garments. After that all the recruits are made to line up and walk in marching order to a shooting range at the back of the town's large brewery where they learn how to handle their rifle, how the bayonet is mounted and removed, how the cartridge is plucked from the cartouche, and the simplest way to bite off the cartridge and stuff the bullet and powder into the barrel using the ramrod. Thereafter five days of drills begin. Only after this does their Dutch company commander, one Captain van Heusen, lead them to the Swedish front in order to reinforce the French siege at Stralsund.

By now winter has arrived. Breath smokes from the officers' mouths and the horses' bodies steam. They bivouac less than a mile outside the city walls. In clear weather the fortress walls can be glimpsed, like a dark blue mirage above the flat snowy landscape. Now and then they are shot at by Swedish gunboats anchored in the roadstead and even if the shots rarely hit anything but scrubs and open fields, misery still spreads among the troops. Rumor has it that the siege is pointless. Because the Swedes control Rügen, necessities and ammunition are still reaching their troops, and the French know this because they have withdrawn their forces to instead fight the Prussians outside of Danzig, leaving the Dutch to defend themselves as best they can against the Swedish bombardment.

But the days of crystal clear cold during which it is possible to take aim or generally distinguish anything in one's sight line are few. For the most part the entire coast is shrouded in gray rain and then nothing is visible, no soaring walls, no enemies, only the sound of infantrymen gathering their rucksacks and pewter flasks, and the constant creaking of un-oiled wagon wheels as the artillery regroups or is sent forward.

They do drills on empty fields, surrounded only by a fog so dense that they can barely make out each other's contours. Early in the morning of one such uniformly gray drill day a courier comes barreling in on horseback. He has a message from the staff. The siege is to be broken. They are to leave their posts immediately.

For two whole days they find themselves on the march, its direction or duration unclear, and dogged by the rumor that the Swedes are at their heels and could attack at any moment or may even be lying in ambush farther up the road, a notion stubbornly denied by the officers. When they finally reach the Peene River the company is in disarray. Of those who were with him in bivouac, only one older soldiers remains, and all the officers, including the second lieutenant, have disappeared. Joseph is nowhere to be found either, and no one he speaks with has seen him.

They wait for a few hours, unsure if they should set up camp and await the rest of the troops or if they should try to cross the river, each man for himself. When they have finally agreed to send off one of the troops to look for a bridge or at least a place where the river narrows and is easier to cross, the Swedes come charging from every direction, as though they had merely been waiting for one of them to break formation in order to attack from behind.

The jostling crush that ensues most resembles an awkward, untidy brawl. He tries to wrench the rifle from his shoulder, but before he can bite off the cartridge someone has torn the ramrod from his hands. Then he is whacked on the back of his head and lands facedown in the wet earth, stamping boots and horse hooves all around and panting and groaning along with demented wailing cries.

When he comes to his senses he finds himself in a convoy of prisoners. A good two dozen men chained hand and foot sit upon two long benches in a covered wagon and no one has a clue where they are being taken or under whose protection they happen to be. The road they are traveling is rock-strewn and rolling. With each lurch of the wagon they are tossed onto and over each other as far as their chains allow. Several of them are badly injured. The soldier nearest to him has a serious flesh wound on his arm which he has bandaged with a dirty scarf. Further in sits a soldier whose ankle is cut open and who is frantic, screaming and pounding his head against the wall, perhaps out of pain or in a bid for the guards' or driver's attention.

The only one who seems to be unharmed is a boy of maybe twelve or thirteen years who is staring blankly ahead. When W. accidentally nudges him, he seems to come to and looks around in horror, as though only now is he discovering that there are other people in the wagon. W. keeps looking at him, and then the boy points to his mouth and shakes his head.

Are you mute? the soldier across from him asks, the one with the wounded arm.

The boy points to his mouth and nods with large, intense gestures.

So they enlisted you as a soldier, did they, because you can't talk back? the one with the arm wound asks, laughing. In spite of their pain and misery several people in the wagon join in on the laughter, and the boy laughs along even though no sound comes out of his mouth.

The prison wagon arrives in Stralsund, and they end up in the very fortress they once besieged. Again he asks after young Richter, if anyone has seen him or knows what's become of him. This is his first experience of war: nothing is coherent, everything dwindles and disappears without one ever being given the time or chance to understand why or even understand anything at all. Is this boundless ongoing folly in fact the basic order of the world?

For three weeks they sit in one of the casemates, thirty men to a cell. Then they are chained up anew, led on board a ship, and carried across the sea to Carlscrona. Though he never does lay eyes on the sea itself. They all huddle together in stowage below deck. Even though it is May, the weather is inclement. Some hours in, they are caught in a violent storm. The ship is pitching, rolling and keeling; and the other prisoners (like him none of them are seagoers) retch and retch until their strength is sapped and they lay on their stomachs covering their heads with their hands as though they've already begun their journey to the Kingdom of Heaven.

Only the boy, oddly, seems unaffected by the passage and the cramped hold. He is forever weaving his way between them, handing out a bit of food or water or bit of tobacco like a greeting passed from man to man. And because he himself has no name, or at least no ability to speak it, they call him many a thing. He becomes the Dryer Dolt who runs up on deck to lay out their dung-reeking, vomit-drenched clothing to dry when the weather finally eases. Or the Weathervane when he needs more than his eyes and hands to communicate. And from that moment on he becomes everyone's friend and confidant. The hardened men love reaching out their arms and pulling him close, or quickly ruffling the mop of hair that hangs over his wild eyes.

And so one day he comes running down into the hold with his hair on end and places his right hand on top of his left palm. The Swedish coast is in sight. The next morning, waters still rough, they are rowed ashore in long sloops.

After another two weeks in a fortress, they are taken all the way up to Stockholm where they arrive on the summer solstice. Through the bars of the prisoner's wagon W. sees the city opening up around them, the sky mirrored in the water, and the air shimmering and shining with light even though, to go by the time of day, all should be sunk in the deepest night.

AFTER HAVING SPENT TIME IN custody on what is called "Långholmen" at the outskirts of the city they are taking in a prisoner's convoy south to a place by the name of Södertelje. A canal is to be dug there that will connect Lake Mälaren's harbors with the sea, a task, as it slowly becomes clear, that has been attempted many times before. Either the canal had been dug too shallow or too narrow or changing the course of water is quite simply a feat too great for ordinary mortals, for while the work lay idle, the forest has once more burst from the granite where the canal outlet was meant to run. Where they are taken nothing has yet been dug. There is no water here, only scrub. They begin by picking up and carrying away stones. They are called out into the dawn, allotted levers and spades, split into working teams of a couple dozen each and then made to walk in line, ropes slack between them, and dig. Even before they have begun, the sun has risen high and they're drenched in sweat, backs burned red, mosquitoes whirring around them in furious swarms.

Later, as autumn nears, when the air has become crisp and dry and the sun has sunk so low that a damper of shadows seems to have built up between the straight-trunked pines, they are made to carry sand and stay up a bank with the help of logs. The air is high, and it is so quiet that the blows of the axe echo like shots through the forest and they can even hear cowbells clinking and alien voices shouting to each other even though the nearest farm is several *fjärdingsvagar* away.

Even though the old slope of the canal is lined with water troughs, like those used for cattle, the foremen hardly allow them any relief and the fare is the same starvation diet as in prison, watery porridge and salted herring that causes their thirst to burn with every breath. Yet it is more tolerable than at the fortress. They are allowed to congregate at night and mix with the Swedes, even though many of them could hardly be called hospitable or even friendly. He understands that people are outraged that the country's monarch is using prisoners of war to do work that could have gone to locals, provided they were fairly paid of course. The latter he heard from a fellow named Olofsson who says he once was a prison guard but then fell foul of the law himself and now (half free, half captive) runs a small variety store on the prison grounds. When W. tells him that he once was a barber, the man rents him the back of his shed, where a curtain can be hung, so that W. can set up a shaving parlor. People do want to be properly groomed even if they are among strangers, and even though most would prefer to spend their few saved coins on whores and schnapps, there are many who pay him a visit behind the curtain, not so much for the sake of shaving, but for the chat. Unsurprisingly most of the customers turn out to be like him. They have traveled aimlessly, gone from job to job having succeeded at nothing but getting on people's wrong side, then they enlisted in the military and were captured and finally ended up here. Strays like him are always on the run from justice in one way or another. One of them recounts having murdered a man for molesting his wife by hanging him upside down from a stable post and then cutting his throat like fat stock. Have a think about that, Woyetz, he says, leaning his head back in the chair and exposing his throat, what you've got here is someone who knows his way around a knife!

It is in this way, through the shaving parlor's customers, that he comes to hear of the Swedish king's plans to go to war with the Russians, and if this can be a way out of captivity for the most capable of Swedes, then it can also be a way out for him: *take him too, he's a crack with a knife, he's proven himself already.*

The officer who is presented with new recruits in this manner pretends to be amused. His face is like a donkey's, slender and with bright bulging eyes. He smiles with bony teeth—more a grimace than a smile—and signals to the adjutant to write up his name, too. *Johann Christian Woyetz.* (Spelling is difficult; when asked to spell it himself he can't.)

And so it was, Herr Hofrat, that I was entered into the ledger again and caught this early glimpse of the great war while I was in the far north. But I did not lay eyes on the Russians then, this I can assure You, even though I thought I had arrived in Hell itself, if Herr Hofrat can imagine a hell made not of flames but of ice and snow.

IT ALREADY BEGINS AT THE ship's crossing. The weather is dreadful. In Gefle they are made to wait for days before the vessel can leave the harbor and when they are finally able to set off the ship does not sail to the Finnish mainland but to Åland, where they disembark to fortify the troops from the Södermanland regiment who are already in place. He and thirty other men are billeted with some of their officers by a well-to-do farmer called Wilhelmson. Even though the farm is among the largest in the parish the house fills up. They sleep where they can. Some sleep in the stable where the animals give off a bit of heat. But most of them sleep before the fireplace in the large living room, where a constant stench of sweat and wet woolens mixes with the sour bite of peat that the farmers use for fire, the smoke of which rolls into the crowded room like a gray fog, so thick they can barely see through it.

The farm's master has five children, three older boys and two girls. The elder girl is a shy thirteen-year-old who is jealously guarded by the farmer and his sons; the younger, Hedwig, is five.

Hedwig is the opposite of her older sister: unafraid and curious about everything.

One night W. shows her a small tabletop game that he has made. The game consists of nine square wooden blocks, each one the size of a child's fist and with an image on each side. A joker wearing a tricorne and bells; a princess in a crown; a coach and coachman; a hunter with a horn; a boat with a long oar. Each picture is different. On certain blocks only symbols are painted: animals, trees, stars. He moves the blocks around on the wide timber table in the middle of the large living room so Hedwig can choose one at random. Then he says *Katze* because the image on the block is of a cat. He might also say *Stern* or *Mond*. And Hedwig brims with laughter at this unexpected pleasure and climbs onto his lap so she can teach him what each thing is called in Swedish and each time he pronounces the name incorrectly, so she puts her face close to his and with surprising might pinches his cheeks and lips with her fingers and contorts them so that the words come out right (*katt, stjärna, måne*), at least until her mother comes running and snatches her daughter from his arms.

It's no more difficult than this to be German amongst these alien folk. Often a few simple everyday words and friendly gestures suffice.

In the evenings when the other soldiers sit smoking or playing cards he helps the master mend straps and tack. He has his leather pouch with him, in which are scissors, needle and thread, and all manner of scraps, and he attends to the company's trousers and uniform jackets or their gray capotes if they're worse for wear and is thereafter known as the German Tailor. He is given extra rations of salted pork and peas and schnapps in exchange. A tall crookbacked carl, a corporal by the name of Struwe, jokes that he should be given a *royal medal* for his care of the equipment, the king being as he is more interested in pomp and circumstance than his troops faring well in the field.

There is constant talk of this king, Gustav by name. In the eyes of many he seems to be as little revered as the jester adorned with bells on the underside of one of Hedwig's wooden blocks.

At first the days are calm and uneventful. The reveille is sounded when it is still dark and only the farm dogs are barking. They line up on the long rock slab next to the jetty and hold morning prayers. One of the men, usually a young cobbler's apprentice by the name of Falck who has a lovely sonorous voice, intones a psalm and the rest of the men join in. Then their company commander, Sergeant Kwast, an older stocky man with a grizzled beard and protruding eyes, steps forward and issues the day's orders. They take long tours down the coastline and spy out distant capes and isthmuses and more often than not Kwast insists that they go by boat because this way it's easier to scout the coast with its many islets and skerries.

The weather is still, gray and misty but not cold. On some days a white fog wraps itself around them like a pale, cold hand and all that interrupts the stillness is the sharp creaking of the oars in the oar locks or waterfowl taking flight, pinions swiftly striking the surface of the water.

But soon the weather worsens and in a week's time the storms come thundering in with stunning force, and after the final tempest has come and gone it begins to snow and when it stops hardly a chimney stack can be seen above the white peaks that have risen up where the wind has held sway. The master-at-arms arrives with horses from Sund, which they hitch to sledges but it's not long before they are forced to turn back because the driving snow has made every road impassable.

And the winter storms keep coming, and the ocean is open and cold. Within a few weeks he learns to fear the sea more than anything else. It transmutes from day to day, nigh on hour to hour. At night, when they've huddled around Farmer Wilhelmson's hearth, the wind can be heard wailing in the chimney and the billows hammer and pound as though the waves were washing right over the ridge of the roof. At reveille the next morning it is as though the world has ended on the rocks where they hold morning prayers. There is no sea beyond the jetty, no sky besides, only an abyss from which an icy smoke rises, as if Death were breathing in their faces.

But Sergeant Kwast and the other officers fear the storms and the snow less than they fear the cold they know is imminent, the *true* cold, when the ocean hardens and everything freezes over. As soon as the storms have abated and a moment of clear weather prevails they are sent out by boat again, even though the boats are hardly seaworthy and they themselves are hardly used to keeping anything afloat in such rough seas.

The days are short now. The sun dissolves in showers of sleet or frozen rain that in a breath drifts in from the sea and the darkness falls more quickly than anyone can fathom. Scarcely have they met the gaze of the sky, where the sun moves like a blackjack behind the clouds, before the land vanishes from sight. The wind picks up and sharp grains of snow ricochet off the water like the sting of a whip. Of a sudden, the sea is choppy, the boat pitches and drops, batted around by the waves. He sees Gustavsson, who is at the oars, stand up and point at something none of them have a chance to see before something hard collides with the underside of the boat and everyone is flung overboard. He finds himself half-submerged in water. At the last second he manages to grab hold of the gunwale only to feel the boat being ripped from his hands. An icy wave breaks over his head and hands, then another. When the water withdraws he thinks he can glimpse bare rock through the spray. Somehow he manages to gain purchase with his legs and arms (he has lost all sensation in his fingers) and pushes his way through the slush to firm ground. Only then does he dare lift his head in the sharp sleet. But none of his comrades are to be seen and the wind tears the words from his mouth before he has a chance to call out their names.

He has had many notions about the war, the cold order of iron, the courage in facing an enemy on the battlefield; but no one has ever mentioned the loneliness a soldier feels when he has lost his company and suddenly has nothing to arrange himself around, no commands, nothing, and nothing to take aim at in the snow that keeps falling and falling and packs into ever denser drifts all around, nary a speck of visibility when the darkness cinches tight around him like a sack. He roams for hours, the wind howling in his ears and the grains of snow so sharp he struggles to keep his eyes open. Then he feels a patch of bare earth beneath his boots and something hard against his palms, a wall, then he collapses from fatigue.

When he comes to, the worst of the storm has blown by and the sky is a gritty mass of racing clouds, faster than anything he has ever seen, as if there were a second sea above the sea. Instead of trapping him in a snowdrift, chance or luck has led him to a clean-blown slope overgrown with tufts of dry yellowed grass on the backside of a timbered barn wall. Aside from the board wall, stripped white by salt and wind, there is nowhere to fix his sights. The scudding, oddly granular sky offers no clue as to the location of the sun, and had he known he still would not have understood in which direction to set his course.

He trudges through the snow. The farther inland he comes the denser the sky. It sags, a vast and swollen udder, above the snow-covered fields.

In the far distance, by the now-sharpened line that splits earth from sky, a lone barn peeks out at the edge of a field thick with snow. Fatigue makes his legs, frozen stiff, slip and slide beneath him, until he is finally sunk to his waist in the loose wet snow and has to use his arms as shovels to keep trudging on.

But when he looks up again, the barn is as far away as it was before. All that has transpired is a realization that this barn is the same barn from which he set off earlier in the day.

He has returned to the very place he was before, but from a different direction.

He stares at the empty barn. At length flames erupt from the stone foundation and lap up the white wooden walls. When the barn is all ablaze it slowly begins to levitate, it rises like a burning boat into a sky that has ceased all motion and returned to naught but darkness.

WHEN HE IS FOUND AFTER three days he has frostbite wounds on his face and underarms and his mouth is in tatters from the bark and pine needles he has tried to choke down.

They had gone out with a sledge and first found the boat splintered against a rocky bottom half a day's journey from the coast. Falck, the choir singer, is dead, he is informed, his skull dashed against the rocks. The others in the company have all made it out in one piece, except for a man by the name of Renberg whose legs have had to be amputated.

He and Renberg share a bed in the cottage hospital in Ödkarby. For his bedmate and for anyone else in the room who cares to listen W. recounts the weird vision he had: of the barn he watched burn and rise into the sky. Maybe it was the Lord's way of telling him ascension is nigh, someone suggests from a bed across the room. But beside him, Renberg is of a different mind. He is sure it is the Freemasons. Did he not see another two glowing streaks to one side of it? W. says he only remembers the barn. That would be the Freemason's, then, Renberg says, sure of himself.

That same night he wakes up to deep moans and gasping beside him. Renberg is lying on his back, chest heaving like a bellows, and his face is covered with a thick film of sweat. W. reaches out a hand. Renberg's body is hot with fever.

It's punishment, a voice whispers right next to him. It's his punishment for taking *the word* in his mouth.

The medical orderlies have bound rags over their faces. They say it is against the smell. But W. sees that they are rat-faced behind the cloth.

Still he doesn't have the strength to resist as they tear and tug at his body with their claw-like hands. Again he is out on that rough sea. They are being tossed around in a ship so sodden with frothing waves that the sea is barely visible and someone at the helm is shouting, Don't say it, don't say it, and when he asks say what, what is it that I should not say, the answer comes: *the word, the word . . . !*

Does he ever say the word? He isn't sure.

The thought of the word, and what may happen to him if he in fever's torpor has said it nonetheless, torments him until the moment the orderlies arrive to carry his body into the snow outside. There he must lie as they go around to the various cottage hospitals, fumigating them with spruce twigs. He looks at the blackened corpses that have been dragged into the snow. There are now no more than a mere handful left of the twentysome men that were in the cottage hospital when he was admitted.

The Wilhelmson's farm has been fumigated as well. Only the farmer and his wife and the oldest children remain. The youngest, Hedwig, also died of dysentery.

They bury her in the Saltvik cemetery. Family and farmhands and neighbors stand side-by-side in sables at the grave, like a ruffled murder of crows against a backdrop of trees swaying uneasily in a cruel wind from the frozen sea. Kwast's company, or what remains of it, has convened. Because Falck, the apprentice cobbler, has given his life there is no one to give the starting note. In the end Gustavsson steps forward and leads the song. A mighty Fortress is our God, a sword and shield victorious, they sing as the ice-wind snatches the words from each verse.

In the evening he sits as he usually does, head on hand, the blocks beside him on the table. He turns the blocks over one by one, but the pictures on the sides have worn away if they were ever there to begin with. It was all in his imagination, as Renberg or one of the others in the cottage hospital might have told him.

And yet it is as though he can still feel the warm heft of the girl sitting in his lap.

At night the wind drives over the roofs, and the lever of cold prizes and distends the house's log walls. The next morning, after reveilles, marching orders are given. Russians have been spotted in the inner archipelago.

TEN DAYS LATER THE SWEDISH king is deposed and the Russians have taken Kumlinge. Horses and wagons are hastily ordered in. The artillery is to lead the way. When the carts do not suffice birch trees are cut down and makeshift sledges are made. Those who manage to squeeze onto a sledge are lucky, the others must make do as best they can.

Even before they're out on Eckerö Island the troops are so scattered that the vanguard loses contact with the men at the back. Rumor has it that several wagons have sunk into the snow which has gone soft and slushy after a few days of unexpected thaw and the sick must endure being left behind. In spite of the sound of sporadic inland firefighting they have no direct contact with the enemy.

Two days after the sudden decampment they set off across the ice, their course set for Signilskär.

After an initial day with sharp March sunlight, so sharp they can't see a thing in the glare between the frozen sea and sky, more snow falls and then comes a fresh spell of clear weather and biting cold. The snow shouldn't prevent them from keeping up a good pace, but the ice out at sea is not level, rather it rolls and is at times so tightly packed that they must find their way around it as with an actual mound or hill.

It is now so cold that every strip of bare skin burns as though it were being torn off. The cold is like an iron pin rammed deep into his lungs, burying itself deeper with each step. He keeps to a cluster with Gustavsson and Field Usher Wennstam, but overall the men seem confused, as though they had not only lost their bearings but also their presence of mind now that there are no longer any landmarks, only sun blindness followed by dusk then night. They deliberate amongst

themselves whether or not to tie ropes around each other to keep anyone
from going astray, but neither do they have enough rope or reins, and
who wants to be tied together when what matters is marching as fast as
possible and there aren't enough provisions to go around anyway and so
it's up to each man to fend for himself and reach the Swedish mainland
as fast as possible.

At night the sky is so boundless and dark it seems it would only take one
more step for him to fall right down into it, as into an upside-down well.
And the constellations stretch all the way to the horizon. We believe that
the night sky is darkness filled with unmoving stars, the young doctor
used to say, but in fact the opposite is true, as Woyetz understands. The
stars are in constant motion. Not a day passes without their falling. It
is the same whether one is on Baltic Sea ice or in a prison cell or in the
fecal stink of a dark cottage hospital. All around us is God's sky, ceaselessly falling.

And at this thought, he falls, too.

Or more rightly put: on the inside he continues to walk, if but with
short, clumsy steps that seem to stumble on of their own accord, but in
fact he has long since toppled over and is lying motionless in a snowdrift.

Wennstam tries to lift him up by the armpits. Then someone
else comes over and pushes him back into the snow with two strong
gloved fists.

Shhh . . . Can't you see!? The fires!

W. slumps against the drift that has hampered his fall, and at first
he sees nothing but the pitch-black night. Then the glove points once
more and then he sees them, too, faint but clear. Two flickering fires:
they appear to be a few hundred yards apart.

Could it be the Russians? Gustavsson wonders. But Wennstam is
skeptical, finds it incomprehensible that the enemy would reveal himself
at such close range. It would require quite a lot of self-confidence. No,
it's the Swedes, he decides. They're eating horse meat.

And it is this thought, that others from the retreating army could
be so reckless as to sit there feasting on emergency slaughter, that
clinches the decision to head for the fires in spite of everything. This,

and perhaps the ancient draw of fire with its promise of human warmth and fellowship.

They have made it no more than halfway when they are attacked.

W.'s first thought is that this is an ambush carried out by several men coming at them from all sides. Then he realizes it is just one man, ursine fur–clad and roaring so loudly it sounds like the noise of more mouths than this single red maw suddenly gaping beside him. W. whips out his rifle but barely manages to attach the bayonet. The stranger has already knocked him into the snow and so he simply plants his bayonet right into that open, bearded gullet. Still the stranger continues his advance, waving both arms in the air as though he wanted nothing more than for the point of the bayonet to be lodged deeper in his skull. A terrible moan is heard, hands wrapped in rags claw at the barrel of the gun before the stranger stoops over the rifle, which W. has let go of in sheer horror.

He hears the creak of their boots in the snow. The others are already at his side, but have stopped in their tracks.

It's Sergeant Kwast, Gustavsson finally says. He must have lost his mind.

He kneels and lays his head on the man's chest and listens for a heartbeat, then gets up and shakes his head.

Or he thought we were the Russians, someone else suggests.

The gazes, turning to the fires, waver once more. Against the firelight contours of people running to meet them appear. Swedes, thank God. Jubilation as the sundered regiment reunites. W. stays beside Kwast's corpse. His hands, still blue with cold, are shaking.

Finally someone returns with a sledge. They help each other lift Kwast onto it. The bayonet is still in Kwast's mouth, as though he were staked to the ice, the yellowed white of one eye turned to the heavens, bloody mucus and icicles dressing his beard.

You do know that I have to arrest You for this, the field usher says as they walk. It's for the court to decide whether or not You were acting in self-defense.

HOWEVER, THERE IS NEVER TALK of him spending time in custody. After a three-day march when they finally set foot on Swedish soil just north of Grisslehamn, only a few dozen of them remain. Moreover, Kwast's corpse is so deep-frozen that no reasonable person can determine the cause of death. Without many words on the matter, it is decided that the sergeant lost his way on the ice and in a moment of confusion happened to stick the bayonet into his own mouth. After all, several people could attest to this: out there on the ice people simply go mad.

And so he stays with the Swedes. Falling in line is also the best way to remain anonymous. Who is he then, the German Tailor? An apparently decent fellow, but slippery and unreliable; one who gladly ingratiates himself and renders services but when it truly counts is not above sticking a knife in one of his own people? And as the German Tailor, a good year after the defeat on the ice, he too returns to the garrison in Stralsund, which following the treaty with the French is once more in Swedish hands.

But when he adds himself to the army's register again, he does so under the name Wutzig. The name is somehow more robust than the transient and untrustworthy Woyetz. It is as the trustworthy Wutzig that he dedicates himself to repairing the garrison walls and parapets that he alongside the Dutch helped shoot to pieces not long ago.

On the whole it is peculiar to now find himself within that which he once stood without. Yet in some way he remains outside. Even if *by all appearances* everything is as before. He even sets up a small shaving parlor on the fortress grounds and quickly curries favor with the rest of the men. They settle in to his chair, heads and necks leaning back, and he listens and nods and smiles at everything that is entrusted to him in this way. He is simple and good-tempered, as Staff Lieutenant Widebeck tells him one morning while under the towel in anticipation of a shave. More than once he is called to the officers' mess to serve as an attendant there. And it would seem that none of them are in any way aware, when he reaches over their shoulders to pour or serve, that the same deft hand that now so nimbly wields the carving knife and razor blade, just as nimbly thrust a bayonet into one of their own ranks.

THE FIRST TIME HE MAKES her acquaintance it is as one of the so-called soldiers' widows, one of several women who sometimes are spotted peddling their wares along the country road to Damgarten.

It is September, the air is still hot though the day is almost done. The farm where his company has sought temporary quarters is sunk deep in sirupy verdure, the shadows are long and the swallows swirl in the sky. A few of the widows have children on their arms, others are carrying baskets on their backs or are pulling carts full of bread, cured meat, and dried fish. But tobacco and schnapps are also being advertised by voices that seem too shrill and given to laughter and invitations.

As always he is keeping his distance from the others, leaning his back against an old well shaft, a knife and whittling wood in his hands. Down by the brook, shaded by hazels and alders, a few of the farm women are washing clothes, their skirts and blouse sleeves rolled up. It is not the hot sun alone that causes their voices to sound drawling and heavy, but also, judging by their gazes, their suspicions about the newcomers, those who say they are soldier's widows or chapwomen but don't have the decency to hide what they truly are.

Several of the officers have rushed over and are feigning interest in their wares, including barber-surgeon Munther even though he is an old man who barely manages to hobble over with his stiff leg. The women laugh at his clumsiness, their laughter loud and affected. Whereas W. lets his gaze drift into the high leafy crowns where the light clings and quivers as though entangled by the wind and is now trying to break free from the swaying boughs.

Suddenly one of them is standing in front of him.

He feels a shadow cross his face, then a faint fume of armpit sweat and something sweet, a bit sickly. The wind stops rustling and swaying in the hazel bush and he can hear what the woman in front of him is trying to say.

"Water" she says and points to the pewter flask lying beside his knapsack in the grass. With the hand holding the piece of wood, he shields his face and offers her the bottle. She drinks and sits down unbidden, her back to the well mirroring his pose, keeping the bottle in her lap.

She is of solid build, about equal to him in height, but her face is fine-cut, practically concave. Like the bowl of a spoon, it strikes him. But it could also be the shadow from the hazel thicket beside her that is scooping it out. He sees a dark line of sweat running from the underarm seam of her blouse to her waistband. The blouse is ironed and properly buttoned up the neck in spite of the heat.

What will it be? she asks at length, one eye on the whittling wood and knife he has in his lap.

He must have made a sullen impression because she pushes the knife and wood aside and interweaves their fingers, turns his hand over and pretends to study the lines of his palm. You're not Swedish, she says, and then he tells her that he comes from the south, from Saxony, that he was tricked into enlisting by the Dutch, but was captured by the Swedes, and then he let them recruit him to fight the Russians in Finland. He rattles this off like a rehearsed rhyme. It's what he has told everyone else he's met along the way who bothered to ask.

Is that a bullet wound there on Your hand? she asks.

No, frostbite, he says and wants to take back his hand. The officers ordered us to cross the ice when we retreated.

He looks over at the clutch of soldiers.

If there's one thing you learn to appreciate in a soldier's life, it's the camaraderie, he says, this too rehearsed.

At the same time he watches as a few soldiers walk off with a couple of the women from the clutch while their children are left to play by the road. One child, a boy, has stuck his finger in the corner of his mouth and is looking towards the well where they both are sitting.

And yet You keep Your distance? she asks.

She ignores the child, still running her fingertips across his knuckles and wrist.

You have fine hands, she says. For a soldier.

Perhaps you're whittling me a flute, she says and grabs his hand with a desperation that is at odds with the easy smile she's giving him.

Won't You accompany me? she asks and gets up still holding his hand. He is under the impression that she wants him to follow her to town and he starts to say that he's stationed here with his company and can't betake himself elsewhere, no, down there, she clarifies, down to the brook, no one can see us there, and she has already ducked under the hazel's low branches and is hurrying down the slope.

In the gully: a perfume of resin and marshland within the cool shade, sun sparkling on the water washing over rocks and fallen trees, slicked with green foam. Lofty alders raise their leafy crowns above the water and obscure the outside view. The farm maids who were doing the washing earlier are nowhere to be seen. A curious silence has settled over it all. All that can be heard is the water's insistent murmur.

You may look, she says and opens the buttons of her blouse.

The insects whirl impatiently around her. A searing knot of unease tightens in his gut. She looks oddly stiff and unnatural as she leans forward to show off her breasts. You may touch them, she says and grips them from below.

He smiles dumbly and begins to move towards her. Not because he wants to, he doesn't know what he wants. But he has as little control of his smile as he has of his movements. Perhaps he is approaching her because he imagines this is what is expected of him.

Payment first, she says.

He's still holding the thick piece of wood, but with his free hand he digs around for a few coins. No sooner has he pulled his hand out of his pocket than does she grab it and pull it towards her so that it nudges the underside of the breast, which is hanging out of her bodice, then over her belly and down to her lap. Then she turns around resolutely and lifts her basque up over her back. Only two bare rounded buttocks are underneath, a tuft of hair dangling down between them.

He knows he is supposed mount her, and arranges himself accordingly, fumbling with the buttons of his trouser flap. But his sex is slack and because he doesn't know how to proceed, he gives her hips and backside a little rub with the piece of wood still in his hand. The action is not premeditated, more like something an absentminded child might come up with, not understanding the meaning of its actions. She stiffens beneath him, but continues thrusting her rump in his direction. When he happens to push the wood a little harder she yanks down the hem of her skirt, turns around, and screams:

Who does he think he is . . . !?

Only then does he see her face, what must be her *true* face, and it is indeed hollowed out, eyes as large as beans, a vicious stare below hard domed eyelids. Something red is spreading around her nose and mouth that at first he takes for blood or froth but perhaps it's just the sunlight falling through the mass of leaves overhead or the flush that comes from having bent over for so long, and she hurriedly lifts and cinches her bodice and buttons her blouse, already on her way up the bank.

Here, you can have it! he shouts and wants to throw the piece of wood after her but all he manages to do is scare up a dole of wood doves, which rise from the hazel brush, their flapping wings a song.

By then she's already back on the road, taking long halting steps towards the group of soldiers' widows who turn and stare. From the cluster of women, the boy who he noticed earlier breaks away. The boy runs a few steps, then stops with his arms stiff and straight along his sides, like a little soldier. A couple of his own men, the sergeant and Lieutenant Widebeck, turn to the woman who is clearly limping now. He watches her lean on Widebeck's arm, speak to him in distress for a while, then point with her whole hand to the hazel thicket where they had been sitting.

But he has already slid back down to the brook and perhaps they haven't seen him though, of course, they all know that it is him.

A FEW WEEKS LATER HE spies her at the market not far from the entrance to the St. Nicholas Church where she is selling eggs at one of the stands. There are three of them working the stall, four if you count the boy, the first who caught his eye and who comes rushing out and plants himself in front of him in the same brusque, soldierly manner as before.

Soon he lays eyes on her, too: the boy's mother.

But he never would have recognized her had he not first recognized the boy. She is dressed like a different person entirely: a coarse woolen skirt, thick knitted stockings, her blond hair covered with a gray headscarf, under which her hollowed-out visage looks red and swollen.

He watches her exchange a few monosyllabic words with an older woman working alongside her and then take a seat on a stool at the far end of the stand.

It's the way she's sitting, wide-legged but arduously leaning forward, hands on her thighs supporting her weight, that makes him think she's heavy with child. Could it be that his piece of wood impregnated her? The thought is laughable. Still it refuses to leave him in peace.

Could it be that God has had a hand in the game all along?

How is he to know if their encounter wasn't preordained after all?

As soon as he has the chance, he continues prowling around the market stall. The old instinct has been awakened, as when he watched Frau Woost wash her hair or lurked in the forests of Burschendorf to keep an eye on Fräulein Schindel. And as before he has to bring his whittling wood along. It's as if he doesn't dare approach without something to hold on to, as if it had magical powers that could somehow protect him.

But not much is going on around the market stalls.

She stands there all day selling eggs. Meanwhile the boy plays by himself among the vegetable greens and horse apples out on the square. If other children come along he resumes his stiff pose until one of the women calls for him. Towards dusk an older man appears who harnesses a horse to the cart and they all climb in together. She and the boy at the back, their legs dangling over the edge of the platform and an empty water bucket clanking beside them.

The horse is an old hack who moves so slowly he has no trouble following a few steps behind. Once he even waves using the hand that is holding the wood, as if to remind her of something.

But she looks straight ahead and right through him, as if there were nothing to see.

Then one evening she isn't sitting on the wagon as usual, or she might just be hiding from him. It's raining and the boy has pulled a blanket over him to shield himself from the wetness, and why he at first thinks that she too is taking cover under the blanket he does not know. He is lolling a few cart-lengths behind in the sludge when the platform rattles, the blanket slips off, and the boy looks out with his expressionless gaze.

She isn't with him on the platform.

He doesn't understand why this makes him so upset. With long strides, he returns to the market square, and when the chapwomen he queries simply turn their backs on him and continue packing their wares, he is seized by rage and makes threats until a gruff fellow grabs him by the shoulders and chases him away.

He walks into a tavern and asks for Frau Thiessen. This is the first time he speaks her name. Presumably he is puffing and blowing like a horse from the effort because the tavern keeper just stares at him until his face seems to drop, and the man slaps the greasy dishrag on the counter and draws everyone in the tavern into raucous laughter.

The Devil you say, the Swedish soldier's gone mad for the womenfolk! Run along, now. You won't find her here!

He takes shelter under the eaves and looks out over the now-deserted marketplace. From the small stands along Artushof all the way up to the town hall's tower, the rain fills the square like a foreign mass. Inside this foreign mass of rain, two men are fighting for dominance over a third. The identity of this third person is at first unclear to him, because one of the men is gripping a horse by its bridle and the horse is blocking his view.

In the middle of the square the horse begins to resist, is about to rear, and *Hold the beast tight* says one of the men in clear Swedish. And then he sees that it is *her*. But she is barely recognizable. Her hair is plastered to her slick cheeks, making her otherwise wide visage look even more hollow. He also recognizes the two men accompanying her, even though gray coats hide their uniforms. The one is his own lieutenant, Widebeck; the other a corporal who usually serves as the lieutenant's soldier-servant and answers to the name Antonsson.

Automatically he stands at attention when the two officers walk by with the woman and the unruly horse. But even though both Swedes meet his eye, neither seems to recognize him.

Frau Thiessen doesn't even look in his direction, she only sinks lower between her two escorts, and then Lieutenant Widebeck takes a firm hold of her arm, as though she were the unruly horse.

Without knowing why, or perhaps he is simply being true to his nature, as Clarus would say, he follows the two Swedes—but from a fair distance, hidden by the horse who is still anxiously treading the wet cobblestones.

The entourage turns into a narrow cross street. On the far end of it lays a ramshackle building with an inn on the bottom floor from which a muffled roar escapes. Beside it stands a much lower, narrower house, half hidden by a broad elm so crooked in shape it appears to be leaning against the inn. It is to the smaller building that Antonsson is heading while Widebeck waits, the horse's reins in one hand and Frau Thiessen in the other. W. never hears the front door open and only catches sight of the woman across the threshold when she raises a lantern so as to illuminate Antonsson's face.

Antonsson steps aside and points to the lieutenant waiting in the distance.

Then the woman bows submissively and takes a welcoming step aside. Lieutenant Widebeck hands Antonsson the reins and, fist still tight around Frau Thiessen's arm, follows the woman whose lantern has already disappeared into the darkness of the house.

THEY END UP LINGERING OUTSIDE the closed door, he and Antonsson. And the horse.

At first he wants to say something, to explain to Antonsson why he is still here in spite of the gushing rain, his leave having long since expired, but he can't come up with anything so they end up lingering as though they were strangers or by mere coincidence both happen to be present.

He wishes he had his whittling wood with him, or anything else: if only he had something to cling to. But he has nothing and slowly his field of vision shrinks and all becomes a sort of sleep.

Then the door opens anew and Lieutenant Widebeck comes out. This time he looks him right in the eye. *Good evening, Wutzig*, he says, astride the horse whose reins Antonsson hands him, and then he rides off, his soldier-servant jogging behind.

He doesn't know what to do or where to go. The door she walked through hasn't opened since. So he stays in the rain. Inside him is this wondrous sleep and inside the sleep, the door.

It opens again and Marie Thiessen comes out.

She has tidied her hair now and pinned it at the nape of her neck but is still bare-headed, and in the absence of a proper head covering her face if possible looks even more sunken so that when she turns to look at him, it is as though she is both looking at him and yet not. So too is her voice. When she speaks to him it is as though her voice were coming both from inside her and from elsewhere.

You must be out of Your mind to insist on following me like this.

He says nothing.

What is Your name?

He says his name is Wutzig.

Are You Swedish?

He says nothing.

Aren't You afraid Your superiors might see You?

He doesn't know what to say.

You don't know anything about me, she adds, as though he had suddenly made an accusation. I'm married, she says. My husband is in the field.

In which regiment? he asks.

I'm expecting his child, she says.

She brings one hand to her belly.

And the boy? he asks. To whom does he belong?

Now she is the one who is silent of speech.

If he'd had the whittling wood he would have handed it to her now. As a gift, or perhaps a plea. But this time not even the wood would have been enough to change anything. She walks onto the street, which immediately transforms into a sea of rushing water and quickly disappears. Only then does it hit him that not with one word did she betray that she knows who he is or even remembers that they are already acquainted.

BUT HE RETURNS. SEVERAL TIMES at that. He stands under the elm and watches carefully each time anyone enters or exits the inn. But even though he sees Lieutenant Widebeck again as well as several other Swedish officers, sometimes in the company of one or a couple of the soldier's widows they happen to meet along the road to Damgarten, it is deep into the autumn before he lays eyes on her again.

By then he has been standing for so long under the large tree that they have almost grown intertwined. The hubbub from the inn has also become so familiar that he hardly flinches when its door is flung open with a crack and a boisterous party staggers out.

This time it is she who lays eyes on him first, so tries to hide her face in her apron. But now he is holding the whittling wood, and some form of power must yet radiate from it for when he reaches out his hand something in her seems to soften and yield. She turns towards him, without the previous reproach and with a smile that could be taken as heartfelt, had her gaze not slipped and slid in every direction.

And. What is Your name? she asks again.

Wutzig, he says. Again.

Is that Your real name?

Woyzeck, he then says. My father was Polish.

Then you have a secret, too, she says from inside her smile.

I haven't been completely honest with You, she says.

My husband is dead, she says.

He holds the piece of wood tight. And what happens in that moment can't be explained. From inside his great sleep he sees her take one step forward and grab hold of his hands with both of hers. Then she lifts them to her mouth. First the one, then the other. And she takes the wood from his hand and kisses his knuckles. Then she guides his hands down to her lap where new life is already pulsing.

And. What is Your name? she asks again.

And Wutzig, he says. Again.

HIS COMRADES TELL HIM THAT even he, Wutzig, must understand that this wench has never been married, much less is she the widow of a fallen soldier. Has he perchance seen a ring on her finger? And how could she be with child by one who has fallen in the field? Her belly was hardly round when he, Wutzig, got mixed up with her! And does he really believe, as he says he does, that she is in the employ of her dead husband's parents? What kind of parents-in-law would silently look on as their daughter-in-law ran around fornicating with others?

Even he must understand this, he can't be that stupid!

It can't possibly be the child of this husband that she is carrying if he has indeed disappeared in the field. Moreover such thoughts are ungodly. Can't he at least concede that there has perhaps never been a husband—just an endless stream of soldiers who come and beget and die, beget and die all over again? For such must be the lot of the soldier's widow. If one falls, a thousand rise in his place. Never any peace or quiet. Nevertheless, and this is the remarkable part, he *believes* her.

To Clarus he would later say that even though he knows that she is lying, he seems to prefer the lie to the truth. The lie is somehow more capacious than the truth. It is easier to inhabit.

THEY BEGIN STROLLING TOGETHER. BEING seen
in his company doesn't seem to make her as anxious as before, and she
takes his arm as they walk, going so far as to press herself into him when
they meet an acquaintance of his. As though he might otherwise think
to break free from the crook of her arm and flee.

But what does he care about those who walk past laughing or pointing fingers?

Walking with her as if engaged makes him feel happy and a bit
distinctive. He has never walked with a woman in this way before.

The days are unusually open. It is like they are spending time in rooms
full of only windows. Everywhere he walks with her there are new things
to see. The world has become new. Or he has simply been given new
eyes with which to see it.

Of course he does notice that she prefers certain paths to others.
And she does not want him to meet her parents-in-law. This he must
understand, it would be ungodly seeing as she has just lost her husband.

And he is not allowed to meet the boy either. Johann Christian
August. Once he was ever-present at her side. Now he is nowhere to be
found. As soon as he brings the boy up in conversation she changes the
subject. Instead she wants to know in which regiments he has served,
or even the names of his commanding officers. Though she herself can't
account in which regiment her husband served or the names of any of
his commanding officers. Why don't you talk instead, she says. And he
hears himself talking to her. Grandly and at length he talks about the
Russians, about the fires they saw burning out on the ice at night as they

were fleeing. And he tells her about the little girl, Hedwig, the one who died from dysentery, about the game with the painted blocks that gave her such incredible joy.

And he told her of the barn that started burning and rose up into the sky.

She smiles but seems oddly unmoved.

But you've never experienced battle? she asks.

And he? No, no battle.

Imagine that, she says, such a long time in the field and yet no battle.

And she says that he has beautiful eyes. That they are bright and calm when his gaze comes to rest on her. She says she likes that he never has a foul mouth or raises his voice at her.

But when she says such fine and beautiful things to him, she turns away. Whether it is out of shyness or shame he is unsure. Perhaps both.

Now she's looking down and asking if he wants her to be kind to him. And then she takes his hand in hers. When he wants to pull it back she raises it up in a sudden fluttering sweep. They laugh. She keeps on lifting his hand in this fluttering birdlike way before she finally arranges their entwined hands in her lap.

And then she says what she has always wanted to say: ever since their first time, she was already carrying another man's child by her heart. She didn't dare say this to him because he was so good to her. And neither did she dare say anything after because she thought he would leave her if she did. She knows he must despise her for not being pure. But she must have this said, she can't carry it around inside her anymore.

If he so prefers, he is of course free to walk away from her now. She does understand that this may be his preference. After all she is by no means an honorable woman.

But he does not go. No, he sits there, straight as a candle. And smiles: a bit troubled, but still obliging. The smile of someone who knows something important is expected of him, it's unclear what that something is, but nonetheless one is prepared to be obliging.

She looks at the floor.

And after a while when she looks back up her face has returned to normal, her cheeks concave and her gaze roving. As though the shyness had been but a veil she had quickly drawn over her face only to fling it off with equal speed.

And in this moment is everything between them that will always be.

Her shy gaze and his helplessly searching hands.

And the boy, Johann Christian August, is back. Stiff as a soldier, standing straight, his arms stretched along his body, he stands beside his mother, keeping watch.

And so the lies continue.

IN SWEDISH POMERANIA AT THIS time there was a menagerie exhibitor by the name of Henze who traveled through the cities along the coast and out on Rügen with his theater. Now he is back in Stralsund. They see him on their strolls where he has erected a wooden monstrosity, built in two stories like a real house and chocked up on broad trestles. Wide windows run along the structure's both sides, hung with red curtains that are always neatly drawn so that the action inside remains in plain sight. Inside, the theater is made up of several interlinking chambers, the floors and walls of which open up like trap doors. On top is a tower-like room furnished with metal grating that faces in each of the four cardinal directions, like a watchtower. The tower is called the maiden's tower, and inside the maiden's tower is a "maiden": a field vole or a similar animal whose plaintive squeals can be heard far and wide.

When a sufficient number of curious onlookers have gathered round the theater, Henze's assistant steps forward, a gruff man strapped into a leather apron who is called the Hun. When Henze rings his cowbell to mark the start of a performance, the Hun goes up to the cages behind the theater where the baiting beasts are kept (a marten, a polecat or some other animal that Henze has been keeping on a starvation diet for weeks), grabs the animal with a mighty leather-lined glove and holds it up for the audience to watch as it hisses and spits, dangling from the loop at the end of the long pole he always has with him.

Meanwhile Henze plucks a pocket watch from his vest and holds two or three or five fingers in the air. The fingers corresponded to the time in minutes that the hunt will last, everything calculated according to the animal's presumed endurance and strength. The audience is then asked to make a bet by placing their coins in a basket that Henze sends around, whereupon the hunter is driven into the first chamber and let loose inside the theater.

To the cheers of the audience, the game begins.

Or rather, the fight:

For however strong the scent of the maiden up in its tower is, there is always a moment where the hunter realizes that it is itself hunted, when the floor gives way underneath and it falls between the chambers or get stuck between the boards and hatches that serve to keep the walls both upright and in constant motion.

The Hun walks around jabbing the crook of his staff through the window to force the animal to resume its hunt for the prey in the maiden's tower. Correspondingly Henze walks through the audience presenting his pocket watch, while those who stand closest in the throng around the theater in the best case manage to catch a glimpse of a sharp eye or the tip of a tail flitting past a window.

But for the most part only clumsy tumbling and groans from inside the chambers can be heard as the baited beast falls through all the trapdoors and is forced to take up the hunt for the maiden once more, and the Hun prods his crook through the theater's windows ever more irately, and the audience howls and hollers, all the more upset at the poor animal. But in the end time always runs out, and the Hun opens the front door and hauls out the animal, now so exhausted by his own hunt that it clings to the crook as though this instrument of torture were its only salvation.

And the audience cries out its exasperation and anger.

A number of them make their way forward in order to finish off the beast for having betrayed its very nature. But the Hun intervenes, and no one dares set upon him, for he has a crook and glove, and it always ends with the disappointed onlookers moving on and a new bloodthirsty herd appearing and the Hun licking his lips and hauling out a fresh animal from the cage while Master of the Hunt Henze swings his cowbell and accepts fresh bets and coins in his basket.

One of Henze's main attractions this year is an old vixen, scarcely more than a sack of bones wrapped in a shabby fur. The vixen is kept in a larger cage away from the others, in which she anxiously rubs against the bars day in and day out as though she wanted to scrape off the little that remains of her gaunt, starved body, and sometimes her yowls can be heard across the square. It is as though her despair is so deep that only by being in constant motion can she continue to exist and the world around her remain solid, upright, and real.

She only lies down on the cage floor when the Hun hooks the skin of her already chafed throat and forces her into the theater. Henze then goes to and fro with his basket and bell and explains that the fox hasn't tasted flesh in weeks.

Surely You have never before laid eyes on such a wild and hungry beast, ladies and gentlemen, and the question is: will she reach the maiden or won't she? Foxes are cunning animals.

If You bet on the fox, Your stakes will be returned to You ten-fold.

Come now, good people, place a bet before it is too late!

And many in the audience place their very last coins on the starved fox and when she, in spite of this, refuses to clamber on but instead curls up deep inside one of the chambers, they come charging with sundry weapons, which they plunge through the curtained windows, all to spur on the wretched fox, she who can't even muster the energy to rise for the sake of her own hunger.

So one night what everyone must have known would happen sooner or later happens. Suddenly the customary racket from inside the theater stops and when the Hun sticks in his crook and hauls the vixen out, clinging to the crook is but a slack pelt, one eye staring blindly and uncomprehendingly towards an assembly of dismayed spectators.

The audience is unusually subdued as the Hun drags the dead animal into its now pointless cage. As if they to the very last had bet on something about themselves that they thought was invincible. Even W.'s intended covers her face with her hands and turns towards him in despair.

You mustn't bring me here anymore,
It's too grisly to watch!

In retrospect he is convinced that the moment the fear stopped hammering and pounding in the vixen's body it moved into hers and began pulsing and pounding in the fetus inside her. From that moment on, he too carries the vixen's terrified heart with him wherever he goes. Across the river Memel hears how that heart beats, with the same dry clang as the clappers in the bells of Russian churches: a brittle lonesome sound that swells with each interval and accumulates strength so as to finally be heard far and wide. As though the bells have been taken from their stocks and buried deep beneath the earth and yet keep ringing, from inside the darkness, inside the very ground upon which he treads.

Not a day passes without his hearing them.

The heartbeats

The clanging bells

The frightened heart

THE CHILD ENTERS THE WORLD during a thaw day in March the following year, and because he has told everyone that he is the father, a message is sent to him at the barracks. The birth is said to have taken place by the peat sheds, the message reads, and he receives a note with a name and address. But it takes until late into the evening before his leave is granted, and by this time it has grown dark and the melting snow has evaporated into a thick, sticky haze that surrounds him like a wall. Finally, after much wandering and questioning, he arrives at a ramshackle house at the rim of a turbary on the outskirts of town. The turf itself can hardly be seen in the haze, but one can hear the melting snow seeping and running through the peat.

Later he won't be able to account for who actually lives in the house. Her grandparents on her mother's side or her parents-in-law are not among them at any rate, and none of the people he meets will return a greeting or receive the hand he reaches through the open door flap. In fact, an old woman is sent out to block his way. *Swedes have no business here*, is what comes out of her almost toothless maw. Tough and stubborn, she holds her own, her tanned skin stretched across her face as tight as a drum. When finally he manages to get the door to yield the other people inside just stand there staring at him. At least a dozen men and women of various ages. At first he thinks it's the uniform they are reacting to, or perhaps the dialect in which he stutters his apologies, or perhaps it's the frightened expression he must have made. Or perhaps none of it or all of it. A few of them erupt into raucous laughter, slapping their thighs and pointing fingers. Even the angry gammer's face breaks into laughter and her toothless gums cut like a wound across the tight leather of her drum.

Marie lies behind a curtain, on her back on a simple straw mattress under the stairs. Her aspect is glassy, as though confinement has robbed her of all power. Little Heart lies on her chest, her two tiny fists balled up in front of her face, which scrunches into fine folds as she unleashes her cries, head so much larger than her delicate little body.

He takes a seat on the edge of the mattress, carefully as though it were the edge of a real throne, and clasps on her tiny clenched fists with two fingers. With this the child falls silent, at last. Even Marie tuns to look at him with what could be a smile or an exhausted grimace or just an expression of infinite weary. At once, as though she were reading a familiar rhyme aloud, she begins to rattle off all the things he must procure for the child. Fabric for her clothing, a bonnet for her head and a pair of white socks; and a proper cradle with a lovely curtain, preferably in a light and airy muslin.

He makes an effort to listen and commit it all to memory, but as she is talking, footsteps and echoing voices pass through the room, up and down the stairs overhead heavy steps and thuds resound; curses are spoken, a woman is screaming in rage and something tumbles to the floor right beside the curtain.

Still Marie continues making demands, as if the list of things and tasks were endless, or as if she and the child were a world unto themselves, beyond all noise and shame. In the end he enters this world too, for when he comes to his senses and again can hear voices and other sounds, the darkness has already given way and he can see the contours of alien bodies moving like large animals behind the cloth partition hung in front of the cubby under the stairs. Water can also be heard running and dripping, the sound of a scoop being sunk in a tub and water pouring into an enamel basin. Then the linen cloth that is shielding them is torn open and unknown hands reach in and grab at them—again it is the gammer with the drum skin, now stretched tighter than ever. Only now does he understand that she is the midwife.

What is this stranger doing here, she says in the same shrill, flat, and dismissive tone as before. Sitting around here, showing off!

Doesn't he know the child is not his, and even if it were—how would he go about caring for it, a footling soldier . . . ?

And Marie has stopped singing her endless demanding rhymes, and he takes a seat and stares down at his hands, which had yet to feel quite so empty and meaningless.

HE PONDERS HOW WOMAN IN essence differs from man. She says she is the widow of a soldier who went off to war. Before he went away he begot a child with her. Or did he go away and then someone else did the begetting?

Now she goes with soldiers. She says she knows no other life.

One soldier begets, another stands guard. Or takes up the burden when the child arrives.

What does he who begets know about the life that is begotten?

Do a woman's moans encompass a particular certainty from which he is excluded, a certainty like that of the Freemasons', giving her access to a secret place inside all skin, all membranes where there is knowledge that no one else may partake in?

Only on one occasion has he been able to push deep enough into her moans to feel what is deepest inside: a gaping mouth, a small hand opening and closing, opening and closing, only to then let go.

And again he is forced out, locked out.

BUT HE HAS A REPUTATION now. At the garrison his comrades buzz about his industriousness with the womenfolk. He doesn't just knock the whores up, that Wutzig. He takes on their brood. No wonder they're throwing themselves at him! And so as to underscore how desirable he truly is Andres approaches him from behind, grabs him by the waist, and sighs with yearning in his arms—*Take me, Johann; take me as only you can, Johann*—and W. smiles his simpleton smile, twisting and squirming with discomfort and shame.

Even so he can't help but feel a bit flattered. These are his comrades, after all, the lot of them, they mean well. In this world of war and violence and ruin and need, where nothing is what it appears out to be at first glance and everything is in constant flux, comradeship is all that can be trusted in the long run. Believe me, Herr Hofrat, if there's one thing I've learned in my long life as a soldier, it's that friendship can't be valued highly enough!

And they buy him drinks. More than that: they want to get him drunk. Because it's such first-class fun when he gets fired up and tries to play king of the coop and demonstrate how he went about knocking her up. Right there in the middle of the tavern: he pulls down his trouser flap and stands at the edge of a table and starts thrusting while banging the whittling wood against the tabletop so they can see what it looked like when he drove himself into her soft flesh.

And afterwards, for the life of him, he can't understand how something that started with warm glistering sun and hazel thickets and a small piece of wood that could have become something truly fine, a whistle, a flute, a bird, could end with him acting like a crowing fool, who then retches in the nettles behind the tavern's privy.

And then at dawn: regret. The ugly feeling of betrayal that pushes into the part of him that is bottomless. The darkness has not yet dispersed when he starts prowling the turbary, which soughs and flows and drips and gurgles in the gloom.

She is still lying in the cubby under the stairs, but turns her back as soon as he pushes the curtain aside. She says she can't take the reek of liquor on his breath. The house's other inhabitants want nothing to do with him either. As soon as he appears and makes a request, even for something as insignificant as a pail or a washcloth, their eyes go blank or they turn their backs to him with a curse. And so one day, just as he has made a fresh attempt to reach the closet under the stairs, the woman with the drum-skin face appears with a gruff carl in tow. The man stands wide-legged in front of him and holds out his hands and says that he wants to be paid for the bed.

As the father of the child, he'll pay up, won't he?

Behind him people begin to laugh; the laughter that arises is that of when a long-awaited punchline is finally delivered.

So he wants to be a father, but when it comes to paying up, he slinks off!

And on the straw mattress under the stairs Marie turns her back to him and to the crude laughter. Not even the child is offered her breast, though she is right beside her, screaming in a way that seems to shrivel the lungs inside her small body.

And in front of the curtain, the boy Johann Christian August stands guard. Not like he usually does, straight and soldierly, but by looking him right in the face, eyes full of hatred.

EVEN AS THEY'RE SAYING THAT the child belongs to someone else, he knows the girl is his.

And his alone:

Her eyes are a bottomless blue, like all children's are. But they are his eyes.

And if he took another step back, he would see that she has his mouth, too, the same plump, defined lips, the corners of the mouth set in an involuntary upward curve; her hands so dainty and fine, around her knuckles are rosy wrinkles, so elegant only a king would dare touch them.

How is it possible that something not come from his seed can still appear in his image? Even the smile, when it finally springs from her face, is his numbed, shrinking smile.

Could they be bound by a kinship other than that of the body, a kinship of heart or soul? As if in fact the two of them lived beneath a sky other than the one that hangs above everyone else.

But right as he wishes to draw near, Marie slaps his hands away, her voice sharp and dismissive.

You have to go, Wutzig.

She could just as well have said:

This is your life, but it's not for you.

AND THEN SHE MUST BEGIN her rounds again, come rain or shine with the child strapped to her back in a sling. And the boy Johann Christian August follows along as ever to ensure that no unauthorized person comes near.

As for him, he sits silent at one bar or another, unsure of what to do with himself in his despair other than drink up the few coins left over from his measly pay, which wouldn't have been enough even if he had given them to her.

Or so he tells himself.

And they come to her again, the aging lieutenant Widebeck and the other one, Antonsson, who leads his horse and then keeps watch outside.

Now he knows who runs the Angel House, as the house is called because of the long trumpet-playing angel flying horizontally, wings spread wide, over the gateway that leads to the entrance: an old harlot who doesn't allow the girls who rent beds from her to bring their children inside. Instead, the woman with the drum-skin face tends to the girl. So he makes his way to the house by the turbary instead. But now everyone who lays their head down at night in the house knows it is not the mother for whom he is pining, but the child, and they insist he pay even to look at her.

Disgrace has its price. Even for him, it has its price.

IT IS ONE MORNING EARLY in May when the child is still no more than a few months old. At the garrison they are still busy repairing the ramparts. Seabirds shriek and dive in a sky so blue it seems to lack all depth. He is walking with a fully loaded wheelbarrow along the narrow rugged path within the walls when the second lieutenant comes rushing, arm around his hat and coattails fluttering. Three or four men are needed to move a household. The captain has made a promise. It concerns a Swedish officer's family whose furniture is to be shipped to Carlscrona. Four, five responsible men are needed, the sergeant has already chosen who he deems suitable, Wutzig can come along, too. It's an afterthought. It always is.

For the first time since he was at Waldenburg in the young doctor's service, he is inside a rich man's home. White linen sheets cover all the goods that are to be moved, including the grand piano which is the only piece of furniture in one of the rooms. White light streams into the rooms, the furniture, wrapped as it is in white cloths, makes an elevated, almost solemn impression on the soldiers standing awkwardly with their uniform caps in their hands. The family's two daughters are also dressed in white, wearing pinafores and white ribbons. The children are clearly thrilled by the moving staff. A dog weaves between their legs, it too barking happily.

He can't stop thinking of Marie and the child. Each time he visits with her she tells him about the home she wants for herself and the girl, a home that only exists in her fantasies, but still she speaks of it as if it were real.

You can't leave us now, she says one morning. It would be the death of us if you did.

She goes so far as to place a hand on his coat sleeve. Yet it is as though the gaze from those remarkable eyes is directed elsewhere, at someone else standing off to the side. From where he is standing and listening to her, he too can see that person as if he were present, or as if he were said man, but in the guise of this other soldier she's always insisted was the child's father. This other soldier has darker skin and hair and his hand clutches the knapsack strap like a claw. He is off to war, yes, he has already taken a few steps away from her when he catches sight of a jewelry box on one of the tables that has yet to be carried out. Without quite knowing what he is doing, he sticks a thumbnail under the slender snap and opens the lid. The box is empty. Those who have forgotten it here have long since removed its treasures. He barely dares imagine what manner of finery has been stored inside. The box's velvet lining is a magnificent dark blue, as beautiful as the sky above the fortress walls.

If only he could turn around and offer it to her as a parting gift.

Here you go, Marie, this, the most beautiful thing I own, is my gift to you.

And he has already begun turning around and handing her the empty box when the door to the chamber opens with a bang and the two girls come running in, followed by the chambermaid who is worn out from running up the stairs after the children and is now gasping for breath as she leans against the doorjamb. He tries to stuff the box in the knapsack on his back, but because there is in fact no such knapsack, he sticks it down his pants instead. There is already so much bulging and protruding there anyway, and the chambermaid doesn't cast more than a hasty look at him before she hurries after the two girls who are now calling to her from another of the already emptied rooms. And he doesn't give it another thought, perhaps he has already handed Marie the gift and freed himself from the close atmosphere he carries within when the sergeant charges into the barracks where they are sleeping, two to a bed, and they are ordered to stand at attention while the beds are searched and finally the sergeant is clutching the jewelry box as he roars in his face.

And W. I don't know where that came from, sergeant.

And the sergeant. So You're seeing it for the first time?

And W. It was empty, sergeant. There was nothing inside it.

And the sergeant. How do you know it's empty, if this is the first you're seeing of it?

That no object of value except for the empty jewelry box is found among his possessions is hardly considered a mitigating circumstance. Instead it is testified that he has been seen with soldiers' whores. The lieutenant's soldier-servant Antonsson can testify to having seen him outside the Angel House more than once, awaiting officers who had ended up in a fuddled state in order to steal from them. He and one particular slut are said to have been in cahoots. Antonsson has seen them together on several occasions.

And he is sentenced to six months in a house of correction.

It is as though the prison he fled from in Barneck has now caught up with him. But this time he has to share a cell with others of his kind, thieves, vagrants. They too have heard of his unfathomable successes with the soldier's whores and want to feel his member to see if it really is as big as the women boast and when he won't let them near, they spit wads of tobacco in his face and twist his arms behind his back until he feels like he is hanging from a thread of a rope over a precipice and someone is screaming *for God's sake drop the bastard let him drop*, but he can't drop or be dropped because there is nothing beneath him. Or rather: what is beneath him looks exactly like the raptor's trap the young doctor showed him up in the mountain rangeland. The terrain that was no terrain at all, not a ridge nor a slope or even hillside, just a depression in the landscape itself, something solid that had given way, just like he now is blindly fumbling for a protrusion he can cling to only to find something soft and yielding, his own skin, his own hair, his own face. And then he realizes that the crack runs right through him. It can't be traversed, because the more effort it takes to make a running jump, to dare to jump, the more the crack widens, and in the end it's everywhere he is. He doesn't even need to let go. There is nothing to let go of.

She visits him in prison, but does not bring Little Heart. She has nothing with her. Not even food for him. She just sits there, her open hands like an accusation in her lap and her face an empty bowl that never fills with desire or joy, not for him or anyone or anything else in the world.

And she says that once he has served his sentence he can go back to his old life. And if he intends to visit her, then he'll have to pay.

Like anyone else.

And he knows that she's going with others, that there are others who she would rather have as the girl's father. Or what does she care? As long as *someone* takes his place.

At the Inquest of the Detainee (2)
As regards this man's spiritual state and more specifically his psyche:

... he appeared to me neither incoherent nor absentminded, neither highly strung nor lost in confused thoughts and notions. Rather he gave evidence of a good ability to keep his attention on the subject of our conversation. For example, after I had taken some time to write down my observations, he could pick up the thread where I had left it. At times he himself would point out where his memories diverged from the chronology or became mired in irrelevant circumstances, after which he would return to the matter at hand with a natural and coherent train of thought. He immediately understood the meaning of the questions posed to him, it was never necessary to repeat them, and he answered each question quickly and pertinently. He was also able, if so called upon, to reformulate his response using different words and expressions, which was necessary in particular when it came to his state of mind immediately before, during, and after the crime itself. His memory was fully intact. One and a half years after our first meeting, he could still describe the course of events, citing the same circumstances as the time before. His comprehension of objects and facts are, at least when limited to the material world, correct and normal for a person of his spiritual education; even if his psyche, where states of a religious or supersensible nature are concerned, is perhaps prey to certain fallacious prejudices that are not altogether unusual for a person of his class and education, torments that cause him to stubbornly cling to blatantly false ideas. Though I did not notice in him a trace of morbid exaltation, emotional impoverishment,

or conceptual confusion, and after having delved further into these torments I have arrived at the conclusion that he is by nature quick to learn
and his psyche is fully capable of grasping better knowledge.

As regards his spiritual state and more specifically his state of mind:

... I noticed, as during my previous conversations with him, not a trace
of unbridled excitement, irritability, tension, unease, or unhealthy pas-
sion, or for that matter dumbness, absentmindedness, dejection, or
self-absorption, and consequently nothing that would lead me to draw
the conclusion that the delinquent suffered from madness, idiocy, or
melancholy in any form, degree, or complication. However, as far as the
delinquent's own state of mind, I did very soon observe that since my
first examination, through the simple and routine conditions of his prison
life, the good pastoral care he received from the clergy, reading the Bible
and other religious texts, as well as the long solitude and seclusion, and in
full awareness that the doors of death would soon open before him, all of
this affected with it a tangible and most beneficial change in his mental
state. He is much more accessible, more open, more given to conversation
and familiar now, and even seems to have a more considerable need to
communicate with others.

II.
Verdict and Appeal

AUTUMN HAS ARRIVED, THE SUN'S cupping glass has long since stopped wandering from one cell wall to the next and from the floor rises a ferrous chill that in the dawn reaches all the way up to the bunk where he lies. He coughs, half in trance, and his thoughts drift, hazy as the darkness of the early dawn. Johanna sits on a low wooden stool behind the bar at Jordan's inn, her head tilted against the wall, her hair, if possible, even fuller than he remembered it, grey-streaked black cascades in the splintered light the fire in the stove casts around the smoky venue. She is in a deep sleep. Breathing with all her chest, her eyes wide-open and empty.

She gives a sudden jerk, straightens up, and looks at him: right through the dream and the vast distance of time and space.

Is that YOU . . . ?

Her voice rings out like a clap of thunder.

But it is only the hatch on the cell door being pushed open with a bang, and in the gap the wooden mask of the prison guard Conrad's face appears. You have a visitor, Woyzeck, the face says, and in the light of the lantern he sets down on the small table in the cell, the lawyer steps forward, followed by his brother, the priest.

Goodwill and Anguish.

They each stand on one side of his bunk and look at him with distress. Woyzeck, says Mr. Hänsel, as if to see if the name can withstand the serious gravity of what he is about to say. He says that Herr Hofrat, the high-born Professor Clarus, following the end of the interrogation has concluded that as far as W.'s state of mind at the time of the deed, this man was fully accountable and so, from a legal standpoint, he must be considered fully responsible for the crime he committed.

W. doesn't understand a thing.

The last time the two of them spoke the court councillor had by no means suggested that the interrogation had reached its end. Quite the opposite. A reluctant intimacy seemed to have arisen between them. As though inside the bare interrogation room in which their conversation took place another space had gradually emerged, at once within and without time (the only sound is the slow but inalienable scrape of the clerk's pen tip against the page): a more open and freer space. It is in this space that W. tells Clarus about how after leaving Stralsund he made the long journey to Schwerin where again he had enlisted, this time in the Mecklenburger army, only to be flung into the French Emperor's ongoing war against Russia, and what surprised him in this great country was not the rugged, partly impassable terrain, but the cold that suddenly assailed them from God knows where. The Russians could not have wished for a worse equipped army, he says and tells of a Saxon named Papenhafer whom he came to know during the campaign, who carried a temperature gauge that he had fashioned himself and one day the quicksilver in the tube had crept so far down it could no longer be seen. It was so cold that piss froze before it hit the ground. Believe me, Herr Hofrat. The only thing that helped against the cold was pig fat, lard, or ordinary tallow, smearing it on each day and making sure that each strip of bare skin was covered. And of how later in Vilnius, when almost all of his comrades had died, he had been ordered by his company commander to single-handedly transport one of the sledges with provisions and essentials across the winter-frozen river. There were nineteen sledge drivers in total, Herr Hofrat. We were the only members of our company to survive.

And during all this talking, a freer expression has taken hold in Clarus's normally grim aspect, his hands move without touching quill or paper, and as W. demonstrates applying a liniment of fat and tallow to his arms and hands, he rises from his tall throne chair, although this means revealing his modest height, and takes one of W.'s hands in his with a surprisingly gentle, almost tender gesture so as to inspect the skin front and back, and something like a smile spreads across his face.

Clarus. So in the end You are showing Yourself to be a truly clever and reasonable fellow, Woyzeck.

But it is precisely this intimacy for which Mr. Hänsel is now admonishing him. One does not make a pact with the devil, and one does not enter into intimacies with one's interrogator. When W. points out that the lawyer had in fact told him to be as honest and forthright as possible during the interrogation Hänsel objects: Perhaps not quite so forthright, Woyzeck. And: Perhaps not quite so generous with your confidences, says his brother, the priest, who has been standing by the bunk while the lawyer per his custom has been taking measure of the cell with his long strides.

But what is one to do, when something inside awakens that is greater than oneself, that has neither form nor reason nor limits? One must be able to speak to someone!

W. sits on the edge of the bunk and when he looks down he discovers that his face remains in his open palms, while what should have been his face is wet with tears. What will become of me? he asks the face he is holding between his palms, and Johanna, who is still sitting on the other side of the dream with her look of dismay.

Is that you, Johann?

The lawyer and the priest look on with distress. Neither of them knows what to do with a murderer who is crying for fear and self-pity.

In the end Anguish impatiently scrapes his heel across the floor.

Let us pray to the almighty Lord. After all, our destiny nonetheless rests in His hands.

October 11, 1821

The trial at Leipzig's Schöppenstuhl against the day laborer and former foot soldier Johann Christian Woyzeck, concerning the murder of Johanna Christiana Woost, née Otto, widow of the surgeon Julius Friedrich Woost, opens with the prosecutor presenting the fundamentals of Professor Clarus's report on the delinquent and Clarus's conclusion that the delinquent had been hale and in full possession of his senses at the time the crime was committed and from a criminal law standpoint must therefore be considered fully responsible for his actions.

The reasons given are as follows:

1. The murder weapon, the broken-off saber blade, had been procured and furnished with a hilt with clear intent to kill, and this had been done in good time before the murder was carried out

2. During the police interrogation on June 4, the delinquent clearly recalled every circumstance around the murder, whom he had encountered and so forth, and *not on one occasion* did he lie or try to conceal anything

3. Prior to the crime, the delinquent encountered several acquaintances whose help he requested in determining the whereabouts of Frau Woost, and

4. when he had understood that the widow Woost was in the company of his rival, his state of mind further darkened, even more so when, after he followed her to her domicile, the widow Woost spoke the following words at her gateway, which could be confirmed by several witnesses on site:

. . . but I don't understand what you want,

go on home!

what if Frau Wognitz were to come

—and it was only on this occasion, when it became clear to him that Frau Woost would prefer not to be seen in his company, that he was reminded of the saber blade that had been refashioned as a dagger and thus dealt the death blows

(to which follows:)

5. that there exists no contradiction between what the delinquent himself stated more than once during the interrogation—namely that he had forgotten he was in possession of the dagger—and the fact that he committed the crime in cold blood, and this because the delinquent, who must be viewed as a fundamentally simple soul given to fall prey to his emotions, had first allowed himself to be encouraged by the joy of seeing Frau Woost again and then, when she declined his company, was overpowered by an equally overwhelming rage and so dealt the blows that would lead to her death

6. that the details recounted by the delinquent—that his first impulse after the deed was to impale himself with the dagger and in this way take his own life—cannot be taken as proof of insanity, since such an impulse must be considered wholly natural in that a perpetrator's first impulse upon committing a criminal act is to dispose of any evidence of said crime, including himself; when he did not succeed, since there were, in his own words, "too many people around," the delinquent satisfied himself by throwing the murder weapon into the pond only to then try and distance himself from the place, and this "at a runner's pace" as he himself stated during the interrogation

7. to this it must be added that he, when the police officer on site arrested him, had heard these words spoken: God willing she is dead

8. that all of this indicates a premeditated act that not only required thorough preparation, but also coldhearted calculation

9. that the suggestion that the delinquent while committing the crime, beforehand or immediately following, is said to have been a victim of a form of spiritual agitation that went beyond the passionate excitation common among people of his kind, for the aforementioned reason must be firmly rejected

10. that likewise it shall be pleaded that the delinquent himself admits to having acted in the aforementioned manner, in full knowledge not only of the motive for his actions, but also their consequences, and has confessed to all aforementioned statements

Question. Will the detainee please rise!

Answer. (. . .)

Question. Is it true that You Yourself stabbed the widow Woost multiple times with a dagger inside Frau Wognitz's gateway?

Answer. Yes.

Question. Did You deliver these stabs Yourself with the dagger, which was hitherto in Your possession and recovered at the time of Your arrest?

Answer. Yes.

Question. From where and to where did You deliver these stabs?

Answer. From the front, into the chest.

Question. For what reason did You stab Frau Woost with the dagger?

Answer. She must have said something that angered me, then I stabbed her.

Question. Did You deliver these stabs of the dagger with the intent to kill?

Defensor. It was during the police interrogation immediately following the arrest that the detainee answered that this was his intention. The detainee, however, now states that he never harbored such intentions and wishes for the following statement to be committed to the record *[reads]*:

" . . . *now write it down like this, if it's the truth You're after and the truth is what You'll get when I say that I harbored no such thoughts, all I did was I stab . . .*"

Question. For what purpose did You keep possession of the dagger after having collected it from the woodturner?

Answer. It must have been with the intent to stab Frau Woost.

Question. After Your arrest can You confirm that You said: God willing that Woost woman is dead, it's what she deserves?

Answer. The words "God willing she is dead" are mine—whether or not I added "she deserves it," I can't say.

October 12

Pastor Friedrich Moritz Hänsel's description of his encounter with the murderer Woyzeck, the same evening the verdict against him was pronounced:

I found Woyzeck downcast and remorseful in his cell. Thus we jointly sought strength through prayer, whereupon Woyzeck spoke these words: "In truth I have erred." I inquired why he wasted a lifetime without improving himself or changing his ways. W., pale and penitent, then confessed that he had fallen prey to the devil's wiles more than once in such a way that the Lord would not have been able to guide him. These are his own words. I replied that it was not up to God to guide man's every step, but that it fell to each and every one of us to turn to God and seek His strength and guidance. Whereupon Woyzeck replied: "In this too I have erred, forsooth." He went on to confess his pride before God. He said he had been caught up in the devil's yarn and spoke of demons and other of the devil's tools. I rebuked him and said that in the world of God's creation there is only the path revealed to us by Him. Woyzeck then fell to his knees and confessed before myself and the Lord loudly and clearly: "I hold nothing to be true or holy other than the Lord's gospel and my faith in the Lord as it has been manifested and heralded by God's son, Jesus Christ." And when he, full of dolor and remorse, asked whether there was any salvation to be had for him, I replied that for he who openly and without concealing any of the truth acknowledges his sins and admits that he is a reprobate, there is always hope for mercy. Then W. responded verbatim with the following: "Yes, then in truth I am a reprobate, a beast as You say."

Whereafter afresh in prayer we both sought strength in the word of God and asked Him to have mercy on all those who in want of reason or out of folly have strayed from His path.

December 3, 1821

The military submits an appeal of the verdict, in which it is asserted that the detainee acted in a state of soullessness and confusion and so full responsibility for his actions cannot be assigned.

> *The detainee belongs to the type of person whom destiny has flung into hostile territory. He neither has a home nor a roof over his head. He has failed in his every undertaking to advance his station. Thus, he has not known how to find a means of sustenance, for which reason he has become indifferent to life. Directly he has made the following statement:*

> *"... I have long tried to support myself to the best of my ability. I have labored, but no reward has this brought. I have only fallen deeper into ruin. So, it shall go as it may for I cannot help it. I realize that this will cost me my head. I take this fate in stride, as I know that I must one day die."*

> *These utterances suggest a ravaged state of mind, a state best understood as part of the designation "mania."*

May 1822

Proposal to request approval of the petition for clemency, drawn up by Friedrich August the First's nephew, later King Friedrich August II, according to whom the criminal Woyzeck rather than be executed, as provided for in this verdict, shall be transferred to a prison or a hospital where he can receive medical and spiritual care:

> "*. . . Notwithstanding the laws of the land, and in consideration of the position in which Your Majesty has placed me, I take it to be my duty to let my opinion be known, all the more because in this case it is not a matter of which sentence is to be passed but to what extent mercy can be granted, and mercy is by definition above the law . . .*
>
> *Which conclusions can be drawn from this for the State?*
>
> *1. that the State is within its rights to use violence to avert all dangers that may be directed at it as a whole or in part*
>
> *2. that this violence is only to be used to the extent that it is absolutely necessary to avert these dangers*
>
> *Moreover, one hundred culprits escaping with their lives intact is to be regarded as a lesser evil than if a single innocent loses his. For the State, the former is to be regarded as an accident, whereas the latter can only be seen as an injustice. Unfortunate is that which happens without our knowledge or intent; however, an injustice always occurs with intent.*
>
> *So I take it as my obligation and duty to before Your Majesty call attention to my reservations about the content of the expert opinions that have been given in this case . . .*"

III.

The War

[...] this morbid condition is only the product, the final result [...] of a totally perverted way of life, which for so long in an unnatural, psychic and somatic way has become overtense, overfilled, and overexcited by passions [...] the storm in the bodily organism is merely an external reflection of the internal condition [...]

(Heinroth, 1818)

(On heartbeats and demons)[*]

[*] (Presented to Clarus)

1. Of demons I only know that they take many a varied form and they make themselves known in divers ways and not all have faces. They can show themselves at the outermost edge of the sky, where the curve turns red in the evening, and we would all see their limbs were we not blinded by the rays of the setting sun. At nighttime it happens that they may push through the vapors that separate us from the celestial sphere, but then their bodies are shadowed, which are of darkness by nature.

2. The demons ascend and descend across the sky in paths like those of the planets, though not necessarily direct or regular, and when they reach their apex in the celestial sphere, which need not occur at noon, they emit a sound so shrill no human ear can perceive it and so it is taken for the deepest silence. More than once I have experienced the whole earth as filled with the shrieks of these spheres, and even though I covered both my ears the sound was not muffled.

3. I would like to distinguish between the demons that reveal themselves during the day and those who reveal themselves at night as follows:

    a. Even in the middle of the day I can be overcome by an emptiness of thought. Herr Hofrat would surely call it *indolence*, and shortly thereafter I feel beside myself, in the sense of being outside of my own body. I am *aware of* what I perceive, but I know nothing *about* what I am feeling, experience no pain or even tiredness, neither do I feel release, on the contrary, only agony, for I know that this is the work of demons. There are demons that have the power to transform people, snatch their souls for short or long periods of time, without one ever being aware; neither does one know where one is being led, for while one is in the demons' circles all memory or knowledge of what one experiences there is refused.

b. The night demons often draw near right at the verge of restful sleep. They can appear as immense or threatening forms, encourage odious acts, such as fornicating with animals. But they can also possess the most seductive sweetness, with hands as soft as angel down. Their touch can cause shivers of sensuous pleasure to run through the body that do not stop even as the very fundaments of the world tremble and quake. When they withdraw they leave a dark, aching pain in the heart, and a smarting like that of the eyes and mouth filling with ash.

c. The demons of distance distort one's vision and beguile one into believing that what is right before one's nose is in fact far away and inverse. In Russia during the emperor's military campaign I often experienced it in this way.

d. There are even demons that can fill your nightly sleep with drumbeats or a wind slapping a stiff sailcloth. They are never visible for they never cease—they are an echo—beneath the earth they rest like ringing bells, like heartbeats, buried deep.

4. As the demons harry it often happens that I pray for God to avert these visions and punish me for my errors. But even my prayers to the Lord fill with trembling and quaking. It is as though someone were plucking words from my mouth and rolling them like stones. And when I wish to conjure the vision of the Lord God's glory and peace in my mind's eye, this image too is distorted, and it is as if someone were holding my heart with the intent of squeezing the life out of it.

5. Once I saw a building catch fire and rise into the sky.

6. If all that happens in the world is the work of demons, may the Lord Jesus Christ have mercy on us.

HIS FATHER ALWAYS SAID THAT his side of the family came from Volhynia, but when he asks the others in the company where this country is to be found, he is only met with shaking heads, no one knows or they point their arm in a vague direction, southward or eastward or somewhere far beyond the uncertain point on the Polish flatlands through which the entirety of the Mecklenburger column is now on the move, dust and din, the drivers' irate shouts when the baggage-wagons cluster on the narrow roads: campaign chest wagons, wagons with ammunition and provisions, the staff carts and the many company carts loaded with tents and bags, all pulled by horses and mules whose backs are already covered in lacerations from the abrasive harness straps.

It is now June, the sky shines like the white of an eye long into the night, and the hot unclean air is thick with insects.

They travel during the day and sometimes set up camp in open fields and light fires that can be seen from far and wide as in a dream's inverse order, where the nights are crowded but the days are empty. The villages they march through are abandoned in the middle of the day, down to the lone greybeard on a bench next to the church wall or a smith's firm and steady iron hammer ringing out from the darkness of his smithy, hammering that continues even when it is drowned out by the noise of the column: snorting horses and the wagoners' shouts, creaking wheels and rattling chains, the dust being kicked up and the furious barking of dogs that surrounds them as they make their way through populated areas and that makes the draft animals nervous. But if they arrive around evening the streets are often crowded. One pulsing-hot early summer evening in a town he can't remember the name of, it is as if the inhabitants had been waiting by the wayside for days. Not just the bare-legged children with their anxious small faces, who run and beg alongside the convoy, but also the adults of the town, men and women, broad-shouldered smiling merchants who wave and small wrinkled farmer's wives holding baskets full of eggs and vegetables, and *cudów! cudów!* they shout with one and the same mouth, *miracle! miracle!,* and a courageous boy even swings himself onto the campaign chest wagon to try and stop the convoy and *cudów! cudów!* they continue to shout, pointing towards the cobbled square where a statue of the Holy God's mother towers atop a pillar as tall as three men. Even though her head is demurely bowed it seems she appears to be smiling at them, a timid, provocative smile under the curve of her eyelids, a smile that seems to grow larger and happier, brazen even, the closer they come and, when they are standing in front of it, to crack into something ragged, unreal. Only then do they see that her face is hidden under a mask of squirming insects, butterflies, and owlet moths swarming the gilded halo atop the Madonna's head, they cover her lips and eyes and beat their wings and crawl down her chin and cheeks, making her whole face looks like it's smiling, and by the monument stands the town priest in full canonicals, with chasubles and censers—he too is smiling happily, he too is shouting *cudów! cudów!* in chorus with all the others.

When he asked his comrades about Volhynia they name towns, villages, streets, and squares where someone they knew once lived, or where they had stayed themselves, but not one of these names means anything to him, or the places only exist wordlessly in his memory. But this one word did exist. *Cudów nie ma* his father used to say. There are no miracles. Yet there were. The word existed, as did the memory of what it meant. Likewise the expression of joyful devotion in the faces of those who had spoken it. Afterwards he was told that the town had a long tradition of rubbing the Mother of God's face with wax and honey to attract insects at night, one of the Lord God's wonders meant to incite amazement and wonder in passersby and perhaps even cause them to stop and buy some of what the townspeople, men and women and children, rush forth to offer the weary soldiers in the convoy who, if somewhat reluctantly, have now come to a halt at the foot of the Madonna statue on the square.

THOSE WHO ARE LUCKY ENOUGH to know one of the drivers are sometimes allowed to ride on a wagon; but for most walking is the only way. Now and then the march leads through long avenues shaded by leafy trees, but for the most part the landscape is wide-open, empty, somehow leached. He walks as he learned to walk in his many itinerant years. He doesn't measure time by counting steps or hours but by the height of the sun in the sky, the length of the shadows on the ground. The march isn't leading anywhere in particular, it means nothing, consists only of heavy rucksacks and rifles chafing the back and shoulders, the taste of salt on the lips, aching legs that give rise to shooting pains towards the evening, only to settle into a leaden numbness in each limb. And all around and without direction, with no inherent order, a cacophony of sound and smell: the baggage drivers' shouts, the livestock bellowing, the smell of open earth and dung, the tang of excrement left behind by the many companies that have marched here before them, until finally they are called to a halt, fire pits are dug, provisions and tobacco are unpacked.

Over the course of the day the column manages to disperse, and when he finally arrives at camp, sometimes he has lost sight of his comrades, and if he doesn't have the energy to wend his way around the fires in the dark, searching for them, he settles down wherever there is space.

He, otherwise silent of speech, may then feel occasioned to take center stage. Surrounded by more than two dozen young men, a number of which are already half asleep, others anxiously staring into the darkness, he mentions that he has already encountered the Russians: when he was fighting for the Swedes on the Finnish coast. And of course they all want to know what they're like, the Russians, and because what he's saying isn't exactly true, never was he face-to-face with the Russians, he recounts his crossing of the frozen Baltic Sea during the retreat, when the Russians came after them like wolves, he says, and for the first time in his life he discovers that someone is clinging to his every word, he who is otherwise so insignificant, so he can't help but play along in the game of awe, puffing his chest as he speaks, going so far as to interrupt his torrent of words with the odd dramatic pause, sucking back the snot running from his nose or looking to one side as though to mark how rather bored he is of it all. And then he tells them about having just set up camp on the ice and lain down to rest when a wild man came charging, and how everyone had taken the wild man for a Russian and thrown themselves over their rifles but it was he who the wild man was after and barely had he managed to screw on the bayonet before it slipped right into the roof of the beast's mouth and only then did he realize the man so stuck on his weapon was their very own sergeant; and to this very day, he finishes up eloquently, I cannot for the life of me understand how a hale and hearty commander could become such a roaring malefactor, as though he were prey to the Devil himself, and as soon as this is spoken he realizes that what he has said about the bayonet stuck in Sergeant Kwast's mouth cannot be retracted or unsaid.

From that day on people begin to steal away when he comes over and takes a seat with the wood and whittling knife he always has to hand. That is, he is said to have stabbed one of his own officers to death in cold blood, and if he could mistake one of them for the Russians, he could just as well stick a knife into any of them.

DAY BY DAY EVER MORE companies attach themselves with their wagons, and beyond Tilsit, as they approach Poniemon and the river, such crowding reigns on the large country road that they can only advance a short distance at a time. It is as if the entire world has squeezed itself onto one and the same place. Above the sound of snorting horses and lowing oxen (two of an ox cart's four wheels have gotten stuck in a ditch) curses and commands can be heard in a myriad of more or less intelligible languages, German, French, and Polish. The troops must number in the tens of thousands and each one seems to be heading in a different direction—the French cavalry comes riding *down* the column instead of up and past it, the baggage-wagons returning to Tilsit, drawn by the same weary oxen that he had seen dragging themselves along the day before.

An army of this kind is like a great beast, says the pensive Johann Krupp, who as soon as they get stuck somewhere on the road instead of getting angry slowly knits his fingers and starts philosophizing.

It devours whatever's in its way. You'll see, Wutzig.

Indeed, he feels a remarkable mixture of fascination and fear, and of course, relief that the long march to the border is nearing its end, but also a gnawing anguish about what may lie ahead.

When they finally reach the army camp itself, situated on a long slope leading down to the river, the main army has already crossed the bridges laid by French sappers. But when the Polish cavalry was about to cross, the pontoon bridge broke, it was said—the pontoons too low in the water or ill secured—and the horses began to shy. In the uproar several of the officers had walked into the river, horse, kit and all. As duty prescribed, each officer raised a hand in a final salute to the emperor

and swore their faith and obedience to him, Krupp said, for such are the
Poles: men of honor to the death. But the hill from which the emperor
had witnessed it all, a place with a broad panorama across the river and
the flatland on the enemy's side, sits empty now, Bonaparte has already
decamped with staff and adjutants, and all that remains is a piece of tent
canvas fluttering in the wind and two soldiers standing guard next to a
gun barrel on a mount.

In the camp the motley bunting of company flags mixes with laundry,
which also resembles flags, hung on lines stretched between the tents.
Between and below them moves riffraff of all kinds, cordwainers and
tobacco hawkers and village idiots and beggar women, some so eager
to display their charms that they walk bare-breasted, flying in the face
of all that is honorable and decent. Here and there are also a number of
short men with small writing cases on their chests, in the event that a
soldier might think to send off a few last words to his nearest and dearest back home.

Surely they could draft a letter in Volhynish, if you like, Krupp
says good-naturedly.

W. has had thoughts of writing letters, but what would he have to say
to Marie Thiessen in Stralsund who had so deplorably betrayed him? He
could only imagine directing a few words to Little Heart, but of course
she isn't literate and perhaps he has better ways of contacting her. The
image of her fair face escapes him not for a second.

During these last slow weeks he has spent almost all his spare time making pieces for a little board game. He already has the board. It can be
folded out like a table. Now he places it on a patch of earth worn bare
between two tents and arranges the figures in the light. On one side
stands the emperor's army, on the other the czar's. Flanking him are the
marshals, generals, and entire armies with everything from cuirassiers to
simple foot soldiers. He has also carved a one-legged military chaplain.
I'd bet you'd relish sticking your knife in him, says Krupp, who forfeits
no opportunity to tease him. (For some reason he has a reputation as
one who denounced God, probably because of his strange ideas.) And

now the actual military chaplain comes limping with his crutch wedged under his armpit. He bends down and inspects the blocky one-legged piece that is meant to be his likeness.

If you discount the leg, which he says he lost in an accident involving an explosion, he in fact recalls the surgeon Woost, squat and mighty as he is about the neck and shoulders. But his hands are small and weak, like a child's. When he picks up the figures that W. has carved and turns them over in his palm, he does so with care, almost tenderly, as though he were holding small living creatures.

It is silent until the priest wordlessly limps off, and afterwards they can't seem to pick up their thread of conversation, until Krupp releases his fingers, woven like a basket held in his lap, and playfully shoves him in the side:

He's probably not all there, Wutzig, but he doesn't have a bad bone in his body, that one.

W. holds his knife and carving between his pulled-up legs and smiles dumbly. Whenever anyone addresses him he feels like an animal that has been dragged out of his burrow and is shamefully smiling into the far-too-bright light. Like something laid bare, he feels, like a different W., inaccessible to his person but still performing in his name. Who then is this other who resides in the soulless darkness, the one who the hands with the knife and the wood are forever trying to distract from? He doesn't know, and among those who bend over the board game on the ground, not one takes pains to find out.

I'll be the emperor.

Hans Wiener pushes his friend Krupp aside and sits cross-legged behind the Frenchmen's blue pieces.

And all the while the river maunders through the summer heat, and the city in the plains on the far bank is at once incomprehensibly close and strange, as though the agitation and noise in the military camp on his side were but a senseless, unreal spectacle, something flickering by that it does not care about one jot.

AFTER BARELY A WEEK IN the camp, the company receives orders to detach. Before then, they have had to empty their packs of all but the absolute essentials so the same thing that befell the Polish cavalry when they crossed does not befall them. Even though the bridge has now been reinforced and has held stable and steady for the ceaseless flow of infantrymen and artillery units that have been crowding on it since early dawn. The long slope leading to the river and the trampled field beside it are full of hastily discarded kits and cooking vessels. The searing sun is like a tin plate on the backs of their necks as they, close together in the stench of their unwashed bodies, make their way onto the gently swaying pontoons, and on either side of the sagging bridge the river is a creamy brown and green, full of invisible shadows.

On the other side: flatland, sparse deciduous forests, farmland.

And a silence so thick it feels as if they were moving through a viscous body of water. They pass a man's body in a ditch. His lower body is shot to pieces or merely decomposed in the water but the torso is remarkably intact, the scraps of a grayish uniform and the staring eyes of its face surrounded by buzzing flies.

In its vile stench the body lies as thousands of pounding feet march by; as though death itself were lying there, regarding them with its indifferent gaze.

The city, Poniemon, too lies dead and abandoned when they pass through it a little later in the day; only soldiers from their own vanguard are standing guard outside the town hall and jail. They turn onto the large highway to Kowno. All that can be seen are the traces of their own troops that have already walked this road, horse manure everywhere and all manner of muck, junk, garbage. But no people.

They come to a halt in a small village that has suddenly become larger than the world.

GOD IS THE DEAD HOUR in the middle of the day. In the stillness of the sun, stables and barn stalls stand empty and abandoned in the lazy buzz of flies. Not even the dogs are there that everywhere else had come bounding towards the horses or the livestock in the convoy. Perhaps the dogs are hiding, as the enemy is, somewhere at the edge of the next forest or across the fields, shimmering in the heat, a watery grayish blue. During a one-hour stop he, Krupp, and Wiener are ordered to search two farms on the edge of the village. They walk into an abandoned stable and in the shadow-ruffled light two cackling hens appear in a cloud of white beating wings. The hens must have hidden under the roof beams or were simply forgotten when the farm folk left. Krupp skillfully binds their legs and stuffs them in a sack. A sign. And late in the evening when they march into the next village they catch sight of a lone pig in the middle of the road. As unreal as the Godhead it stands there, under a wide-open sky that refuses to yield to darkness even though the midnight hour is nigh. Out of the shadowless light half a dozen half-naked men approach from various directions, crouching, heads squeezed between their shoulders, arms close to the ground, and the pig cries out like an infant but no escape route comes to light. They nail the dead animal to a barn door and slice open its belly, its heavy entrails spill onto the road where they land wet in the dust. The meat is eaten raw because the officers do not allow them to make fire. Afterwards they smear their naked bodies with the blood of their kill and run one by one onto the dead village streets, shouting at the far-too-large sky. Do they wish to display their still unquenched bloodthirst or do they simply wish to eradicate what the future may bring by unleashing their horror in advance? Soon we will all be hanging there, nailed to their outhouses and dwellings, entrails removed and swarms of flies as thick as tar around the bloody remains. Why do they never reveal themselves?

IN KOWNO THEY AWAIT PARTS of the Mecklenburger regiment that are transporting essentials in a barge convoy all the way from Königsberg, and in the morning during formation fresh rations are handed out, a change from the *kapusta* and the dense sour bread they are served day in and day out. When they decamp the following morning they pass a monastery on a small hill by the roadside, it too is said to have served as a military camp for the emperor when he stayed here. Everywhere are traces of the main army's ravages. The army road is so thick with dead soldiers and horses that the air is barely breathable. They take detours. They pass through forests with a carpet of soft springy moss. Blueberries are growing in such abundance that the forest floor is practically shining black. They dig using their hands as shovels and stuff their mouths full and when they finally reemerge from the trees they look like demons, mouths and lips turned black and red from the crushed berries.

They pass Zizmory and towards evening reach a town by the name of Milenany where they stop for a few days. Like in so many other lesser towns in the region most of the buildings are made of thick gray logs sealed with moss. Even the church is made of wood. But the inhabitants have long since fled or have been driven out. Only the Jews are left in the town. They walk amongst the men who have set up camp on the main square in the middle of the town offering all manner of thing, except for the extra provisions they'd actually need. After a dispute with the local Polish commandant, Captain Wirth orders all buildings to be searched. A former blacksmith by the name of Lunzer has joined up with him, Krupp, and Wiener, and together they search through a large merchant's estate right next to the square. In the center of the house is a kitchen with a stove and two beautifully furnished rooms on either end of a long corridor, one with a long wooden bench along the wall like a courtroom bar. As for him, he makes his way to the back room, a small parlor where the light from the low windows falls upon furniture covered in strangely patterned cloths. The room must have served as a nursery. On the floor is a rocking horse with a real leather saddle and small stirrups of polished iron. On carved wooden shelves sit beautifully dressed dolls, their painted porcelain heads wearing small red and violet kerchiefs. On the shelf is also a small loom, so small it fits in the palm of a hand, and a music box that tinkles delicately when he cranks the gently curved enamel handle. But they find nothing edible. Not a trace of flour, grains, or sugar. Lunzer sits on a stool he's dragged into the middle of the room. With his rifle wedged against one shoulder, he is busy cleaning something with a rag. Look here, Wutzig, he says and holds it up. A silver ruble! All around him are rows of objects—copper kettles, cutlery—that he apparently intends to carry with him.

Wutzig, can't you help me carry some of this? he says and hands W. a half-yard-tall samovar. In the next room Hans Wiener is letting loose on doorposts and walls with his bayonet and the rifle butt as though the house were the inside of a living person he can't finish off fast enough.

At night thieves and prostitutes scurry like rats through the camp. He clutches his field bag, his canteen, and rifle and finally manages to fall asleep with all of his belongings underneath him. He dreams he is walking through a forest as large as a kingdom. The kingdom is populated by his wooden figures, which are running around as the church bells peal and swell in the air. The emperor himself is wearing a tricorne on his head and beating a wall with his wooden sword while his other hand lifts up an imperial crown wreathed in towering flames. W. reaches his own hand towards the burning crown and can feel the heat it emanates split the skin on his knuckles. Krupp wakes him with a swift kick to the midriff, and the Wooden Emperor's crown and sword are not all that is burning—the whole town is on fire. Every house in the semicircle around the square where they are camped is ablaze. The fire's roar drowns everything else out. Against the raging wall of fire Captain Wirth is a dark silhouette. Like a weathercock he bends in one direction, then another, and with these movements directs soldiers away who then return as long bucket brigades heaving pails of water all the way up from the river. Others run straight into the sea of flames with casks and troughs and return again, doubled over, hands covering their mouths, while the fire casts its rain of sparks high into a sky that the billowing smoke has turned blacker yet. Amidst the flames, in the fire's beating heart, he seems to be able to discern the Emperor's crown, the one he reached for in the dream. Just as in the dream, it glints and fades, glints and fades, as though to signal something of great importance.

Yes, in truth, Little Heart, the world is a strange place.

Mysterious signs that appear to us in dreams can in the next moment stand right before us in the full glare of reality, clearly etched on the Lord God's own Heaven.

In the dawn, it is revealed that not a single building around the square has survived, except the church, and its bell clappers continue their droning clamor under a sky that even in the middle of the day allows no glint of light through. Afterwards it will be revealed that it was arson and had Major von Moltke and his battalion not sped away the previous day, they would have all burned to death, every last man.

The Polish commandant stands in the middle of what is left of the square and reads aloud from an inventory list while a company officer translates his French into German. Military rank insignia have been recovered in some of the burned-down buildings. It cannot be eliminated that some of our own men were imprisoned here, says Captain Wirth and orders for even the smallest dwelling and cellar cavity to be searched.

But it takes until the evening for the heat to dissipate enough for them to go back into the buildings and when they do, they cover their faces with wet rags to shield against the smoke.

Of the splendid merchant's house not much more than the stone foundation remains. Orienting himself by the stove's soot-blackened chimney, he makes his way to the nursery. In the ashes he finds the wooden horse's stirrups, still hot from the fire. The dolls' small porcelain heads lay scattered like fragile eggshells and their eyes stare at him, wide with surprise. He picks some up and pockets them. If I ever get out of this country alive, Little Heart, I will sew them beautiful new clothes and give them to you.

UNTIL VILNIUS THEY KEEP UP a good marching step but thereafter the terrain becomes more difficult. They have to walk close behind each other, in orderly columns, which means that he can't walk as habit has dictated, by emptying his mind of thoughts and finding rest in each length of a step and the steady flow of movement. Now fresh hurdles and troubles are constant. If it's not swarming insects, it's the heat and the dust working its way into his eyes like the smoke of burning coal and it smarts and stings until the tears flow and he walks half-blinded. They keep turning onto new roads that are wide at first, like real main roads, but then narrow or simply end at the edge of one swamp or another. There they must wait in the sticky heat of the sun while mosquitoes buzz around their eyes, mouths, and noses until marching orders are given and the entire company sets right off in the opposite direction.

Only to be waylaid by marshland again.

It is as though the landscape itself has risen up against them. It pretends to be one thing but is in fact something else. Some can no longer endure the thirst and exhaustion and stumble mid-step and end up lying by the wayside with all of their equipment and no one turning back for them.

Following four days of sweltering heat the sky fills with dark veil-like clouds and afterwards it begins to rain, soundlessly at first, then more heavily, and since they don't have any dry clothes, they sleep in what they are wearing. The wetness creeps in under the skin and lodges itself like a body inside the body, as though his legs were covered with a second skin made of cold. He cannot perform the simplest act without his numb hands shaking. And each town or village they pass is deserted, emptied of everything, or, like Milenany, burned to the ground. A particularly odious stink, rain laced with bitter ash, hangs in the air. Clean water is nowhere to be found. They drink from ditches where horse cadavers and fallen soldiers lie. The eyes of one dead soldier half-submerged in a ditch are staring, frozen in horror, as though he can't stand the specter decay has made of him.

They build rain shelters on deserted fields. The parched earth seems incapable of receiving all the water and within a day the landscape has turned into a lakeland. They spend hours searching for ground that is high and steep enough to set up camp. It has been raining all night, and by dawn the flooded earth reaches all the way up to the sky. They make their way down to the marsh with all the scoops and canisters they can carry. They draw water from three feet deep. The water is reddish-brown and crawling with small red worms; it can only be drunk if you suck it through a sieve made of thin linen cloth. They have nothing fresh to eat, even the few dry rations that remain are rotting in this damp. And the rain keeps falling. For days it rains without pause. No one seems to be able to do anything, not even raise the tents back up after the rain weighs the stretched canvas to the ground. The road they came in on is now but mud, and soon there is no road to speak of, just a large waterlogged field on which soldiers lie, fallen from exhaustion, if not already dead.

WHEN THE RAIN HAS STOPPED and the air finally begins to clear, a detachment of thirty men sets off to forage. Captain Wirth leads the troops together with a lieutenant from another company. Taking up the rear is a corporal leading two horses intended as packhorses. When after half a day's march they are still empty-handed, they decide to split up. The lieutenant continues north, Wirth and his men westward. Near dusk they arrive at what seems to be a large village. The village road is narrow and muddy and edged with long buildings, all built with the same bare, unpainted logs as everywhere else. It is clear that they are expected. Standing outside the buildings, old people point at their mouths, as though they were the ones hungering. Captain Wirth ignores them. At the end of the road, where it turns to muddy fields, lies the church, it too made of wood, and topped with an onion-shaped dome that seems to be made of shingles.

The short road that turns from the village street and leads to the church hill is lined with tall poplars. Below the church hill is a long slope where work of some kind seems to be going on. Overturned rabbit- or bird-cages peek over the tall grass. A flock of crows rises shrieking, making odd wheel and circle patterns in the air only to then settle in the trees. W. tracks them with his gaze. He has a piercing sensation in his gut that isn't from the days-long hunger.

The captain has also seen the movement in the grass and calls over a handful of men and points downslope. Be careful, he says. They may be lying in ambush.

The men set off, crouched, rifles at the ready.

As for Captain Wirth, he dismounts his horse and walks all the way up to the church doors. He looks remarkably small in front of the wide door and the harder he knocks the smaller he seems.

Nothing.

He calls for Lunzer who arrives with a hammer and crowbar and starts battering the door fittings with hard, practiced blows. W. turns around. The villagers that had lined the muddy village street have now crowded down the short poplar avenue. They are standing perfectly still, as if they expected that at least their church would resist the violence to which they are being subjected, or are they resigned to the fact that nothing can ever be resisted?

Then the door gives way to Lunzer's blows and they all flood in, as though the church itself were drawing them into its darkness. A horse whinnies in fright, incessantly. It takes a while for them to locate the source of the sound. In the tumult one of the men is hit by the rearing animal's hooves and crashes screaming to the floor while another clings to the reins with which the horse has been tied and is being dragged through the manure that has amassed on the floor.

This is no church for Christ's sake it's a bloody stable . . . !

Apparently unaffected by it all, Captain Wirth has gone over to the far wall where sacks of seeds are stacked high. The wall where icons and church paintings should hang are empty. Only a whiff of incense lingers under the arches, mixed with the sharp scent of horse piss and wet rock.

The captain is being called for from the church hill, and one of the men that Wirth had ordered to inspect the animal cages on the slope strides resolutely up to the commander and speaks to him in an upset tone. Captain Wirth turns on a dime, one and all follow him to the church hill. W. sees that the villagers are still on the poplar avenue, but they seem to have spread out. Some are even hiding behind the trees, as though they fear the worst.

From down the slope come harsh, abrupt shouts. They are in fact rabbit cages, he can now see. But the men have not gathered around them, but at a spot farther down, near to where the forest begins again. Krupp turns around sharply, forearm over his face, and at this moment the smell of corpses reaches him, too: like nausea rising from the ground itself.

It's three men. They have almost been engulfed by the grass, two on their fronts, one on his back. The eyes are missing from the one faceup. First he thinks the crows still flying overhead have pecked out the eyes of the dead. But upon closer inspection he sees that they have been cut out. As has the tongue. Where once were mouths are now only gaping wounds.

Captain Wirth has squatted down next to one of the dead. The captain's face looks swollen, whether with rage or rigid horror it can't be said. He turns the other bodies over. Flies rise up in clouds so thick they shrink back. The faces of the other two are also disfigured. The corpses are in such a state of decay after having lain facedown that their features can no longer be discerned. On the uniforms, the braids and fittings have been cut off, the boots are also missing, their bare feet are stiff and bluish black in the grass.

Curses are heard among the men, loudest among those who wish to hide their unease and nausea. But Captain Wirth has now composed himself. Dogged, he returns to the church accompanied by his men. The two who had been ordered to stand guard by the church door are now holding a prisoner between them, an old man in a caftan with some fashion of hood over his head: a priest. When he catches sight of Captain Wirth he tears himself from the grip of the two irresolute soldiers and comes running, coattails in his hands so as not to trip over them.

The bearded face is bathed in tears. He shouts something plaintive and keeps trying to grab hold of Captain Wirth's hands. But Wirth, irritated, tears himself free and calls for an interpreter. They all crowd around the interpreter and try to make out what the two men have to say to each other. Captain Wirth wants to talk about the dead French soldiers whereas the priest wants to speak about the church, God's holy space, which he claims Wirth's men have desecrated. There is froth in his beard and his eyes are white with rage.

Bring him with you, Wirth says, then we'll see who's desecrating who.

As they are about to enter the church, the priest seems to recoil, as though only now does he understand the full extent of what he has been trying to withhold, animal as well as seed. He catches his tails as if to flee once more, but the guards grab his shoulders and throw him to the church floor. At Wirth's command they chain him to the iron ring on the wall where the horse had been hitched.

Ask him to tell us who killed the soldiers, the captain says to the interpreter.

In the church his voice rings hollow, almost toneless. As though the words had not been spoken at all. The priest screams in his foreign language, the guards kick his legs out from under him and he falls face-first into the horse dung.

The interpreter squats beside him.

He doesn't want to talk, says the interpreter. He wants us to leave his church.

So, we'll leave him, says Wirth. He plucks a small pocketknife from the breast pocket of his uniform. He walks up to where the priest is hanging in chains and grabs hold of his befouled head. Hold him fast, he says and then begins with careful, pedantic movements, as though he were devoting himself to a fine piece of needlework, to carve the priest's eyes out of their sockets with his knife. The priest's screams practically cause the church walls to crumble; then they are stifled by a thick gurgling. Wirth has already prized open his jaws and when he lets go of the now almost lifeless priest's head, it is to throw the cut-out tongue along with the eyes into the stinking fecal sludge on the floor.

Then both packhorses are summoned and the sacks are carried out. Wirth leads the white horse that was in the church himself, gripping its reins until it too is loaded with seed sacks. The horse falters and shakes his head walleyed, but it could just as well be because of the blood now covering Captain Wirth's uniformed chest.

On the road between the poplars the villagers haven't moved. But they've stopped pointing to their open mouths. Only their eyes are wide-open.

They're trying to starve us out, it's us or them, Lunzer says to him with a broad pleading smile as though he, at any cost, wants to make him repeat the sentiment.

W. doesn't know what to say.

There is a noisy rattling in the silence when someone screws the lid off his canteen and drinks. Dutifully: as though to keep busy.

Where are all the men? someone suddenly says.

Between the rows of poplars, the yellowish dusk behind the villagers sharpens the outline of each and every body—all children and the aged. Even if they tried, they wouldn't be able to resist the foreign soldiers.

Then the bell up in the church starts to ring. The lone clapper's tolls sound thin and hollow at first, as though it was pointless hammering against the empty husk of the sky; but soon each toll grows stronger, they give each other weight, and the ground beneath them quakes, as though there too the bells tolled and wanted to press up between their feet. W. doesn't dare direct his eyes anywhere but forward. Right in front of him rides Captain Wirth in his bloodied uniform. There is something almost obscene in how he allows his body, back and hips, to follow the gentle sway of the horse's rump. It is impossible to say if he is unaffected or if the clanging bells cut right through him as well.

The sky above is still as bright as a lantern, but covered with wisps of cloud, as though God had wished to hold up a veil, so as to put this all out of sight apace.

THEY SIFT WHAT FLOUR THEY have and mix it with water and roast the bread right over the fire and eat it as it is, hot, outside burned, raw inside. The strange sleepiness lingers and makes it so that nothing really catches the eye. Or rather: he doesn't quite know what he's looking at. His own and his comrades' hands greedily and guiltily reaching for the scalding bread on the gridiron over the fire, or the back of Captain Wirth's hands carving into the priest's face. The raw bread, the priest's swiftly quelled screams, the blood flowing into the horse manure, the church floor, the earth where the bell clapper and the heartbeats pound. He covers his ears, but the tolling bells can be muted as little as the awful light from the sky can be removed. Do you think the dead can return? Lunzer asks, as though he had been sitting there thinking the same thoughts. No peace is to be had in this light.

WHAT FOLLOWS ARE LONG BLAZING days, the sun quivering over the flat horizon as if suspended in a viscous brew, and the very ground upon which they tread is so dry it feels as though with each second it is about to crumble and fall beneath their feet. Inside these days the hunger is like a bone in the body gnawed clean. The hunger bone runs from the parched soft palate down to the pelvis and is ground through with a hard dull ache made worse by each step. In this fatigue, rumors flourish. It is said that the enemy has amassed a great army and is waiting for them to get just weak enough so that they can attack from behind and cut them off from every line of retreat.

How long do the Russians intend to retreat into this country that isn't anything, only a wide, scorched terrain with no horizon?

The column with the supply and campaign chest wagons moves slower and slower.

Nor are the promised reinforcements of provisions and troops moving any faster.

One day they catch up to a French food train, so heavily loaded that the oxen pulling it can hardly progress. The officers' horses are there too, at least half a dozen bound to the final wagon in the convoy. The sight of the horses unleashes new rumors. Have officers also been made to offer their lives at the front? Or have they ordered fresh animals in order to flee?

The horses are clearly well-fed, but they are nervous animals that spook and threaten to rear when the Mecklenburger infantry tries to squeeze by on the narrow muddy road, and suddenly it is as though this worry goes on to infect the lot of soldiers who have been marching for days without proper rest or food. Half a dozen men descend on the field kitchen, and the grenadiers guarding the supplies prepare to open fire. It would have ended in bloodshed had not Major von Moltke and two other officers come to the rescue and after a quick exchange in French put an end to the skirmish.

Like two great landmasses the two columns part ways, the Frenchmen are forced to step aside and the Mecklenburgers struggle to pass by. Expletives are exchanged and the officers' horses shy away and twitch their ears, as unsure of how to conduct themselves as the foot soldiers who have nothing to look forward to but more hunger and misery.

That night the possibility of deserting is heard being openly discussed by some. They've put one over on us already, Wiener says, who is heated by nature. The major is confident of a victory, Krupp replies, referring to von Moltke who, of course, none of them have heard say anything that might confirm or refute this notion. Someone else objects, saying that those who set off now are only turning themselves into willing prey for the Cossacks who run riot in these parts. The Cossacks, Wiener replies, when did you last see any Cossacks? They're just trying to pull the wool over our eyes, frighten us, but I'm certainly not going to let myself be frightened.

Meanwhile Lunzer, the smith, is sitting there, polishing his silver ruble. What if, he says to W., it was this mad bunch who gouged out our men's eyes and the priest was innocent? I mean, what if he was just trying to protect the people of his church?

It is clear that he has taken the trouble to think this through.

THE NEXT MORNING THEY REACH Bobr, a town by the river of the same name. The narrow, winding streets are unpaved and are so full of refuse and animal dung that it feels like they're wading along with horse and cart. The only reasonably clean place is the square in front of the church. There they set up camp, and in the afternoon he, Lunzer, and a half dozen other men are ordered to build ovens as a wagon train with supplies is expected in the evening. They labor with renewed vigor knowing that provisions are on their way. It is well past the summer solstice and the red evening glow is dampened and has a darker tone, like that of lead or ash.

Yet the heat remains as paralyzing, the air is stagnant, heavy and stifling. They sleep where they can on the square next to the church or in the stinking side streets, back-to-back and huddled close so as to protect both limb and property.

As soon as twilight has fallen, shadows loose themselves from the dark. One shadow finds its way to the abandoned stable beside which he and Lunzer are sleeping in the stench of horse piss and offal. Unlike the whores who follow along with the convoy, this one is not old, but thin as a rake and clearly deranged. When she speaks her lower jaw moves as though her mouth were going in a different direction than the rest of her face and out of her mouth rises a foul, viscid stench of spirits. She is waving a bottle, her arm as long and pointy as a stick that tips over as though of its own accord.

Lunzer takes the bottle from her and drinks as though he could drink up the darkness and hunger and dejection in one big gulp, and when he lays with her he moans more than he usually does. *Give me give me give me,* he says again and again. It isn't clear what it is he expects to get from her, more of herself or more of the booze?

A few hours later when the sun is again boiling in the sky, Lunzer is sleeping with both his arms outstretched as though he had surrendered and was ready to rise up to heaven. Farther down the side streets others lie sleeping. Heavy shadows move over and between them with the same lax pace as carrion birds taking their time flapping their wings, only to swoop down on the next available corpse.

Not even the soldiers who have been ordered to stand guard manage to shoo away the pack of thieves. One of the sentries is sleeping, his back to the church door, the butt of his rifle wedged between his legs.

The next night they hear the transport approaching. It seems to split the darkness and from this fissure spills a violent noise. They hear the foremen shouting at the draft animals and whipping them up the riverbank, wagon wheels creaking. Presently they seem to be everywhere, the men with their cries and shouts and the oxen with their lowing. On the square several soldiers have already sat up, sure that the order to light the ovens will come soon.

But all of it is a mirage; a hallucination of the ear or gut.

When the quartermaster turns up at dawn the next day all he can do is shrug helplessly. No transport has yet to arrive. They are served the same stinking *kapusta* as always and before dinner they are ordered to fall in line and march off. A few days later they cross the Dnieper near the town of Osza and head for Smolensk, also abandoned by the retiring Russian army. After yet another long day's march, they arrive at a town by the name of Dorogobuzh.

Farther east they do not come.

FROM ONE DAY TO THE next the cold arrives. Like the flip of a hand. Like this, W. says and turns his palm over so only the back of his hand is visible. From behind his desk Clarus can even see the wound that runs like a map across the prisoner's hand, bright against the blackness of the veins. The cold rides in on the northern winds and stays for weeks. It is like a damper has been opened in the sky. Highest up in the town is a fortified castle that offers a panorama of the landscape that stretches for scores of miles on these clear icy days. It is this castle, as well as the palisades down by the river, that they have been ordered to reinforce. From the parapet at the top of the castle W. looks out over the river with its long bends and windings over which sunlight dances and the shadows of clouds glide, as they do over the patchwork of forests and small fields all around. At closer range he can see the pontoon bridge leading to the outlying districts where the country road splits like the fork of a branch. To the right the road leads to the city Tver and the Volga River and to the left to Dukhovschchina and the main road to St. Petersburg. The villages along the road are unreal in their stillness, as though a paralysis has set in—not a soul is in sight between the buildings. Only church bells ring out their unending clapper-song: the churches are easy to distinguish with their vaulted onion-shaped domes, some painted whereas the rest of the buildings are of the same uniformly gray timber.

For three weeks they hold out up here, and with the cold comes a darkness that is more than the absence of light. Day after day from the castle he can see how the very landscape dissolves into a misty gray haze. Smoke and fog drift across the river.

Rumor has it that Napoleon left Moscow after the whole city was set on fire, meanwhile the Russians are moving in from the south and north to try and cut off their line of retreat. They could arrive at any moment now. It is also said that their own regimental commander has returned to Königsberg along with a handful of officers and an adjutant and has handed over command to Major von Moltke. It is said they returned to arrange for supplies, provisions, and clothing, so that they could take up winter quarters here if need be. But nobody believes this. If the French Lilliputian's own officers are deserting, then what's to become of us? Lunzer asks.

As for them, they have nothing. They stuff their boots and clothing with straw and smear any exposed skin with fat and lard. Lunzer has wrapped himself in a thick bear fur that he picked up along the way and has greased his head and neck and hands and bound them with rags so that only his fingertips glow red in the firelight. They are quartered in simple barracks left behind by the Polish regiment that had previously held the town, mostly boat sheds and harbor magazines down by the river.

They play cards and dice to keep their spirits up, the prize is cheap vodka or a thick stringy soup with gray fatty lumps that someone says are of dog.

I'd bet my last coin on the major general and his entourage never coming back, Lunzer says. Why don't you wager the fur instead? Papenhafer, the Saxon, is asking. He has his temperature gauge with him, its quicksilver tube has not moved an inch since he first presented it, so no one will take it as a pledge. Lunzer's fur is preferable. People ask how he came by it. I bartered with a pack of tinkers, he says and laughs, that quick sideways glance of his betraying the lie.

It's like that Lunzer has a certain magnetism with things. Somehow everything ends up in his hands. Like the silver ruble he is constantly taking out and polishing as though everything, their survival, yes their very presence here on the edge of the steaming black river, relies on him keeping it as shiny as possible.

During the night the wind picks up and brings with it a crackling rain of sparks from the fires that have been lit by the shed where the grenadiers and musketeers keep. When his already aching belly can no longer handle the alcohol and putrid soup and he walks down to the river to relieve himself, the night above him seems infinite. As though it alone truly existed, and each new day were merely a faintly sparkling haze below: a shadow-day of smoke and flame soon to be swallowed by the night again. When Napoleon's armies triumphed in Jena, sparks rained from the sky. But now the sky seems dulled, as though shaded by a hand. Somewhere below the misty sky above the city hovers the castle where Major von Moltke and the remaining officers have entrenched themselves, awaiting further instruction.

FROM ATOP THE CASTLE'S PARAPET one afternoon he sees the sun halve and then sink into a fringe of clouds above the horizon like a ladle into a pot. Then he sees a handful of cavalrymen galloping down the far bank of the river. From the distance comes the rumbling of cannons. The sound is dull, like a constant tremor under the earth. Impossible to say if the shelling is waning in intensity or the opposite, it's slowly drawing near, as though hidden in its dark cloak of sound.

Then at dawn come the decampment orders, and if it wasn't clear before, it is now: the officers have abandoned them. The officer's wagon is not harnessed, only the baggage wagon is, and Captain Wirth and the other officers keep riding up and down the column, not to urge them to step up the pace, but to hide the fact that they are not in full strength.

At dawn: mottled cloud cover overlain with a thin veil, a keen wind from the north with grainy snow that whips their faces like a stinging hail. The snowfall intensifies along with the darkness, but no break or rest is granted. They march all night in the thick snow as though inside a tied-up mitten and when they reach Smolensk at dawn the snow-covered fortress walls look alien, as though the entire town had disappeared into itself.

They wait for two days under a slowly clearing sky. When darkness falls they light fires to guide the troops, and right before the second day dawns, the first column of French soldiers arrives. As though the darkness itself had spit them out: in the firelight they stand out like ebon shadows against the white snow. The army is flanked by horsemen who, as soon as the troops begin to arrive, turn around and ride back to the rearguard. The column is so spread out that a day passes before everyone has congregated and the parade ground outside the city walls becomes one giant army camp.

By this time several columns of captured Russian soldiers have also arrived, chained together. Most of them have bare rags left on their bodies but they seem to be in better shape than their captors. Several of them are actually standing tall and looking straight ahead, apparently unaffected by the blows and curses raining down on them.

Among the roadside onlookers is Lunzer, clad in his great bearskin. For every clutch of prisoners that passes by in the column, he spits in his hand and twirls the silver ruble between his fingers.

ONCE THE SNOW FINALLY SETTLES, the temperature continues to drop. The air becomes clear and dry. The midday light falls as though through a deep well, the edges of which are clad in a cold made of sharp, biting iron. With each passing hour the cold pushes deeper into the lungs. Faces and hands go numb. In the wind, which again is driving the snow towards them, their field of vision shrinks and the distance grows between the main column and that of the prisoners and wounded. Come night, the two of them could just as well be walking on their own, he and Lunzer, who labors clumsily along in his heavy fur. He knows it and clings to W. like an animal, eager and helpless.

After darkness sets in on the fourth and fifth day after the departure from Smolensk, they reach the Odrov River. Another thaw has set in overnight. Sappers have laid a pontoon bridge that sways and sags under the pressure of the water. The shore is covered in ice banks worn smooth, which they must traverse in order to proceed. Before they even reach the anchorage Lunzer falls to the ground and slowly glides into the water. Had the heavy bear fur gotten wet, he surely would have been sunk at once. But W. and another man from the company manage to pull him up in the nick of time.

So he stands there, shivering and freezing.

Of the once so industrious and astute Lunzer has become a pitiful, trembling tatterdemalion.

And so they are back in Bobr. The city with its narrow winding alleys is barely recognizable in the cold and snow. The tightly packed, leaning wooden buildings with snow up to their eaves might protect against the stubborn wind but they do not allow for a view. The city is like a cage in which they sit like defenseless game. Within a few hours a rumor starts circulating that they are being attacked, but it turns out to be the main column returning.

Now they find out that the main road to Minsk is barricaded, and the czar's troops have broken through this part of the front.

They are surrounded.

In a rage, one group of soldiers attacks the Russian prisoners of war. W. looks on as three prisoners' skulls are crushed and their faces cut to pieces before some officers finally manage to intervene.

Slowly the column sets off again. But they are all mixed up now. Once they had walked in good order, each regiment for itself, but now it is as though the country has spit them up in glorious disarray. Among the Mecklenburgers are also soldiers from Hessian and Westphalian units. Now the enemy's artillery fire is a steady rumble that seems to come from everywhere, or is it but a ringing echo that arises as they march through a landscape so frozen stiff and barren that nowhere can a sound gain purchase.

EARLY ONE AFTERNOON, WHEN WHAT little remains of the light is about to vanish below the horizon line, the path leads through a dense belt of forest. Snow-covered pines rise up on either side of the column like tall, stiff sentinels.

The officers are on the alert and send out a few men ahead on reconnaissance. They have barely made it to the bend in the road before they come rushing back, arms flailing wildly. Farther up the road, in what looks like a clearing in the forest, two overturned wagons and horse carcasses can be seen and on the hillside are several corpses, contorted all, their blood and guts spilled in the snow. Their faces and the exposed parts of their hands are lightly dusted with snow, but the hoof prints are still deep in the snow, and excrement streaks the road.

W. is standing by a sledge, the runners of which are sticking from a snowdrift like goat horns, and he is just about to call Lunzer over to help him pull the runners free when someone beside him points to where the road disappears into the thick forest.

At first the strange horsemen are almost impossible to distinguish from the massive wall of pines. Then it is as though the tree-shadows are breaking free from themselves. The riders surge out to the flanks and some of them seem to be leaning over their horses at a precarious angle.

From right behind him, Captain Wirth bellows his orders.

Then follows the tremendous crash of musket fire.

This only succeeds in dispersing the group of Cossacks. Some of the riders retreat slightly, then deftly turn their horses around and come charging back. One of them streaks past W. at such close range that the man's gaze is right in his eye. He manages to glimpse the gun the moment before the shot is fired, hurls himself out of the way, and smells gunpowder and the sour stench of animal sweat from the horse's hot body as the Cossack sweeps past in a thunder of beating hoofs that spray his face with snow.

Nearby Lunzer, swearing to himself, has already bitten open a cartridge and poured the gunpowder in the bore and perhaps it is this fact, him having already managed to load and raise the rifle, that causes another charging Cossack to take aim over his shoulder and fire off a shot. It looks like Lunzer's left leg has been blown to pieces. Bloody scraps of flesh fly into the air as Lunzer spins half a turn and falls sideways into the snow.

W. cowers until the shooting has stopped and the beating hooves have disappeared, then runs to Lunzer who is hunching in the snow, his leg stretched out in front of him at an unnatural angle. His face is pale, bloodless. W. grabs hold of his shoulders and presses his face to his lips to feel if he is even still breathing. A long moan escapes his mouth. He makes an attempt to raise his torso but the pain runs through his body like a spasm and he falls wordlessly to his back.

He's not going anywhere in that state, someone shouts.

Two men come trudging through the snow. One of them elevates the wounded leg while the other wraps it in a cloth. W. manages to free the sledge from the frozen drift and together they lift Lunzer's heavy body onto it. From the supply wagon, a rope is thrown out, which they quickly tie around the runners. And right then Captain Wirth rides over.

Let it go, is all he says.

And when none of them can bring themselves to obey he walks over himself and unfastens the rope that is attaching the supply wagon to the sledge. Wirth's gnarled face bears the same expression of contempt and slight disgust as when he stood in front of the priest in the village church. He mounts his horse, marching orders are given and the full column sets itself in seemingly reluctant motion and is then swallowed by the forest as if it had never existed.

THERE ARE PERHAPS FIFTEEN WOUNDED who are left behind in addition to him and Lunzer, and the column is now so spread out that it takes almost twelve hours before the prisoners of war and the injured others reach them.

Evening arrives and swarms of crows circle the sky above the still-unburied corpses upon the hill. Huddled together, they listen to the moans of the injured. Then darkness comes and no one dares light a fire for fear of the Cossacks returning. In his mind's eye, he sees them breaking free from the massive tree-shadows, wave after wave come charging, rifle or saber raised high. Never before has he experienced, or thought he would experience, such fear: as though the night and its icy cold were neither night nor cold, but a living malevolent being just waiting for the moment their vigilance waivers to ravage them, or as though this ravaging were already happening, and all they could do was lie there, stiff with cold, and wait for it all to finish and then at least the agony would stop.

In the first turquoise-green hour of dawn he hears them coming. He hears the stamping and snorting of horses, harnesses clinking and rattling in the cold, and wagon wheels creaking and grinding. Someone shouts *halt* and then it is again full of people running around and trying to care for the wounded and injured.

Lunzer's leg wound is tended to by a barber-surgeon. He stays on his back on the sledge, but his pale face is turned to the sky: as if he only expected help from above. Then the sledge's runners are tied to one of the draft horses and they continue through the forest and across snow-covered fields.

And now the Russian troops' artillery fire can be clearly heard. Dull toneless cracks that echo deep under the ground. Ever closer, ever denser, comes the roar. It is as though they are not fleeing their fate, but dragging themselves towards it, resigned and without haste.

NO ONE, NOT EVEN YOU, Herr Hofrat, can conceive of the tragic end our army met. We were supposed to have moved to Borisov, but our orders changed at the last moment. Later we found out that the Russians had already captured the city and were guarding the bridge abutment and firing upon us with their artillery from various positions along the road leading there and away. So we had to join the northward-bound prisoner column led by a Württemberger company, but on several occasions we had to await passing foreign cavalry, and new wounded men were constantly joining our column.

It was like Doomsday itself. So many sick and injured. Some with injured legs or arms, like Lunzer, others with half their face blown off. Some being pulled on sledges like the one on which I was pulling Lunzer, or on makeshift stretchers made of simple boards with fir branches between. Others walked with only their comrades to support them, who were also so weak and battered it looked like they might drop at any moment.

By the riverside, tens of thousands were already waiting, and only units that were still in combat were crossing the lone bridge that had been laid out. Again and again officers arrived to say we were next in line, but there was always someone else who was let across first. There is no justice in Heaven, Herr Hofrat understands. The poor and sick are always last to be granted entry, if they are allowed in at all. And as though God had wanted to demonstrate his lack of mercy for us in particular, there followed a few days of thaw. Large brown patches had already appeared on the ice, the waters would soon be unleashed and sweep the bridge along with them, and if the Russians closed in we knew our own would prefer to blow up the bridge on their side, then those of us who were left behind would only be able to hope for the enemy to show us a quite inexplicable mercy.

Two days and two nights this Doomsday lasted. Beneath the sky it flamed as though with burning fire. The troops that were down by the river, or hadn't yet managed to take shelter, were fired upon ceaselessly from the Russian positions in the hills, and those who had yet to reach the bridge abutment tried to build ramparts as they fell back, and in this incessant cannonade, this constant din of artillery fire and officers shouting orders and shrieking horses dragging entire wagon loads down with them as they fell, we were supposed to approach the riverbank and take up positions where our troops were the most vulnerable.

When orders were finally given to cross the bridge, darkness had long since fallen, but the firestorm in the sky had turned the night into the brightest day. We were among the last, and there was an unprecedented crush at the foot of the bridge. I had to pull the sledge with Lunzer myself the last bit, and I think I must have already begun to fever because what flew into my head was that it wasn't Lunzer on the sledge but a terrible beast who was resisting with all its might, and when I turned around, I looked right into the maw of the beast and there it glowed like the sky above.

Whatever I did, I knew I could not pause, or stop pulling, or lose sight of the column in front of me for even a second for then all would be lost.

And yet I seemed to be slowly overcome by a great sleep.

The last thing I remember is an army of black crows, the kind that eats fallen soldiers and draft animals, and then a row of spread-out birch trunks shining, white as signal flags, though only darkness lay between. The birches seemed to be animate, as though the bark were giving off its own light.

Little Heart, I thought I was in the Kingdom of Heaven.

WHEN HE WAKES UP, EVERYTHING is bright and frozen stiff again and as silent as the grave. In front of him stands a hulking fellow, more than twice as tall as his own shadow is long, rifle pointed right at them; and beside him stands a man without a face. Both are wearing the French army's blue uniform coats, but the faceless one has a Russian fur cap pulled over his head. Thinking at first that they must be dragoons out looking for deserters, he rises from his bed of spruce twigs and begins to report and explain. How their company was ambushed by Cossacks, how they followed along with the prisoner train and were among the last who managed to cross the river but then fell behind or rather were left behind by the convoy of sick and sought shelter on a wooded hillside, this very hillside. The tall one doesn't seem to be listening. He is looking at Lunzer, still on his back on the sledge. Joost, he says by way of introduction, and over there is Dinkel. He means the faceless one. Then he kneels next to the sledge, unwraps Lunzer's bloody bandages, and gestures for water from W.'s canteen. Together they try to clean the wound which has gone black around the bullet hole. On the other side of the leg, just below the thigh, the leg is so swollen the knee cannot be bent.

No use, Joost says. It needs a barber-surgeon.

W. says nothing. The trees that had been dripping with moisture have hardened again. A clinking forest.

How did he get here? Joost asks. Did you pull him on the sledge?

W. says nothing. Joost looks around. What had been snow is now solid rolling ice.

Not sure if the sledge can be pulled now without falling over, he says at length.

Why don't we just shoot him? Dinkel asks.

Dinkel's voice is like his face: absent. But it also contains rage. The image of a cloth beating in a strong wind appears to W. Whether the wind is Dinkel's hoarse whisper or the rage itself, he does not know.

One doesn't shoot people like animals is all Joost says.

THEY STUMBLE ONWARD OVER ICE and crusted snow. Joost and him take turns pulling the sledge on which Lunzer lies, the ruins of his leg splinted and wrapped with a fresh bandage. Dinkel doesn't pull. He walks ahead of them as though to reconnoiter. No sound can be heard. Only the hollow scraping of the runners against the ice crust and Lunzer's long, heavy moaning breaths. If the sky had once been a fire, the interior of which couldn't be seen, it has now become a crowded dome, so crowded that the sweat squeezed out of their bodies could just as well be the condensation on the inside of the dome. As they are walking he can't help but feel that each tree, each forest edge, each open field they pass is only there to hide something else. When they are finally forced to stop, about to drop from exhaustion, the landscape pauses too. The forest and the empty fields stare at them as though awaiting their next move.

The cold is on its way back. He can feel it rising from under the ground and snow. When dusk falls everything around them seems to be breathing frost. In spite of the cold, Joost refuses to make a fire. They're hiding among the trees, he says. If they catch a whiff of smoke they'll be on top of us in seconds. He doesn't say who *they* are. The Russian vanguard, Cossacks, roving brigands, perhaps only armed elderly villagers who have gone into the woods?

Dinkel takes Joost aside and speaks to him, placing a familiar hand on his arm. Standing in profile, his cheeks and chin are obscured by his coat collar but his high forehead, nose, and the hollows that must contain his eyes are visible. As is the tiny, wan mouth with its slight pout. It can't be said if those negligible lips are smiling or if it is a matter of lips at all and not just a thin score where the cheeks merge into what should be chin. W. wonders what sin of Cain Dinkel is guilty of to have been condemned to carry this half-face around for his earthly life. Now Dinkel is again turning his crooked back to him and pointing over his shoulder in Lunzer's direction and from a distance it's clear he has set his sights on Lunzer's great bearskin coat. W. sits beside him on the sledge, cringing in fear. It is not the same fear as when they crossed the swamp and each and every second man dropped from exhaustion. Or when the shadows of the Cossacks loosed themselves from the forest edge and the strange horsemen came charging at them. It is a hard, gnawing, and continuous fear that slowly erodes him from inside. Like the hunger does. And like hunger, this fear not only eats away at his physical strength, but also his sight and hearing. He knows that Dinkel could blind and stun him, rob him of his last rational thought, if Joost allowed it, and he could do so unseen.

They divide the night into shifts to help keep watch but in fact it is mostly Joost who is on the lookout. Dinkel sleeps or whatever it is that he does behind that nonexistent face, and Lunzer's pains are too great for him to be of any use. Several times he wakes from his feverish half-torpor and flails around as though to defend himself against invisible assailants and when W. bends over his face he sees that it is slick with sweat.

When it is dark the constellations appear in the sky as though etched in brittle glass, and the cold is a hard and metallic thing that can be touched, and the smell of snow is rough and wet in the air.

When daylight squeezes through the sheltering treetops, Lunzer's leg has swollen to twice its size and a foul stench rises from the wound. They go on for another few days but Lunzer is now in so much pain he hardly has it in him to lie on the sledge. The slightest jostle or jolt causes him to give forth a long howl. It is clear to them that soon they won't be able to make any headway and Lunzer knows this too. When he is awake his gaze flits anxiously between them. He looks at W. with a silent, expressionless appeal, as though it fell to him alone to save or deliver him from this torment.

ONE MORNING JOOST MAKES HIS way to the road with the long telescope he wears in his belt, and ends up standing at the roadside with the telescope pressed to his face. Then he turns around and waves Dinkel over.

It is a hazy, faintly sunny day, and the ice fog closest to the ground makes it difficult to see the contours of the landscape. Only after a while can something that appears to be riders on horseback be discerned on the horizon. It is as though they are emerging from the blinding light itself, but separated, torso parted from horse, so that the number of riders is uncertain. But Joost is sure. There is only one. Dinkel wants to go for his rifle but Joost signals for them to go back into the woods. No weapons. On the sledge, Lunzer has also understood that something is afoot and makes an attempt to prop himself up on his elbow. He has froth in his beard, wild eyes. Joost strides onto the road and gestures with both arms at the lone rider who slowly approaches, leans forward in his saddle and then peers at the wooded hill where Joost is now pointing. The man is unarmed as far as they can tell. Joost continues pointing and finally the man dismounts, lifts off the black bag that was bound to the back of the saddle, and walks over, bag in one hand, reins in the other.

As the two approach, they hear Joost speaking French and the man clearly understands him because he's nodding and looks dogged, but not afraid. He is thickset, dressed in a double-breasted justaucorps and knee-high boots. His face is almost spherical, clean-shaven but has bold, bushy eyebrows. A doctor. If nothing else, the black bag makes this clear. His face expresses a calm, patient resolve. Where W. is from, a doctor would never pay a visit in anything less than a buggy. But this doctor rides alone on horseback. Which great distances has he not covered astride this beautiful beast?

The doctor removes his fur hat and exposes a curiously bald head.

Joost keeps chatting with him. Together they walk up the wooded hill where Lunzer is lying on the sledge, his swollen leg stretched out before him as though it were a foreign object that did not belong to him.

The doctor lifts the blanket with which Lunzer has covered his leg. W. thinks he sees it throbbing beneath the black scab and the sweet rancid smell that rises from the wound nauseates them. The doctor says something to Joost in French and shakes his head. He's saying that the leg has to be amputated and for this he does not have the means, Dinkel explains to W. Joost is insistent, takes a fistful of coins out of his pack. The doctor retreats a few steps, smiles, and wards him off with a wave of the arm.

Dinkel plants himself behind him, rifle raised.

Si ça peut sauver la vie de ce pauvre homme, Joost says.

They make a fire, melt snow in a pot. The doctor wets the rags in the boiled water and takes them out with the tip of the bayonet Joost has screwed off and handed him. Lunzer screams like a madman when he realizes what they are going to do, but Dinkel stuffs a rag in his mouth and W. and Dinkel lift him up by the underarms so that the doctor can reach around the leg. The bayonet isn't sharp enough and the doctor has to prize and press using his whole body. Even with the rag in his mouth, Lunzer's screams can be heard far and wide.

Joost takes the rifle and walks onto the road to keep watch.

Only when the bayonet reaches the bone does all go silent. Lunzer has fainted with Dinkel's fingers shoved in his mouth.

The doctor kneels beside the sledge and carefully begins to wash the wound with a liquid from an apothecary jar that he has taken out of his black medical bag. He then unpacks a piece of clean linen and dresses the wound again. W. hears the soft sound of Joost's boots in the snow. Move aside, he says in German. W. turns around. Behind him Joost raises a wooden club high above his shoulder and with great force swings it into the back of the doctor's head. The man falls forward, his face on the needle-covered forest floor. Joost straddles him and continues beating him until that bald skull cracks open, revealing the slurry of blood and gray matter underneath.

A long silence follows. The only sound is the wind up in the pines.

How are we going to get Lunzer on his feet? Dinkel asks at length.

We need the horse more, Joost says.

They rustle up some branches and leaves and cover the corpse.

Joost opens and takes stock of the contents of the medical bag, then ties it behind his saddle. With their combined strength, they heave up and tie the still-unconscious Lunzer to the back of the horse and set off, sledge in tow.

THEY TRAVEL NO MORE THAN a couple versts at most before Joost stops again. The two others stand around him and the horse like disciples around a prophet. He must have been on his way somewhere, he says. Who? Dinkel asks. The doctor, says Joost. He must've been on a call. And with that he turns around and sets off in the opposite direction, back along the road they came. Dinkel protests but it is Joost who is leading the horse carrying Lunzer and it is he who has all the supplies and the sledge so they have no choice but to follow.

After some hours the dry icy wind begins to carry a clear note of wood smoke. They turn off the road and follow a short, sloping stone wall that runs along the edge of a dry creek bed, black like a wound in the snow-white landscape and overgrown with sallow and osier. The wall, like the creek bed, ends at the edge of a field and sitting on a log out on the field is a farmer. He has a little leather haversack on his back and his hands are resting on his kneecaps like two heavy wooden blocks. In the light of the low-slung sun his face is almost white and the shadows beside him are long. They come to a standstill at the headland but even though the horse is impatiently stomping and snorting in the cold the man doesn't seem to notice them. He keeps staring at the white sun glinting on the horizon.

Maybe he's deaf, Joost says.

They walk onto the field and approach the unmoving man in a wide skirting formation. The man continues his silent staring. Only when Joost throws the stone does he turn his head, but then to where the stone has landed and not towards them, even though they are now only about a dozen yards away.

He's blind, Joost says.

Now their shadows are on the old man's head and he is smiling at them as though the smile were a message they should be able to interpret. Joost tears the haversack off the old man and dumps the contents onto the snow. Nothing but an empty tin and some tobacco. The man mutters into his beard. W. leans in, listens for a moment, then turns around.

I think he's asking if it's the doctor who has arrived, he says.

Tell him he should be grateful anyone's here at all, Joost says.

W. doesn't know what to say.

But the old man seems satisfied to just have asked the question. He gets up from the log, then bows farewell without looking at any of them and sets off across the field. Halfway there he slows down, pauses but doesn't turn his head, as though to ascertain whether or not they are following him, then keeps going.

They linger for a while, unsure of what to do with themselves. On the other side of the field a grove peeks out. Over the trees and across the field flies a flock of cawing crows. As they come closer, they once more see the wall creeping out of the snow and the frozen mud. It is the same wall as before, built by the same hands. But now it surrounds a small house, built of sturdy rough-hewn logs, almost black with lichen. Behind the house is a stable and a shed, and behind these a cluster of gray-bearded roofs belonging to other houses and outbuildings in a small village, apparently untouched by the war that has ravaged and burned everything else along the road they have been traveling.

They walk into the forecourt and from out of nowhere a dog comes racing. The dog is stopped by the length of its leash, but the horse gets nervous and backs away. W.'s first thought is: why didn't the old man have the dog with him? Then he understands. The old man must have been out on the field waiting for the doctor. From inside the house a woman's voice can be heard shouting. So the dog is guarding the house. Watchfully, they continue to move across the forecourt. Again the dog runs at them, again stopped by the leash. Joost stuffs a cartridge into the mouth of the rifle, pours gunpowder in, aims, fires. The shot rings out like a clap of thunder and the fallen dog lies on the ground like an empty sack. The house looks like it wants to sink even deeper into the ground. A shadow appears in one of the windows. Joost approaches, brings both hands to his mouth and calls for the old man to open the door and come outside. No one comes, but after a while the door glides open as though of its own accord. Joost grabs hold of the doorknob and signals for the others to go inside.

In the smoky darkness, they see a table, and then at the back, closest to the window, a bed. In the bed lies a woman who's trying to get up but she only manages a few steps before she stops, one hand on the edge of the table, the other pressed to her heavy belly. The woman has large round eyes and her face is drenched in sweat. She says something in an upset voice to a deformed boy who is lying on a bench or shelf above the stove. The boy makes no reply. Reluctantly, he clambers to the floor, then stands there with a yapping smile directed at all and none but still won't stop. An idiot.

At least there's a hot stove, Dinkel says, opening and closing his hands with slow, soft movements.

Joost enters. He's dragging Lunzer across the threshold by his armpits.

Make way for him, he says and pushes everyone aside, even the woman, who falls helplessly to the floor and starts whimpering and rocking, her arms around her belly.

Joost lays Lunzer in the bed next to the window where the woman had lain, then says to Dinkel: Go out with that one and see if there is feed for the horse. Then come back and boil some water on the stove.

He smiles.

W. thinks this is the first time he's seen Joost smile. He has just beaten a man to death with a wooden club, but now he is smiling.

Upon hearing Joost's voice the old man got up from the table and is now fumbling insecurely for his hand. When he finally gets ahold of it he starts bending and bowing deeper and offering thanks and saying Herr Doktor. Everyone, presumably the old man too, knows it isn't the doctor who has come, but no one lets on otherwise.

Dinkel comes back into the house, without the boy, and walks over to the worktop and rummages among the dishes and pots. It all crashes to the floor. W. notices that Dinkel's hands are shaking.

Is there not a single person of sound mind in this house?

He crouches down next to the woman who is still lying under her giant belly on her back on the floor. He fits his body along the woman's, his faceless face to hers. Her eyes are white with horror.

Where is your husband? he whispers.

You know where he is, Joost says.

And the food, where have you hidden all the food? Where is the lard, where is the sausage?

The woman screams. It is a scream that comes from deep within, as though she were breaking apart somewhere, and her hands reach for Dinkel who is now pressing a heavy knife, taken from the countertop, to the woman's throat.

Stop, Joost says. It's not like she understands.

But Dinkel doesn't stop. He starts slapping the woman's head and neck with the handle of the knife. When the woman, screaming all the while, rolls over and tries to curl herself around her defenseless belly, he grabs her arms and yanks them over her head.

Hold her hands in place, he hisses.

No one seems to hear.

Then Dinkel lets go of the woman's arm, takes fresh hold of the knife, and drives it with all his might into her belly. The woman's scream is stifled by a dark gurgle. The hands that were flailing wildly in defense, pounding Dinkel's head and shoulders, freeze midair, as though trying to grab at something up high, then fall slack to the floor. The woman's head is thrown to one side and a mighty stream of dark blood wells from her mouth. Far from stilling Dinkel's ire the woman's sudden laxity only seems to further spur it on.

If you can afford to give birth to a little soldier boy, you have food to spare for us!

He kneels next to the lifeless body and stabs and drags the knife around her belly until her intestines spill out along with what's left of the woman's uterus. Beneath the layers of mucus and blood smearing across the dirty floorboards, the fetus's head is clearly visible, as is its curled-up body. Dinkel has blood up to his elbows when he finally calms down, chest heaving as if in convulsions, and the lips of that little mouth are quivering. But he is done speaking. It is so quiet in the room all that can be heard, beyond Dinkel's long wheezing breaths, is the leisurely trickle of blood still flowing from the dead woman's body.

W. notices that he is standing there and smiling. He doesn't know what to do with himself or where the smile is coming from. He is as little able to guide the actions of his mouth and lips as he is to stop the sleep rising in him like a tide.

They might have stood there for an eternity had Joost not suddenly said:

Where has the blind man gone?

W. turns around, as though only now is he becoming aware that he has a body and two pointless hands right in front of him which had done nothing.

But the old man isn't there. They are alone in the room with the dead woman.

He must have run to the village, Joost says. Go after him.

W. opens the door and steps into the sharp white sunlight, with the feeling of stepping off a cliff's edge. It is as if he himself were blind, or suddenly surrounded by the sky on all sides. It takes him a while to blink his way back to something that resembles sight.

The horse stands with hanging reins next to the dead dog. Nearby, beside some of the outbuildings, the boy lies on his back, his slit throat like a gaping second mouth and his long arms stretched out as if in prayer. The doors to the stable and shed are open but inside are only wood chaff and shadows thick with cobwebs.

The blind man sits out in the field on the same log as before, in the same position, his hands like two chunks of wood atop his closed knees and his face turned towards the sun, now even closer to the horizon. Tears are streaming from his eyes but still he is smiling.

W. bends over and fumbles after the few Russian and Polish words he knows. He has to ask where the country road is. They must find their way back to the road. Right now nothing is more important than this.

Gingerly, he lifts up the old man's arm, pulls back his wide soiled sleeve and with his fingertips draws on the old man's bare forearm, then on his wrinkled palm: the road they walked an eternity ago, the road that led them along the long dry creek bed, with the wall that encircled the farm and the farmhouse. And once he began drawing with his finger on the man's forearm he kept going: the horse, the dead dog in the yard, the boy on his back with his arms spread wide as though he wanted to embrace the sky, the dead woman with her dead child in the blood on their dirty kitchen floor.

The blind man turns his face towards his exposed arm, then turns around and points with the other arm to the far end of the field.

W. stands up.

From the neighboring village comes a dog's stubborn bark.

The crows draw ever-tightening circles, then fall from the sky.

THE HORSE PROVES TO BE more of a burden than a gift. Their pace does not improve as Lunzer is the only one on horseback, and the others must make do on foot beside him. And they have to keep to the country road because the lesser roads and sled trails in the forest are often so snowed over that the horse sinks in and every time they look for a shortcut it feels like they're using up their few hours of daylight trying not to get stuck in snowdrifts or mud.

What little horse feed they looted from the farm soon runs out and the horse grows ever weaker. Sometimes it just stands there, snapping at defoliated branches at the edge of a forest. They set up camp for the night in low-lying places, in gullies, behind rocky outcrops, once in an abandoned post house. They search for flour or seeds in the remote farms they pass but most of it has already been plundered. They see imprints of hooves and cartwheels in the snow, also tracks and wild animal droppings, but don't dare use what little remains of their gunpowder because one shot in this countryside's far echoing silence would give them away at once. There is no time to wait for small game or fowl to wander into the traps Joost lays.

They cook a soup of roots and deer moss and vomit in the snow and Joost sits guard by the fire with his rifle over his knees.

Traces of war are visible everywhere. It is as if a great devastating fire had swept through the land, indifferent to everything. Charred buildings with soot-blackened gable walls or chimney stocks against the low winter sky, decomposing animal carcasses and human corpses left in ditches or out on fields or in the midst of a thicket, half-ravaged by the animals that found it, now covered with a merciful layer of frost.

But there are also villages, sometimes only a few hours off the high road, that seem entirely untouched and where life continues as though there had been no war. Women in long skirts and with thick kerchiefs over their heads pluck beets from the earthy fields, men drive fully loaded horse- or donkey carts along the roads, dogs run around their barrow wheels barking. They take what they can of the wasted beets that have fallen off the carts and hungrily bite into the hard, earthy peel or chew the greens rendered into a smeary slush by the frost, and then seek shelter in the forest until they have put enough distance between them and any inhabited areas and the dogs have stopped their barking.

ONE MORNING THEY COME UNDER attack.

They have deviated from the army's route to avoid populated areas and are following an old sled trail through the snow. Felled trees form the base of the corduroy road but the snow is thin between the pines and the hoofbeats and the sledge runners crashing against the logs prevent them from hearing the approaching bandits until one has already charged at them and grabbed hold of the horse's reins.

W. lets go of the sledge that he has helped to keep steady on the slippery logs and reaches for the rifle on his back.

Then he sees that fully armed men are also standing between the trees.

But the one who is closest is only a boy. And uncertain. He can tell by the twitchy way he swings the barrel of his rifle between W. and the sledge and the horse sharply tossing its head in an attempt to parry the strange body hanging from the reins. Wavering, the boy lowers his weapon, and W. catches a glimpse of his horror-struck eyes before Joost shoots and the boy collapses as though someone had cut the invisible strings that were holding him aloft.

At the sound of the shot the horse breaks free, the man who was hanging from the reins falls to the ground with a thud and the two other assailants flee into the woods.

Lunzer fares worse.

The rope binding him to the back of the horse keeps him from falling but also from sitting upright due to his missing leg. They watch him grab for the horse's mane but the horse rears and Lunzer falls forward only to get tangled upside down in the harness as the horse, shrieking wildly, rears and bucks, and suddenly it stops, oblivious to everything, and bends its head to the ground and quests with its muzzle through the snow at the wayside.

When Joost, Dinkel, and he finally make it to Lunzer's side, his face is bathed in blood and clay, and his right arm is jutting lifelessly from his body at an unnatural angle as though it were broken or dislocated. Only his mouth and eyes remain on that bloody face, both wide-open in pain.

It's over for him, Joost says.

So shoot him, Dinkel says, but Joost just scoffs and turns away.

Don't you think we've wasted enough gunpowder already?

Then Dinkel bends over and starts stripping Lunzer of his clothes, first the fur and the justaucorps underneath, then the trousers and under-pants, paying no mind to the bloodcurdling scream Lunzer unleashes when Dinkel stretches his broken arm overhead.

Finally the blacksmith's massive body is lying naked in the snow, his skin strangely bluish, like milk thinned with water, except around the red, swollen stump of his leg sticking out from the rags with which they tried to secure it.

Joost turns each garment inside out.

Here, he's your companion, he says and tosses the silver ruble to W. who receives it with the same sleepy idiot smile as when Dinkel killed the young woman.

In the silence only the high wind moving through the pines can be heard.

W. stays put and looks at Lunzer who stares back with indifferent feverish eyes. Joost has already packed the bloody bundle of clothing in the sledge and sorted out the tack. Now he is riding the horse along the corduroy road with Dinkel in tow. Neither glances back. W. has to run to catch up with them.

DEJECTION DRAGS HIM DOWN LIKE a bog. Each step he takes grows heavier, each pause a prayer for respite, for the chance to lie down a little longer, forever, to not have to get up and take another step. The fact that they can now take turns sitting on the horse does not bring any relief. Hunger aches and grinds in their bodies. Like a wild animal that has clawed its way in so deep its teeth sink through to their very bones. And even though he is wearing Lunzer's thick bearskin fur, and every exposed patch of skin, face and hands, is wrapped in thick rags, the hunger seems to have robbed him of his every defense against the cold. Moreover, the thick fur collar is full of lice that have been animated by the faint heat his body is still radiating and are spreading a searing venomous itch across the base of his neck and scalp, possibly a worse scourge since he can't scratch without exposing his skin.

These can't quite be called "days" anymore. No sooner had the gray haze of dawn appeared than does it fade away again in the darkness. Often they don't bother to find a camp for the night but keep walking until they drop. Had Joost not the strength to look for dry wood to light a fire, they would have frozen to death on the spot. That such fires could be seen from several versts away is no longer a consideration.

But often they don't even have time to make a fire before darkness falls. It is as though a hangman's hood has been pulled over the sun and the blizzard sweeps in like a fog of sharp frozen grains on their faces. On certain days no signs appear. Only the driving wind in the treetops over-head and the sudden crack and snap of frozen tree branches all around, as though the forest had opened its mouth and begun speaking to them.

If they're lucky they find a spruce or a windbreak to huddle behind. Against the wind and the whipping wet or ice-sharp granular snow there is no other shelter. It is like being enveloped by a vast blindness. In the howling storm W. sits tight as though in a small corner of his own skull while what was once his body slowly goes numb and disappears, and all that he can think about is what will happen if he ever catches up with his old comrades again. Once they see which regiment, battalion, and company he belongs to, surely they will shoot him like they did the other stragglers: those who were sucked down by the mud and swampland on the road from Vilnius and then did not have it in them to get back up.

Stragglers or deserters, it's all the same. In the eyes of the powerful it doesn't matter why you waver or fall out of step. All you have succeeded in is demonstrating that you are an incompetent good-for-nothing who can't even handle the spasms and the slow numbing pain inside your own body.

But perhaps they won't make it that far. Perhaps their journey will take so long that not even the war will still exist when they finally arrive? Will he be able to recognize himself then? Will there be anything left of him for anyone to recognize?

BUT WHEN THE END FINALLY comes, it isn't as he imagined it. They have caught up with parts of the rearguard, if one can even speak of a rearguard now that all units have long since been mixed up. Everywhere are clusters of stray men banding together for they know they have no chance of surviving on their own. And while they are distrustful and keep to themselves, all are equal before hunger and so no one can keep themselves from crying out for food. *Courage!* one shouts. Another cries for help. *Hilfe!* The three of them dare not heed any of the cries. A cry for help could be a trap.

They are so used to Joost protecting them that they barely notice when he disappears. But after the encounter with the other stragglers the otherwise composed Joost has also started to behave strangely. Sometimes he seems forgetful and negligent, other times he acts with hitherto unthinkable aggression. One morning, after they fail to properly lash their blankets and supply sacks to the horse and everything tumbles to the ground, he drives Dinkel ahead of him, his rifle butt raised like a club, and doesn't stop beating him even as Dinkel falls to his bare knees and begs him to stop.

For the rest of the day Joost is nowhere to be found. By dawn he has returned. But now he starts to up and leave camp more frequently. It could be the middle of the day or early in the dawn. They assume he is out looking for sustenance but can't be sure and neither dare express what they both fear: they have become a burden to him just like Lunzer once was to them and he is about to abandon them. They don't dare say it because they know that neither of them could take a step in any direction without Joost, they are lost without him.

So one morning, when they have set up camp right at the edge of the old army road, a faint rustling is heard in the grass, frozen stiff on the field behind them. Thinking it's Joost, Dinkel gets up to strap on his part of their load. He has just leaned into the horse's withers when two men attack him from behind.

W. is sitting by the edge of the forest and sees it all happen and yet not. The men are wearing thick fur hats with earflaps like the doctor's, but they are too fair-skinned to be Cossacks. Only when he hears one of the men screaming *take the other one's weapon!* in clear German does he understand that these are his people. Alarmed at hearing his own language being spoken, he doesn't know how to act: should he stay by the wayside and try to pretend he isn't there, or should he get up and try to avert it all, and he manages only to fumble indecisively with the rifle in his lap before he is dealt a violent blow to the head.

He never does register from where the blow came, only the moment after when rough hands dig inside his clothes.

Then a shout is heard. The horse shrieks. A rifle thunders.

And all falls silent.

WHEN HE COMES TO, A beard full of yellow teeth is hovering over him. It takes a while for him to understand that this is Joost, and Joost is screaming at him at the top of his lungs. At first he can't tell if Joost was one of the attackers, or if he has once more come to their rescue in the nick of time. For one sickening moment, uncertainty sets the ground beneath him asway. Then Joost grabs him by the armpits and forces him to his feet.

The blow must have knocked him unconscious. Feeling around his neck, his palm becomes coated with sticky blood. Sitting out on the road is Dinkel, head in his arms, and beside him lies the horse, shot down. The shot must have hit the animal in its loins. The horse's hinds are on the ground, as though something were weighing it down there, while it uses its head and that long neck to make fruitless attempts to rise up.

We have to finish it off.

Joost is more yelling the words than speaking them—or so it seems to W., who is still half-stunned after the crack of the rifle. Joost then points at the gun bore and ramrod in his hands while shaking his head.

We're out of ammunition.

Faceless Dinkel sits on the road as though he had just fallen from the sky and can't figure out how to get up. It falls to W. and Joost to stand for the slaughter. W. uses both arms to restrain the careening neck while Joost beats the horse's head as he did when he finished off the doctor: switching between using the rifle's butt and a heavy piece of wood. The animal's back body is rigid, only its hind legs quiver and kick, the twitching movements ever smaller. But its wide chest continues to heave like a gigantic bellows, its lips peeled back from the teeth, eyes wide with fear. W. hugs the animal's withers and neck even harder and finally tears spring from his eyes. He doesn't know if he is crying for himself or for the dying animal. When the horse's resistance eases a bit Joost drops the wooden club, takes out the bayonet, and cuts a deep slit right across its throat and the blood washes like a river across W.'s splayed legs.

Because they have no cooking vessel, they eat the horse meat raw.

It is still body temperature as they eat.

After they've eaten Joost disappears again, and again without a word as to where he plans on going, when or if he means to return. Dinkel and he sit on the grass for hours, terror-stricken, the bloody horse cadaver stiffening in the frost.

When Joost finally returns, it is with a sack of salt. Neither asks where he found it. On Joost's orders they cut the horse meat into thin strips with frozen fingers and place it in the salt. Then they make a fire.

The fire, and the sickening stench of fatty meat, entices the crows. They soar in the darkness like a vast black shield cawing overhead. After eating, they pack as much of the salted meat as they can carry, and it is in this state, without a wagon or pack horse and weighed down by their burdens, that they finally approach Vilnius.

PEOPLE ARE EVERYWHERE. WHEREVER HE turns his gaze he sees other soldiers stumbling along, in front of or beside him. They walk alone as mechanically as he, with long, lumbering, resigned steps, looking straight ahead or down into the snow, and all around landscape and sky are full of strange signs. The sky, though already midday, is jet black, as if the day had been turned inside out, while a weird shine emanates from the snow, as if lit up from within or all the light left in the world were level with the ground.

He walks with a constant tremor in his body, whether it is the shivers or a displaced subterranean mass he does not know. Is this why the trees are leaning over the road, as though they were bent by a great brace? Is this why the moon has cloaked itself in an ashen coat and the flights of birds are making such odd formations? Is this why the crows are wheeling high up in the sky? Is this why the plowshares remain on the fields, frozen into the hardened earth like massive teeth?

He thinks someone should bear witness to all this strangeness. The world's natural order is disturbed. Nothing is constant anymore.

Then it is as though something is placed upon his shoulder. Not like a burden, more like a brotherly hand or a face resting on his cheek and breathing against the nape of his neck, and then it speaks to him in a hot whisper. *Return. To your. Archetype. Human.* Says the voice. Loud and clear. These words alone. But when he turns around no one is there, no Joost, no Dinkel, only hundreds of other men, soldiers from regiments and battalions that can no longer be identified, who stagger on in stinking packs, some on crutches, or are they being drawn on carts or sledges of the kind he once pulled Lunzer on?

But where are these hot, soft breaths that brush against his neck and back like a dear and friendly hand coming from? Curious words from a poem the young doctor would read aloud come to him with such force that he can almost see his former master in front of him, pacing up and down the library, an open book hiding his face and the writing cabinet's wings spread as though the entire world were wide-open.

Ach aber unsre Seelen sind an Bücher
Geheftet und an todte Tempel. Diese
Copien des Lebendigen, mit viel
Irrthümern abgenommen; sie,
Sie ziehn wir Gottes hohem Lehrstuhl vor.

Deshalb die Strafen, die von jener Irrung
Uns unvermerkt ereilen. Zänkereien,
Unwissenheit und Schmerz. O kehrt zurück,
Zu eurem Urbild, Menschen, und zum Glück.

As he walks, and this alien breath keep panting on his cheek and neck, a little bell rings. He turns around but sees nothing but the same stumbling swarm of frozen-stiff and hungering men. Then his cheeks heat up even more and the ringing bell can be heard even more clearly, now followed by a prolonged scraping sound. When he turns back around, he sees a peculiar gray creature walking towards him with slow rocking movements. At first he thinks it must be a monster, maybe a demon of some kind, because it wasn't there before. The creature jags ahead and sideways, like a bear, and exactly like a bear its body seems covered with gray or brown skewbald fur. But the creature does not seem to have forelegs. Nor does he see a snout. Knees trembling in fright, he reaches for his rifle. But the creature doesn't stop, draws nearer with unremitting steps. Then he sees that what he has taken for a terrible beast is in fact a handcart full of clothing and equipment of all kinds—he sees uniform coats, shakos, gloves, and cavalier boots—stacked atop each other, layer upon layer, and the entirety of this great load is being pulled by a single person: a short little man whose bald pate sticks up like a lizard's cracked leather head between the two shafts in his hands. And just as ancient seems the man's face when he finally slows down, stops, and looks at W. with two small eyes that squint and peer anxiously, as though he too were blinded by the half-light.

What have You got there? W. asks.

The man attempts a smile.

W. moves closer.

Then he sees an arm hanging out of one of the coat sleeves, from under the shakos a head stiff with cold stares back at him. In fact each item of clothing still contains the body that had once worn it.

What grisly load is this? W. asks.

But the man continues smiling and peering. Then he lets go of the wagon shafts and runs off like a child, moving light and free, and the whole load topples over and on the frozen ground lies everyone he knows inside their tattered uniforms: Wiener and Krupp, and Flotchser and Schmidt and Kuhfeld and Papenhafer, even Lunzer is lying there wrapped in his thick bearskin fur. Which is impossible, because he is wearing that very fur right now. But now the fur is stabbing and pricking him as though it were lined with thousands of needles and:

HALT! W. screams.

But the man, if he was even a real human being, has disappeared, only the crisp jingling of the bell remains, as though the bell were hanging just out of reach below the sky and were moving of its own accord. And so: the awful load that lies spilled across the road as far as his eye can see. He wades through the bodies as if this were the bottom of a dry ocean bed, and finally he can do no more than to fall prostrate into the snow.

SOMEONE LEANS FORWARD AND SPEAKS to him. He can't tell if it is God or Captain Wirth or a third party. But it sounds like Captain Wirth. Has he found his way back to his company? Beneath his eyelids is a pain like that of chafing grit and the light cuts like a knife right into his cranium. He lies somewhere in the midst of what seems to be a great hall with whitewashed walls, the ceilings so high that every sound and voice in the room seems to catch, clinking and brittle, under the rafters, ready to crack and crash down on him at any moment. Next to the bed stands Captain Wirth and Köpke, the barber-surgeon. Both are smiling at him from behind their stiff beards. But how is he to know that this too is not a dream? Wirth has a chilblain as large as a hand across one cheek and both hands are bandaged. So he is yet alive. How can that be? He can sense that burning breath that grazed his neck and cheek even now; dead skin, dead hands touching his still-living ones.

HE IS IN VILNIUS. IT'S snowing. But the snowfall is so light that it most resembles motes of dust whirling in the air. He legs are so weak that the field usher has to support him, and the cabbage soup they gave him is burning in his gut and causing his head to swim with each step. They arrive at a warehouse, the gate to which is guarded by two gendarmes. But when they are granted entry, W.'s legs begin to tremble and he refuses to go. The guards shout at him but finally they give up and leave him sitting outside in a snowdrift next to a long sledge, one of the nineteen that were part of the convoy from Königsberg. From the field usher he then receives one lined winter coat, one pair of lined gauntlets, new trousers, stockings made of wool, and a padded cap with earflaps. With these items in his arms he walks through the city. It's odd to sense the hollow ring of cobblestones under his boots. Everywhere are buildings he recognizes. Though they appear in a new light. The people hurrying along the streets are also of a different kind. Unreal, ghostly: as though they only become visible the moment they squeeze past him, then disperse and dissolve into nothingness again.

Through the low, leaded windows of a tavern he thinks he recognizes Joost's stately figure. Is it possible that he too has survived? He tries to remember when he last saw him, but when he digs through his memory he fails to find anything. He remembers how they slaughtered and ate the horse, but is not sure if Joost was still on their side then or if he had already gone over to his countrymen. He decides to go in anyway. In the tavern is such a deafening noise that his senses slip for a moment. All that is keeping him upright is the press of human bodies. But they are friendly, these bodies. He hears them shout—*is that you, Wutzig . . . ?—how are you, old boy . . . ?* Someone has placed a glass of schnapps in front of him on the bar. His hand reaches for the glass, but even though he can clearly see his fingers wrapping themselves around it, the glass won't budge, he can't even feel his own hand. But he can feel the bitter burn of schnapps in his throat. It is so strong tears spring from his eyes and again his stomach tries to turn itself inside out. Again the glass is on the bar, and again he tries to wrap his fingers around it, but nothing happens. It is as though only a small part of all that is going on around him is actually happening. The rest isn't. How is that possible? *Joost . . . !* he wants to call out. *Joost . . . !* he calls out. His calls catch under the ceiling like they did in the echoing hospital room. He looks to the bar, but now there is no glass. And when he turns around to ask for the glass back, Joost is standing next to him and saying:

Wutzig! Your time has come. The executioner has arrived.

And Joost points to the stairs leading to the street where the executioner is standing. It is the same man who was dragging the carts with the uniforms containing the dead soldiers: the same bald head and plump, stocky toddler's body. The executioner carries W.'s items of equipment in a bundle under one arm and with the thumb and index finger of his other hand he is pinching Lunzer's silver ruble.

Looks like You forgot this, Wutzig.

And suddenly he is surrounded by Joost-skulls and Dinkel-chins. There have only ever been these two here. And W. screams in terror. He screams as though the scream is something inimical and alive in him that he can't manage to expel.

UP CLOSE THE EXECUTIONER DOES not look quite so grim. His head is bald and even though his eyes are set deep in their hollows his cheeks are as smooth as a child's or a priest's, the rest of his body with its chubby arms and thighs contribute to his oddly child-like impression.

But the smile he directs at W. is that of a grown man's, teeth hard and white.

A tub of hot water is carried into the chamber along with washcloths and two jugs with water for rinsing. W. undresses and the executioner helps him into the tub, hands him a mirror and shaving equipment, but though in his day he has barbered noblemen and officers alike and his hand with a blade and brush have always been praised, a fact he now takes pains to explain to this person who may yet be his executioner or his benefactor, his arms are so weak that the equipment simply slips from his hands.

So the executioner must wash and shave him. Soon the scalding water turns murky and the skin that once was numb feels as delicate and sensitive as a child's when the executioner runs the blade across it. Washing reveals the discolorations on his face, his arms and legs. He thinks of Lunzer's mutilated naked body in the white snow and the old man sitting on his log in the field awaiting the doctor who was to deliver his daughter's child.

Come, show me the way, W. had said and the blind man had shown him the way by running his fingers along the veins of his forearm, and:

God have mercy—what have I done . . . ! he says and grips the tub with both hands so violently that the filthy water sloshes over the edge and onto the floor, where the executioner waits, looming like a specter, with a towel and dry clothing.

Afterwards he is sitting at the kitchen table and eating beer posset with the executioner's family. It is the first time in many months that he is at a real table. It feels grand and a little unreal, like in church.

The executioner has five sons who all dress identically to him, in shirts and white loden trousers. They all sit up straight around the table as the wife runs back and forth to the stove with the bread and the pitcher of milk. Perhaps it is the unusual setting, or the even more unusual fact that he is apparently a guest in this house, a demanding guest moreover, dirty and maladjusted, or perhaps it's the feeling that he has to find an explanation for his wretched state, that makes him tell the executioner about his daughter, the most beautiful creature the world has ever beheld, so wondrously beautiful that her feet alone tread upon the surface of the earth while her true being was in the Kingdom of Heaven, and how she was wedded to a prince from a foreign realm, Persia he thinks it was, and though her father (W. points to himself with a trembling hand) may be an insignificant person, hardly worthy of even a glance from such a fair woman, he is and will always be his daughter's father, and this is the reason he collected gifts for her everywhere the war took him, collected them with the hope of one day laying them at her feet, his dearly beloved. It was also the thought of the happiness he would feel upon handing over these many gifts that kept him alive during these hardships that no normally constituted human should ever have to endure. But the demons had done their utmost to disadvantage him: time and time again they had risen into the sky so that her image faded before his eyes. But he knew she was up there, looking down upon and watching over him and never did he doubt this even though the demons had covered the sky with fog and thick billows of smoke and cloud.

As they speak the executioner's gaze is trained on him. His five sons are also watching him: five pairs of eyes staring at him from motionless faces.

What happened to all the gifts he collected? the executioner wants to know.

And then W. drops his gaze into his empty but clean-scrubbed hands.

I had to leave it all behind, he says.

A moment of silence reigns around the table. Then the wife starts clattering with pots and pans again over by the stove.

You are a good man, Woyzeck, the executioner says. But now You must choose to take fate into Your own hands. In time, believe me, You will see Your daughter again.

IT IS ONE OF THOSE days that January can bring, with an unexpected thaw and a mild, strong westerly wind. The riverbank is covered with grass, dead and beaten after the snow and the biting cold. The river runs high. Ice floats on the water. On the bank stands the one-horse cart that brought them here and, a short distance away, the horses that the executioner has unharnessed and are now peacefully grazing in the grass. The image of the horse grazing against a vast horizon of grass and a blustery gray winter sky makes him wonder if what is happening is really happening and not just something he once saw in a dream. Hadn't the horse been wounded by a stray shot? He has a clear memory of him and Joost slaughtering it and eating it up. Could the horse have been resurrected on this, the last of all days? And what has become of his former company? Has it also risen from the grass like a miracle and crossed the pontoon bridge that once carried them to this foreign land? He remembers the story of the Polish cavalrymen who misstepped on the bridge and fell in and how man and horse parted and each drifted in their own direction, but how the Polish cavalry officers though they were being swallowed by whirlpools praised and extolled the emperor to the last—*long live the emperor, death and honor* . . . But there is no bridge left. Only the two riverbanks, overgrown with grass. And the river itself rushing by at astonishing speed, full of ice floes and sundered tree trunks and branches. On the edge the bareheaded executioner stands watching him. W. turns around and waves. His escort waves back. Then he climbs into the ice-cold water. But after a few strokes it is no longer the water that is carrying him along, but the river's edge with the executioner and the grazing horse that are quickly drifting from view. When he has dry land beneath his feet once more, they are long gone.

IV.

The Candlemaker

Conversely, however, the bodily life, which is received into the consciousness and which cannot be experienced without it, is susceptible to attack by every human sickness (if, indeed, it is not actually being attacked) and, depending on the extent and nature of the diseased state, may indeed become diseased, since the entire man is only one life.

(Heinroth, 1818)

(Sing for me)

1. Love is a child. It walks barefoot or wears white socks. It knows nothing of thresholds or walls, and only of windows through which the beloved can enter.

2. Love has a laugh that begins in the eyes but ends in the belly. It understands nothing, only that its beloved is coming.

(The beloved's certain departure cannot love comprehend. Love cannot comprehend that anyone must depart.)

3. For love, everything happens, even what has already happened and what will happen, as if it were happening now and for the very first time. This is why, for love, there is nothing but joy.

4. Love knows all about what is happening, but it is innocent of it all.

5. Love has warm, soft hands and eyes that see stars at night and trees that can only grow if the sun is in their eyes and so do not know that they are growing.

6. Love is blind and blinds but it beguiles and is not beguiled. It casts no shadow. Nothing conceals it or keeps it hidden.

7. Love says to death: you exist but you cannot take me.

8. Love says to death: I too have a darkness. But love's darkness is the opposite of the darkness of the grave. In love's darkness all is stitched together anew, all the seams that have split, all the threads that have been torn off.

(And so you are born again, Little Heart.)

9. Love casts its own light on the world. Come, it says, I'll explain it to you. But love explains nothing. It only shows you what you already know. That lips are hot, hearts throb, and the groin is warm; that nothing is used up just because it has been done once or a thousand times. Everything can always be done again. It is not time that measures the weight and power and age of love, only the body that remembers what it has always known.

10. God is happy. He wears a hat on His head that resembles a crown.

SO, IT WAS AT THE start of this year, right around when the light changes, that he climbed ashore on the far bank of the Memel River. Who was he then? A person who no longer recognizes himself? A settlement where someone else had settled, someone he doesn't know and to whom he normally wouldn't dare show himself? But how do you go about not being seen by someone you carry inside you? He doesn't know. All he knows is that he must keep away from other people. If he meets anyone on the road, a horse-drawn carriage or a fellow lone wanderer, he skirts into the forest or turns off on a field and if this isn't possible he keeps his eyes on the ground. Each step is taken as though it were the only step, each object viewed as though only this object existed. Above all he takes care not to let his gaze drift to the sky. From early morn 'til late, the sharp end-of-winter sun weighs on his neck and shoulders and the light radiates from what is left of the snow on the fields and gleams like quicksilver in the ditches and watercourses.

The sun: this enormous red-hot globe that births and devours itself in the same breath.

Krupp had told him that the Freemasons, *the initiates*, knew how to use the rays of the sun like weapons. They lull those they wish to annihilate into arrogance. They take them by the chin like this. (Krupp had demonstrated by grabbing his chin with one hand and forcing his face skyward.) And at that moment the rays from God's flaming eye slice like a sharp knife into the eye and down to the seam at the bottom of the heart that tethers us to life. Lately he has been feeling an ache and tug at this heart-seam. Even when he is cautious and walking with his eyes to the ground it is as though his heart strains and pangs and his pulse becomes quick and restless.

But the sky burns and keeps burning, scalding.

Even at night when the sun is not in the sky, it burns.

He catches the light he needs in other vessels. He goes from farm to farm searching for mirrors. Wherever he can find them: a small swift stream on which the flashing light is as sharp as fish scales, or in a lonely barn window sunk so deep in the twilight of oblivion that the darkness seems to be welling up from *within* the buildings, from within the trees' stark ebon shadow where the cattle can sometimes be heard bellowing as though their bodies were being cloven by the long blows of an ax.

When he is sure that the farm folk are in the fields, or among clattering milk pails in the darkness of the barn, he sneaks into the houses and searches for fine objects, anything that can carry or is capable of reflecting light, like the enamel of a milk can, the glass of a hand mirror, or a few small coins he finds at the bottom of a clothing trunk and that have been rubbed so smooth they seem to glow of their own accord. He finds small mother-of-pearl buttons, sewn to a dress made of a lovely crimson brocade. He bites the buttons off their threads and rolls them up in wadding and stuffs them in his pocket. Wrapped in the red brocade fabric are also shards of glass and mirror, kept there so he won't cut himself when he takes them out to look at them.

This is how he carries the light within instead of without. It's like carrying water in a pail. Of course one never carries the water itself, only the pail, afraid that what is invisibly resting inside will spill out.

And in this guise, a lightmaker in his own right, he sets off for Stralsund one morning to once again see the child he left behind.

It is March 1813. Six years have passed since he, as a young recruit in the Dutch Army, assisted the French in an attempt to starve the Swedes out of Stralsund and almost three years since his Little Heart alighted upon the world.

Just like on that day there is a thaw. Snow tumbles from the roofs and meltwater is streaming through the pipes and gutters, pattering on and pounding the tin roofs and cobblestones. It's like music all around him, as though there had been no war and distance were only an invention or imaginary. As before, the market stalls on the square in front of the town hall stand close together beneath colorful awnings, the fringes of which flutter in the wind while the chapwomen crow like roosters, trying to drown each other out. Among all this jostling and hauling through the muddy melt, the odd Swedish soldier appears whom he takes the liberty of greeting with a gallant gesture even if they wouldn't ever recognize an old comrade-in-arms in a beggar-lout like him.

The only one who seems to recognize him is the old master of the hunt Henze, who meets his gaze for a moment before continuing to load his cages onto the waiting wagon. Henze himself has shriveled with age, and the two bitter dips in his cheeks have narrowed into deep furrows. There is no Hun in sight, no baiting beasts either; on the other hand in one of the cages that has already been loaded onto the bed stands a half-naked boy barely ten years of age, following the passing cart wheels with wandering eyes.

But the stall where Marie Thiessen used to stand, along with the old woman and the older man whose name he never learned and who'd pick them up with his cart at dusk, is nowhere to be found.

On approximately the same spot, a muscular man runs a vegetable stand. W. approaches with his usual anxious, evasive movements, finally bowing politely and asking the man if he recognizes the name "Thiessen" and describes both Marie and the elderly couple in as much detail as he can. The man has a rubicund face with large fish-like eyes that stare straight ahead, neither looking at him nor at the root vegetables that his strong callused hands are rummaging around in. Suddenly he stretches out his arm and points towards Mühlenstrasse and says:

Frau Wienberger has gone home to rest but the children are playing over there.

It is impossible to tell by that fish-like gaze if the man has understood the question or has spoken just to have something to say, still he heads in the direction man is indicating, towards Mühlenstrasse, to the peal of hammering: stubborn and resounding, like the iron strike of a church bell.

The hammering is coming from a livery stable behind one of the merchant houses. Inside the open stable door he glimpses horse rumps in narrow stalls and nearby, next to a workbench that has been dragged into the spring light, two men are holding a wagon wheel against an anvil while the blacksmith himself, a brawny man with a large black leather apron around his waist, is straightening out the axle with heavy strikes of a club.

Only when the smith takes a break and lowers his club does W. catch sight of both children. Apparently they live in the livery, or at least are playing there. It is her brother, Johann Christian, whom he catches sight of first.

So big he has grown, the boy, and looks even bigger because he has outgrown his overalls, which barely reach to his calves. He has adopted the slovenly gate of an older boy, as though to show off for the girl who runs to hide behind some tables and chairs set out in front of a basket-maker's workshop. The girl crouches in that intense way small children do when they want to remain unseen, but she can't keep herself from peeking out, only to then boldly, and with an odd laugh as strong as it is bright and gasping, flee her hiding place and dart in between her brother's legs. Her brother? Half-brother, rather. But it is clear they share a mother. The girl has her mother's slightly sunken face, like the inside of a wooden clog, even though she has the round rosy cheeks of a healthy child, a small mouth with beautifully shaped lips and tousled blond waves that whirl in the air when she jumps and takes small dance steps on the paving stones. It is his blond hair, his pale skin, his shapely but slightly weak lips. Anyone watching her play could see this. One of the Lord's miracles is standing only a few steps away from him. Trembling with excitement he crouches behind the basketmaker's cages like a criminal and dares no more than to peek out from behind the wickerwork to assure himself that the children are still playing in the alley. But soon they get distracted and run off. But the girl's loud, bright laughter lingers like a glittering veil below the alley's narrow canopy of roofs. It is an unusual laugh. It begins as a dark gurgle deep in the pit of her stomach and only bursts out once it reaches the mouth, like wet butterfly wings only unfurl after they free themselves from the pupa and then hang weightless in the air.

Towards evening he seeks out the tavern near Knipertor and even though he barely has enough money for a proper bed he liberally orders food and beer and a half-stoup of schnapps. The miracle that has occurred must be thoroughly pondered. He can't believe he has seen his daughter; it's as unbelievable as paradise being found somewhere here on earth, which otherwise only has space for walls and fences. The schnapps soon goes to his head and because he isn't used to being in rooms with regular walls he soon becomes rowdy and falls over and when help is offered he becomes loud and waxes drunkenly on about his daughter who is more beautiful than the Princess of Persia and who wears a crown adorned with a veil of rippling laughter. He demonstrates with the mirrors and the red brocade he has draped over his head and in which prances about, laying it on thick, and at first he is laughed at, then he is scolded and thrown out of the bar.

But they can't throw out the joy of having seen her again. She is a small flame that he must keep cupped in his hands so it won't be snuffed out. He holds her in this way all night long, and early the next morning he goes out again, and this time he has all his treasures with him.

HE NO LONGER GOES UNRECOGNIZED. The smith watches him from within the darkness of the livery stable, as does the basketmaker who has swept and rinsed the street clean of straw and horse manure and is now, broom wedged under his arm, tracking him suspiciously with his gaze. Piece by piece he lays out his mirror shards. It is important to position them just right. Little Heart is not meant to see the mirrors, only the light they catch. So he must also take her steps and glances into consideration. He covers his head with the crimson fabric so that the sun can offer its guiding light without dazzling him and then he tramps, up and down the street, arms flailing. To an outsider, a blacksmith or basketmaker for instance, it must have looked like he had an invisible tape measure between his ankles that he was trying to stretch to its limit. After having taken one such or a few long measuring steps he squats down to join two mirror shards or to separate some that have ended up too close together. And so consumed is he with these activities that he doesn't feel the crowd closing in on him. The majority of those flowing in are gentlefolk in their Sunday best on their way to church, several stopping to help him find what they think he has lost. But more than people are on the move. Beating hooves draw near as well, the rhythmic rattle of wagon wheels. Suddenly someone grabs hold of him from behind and chides *Watch out you fool!* and when his cloth veil is torn off, the blacksmith is there, standing wide-legged with both hands gripping the halter of a snorting horse. The coachman swears and hurls a tobacco-stained wad of spit at him before the equipage keeps moving towards the livery. Inside the carriage itself a terrified traveler leans forward, but by then he has already seen the mirror under the wagon wheel and at the same moment he catches sight of the girl.

Both are standing there, brother and sister, in the middle of the street, the boy in properly fitted pants now, shirt and vest, the girl in a beautiful blue-patterned dress with a lace collar, a white apron, and white stockings up to her knees. He rejoices at the sight of his Little Heart. At the same time disappointment and torment weighs on him. Dressed up as she is, she wouldn't dare search for the mirrors, if she dares move at all under that tightly knotted bonnet. He wants to wave at her, or make himself known somehow, but the girl has already walked into the street, turned around, hopped forward twice with two feet, her arms crossed over the bib of her apron, as if about to play hopscotch, while calling out to her brother who seems stuck in his shoes and is making angry, impatient grimaces to get her to stop playing.

Little Heart, W. whimpers invitingly, but his girl's eyes are already fixed on the street. She has spotted one of the mirrors. He quickly takes out another mirror, catches the sun in it and directs this light at the shard in the street so that the reflection flies into the girl's face. And the laugh that bursts out (as she cups her hands over her eyes)—the laugh that comes from the pit of her stomach and flies from her body like a shriek—makes time itself stop. And for a moment everything is still, the light and the girl in the street and the dazzle in her eyes that she is now slowly lifting off between her hands as though it were a fragile and precious thing.

Then everything is shattered by a sharp call from across the street— *Sophie!*

No more than five arm's-lengths away stands Marie Thiessen with an infant on her arm and wearing an expression as if he were the one she were calling, not her daughter, who immediately runs and hides behind her mother's legs. Behind her, half a head taller, stands a broad-shouldered older man that he immediately recognizes as one of the men helping to hold the wagon wheel on the anvil while the smith hammered the crooked axel into place, clearly uncomfortable in his Sunday clothes which look like they have been draped over him.

W. averts his eyes and tries to move on. This causes Marie to take yet another determined step forward. She has her weight on one leg, which is pushed forward to balance the weight of the child who now is hanging from her arm more than resting against her chest.

You're not supposed to be here, Wutzig, you'd do well to be on your way.

He searches the cobbles for the shards he has laid out, but all he sees are more feet and legs.

This isn't your child, Wutzig. There's nothing for you here.

She says this in the same harsh, accusatory tone that she used to say this is your child, Wutzig, you must provide for it.

But you said it was mine, he says now.

His words, however, are only a feeble glint in one of the mirror shards. All they reflect is an image of his own powerlessness. Marie Thiessen stands firm, legs wide, inside these words that in no way resemble the young woman he once knew.

Whatever I said, I said because I needed someone to protect me, but you were never more than a weakling who couldn't be counted on, who stole and drank and landed in prison.

I wanted your hand in marriage, he says.

Who'd be so stupid as to marry a soldier? she says. That bony mouth is a barb of scorn. Her head leans away from her body as though to create distance between him and her curt gibes.

But I thought you wanted to marry me, he says.

I only said it so you'd see that I was decent. Now I've met a proper man, Wienberger is his name, here he is, by my side. This is his child in my arms, and he has been so good as to take on the other two as well, and he will finish you off if I so much as say the word . . .

She points to the alley where Wienberger is standing. It takes a while before everything becomes clear: so the man in his Sunday clothes who was helping out in the livery is the father of her children.

But can't I see her again anyway, he says.

No, now shoo!

And then all at once, everyone comes towards him: as though the houses, alleys and gateways that had been holding them captive decided to let them spring free without warning. Even the smith appears, his chest covered in a silk-lined vest and plucking a thick watch from its pocket, which he gives a hasty glance before booming: You have one minute to disappear, you rascal!

Then the first rocks come flying, from where he does not know, he only hears someone shout: *Get him!*

The first is followed by many more: a rain of stones. He wraps his arms around his head and runs away cowering.

Halfway out of the city he hears hoofbeats behind him, as though this nightmare had no end. Again he is under the crimson cover as the unfamiliar team nears and tries desperately to tear the cloth from his head, but there is no cloth. He is in this world now and his head and eyes are exposed and vulnerable to everything.

It's just Henze driving past in his wagon.

In the cage at the back, facing away from the animal-baiting theater's side-scene walls, sits the lean half-naked boy from before, hands around the bars and eyes fixed on the road dust that the wagon wheels are whipping into a whirl.

ON HIS WAY OUT OF the town, he passes a large open field at twilight. At the edge of the field the sun is on its way down and the light is so strong that the shadow from his body doesn't stretch and deepen as it should at this time of day but shrinks and pales beneath him. He continues along the road next to his quickly shrinking shadow until it dawns on him that it is not time that has stopped, but the sun that is stuck in the sky. Instead of continuing to sink it is suspended, swelling in the sky like a piece of apple stuck in the throat. And as the sun grows larger, the light around him intensifies. It is as though he were being suffocated by all the light and waking from this suffocation is not possible because you cannot get out of what you carry inside you.

And because the light has pushed everything else in the world away, time no longer exists.

And because time no longer exists there is no day and no night.

And neither is there sleep nor waking.

Nothing exists.

He stretches out on the roadside and screams right out but his scream is like the light. It is everywhere, and so it can't be heard.

V.

"Beast"

A soul is a force which is nearest to another soul. If an impure soul can corrupt a pure soul, it follows that a healthy soul, the force of which lies in God, can also make a sick soul healthy.

(Heinroth, 1823)

Now stop screaming, Woyzeck, or else I'll strap a muzzle on You . . . !

Herr Conrad's wooden face appears in the cell door, lit up by the flickering light from the lantern he's holding at shoulder height. The prison doctor was here not long ago, he says to the person accompanying him into the cell. The delinquent lacks nothing, I'll have you know, reverend. It is but the fear of what lies ahead.

W. sits on the edge of his bunk, his arms wrapped around his chest. In spite of the raw cold in the cell the skin on his hands and face is slick with sweat and his entire body shaking, and he is still shaking even as the prison chaplain puts an arm around his shoulders and sits down next to him.

Only a few months have passed since they last met, but when Pastor Oldrich takes off his hat and kneels next to the bunk, a white streak can clearly be seen running through his once coal-black hair. Pastor Oldrich takes the silver ruble from his vest pocket and places it on the edge of the table where a handful of writing papers are already spread out. In the light of the candle that Conrad placed on the table, the cell's walls twitch and seem to be contracting.

Woyzeck. My confessor, Pastor Hänsel, has been kind enough to ensure that I have access to paper and writing tools here in the cell and now calls upon me to write in order to take my leave and ask for forgiveness for the pain I have caused everyone so that my steps will be lighter on the day that I ascend the scaffold.

But I do not know what to write, reverend.

The only person to whom I can imagine writing is the woman for whose sake I am here, but I am so assailed by evil thoughts that I lose the thread entirely.

Pastor Oldrich. What kind of thoughts beset you, Woyzeck?

Woyzeck. I dreamed that the husband of the woman I killed was waiting for me in the afterlife.

Pastor Oldrich. Who?

Woyzeck. It was in the dream almost as it was in life. My foster father and guardian Master Knobloch had tasked me with dressing the dead in wigs. But now it wasn't an individual morgue I was being asked to enter but a large battlefield where riven and ravaged limbs lay strewn everywhere. All I found of the surgeon Woost was a hand. I knew it had been lying there the whole time, waiting for me to arrive in the dream and catch sight of it. And indeed: as I stood there the hand froze, became black and hard, not like decay but like it was being consumed by fire, and as I looked on, it turned into a crucifix, a black crucifix, black as though scorched through.

Pastor Oldrich. But dear child . . .

Woyzeck. I dare not trust anyone or anything anymore. Wherever I go it is as though things are changing. It's the war. It twists the mind of even the most sensible men.

Pastor Oldrich. There is nothing to fear. Not of the living or the dead for that matter. God always protects us.

Woyzeck. Did you know I once partook in the killing of someone like You? A man of God.

Pastor Oldrich. You killed a clergyman?

Woyzeck. The captain poked out his eyes. And cut out his tongue. So he could no longer see or speak. And this happened in the middle of his own church. Tell me, reverend, where was God's hand of protection then?

Pastor Oldrich. To doubt is human, Woyzeck. Especially as one feels death drawing near, as you do.

Woyzeck. It is not death that I fear. It's that I can no longer tell the faces of the living from the dead.

Pastor Oldrich. What do you see, Woyzeck?

Woyzeck. Answer me this instead, reverend. Is it one of the Lord's miracles or the Devil's false light and glamor that allows me to see a blackening crucifix in the hand of the surgeon Woost? And as I return from the war and all has been robbed of me, who then is sitting on my shoulder invisible to me but breathing on my neck and cheek? Let me tell You, reverend, the only times God has appeared to me, in truth and might, it is as false light and delusion.

Pastor Oldrich. God does not disguise himself. The true God always reveals himself in the guise of truth. The world is full of signs. Our task is but to interpret them correctly.

Woyzeck. But the signs that come to me are not sent by God. They are the work of demons. It is these demons who make me unable to tell the difference between what is holy and what is mere idolatry.

Pastor Oldrich stares ahead unblinking.

Woyzeck's hand lies open in his lap.

The cell is throbbing.

Pastor Oldrich. Faith alone can clearly distinguish between what is holy and what is mere idolatry. Be advised, Woyzeck, words are not to be toyed with. Once you have uttered the word "demon," the window through which *the Beast* can climb through is open. That much is certain.

Woyzeck. I swear I felt someone breathing against my neck and shoulders.

Pastor Oldrich. It was God's protective spirit blowing on your cheek, like he blows on the dome of the sky each afternoon.

Woyzeck. What do You know of demons?

Pastor Oldrich. I have encountered many wrongdoers in my life, and many of them have thought that I too was in the hands of evil forces. One thought I was Death itself and spat right in my eye.

Woyzeck. And how did You punish this man?

Pastor Oldrich. I shall confess something to you, Woyzeck. I don't believe in God's punishment. I only believe in man's salvation.

Woyzeck. And what does God do?

Pastor Oldrich. He leaves it to us to save ourselves. He has given us that power.

Woyzeck. And how is one whose hands and feet are bound to manage that?

Pastor Oldrich. He has even given us the power to break our chains.

Woyzeck. I am a murderer. I have committed the gravest of all imaginable misdeeds.

Pastor Oldrich. That may be, but before God it doesn't matter.

Woyzeck. I don't understand.

Pastor Oldrich. Because everyone, even the worst criminal, knows that a higher right to punish does not exist. All that exists is the power to do so.

Woyzeck. So punishment is not incumbent on God?

Pastor Oldrich. I won't keep the truth from you, Woyzeck. All you can hope for is reprieve. Sooner or later the trial will demand what belongs to it, you will never get away. And if you ask why this is so, why you are being punished, I can answer you at once. A man is punished because the king must always appear to be stronger than the crime committed. It is the sole condition and privilege of worldly power. That it must without fail appear stronger than all else, even God.

Woyzeck. But God knows that I deserve my punishment.

Pastor Oldrich. God needs not punish, Woyzeck. He is already all-powerful.

Woyzeck. Reverend, are You trying to lead me astray?

Pastor Oldrich. I am not leading you astray. Like you, I have also sat in a cell.

Woyzeck. For which crime, may I ask?

Pastor Oldrich. In my youth I thought that if man in God's image was given power over his own life, instead of ceaselessly having it taken away from him, then misdeeds such as the one you committed need never take place. Neither would any justice be required other than that which has been ordained by God.

Woyzeck. But how are we to know what is just according to the law and what is just according to God?

Pastor Oldrich. Signs are given, Woyzeck, without end signs are given that salvation is nigh. Perhaps the spirit that touched your cheek and neck was one such sign. It is in this way that God chooses to reveal himself to us.

Woyzeck. Once I saw the entire map of the world drawn on a blind man's arm. It was horrifying.

Pastor Oldrich. God does not intend for us to acquire such wisdom. Do the letters know anything of the book in which they are written?

Do we poor people know anything about the world we have been flung into except that there is a form and a will that binds us?

Woyzeck. And what will would that be?

Pastor Oldrich. God's love.

Woyzeck. And what is God's love?

Pastor Oldrich. God's love, Woyzeck, is the dream that keeps us forever awake. We only need open our eyes. Then we will know.

Pastor Oldrich bends down and picks up the Bible from the table in the cell.

Pastor Oldrich. Reason exists. And the law exists. But so does love. In the great book it is not only written how justice is administered, but also how God reveals himself in people and how the world is made through all that is revealed. Perhaps instead of writing and asking for penance and forgiveness, you should have a read of that book, Woyzeck.

Again Woyzeck brings both his hands to his face.

The darkness in the cell.

Inside the darkness: the cell like a great beating heart.

THE HATCH IN THE CELL door now opens at all times of day and Conrad peers in. His face seems to be heated up from below by light of the lantern he is holding up to the opening, but behind this light his eyes are cold and clear with hatred.

It is as if he cannot stand that W. no longer fears him, no longer recoils from his crude jokes about the imminent light at the end of the tunnel, no longer beseeches his benevolence. He just lies on his bunk, slack and lifeless, or sits motionless at the table in the same position hour after hour without so much as touching the Bible and the prayer book that the good Pastor Hänsel brought with him, nor pen and paper, unless it is to fold the pages into figures.

So what they say is true, he is an ignoramus, illiterate.

Conrad can't seem to help himself anymore. For two years he has faithfully kept watch over this murderer. He believes he is owed something.

Soon You will stand before Your maker, Woyzeck.

Our Lord passed his final hours in prayer, but what do You do, sitting here and slumbering like some sort of beast?

W. hears Conrad kick the chamber pot, rattle his keys, and slam the door's bolts shut with a crash. But he perceives Conrad's rage like he perceives everything else that goes on around him. Anew it is as though he has fallen into the embrace of a great sleep. Or is it the greater wakefulness of which Pastor Oldrich spoke, the one that can only arise deep within dreams.

Here the cell itself seems to transform:

Cracks open in the stone walls, long grooves inside which cold moisture flashes. Along the rims of these crevices grows moss: it begins as a brittle line along the groove of water, then ever wider and more abundant. He puts his fingers to the wall, feels the damp finding its way past the round of his nails down between his knuckles and coming to rest wet around his wrist. When he brings his fingers to his lips the water tastes fresh and pure, like nothing he has ever tasted before. But there is also something behind the salinity, a sourness he can't get enough of. He licks and sucks his fingers, his arms, presses his face to the wall, which is now carpeted in green. Everywhere sprouts shoot up from the web of moss: like small callouses. It soothes and lulls but also chokes, stifles and chokes, and deep inside the choking he hears Doctor Stöhrer speaking sternly to him.

No, You can't leave us now, Woyzeck; not now that we are so close

—and someone roughly shakes his shoulder—

Wake up, Woyzeck, wake up

And when he opens his eyes he doesn't find himself in a dream. Instead, it is as if all of reality has moved in with him: in the cell. They crowd around the bunk where he lies, as if they had been standing by his bed the whole time. It is Hänsel—the lawyer—and Hänsel, his confessor, Prison Commandant Richter; even pale Pastor Oldrich can be glimpsed by the door. When he finishes mopping the fever sweat from his brow, Doctor Stöhrer straightens up.

Would You be so good as to stand, Woyzeck?

After he tries and fails, the doctor takes a firm grip under his arms and lifts him from the bed by his own strength. Mr. Hänsel stands at the front with a sheet of paper in one hand and an ambiguous smile.

Someone seems to be rewarding You for Your penitence, Woyzeck, he says. The king in his most gracious benevolence, lets it be known that a stay of execution of the death sentence has been granted, pending a new examination of your state of mind. To our great pleasure, Herr Hofrat, Professor Clarus, has also agreed to hear You for a second time.

And then he reads aloud from whatever royal letter of clemency he has in his hand. And all bow their head and listen, since it is for this sake that they have gathered in this lushly blooming cell. W. alone is not listening. Standing at the edge of those surrounding him, the only one not bowing his head, the prison guard Conrad is looking right at him.

WOYZECK. Doctor—everything's going dark on me again.

Teeters, almost falling onto the steps.

DOCTOR. Cheer up, Woyzeck! Just a few more days and it'll all be over.

He prods at glands and points of the thorax.

The effect is palpable, gentlemen, palpable.

—Just wiggle your ears for the young gentlemen while we're at it, Woyzeck.

I meant to show you this before. He uses the two muscles quite independently.—Go on then.

WOYZECK (*embarrassed*). Oh, Doctor!

DOCTOR. Do I have to wiggle them for you, you brute?!

Georg Büchner: *Woyzeck*

AND SO EVERYTHING MUST BEGIN again. Again he must be examined by a doctor. His eyesight and hearing are to be checked. He is also to be auscultated, as if something had grown inside him that wasn't there before, when in truth it is the opposite. He has grown thin, arms and legs gone scrawny, jowls sagging, and he is losing teeth. But it is the same interrogation room as before into which he is led, with the same filing cabinet next to the wall, the same high desk with a chair that looks like a judge's seat with its narrow armrests and a high back; the same writing set and ink pot, the same bell from which a metal cord runs along the cornice through a hole in the wall to an identical bell on the other side where the police guard is sitting in a sentry box, waiting for it to ring or not to ring at all.

And it is the same Clarus:

He sits in his tall, slender chair as if he hadn't moved an inch since they last sat in this room. Short, chin in his cravat, and his eyes, if possible, even more watery. Even that turtle smile, the small gray teeth inside his pursed, wrinkled mouth, is the same.

Clarus. Woyzeck. It would be a lie to say that this gives me pleasure. Not for one moment do I think this renewed investigation will produce a different result for the detainee than the one already established. Regarding the visions, as emerged *ex post facto* during the inquest, too much weight should not be assigned them. As my esteemed colleague Professor Heinroth has exemplarily demonstrated more than once, it is not unusual for a delinquent to stage illnesses and morbidities from which he claims to suffer in order to elude a verdict and just punishment.

Is the detainee in agreement?

Woyzeck. Excuse me, Herr Hofrat . . . ?

Clarus. The question was clearly put. Are you a malingerer, Woyzeck?

Woyzeck. Excuse me, but I don't understand what Herr Hofrat means.

Clarus. You are resisting a fair examination of Your case, because You believe that if only You were burdened by illness You would escape Your punishment.

Woyzeck. I can assure Herr Hofrat that I have only told the truth as it is and have not in any way tried to conceal anything.

Clarus. Good. For what is concealed will always come to light sooner or later. Reason enlightened by the spirit is such that it frees itself from soulless matter like light from the gloom that hides it. By now we have understood that You are a soulless person, for only a soulless person could behave in the beastly way that You have. Nevertheless it is of the utmost importance to clarify whether or not You acted as a result of fleeting mental excitement or committed Your deed with the coldheartedness characteristic only of a creature bereft of all Christian moral.

Woyzeck. I beg to call Herr Hofrat's attention to the fact that I have always done my duty.

Clarus. And what is your duty?

Woyzeck. I have always done what my commanders have commanded and I am an honorable and upright person.

Clarus. But duty is not a question of the sort of man one is, but rather of where one belongs.

Woyzeck. I do beg your pardon, Herr Hofrat, but I simply do not understand.

Clarus. In the animal kingdom, Woyzeck. You are an animal. A soulless beast. An animal can be stubborn for the moment, a mule who refuses to bear his burden. But in the end it still performs the actions it has been trained to perform. Countless are the stories of draft animals faithfully carrying their load until they collapse. But inside the animal also rages! It tugs and strains at its drafts not understanding that the harness is there to restrain it, and on some occasion it may occur that a spark of daylight penetrates this soulless darkness and the animal realizes that by mounting resistance he can cause his coachman and master to relent. But since there is no morality that can chastise such behavior, the animal only has ruin in mind. It wants to make its master grovel before it, so that rather than pulling its yoke it can follow the path of sloth and a general lack of restraint.

If You are a malingerer, Woyzeck, it is only because the sympathy others have shown You has led You to believe that the very laws we all must follow do not apply to a vulgar character such as Yourself.

W. cannot understand why the otherwise pedantic Clarus has become so agitated. Is it, as Mr. Hänsel suggested, only because he has been forced to go through the trouble of examining him again, or because another professor would have otherwise disputed his rank? Whatever the case, he finds it best not to say a word. Clarus takes a long look at him, then rings the bell. The guard, pale as candle wax, appears in the doorway.

Clarus. Guard, would You be so kind as to ask the archivist to bring in the delinquent's files?

W. is still on his feet when the guard returns. Even Clarus stands. The high arms of the chair are barely the height of his shoulders. Something, W.'s apparent indifference or perhaps Herr Hofrat's lesser size, causes the guard to hesitate. And so they stand there, all three, the guard with the file folder outstretched, Clarus with his eyes fixed on W.

Clarus. So we intend to pick up the investigation from where we left off. I would like to ask the detainee to once more account for what happened on the night when he, for the last time, met Frau Johanna Woost, then murdered her.

BUT HOW IS HE TO explain what he himself is unable to understand? How did he intend to use the broken-off saber blade, why did he
beg for eight groschen in alms so he could afford for the woodturner to
repair the sword by giving it a hilt? What crime was he thereby atoning
for or committing again? It must have been something, why else would
he have been so keen to hide the sword-turned-dagger—even from
himself? So much so that he only thought about the fact that he was
carrying it when he finally caught sight of her shuffling across Rossplatz
and was standing before her, naked and empty-handed as ever, while her
hands were otherwise engaged, her mouth and lips and hands otherwise
engaged, otherwise straddling and grinding into other men's bodies,
grunting and dangling her heavy breasts over them, whereas she had
only flashed him an icy glare with that squinting wolf-eye *Go on, take
a long good look, Woyzeck, that's all he's good for* and how can he explain
the mix of arousal and loathing he feels when she says this, explain that
the more liquor-reeking bile she spews over him, the more she screams
at him to *totter on off,* the more eager he feels, an ever-clearer certainty
is throbbing inside him, there must already be someone in her room,
someone up there waiting for her, if not one from the City Guard with
whom she strolls then some other soldier, that this is the reason why
she is so eager to get rid of him. And how can he explain that it is the
shame and despair but also the excitement at the thought of this *other*
that makes him want to grab the hilt of the saber sword right then, even
though of course he knows that there can't be anyone up at her place
now, that there isn't anyone here but she and he, and there will never be
anyone other than she and he, and then stick the saber blade into her

belly. He can feel the sword going in all the way to the hilt and the hot blood spilling across the back of his hand and forearm and he pulls it out and sticks it in, pulls it out and sticks it in, he doesn't know how many times he sticks it in until finally she gives up and turns towards him, first pressing both her hands, then her head against his chest, as though she wanted to nestle into his arms, only to then, when the blood gushes from her wide-open mouth, collapse and lie there on the worn, dirt- and mud-soiled stone floor while he, bloody dagger visible to all, not only those who, horrified at the sound of her death cries, have paused outside on the street, but also those who come running from the neighboring buildings, taking a few uncertain steps out into the faint yellow remains of the evening light only to then, body bent forward and taking long, somehow drawn-out steps, seek his way down to Rossplatz, not quickly, not slowly, but with the bounding strides used in the military, so as to, upon passing the pond in the middle of the square, throw the bloodied saber blade away, then pause, stop mid-step, and allow himself to be arrested by the gendarmes that have been chasing him the whole way and who now are locking both his arms behind his back as he, according to several of the many witnesses, can be heard saying over and over again *God willing she is dead, God willing, God willing.*

Woyzeck. It wasn't me.

    Clarus. What is the detainee saying?

    Woyzeck. I can assure Herr Hofrat that I am innocent.

    Clarus. You are innocent?

    Woyzeck. It was never my intent to kill her. It was an accident. An unfortunate coincidence.

    Clarus. The detainee presently asked to introduce to the record that soon before the deed he heard a voice "saying stab 'er stab 'er." Is the detainee now admitting to have lied on this point?

    Woyzeck. It wasn't me.

    Clarus. So the detainee was acting on behalf of another?

    Woyzeck. [his face in his hands] How could I kill the one I love?

    Clarus. [ringing the bell, to the guard who appears in the door] Would the guard be so kind as to escort the detainee to his cell. *[to the clerk]* The interrogation will continue tomorrow when the detainee has composed himself.

LEIPZIG: ONE EARLY AFTERNOON IN December, in the air a distinct note of wood smoke mixing with fresh horse manure. Above the wide fortress wall and the towers of both the St. Nicholas and Thomas churches the sky is a sulfurous yellow, the black clouds full of snow that has yet to fall. Sandgasse, where Johanna Woost secured room and board, is a narrow unremarkable alley, lined with dilapidated wooden houses and small workshops that look like they wobbled out into the alley and simply stopped, baffled that they have not yet collapsed. True to his habit he has already prowled around the neighborhood several times, trying to gain an overview, to see what kind of people are coming and going. After a while he stops a boy who has just slunk out of the next-door gateway and asks if there is a Frau Woost staying at this address. The boy gives an earnest nod, as though a pastor were asking. In that case, could the boy run in and ask if she would be so kind as to come down? The boy nods, more out of fear it seems than an actual willingness to be obliging. Therefore, he is so bold as to follow the boy through the gateway. The landlady, Frau Wognitz, is waiting in the darkness of the stairwell, she must have already seen him palavering with the boy: a small woman with barely any hair left on her crown, so upset that she has to cling to the handrail with both hands to keep herself from falling over. *Didn't I say no gadding about in the house?* she screeches as soon as W. enters. *What is the man's business here? Get rid of him!* The boy takes careful hold of his hand, as though to direct his attention away from the landlady's screeching. I know where Frau Woost is, he says.

They walk together past the old fortress wall, then up the Brühl, silence reigning as it does when it is about to snow, as though the city and the sky were enclosed in a sphere of clear glass, where each object seems magnified and every sound echoes. Persistent hammering can be heard from afar, the blatter of a post chaise going by, clanging hoofs and creaking tack. He watches the boy running a few steps ahead, his cap at a jaunty angle, and he thinks of the time he and his sister Lotte took this path: it must have been a winter afternoon like this when their mother was still working at the laundry, and how the sky was high and clear and clean-swept, as it is now, and how it suddenly started snowing and they both tipped their heads back to catch the flakes on their faces, and how the buildings around them looked so high and mighty when seen from this angle, as though the buildings were trees growing downward, basements in the snow-filled sky and roofs at street-level, everything topsy-turvy, so that when they righted their heads it was as though the snow were whirling upwards.

Dearest sister, he wonders, where are you now?

JOHANNA IS SITTING ON A stool beside the bar, thighs spread wide, hands open in her lap, palms turned up as though she were cupping two invisible bowls. Presumably she has fallen asleep in the heat of the stove for her big body has slumped, as it were, from the shoulders down whereas her head is tipped back against the wall, and in this slumber the firelight flickers across her bared face so she seems to have no eyes, or are her eyes but two empty eggshells turned up to the smoky ceiling.

She might not have seen him, but others do. (He does not know them yet, but he will soon.)

In a far corner of the room, around a large round table permanently reserved for them, sit brazier Warneck's two assistants, Kloos and Binder, one large of build, the other slight and thin as a string; as well as the carter Potsch, who drives for the wool-wholesaler Campe, and Bon, the butcher's son who is forever rolling a fistful of coins from one hand to the other. At the table is also the apothecary Johann Thellmann, an odd bird in this company with his aristocratic profile and small round glasses, always faintly smiling as though he were in possession of some secret morsel of bitter knowledge to which no one else could lay claim. The same Thellmann will later become one of the police's lead witnesses because he was on Rossplatz the night a woman's dreadful scream pierced the sleepy evening calm and shortly thereafter watched as the crowd, compressing as though of its own accord, ejected a man holding a bloody dagger.

But all he is holding now is the letter she once sent to him, folded and thumbed so many times that neither name nor address can be discerned any longer. (But then again he has also had it with him for months and years, carried it wherever his company had been commanded, taken it out some evenings to read, or asked someone else to read it aloud for him, just as he imagines someone else must have written the letter on her behalf—he has a hard time imagining many of these words coming out of her mouth, and the excessively scrolling handwriting could hardly belong to her either—and he wonders who she was picturing when she imagined the addressee of these lines. The spindly young apprentice, ever afraid of a thrashing, who spied on her from the landing above Master Knobloch's shaving parlor as she doused her hair in the tub? It could hardly have been this crooked and curbed thirty-eight-year-old standing before her now, with hands that are at times run through with such violent tremors he can barely manage to bring cup or cutlery to his mouth, much less run lead across paper.)

He stammers something, takes a step into the room, and then Johanna opens her eyes and fixes him with a gaze that is unsympathetic but surprisingly alert. Then she gets up from the stool so abruptly it crashes to the floor, and stands for a moment with her back to him as she sweeps her hand up to better the tangled long gray hair sloppily fastened at the nape of her neck. When she finally turns around, her face is a single wide smile. *Johann?* she asks too loudly, as though she were still trying to convince herself. He wants to be convincing, too, and so awkwardly holds out the letter to her. But she has already taken both his hands in hers. *Johann! Is it really you?* she asks and casts an anxious look into the room where the other guests are in a rush to pretend to be in conversation.

She takes a fast grip of the hand that is holding the letter and leads him aside. They walk through a small passage behind the inn's kitchen, up the creaking wooden stairs to a room directly under the roof ridge. A bed stands in one corner on which is piled a mass of stray garments and a chamber pot and two empty wooden plates.

He is still holding out the letter as though it is all that can confirm he is the person she believes him to be.

But *Johann, is it really you . . . ?* she asks for the second time, and what started as a smile grows far too large, a grimace of pain, and of a sudden a whimper escapes her and tears streak her face.

He imagines that she has remembered the other letter, the one that he in youthful arrogance wrote to her now-dead husband, and again he self-consciously thumbs the letter she wrote to him, tries to hand it over again, but thinks better of it and wants to get rid of it but can't find anywhere to put it and ends up standing there fumbling as he mutters:

My sincere condolences for loss of your husband, Herr Woost, I truly am sorry.

Oh, Johann, it's not that, she says and wraps her arms around him. I'm just so happy to see you again!

IT IS SHE, YET IT is not. Her thoughts have become slower and her body heavier, so heavy that when she makes her way up the stairs to Frau Steinbrück's rented room one might have the impression that this body does not in fact belong to her and is but an undue burden that she is forced to bear day in and day out. But at times she can set it aside and forget it, as when she sat on the stool at Jordan's bar and her body was simply there, parted and open wide, as though living a life entirely its own, beyond intent and thought. Or as when she is laughing and her entire face becomes one big mouth, her rough tongue in the middle.

He can't explain it, but somehow she frightens him.

It is as though the second Johanna forgets herself she becomes something far greater, able to consume or crush him out of pure thoughtlessness.

There is also her way of looking at him when she *is* awake. After all, he remembers them from before: those angled wolf-like eyes and their anxiously roving gaze. Their calculating yet evasive quality. As though she does not want or dare to truly look at him. Instead, as soon as she sets eyes on him, that great maw splits into a broad smile or a laugh. It is hardly because he presents a spirited sight, more like she's trying to spirit herself away. As though she wants for something inside her to go unnoticed and so plants her smile in the way so that none need see it or even suspect it's there.

It is the same with what she has to say to him. Words build up like a wall around her. She wants him to talk. Of his fates, she says, when he was a soldier in the war. Tell me everything, she says, but in fact she does not want to know. Usually he can't speak because words fail him.

But now it is because nothing can penetrate this wall of laughter and words that she erects between them.

Instead *she* does the talking. She tells him about Woost. I never loved him, she says in an almost mirthful tone. When I married him, I was only fifteen. All he wanted was some pretty thing to show off. When we were in the company of other menfolk he said how splendid and beautiful I was, but when we were alone he was so limp and pathetic between the legs all there was to do was laugh.

(—But that's not true, he wants to object.

He remembers Woost's rage when Master Knobloch let his stepdaughter into the shaving parlor where men lathered in shaving foam sat in a smiling row, and how Woost screamed and swore and beat her afterwards. He was of small build, Woost was, but he only needed to set foot in a room to make others cower. He remembers the sound that slipped out of the bedchamber when they spent the night: the lusty whimpers of love, and all that strained, burst, and yearned to overflow in him as well, lying there below, listening but unable to imagine the half of it.)

And now she is saying that after Woost's death she was not considered good enough to marry. A passing diversion, for that she was suited for most, but hardly was she a suitable match. After all he only left debts behind, that Woost.

Not that he should imagine a dearth of suitors, she says just as suddenly, in a different tone, almost threatening. Then she begins listing them one by one: names of merchants and tradesmen in the city that she knows he cannot match to a face and therefore can toss around haphazardly. And so she fibs him a palace full of lies, where each sentence she utters is contradicted by the next, where inside becomes outside, warp becomes weft. And altogether it's actually incredibly strange. Had he not tumbled down the stairs in his youth, because he had fallen for her, as rumor had it, she would have not so much as cast a glance his way.

(Perhaps, he will later think, the terrible distances are what create this apparent affinity between them. The expanses of forest and hard-frozen wilds he has covered in marches that took days and weeks and during which he eventually lost all concept of time and thought.

And perhaps it is the same for her. Years have passed, but they contain so little.

Perhaps this is why she is so verbose but has so little to say. Perhaps this is why the palace of lies they are building between them resembles most a temptation. What do I say to you if there is nothing to say? With what will I hold you tight if I don't even have hold of myself?)

Still inside of those palace walls something like intimacy emerges with time. With all of these names of rich and well-to-do widowers that she claims have asked for her hand, with all these hardships he has endured and all the badges of honor he claims to have received, they are furnishing small rooms inside the large palace: not gorgeous showrooms but small apartments of lies, illuminated not by a steady outward shine, which they would not have been able to weather in any case, but only by the gloss they were willing to grant the humble stories they fabricate for each other for the time being, and she says that he's a true adventurer, isn't he, that Woyzeck, and what couldn't they get up to together, she and he?

So then it happens—the inevitable—the conversation turns to money.

It starts with her saying from within her large smile that she doesn't know what Frau Steinbrück will ask for his lodging, at first she will pay for the room, of course, she has a small sum put away, but in the long run the two of them will have to figure something out and might he be able to advise her? And he leans idly back in his apartment of lies in the palace they built together and tells her about the rich Jewish pawnbroker of Dessau to whom he was once in service, he tells her that he wrote the man a letter when his regiment disbanded and was at a loss about where to find work and that Herr Schwalbe replied that he was no longer in need of his services for he had fallen ill. And now Johanna moves closer in the apartment of lies. She wants to know what illness the Jew may have been referring to and then she says write to him again, Johann, write that you're coming back to him, write that you're doing it out of compassion, then he cannot deny you, and stay as long as it takes, then you can lay claim to part of the inheritance afterwards.

And now her anxious, angled eyes shine and her tongue is thick and heavy in her mouth which is open in laughter. Even her body is laughing: for the first time as if it truly were a living part of her. And she says he must promise to write to this Jew at once, not let valuable time go to waste, so we don't squander the opportunity.

Yes, she does in fact say "we." The two of us. She and he.

So perhaps we can afford to figure something out together after all.

Then she says that he may touch her now. She knows he has always wanted to. He's a man now, Woyzeck. Is he not?

SO HE SETS OFF FOR the Jew in Dessau. To find out about the darkness, as he would come to say afterwards. He had just installed himself at Frau Steinbrück's, comfortably besides, in a room with a bed of his own stuffed with straw. Nonetheless he goes. Because Johanna wants him to. He even tries out saying because *his* Johanna wants him to, and it's funny how small he becomes when the two of them are mentioned in the same breath, small and insignificant, a small stick she can use to point in any direction she wants to go.

Schwalbe the Jew does not seem the least bit surprised to see him even though half a lifetime has passed since he was in his service and it was made clear that his services are no longer needed.

I have come out of compassion, W. then says, and Schwalbe says that since he has already traveled so far he might as well stay, as if he, not W., were the one performing the compassionate deed.

It is difficult to say what is ailing Schwalbe. He was thin when W. was first in his service, he is even thinner now, and if he was reluctant to move anywhere then, now he sits stock-still on a few pillows he has placed in the sleeping alcove he has furnished for himself in one of the rooms facing the street. With a voice as fine as a spider's silk he says that his back has become a painful column and if he shifts his position in the least, the pain will knock him to the ground.

W. brings him hot water and a washcloth, but Schwalbe only draws his blanket tighter around him with his talon-like hands. Behind the skin's folds and bruises, his carotid artery stands out like a fine seam. It quickens at times, as if to say these heartbeats may be numbered but the body still lives on. With the cloth W. carefully washes his forehead which curves as sharply as a helmet's brim over his malar bone until the Jew asks him to help fasten the phylacteries and then he performs his prayers with barely perceptible nods of the head, his gaze turned to the far corner of the room.

The prayer ritual is repeated at least five times a day. It is how the hours of the day are measured. But even between prayers Schwalbe sits with his gaze fixed on the darkest, farthest corner of the room. When W. asks to where he is staring Schwalbe replies that he is waiting to see the Lord again. But there's nothing to see, W. says. Schwalbe then replies with his thin voice that in the Hebrew language spoken by all Israelites there are two words for darkness. The one is *khoshekh*, which means darkness as during the night when nothing is visible and the other *araphel*, which is the denser darkness from which God appears. It was out of one such darkness that God appeared to his people and afterwards Moses said to the people: *Fear not: for God is come to prove you, and that his fear may be before your faces, that ye sin not.*

In which way has Master Schwalbe sinned? W. asks.

To this the Jew offers no reply, he only continues to stare into the empty corner of the room where this other darkness resides.

While he was healthy yet, Schwalbe had sat in this way. Straight as a candlewick, legs folded under his body, he sat behind the drapery that split the antechamber from the rest of the pawnshop, keeping an eye on the mirror in anticipation of the next customer, and then the next. There was no end to the waiting. Schwalbe didn't move, neither did the curtain, and of the great rooms beyond the curtain no one knew a thing. W. wishes sometimes that he could also be this patient, to at once keep an eye on the world and be removed from it, in this way surely many a thing would have remained undone, but he is far too restless and impatient by disposition.

While Schwalbe waits for the Lord to finally appear to him W. prowls the back rooms of the house. The Jew's house may look bent and anxious from the street, with only a simple stone façade facing the sloping cobblestone alley, but the rooms that face the garden seem innumerable. All of them are connected by passageways or half-flights of stairs that open onto each other like small boxes and not all of them have a real door with a handle and fittings; in front of most rooms only dusty draperies hang. In turn one or several of Schwalbe's employees always sit guard outside, mostly older men who in an eerie way resemble Schwalbe himself, the same bony limbs and damp eyeglasses. None of them greet him with any measure of enthusiasm, but this does not stop him from pushing aside the heavy draperies and going where he likes.

The rooms are filled with a lifetime of accumulated junk, all that has been tendered to keep the creditors at bay but never redeemed: credenzas, tableware, lead-darkened mirrors with flaking gold leaf, putti, bedsteads with cracked plaster ornamentation, books piled seemingly at random on crooked shelves, wall- and grandfather clocks of which several are still running, as though they were measuring a time entirely different to that which prevails in the rooms facing the street, or in the measurable world at large, a piece of stalled time, not the time that passes and disappears but the time that has been left behind, the *remnants* of time. In fact it does not surprise him in the least when in one of the inner rooms he comes across the young doctor's writing cabinet, the crack in place, as plain as it was on the day it took shape as they were leaving Waldenburg and the cabinet fell to the ground because it had been so sloppily secured. The crack still reveals what was never meant to be visible in the interior of the cabinet: the small numbered drawers with their enamel work and the wing doors' interiors with the black- and red-painted ink landscape with the slant-eyed men with their queues and the women embedded in thick swaths of fabric. And farther in, by the compartment where he kept the picture of his mother and himself as a child, hangs the young doctor himself, like the pendulum of a clock in arrest mid-motion, legs up, head down, eyes that have taken on the shape of a quail's egg and the color of their skewbald shell.

After ten days Schwalbe's carotid artery stops pounding and he is sitting motionless, his eyes still fixed on his empty corner where even now nothing has appeared, at least not as far as W. can ascertain. Where once they had been alone in the room facing the street, now people are whirling around the old pawnbroker. They stream in from every room, from inside the house and from out on the street. They have torn slits in his clothing, which proves that they are sons of his, every one. An impossibility, of course: one single man, who distinguished himself in life by not moving so much as an arm's length from the place where a simple cloth curtain separates the visible world from the invisible, can't possibly have sired this many sons. In that case where are all the mothers?

W. receives no answer to that question. Cloths are hung over the windows and all the mirrors are covered and he must resign himself to being driven into the kitchen while the corpse is being washed and turned to face the wall and the sons sit down to sing the Kaddish for their father.

After many long hours one of them enters the kitchen and informs W. that his services are no longer needed as of now. When W. inquires after payment, the little man who now looks exactly like his father (yes, even the voice is the same) says that he can go ahead and take what he's come to take. No one will stop him. But W. doesn't know what he is meant to take, or he hesitates for too long: the son has already left him and rejoined the other mourners in the room, which is now but a darkness.

IF JOANNA IS DISPLEASED BECAUSE he has returned from Dessau without so much as a *kreutzer* in his pocket she doesn't show it or at least she hides it well. Perhaps there is a stiffness to the smile she gives him and perhaps she lets her heavy body linger a little too long in front of the steps and thresholds, as though to exhale and draw new breath before she throws herself into what she has now made up her mind to do, her gaze always to the side, expectant, mistrustful.

Nevertheless she continues seeing to and supporting him with maternal solicitude.

When Frau Steinbrück demands more in payment for the musty unheated room she has rented to him, Johanna convinces Widow Knobloch to let him live in one of the two rooms her mother rents from brazier Warneck: the same little room with a stove and a sleeping nook where she brought him when he sought her out at the inn and where she would often withdraw when resting on the stool next to the bar was not enough.

It's the least we can do, she says when her mother objects, Johann was like a child in the house when he served as Father's apprentice boy.

And so Frau Knobloch moves out her clothing trunks and he moves his knapsack in and his shabby soldier's boots, which are now the only thing he owns. The room resembles a dusty attic cubby, but with an iron stove in the corner. It sits at a sharp angle facing the stairs, and even the smallest sound penetrates its rickety door: the running of maids on the stairs, the clanking of pots and pans from the inn's kitchen below, and the hoarse voices at the bar which, the longer the night wears on, rise up like a chorus of shrieks and loud lusty roars.

There is a window, a single one, facing the brass foundry in the courtyard. In the courtyard grows an elm of such immense girth it seems to be bursting from the small crooked toolsheds around its trunk and stretching the tips of its branches high above the roofs of the surrounding buildings. When the sun rises above the tiled roofs as spring draws near, the tree branches draw mighty shadow monsters on the building across the courtyard.

Despite the heat from the stove, it is still so cold that he has to seal the drafty window casings with burlap. Still the window fogs over each morning with the damp that sits in the walls and each morning he must wipe away the fog to bring the tree into being again. He does it with relish, branch by branch, until the whole tree appears in the slanting sunlight, as if reborn in the dawn's gray haze.

In order to apply for work with brazier Warneck he makes, on Johanna's urging, several sketches of fittings for wardrobes and doors, items that Johanna knows are in demand. But Warneck has no patience for *curlicues* as he puts it when W. turns up at the foundry to present his sketches. Rudolph Warneck is like the tree in the courtyard. Everything about him is strong and solid, from the thick forehead and the canine droop of his cheeks to his chest and those wide legs which he has stuffed into a pair of high-shanked boots. He assesses the new arrival from top to toe as though he were inspecting an animal: is it capable of work or is it only fit for the slaughter? He doesn't even look at the sketches. *And this they call a soldier!* he says, gruffly clears his throat, then spits on the gravel. Beside him stand his two helpers, Kloos and Binder, and they follow suit: they clear their throats then spit on the gravel. Kloos, the larger of the two, barely reaches to Warneck's shoulders and Binder isn't much bigger than W. himself. But Binder is the one who wants to be the toughest when it comes to throat-clearing and spitting out words. *That one couldn't reach a teat even if you lifted him up to it,* he says and flashes a tobacco-stained grin and so Warneck rewards him with an appreciative thwack to the neck with his giant hand, whereupon the three of them turn and go back inside the foundry.

But Johanna wastes no time. On the very same day she speaks with one of the foremen at wholesaler Heinrich Wilhelm Campe's wool magazine near Hallesches Tor, who promises to give him temporary work as soon as some is available. Employment is of course out of the question, not for that kind of labor. He must get himself added to the foreman's list each morning and then wait for his name to be called if there is an opening.

The wool magazine is a giant three-story building. From early morning to long past the afternoon bell, young men and old (no distinction is made) are busy sorting the seemingly endless mountain of wool that is unloaded each morning down on the courtyard. The wool is then hauled up by winch and crane to the various floors where it is then cleaned and sorted according to sort and grade, the latter is ceaselessly called out by the foremen—*prima, secunda, tertia, quarta!*—there is a persistent stamping and shouting while the wool is bailed and bundled and packed in sacks that are carried down to the loading bay at the back of the building where the sacks again are sorted and weighed on a giant scale. Their weight is noted by an accountant and a controller who sit behind a large table out in the open, then the sacks are loaded onto large wagons to be shipped into the wide world, to Egypt or China.

On the days his name is called, like the other day laborers he either works in sorting or in packing where the already-sorted wool is stuffed into sacks. Wherever he is sent it is hard and tiring work. He soon gets splinters in his hands from the rough wool and the lint bruming in the air makes his throat swell, his eyes sting and tear up until it's almost impossible to breathe and the whole world is one great haze, punctured only by the lacinate, itinerant shadows of the other day laborers as they bend and haul and of the foremen walking around urging them on with disembodied voices that fly through the air like the long licks of a whip.

Buckets of water are by the entrance to every room, and now and then a lukewarm pocket flask makes the rounds. He receives it each time and fortifies himself with one or two big gulps and by the afternoon his head is as heavy as lead. All strength has been leached from his arms and legs and he sits on the floor leaning his back against the wall in the streaks of light filtering through the high, grimy windows, until the foreman's long shadow unfurls before him like a flail and flogs and flogs him until finally he drags himself to his feet, pours a scoop of water over his head and goes back to the packing area where the mountain of sorted wool grows higher and higher with each passing hour.

Finally the foreman blows the whistle, he lines up to receive his daily wages and staggers down Nikolaigasse all the way to the Golden Goose. Inside the courtyard stands Warneck, his leather apron as tight as eel skin around his waist.

You swine! is all he has to say, without a note of gravity, and without moving so much as a finger, only the bitter, gray glare of his eyes below his thick eyebrows: the eyeballs of a giant on which his pitiful self can be seen crawling like an insect in the far too great, almost searingly clear light. From one side of the fenced-in courtyard to the other he crawls, until he finally reaches the entrance of the inn's kitchen, escaping Herr Warneck's gaze, and shuffles up the two narrow, creaking wooden stairs into the little loft under the roof ridge where he vomits in the piss pot then tumbles into bed.

JOHANNA COMES TO HIM. THROUGH the crack in the door he hears the wooden step creak, her heavy, ragged breaths; and her smell, which he'd be able to recognize from several blocks away: slightly sour up close, but with the rounder roughness of wadding or wet flax yarn. Now even the scrumptious smell of frying wafts through the crack in the door. She has brought food for him even though she knows that innkeeper Jordan, who is strict with his portions, forbids it.

I do know he, Johann, doesn't have it easy.

Her heavy triangular face in the door with those wry looks she endlessly tosses out, as though she feared Herr Warneck would show up at any moment or someone would call for her down at the inn.

But no one calls at this time of day, it is after dinner time; the few guests that have already made their way to the inn are sitting on their own with many tables between them.

You eat as if you've never seen food before, she says after sitting down next to him on the bed. Don't soldiers get anything to eat?

One gets used to going without for a long time, he says and keeps shoveling the food down.

And how does one get used to it, going without?

He doesn't know.

Is it the same with womenfolk? she says. Does one get used to going without them, too? Or are there plenty to hand along the way?

Whenever she comes to him she is restless, a chastened anxiety about her, but now she does in fact want him to talk. Not about Russia or the war, but about what actually happened when he was as a wigmaker's apprentice boy and fell in love with a stranger's wife. Ever since he was once incautious enough to speak of this, it's all she wants to hear about. What was it that a lusty but timorous young man actually saw through the crack in the stairs one morning when foamy hot bathwater was being procured in Master Knobloch's kitchen? And is her hair still as beautiful? she wants to know and unfastens the barrettes that secure it atop her head and lets it fall across her collar and back. Does he think anyone today sees her as he did when she was still young? For wasn't this what he wrote to her husband? (Unfortunately, this too he has confessed to her.) But you never wrote to me, she says now, and does he hear genuine reproach in her tone or is she only poking fun at him? You must have been to many unfamiliar places. Did nowhere make you long for home?

How is he to respond? War leaves one mute and indifferent. Everything simply glides past. Nothing can touch one or stick. For what sticks will sooner or later draw misfortune along with it. Look at Lunzer. He wanted to get his mitts on everything. Women and furs and silver rubles, and it weighed him down until he could no longer manage to stand up, instead he lay there with one leg lopped off, naked as a piglet in the snow. He looks up and sees her sitting there amidst her loosened hair and maybe she sees it on him, or maybe she's just losing her patience. She starts fidgeting, shaking her shoulders and arms as though lice had crawled under her clothes, and says that she has been here far, far too long and they are waiting for her down at the inn.

She can't attend to him alone, now, can she? she says.

He says that she must stay with him. For a little while at least, he says, softening it with a smile. Or maybe he can visit her on Sandgasse later, at Frau Wognitz's?

But then that otherwise so very wet mouth closes and becomes dry and stern. No, he must never show his face there. Frau Wognitz will not tolerate menfolk running around the house, she says and gathers her hair and ties it up with angry tugs.

But then she smiles and says that if he wants she can come back, later, at night after Herr Jordan has closed up.

And so she takes the plate, the beer tankard, the cutlery, and leaves.

And since she said she would come back, he waits. Waits until the noise from the inn has waned, the clatter of plates and gushing water from the kitchen has stopped, waits until the farmhand has taken the slops to the pigs, Warneck has closed the gate to the courtyard and Jordan and his wife have finally gone to bed (he hears their footsteps in the rooms beyond the stove wall). For a moment he wonders if she will come at all, or should he dare to light a candle to signal that he is still awake. Then he hears a door open and close downstairs, and footsteps on the stairs. But of another sort now: not as heavy in its reverberation, her breath hoarse as she struggles to hold it back. The door to his room opening and slowly being shut, the sudden heft of her when she is standing close to him and undressing and then the smell of her hair and the skin of her neck and shoulders when she heaves her body on top of his. The bed creaks under their bodies' double weight and she whispers panting against the side of his face that they have to be quiet now so they won't wake her mother, who is sleeping in the next room, be careful Johann, she says and reaches one arm behind her to grab hold of his member.

And in the beginning they are, careful.

She leans forward with her head pressed between jutting shoulders like an animal, but soon she starts driving her groin backwards harder and small short laughter-like sounds escape her pinched lips.

It is as if a great laugh is hanging above her, and she is trying to reach it with her full body, but the laughter keeps eluding her, rising higher, and then she too must stretch higher in order to reach up to it, and finally her whole body careens with each cast and the wooden frame of the bed beneath them, yes the entire attic room, rattles and bends with this laughter, and when he tries to put his hand over her mouth she guides the whole thing into her mouth as though she means to swallow it. And then that glowing heat pressing up in him can't be resisted anymore. Nor the laughter, nothing in the world can be resisted. She wraps both her thighs around his and sticks her hand between his cheeks to press the stiffness even deeper inside her and now the laughter is a screech and the whole bed is rocking and shaking and sliding across the floor, and then there are people in the stairwell who can be heard shouting something that sounds like for God's sake shut up you're waking up the whole house; but she doesn't hear them, she's inside the laughter, her whole body is quaking with this laughter; and so she falls forward over him with her full weight, enfolding him in arms and breasts and legs and trunk, and only when he says that he can't breathe does she roll her body laboriously to the side and lie panting beside him in that damp smell of their sexes spread and the sting of armpit sweat.

After a while she reaches her hand down and takes hold of his shrinking, now almost delicate, limb and holds it between her thumb and index finger:

Imagine, Woyzeck, she says, a little soldier.

AS SPRING APPROACHES HE FINDS work with a book-binder called Wehner in Volkmarsdorf, work to which he is better suited because of his frail constitution. But the days are long. He has to get up at the crack of dawn, so early that when he wipes the fog from the window, the tree in the courtyard cannot yet be seen.

On the road he meets farmers on their way to the markets in town. Slumbering, they sit up on their coach boxes as the horses trudge along in the darkness out of old habit, sometimes a softly shimmering lantern hangs from the frame of the seat or the wagon's front axel so that the light slung through the wheels' spokes during the journey creates a strange, revolving shadow monster on the gravel road where he stands.

Even though he has spent an entire soldier's life on foot he now notices a pressure in his chest and what happened on the drill ground outside of Stralsund happens again—a sensation like a succession of sharp pinpricks in his heart, and like then he gets the feeling that a Will, some Higher Power, doesn't want him to follow this path and that the casting light and pricks to his heart are meant to force him away from there.

It takes him several hours under duress to make his way to Volksmarsdorf in the mornings, and often as long in the afternoons, even if the road is easier to follow in the daylight, and when he finally returns to that little room under the roof ridge he hardly has any feeling left in his arms and he feels the fever rising inside his body like the ice-cold water rose under them in the marshland east of Vilnius.

His only comfort in those moments are the books he carries home from Wehner's workshop, books that need binding or a bit of glue on the spine.

For as long as he can remember he has had this wondrous, almost rever-ential relationship to books. The reverence comes from all the knowledge that is collected in them, of course, but mostly he likes the feel of their soft or hard bindings, their soft silk moiré or blind stamped covers, gently leafing through the stiff pages, breathing in the sharp scent of printer's ink or just the old wood mold that rises from them. In good moments, the handling of books yields the same satisfying self-forgetting that oth-erwise only physical labor can yield, though rarely: a sense that the hands know what needs to be done, so the thoughts are left to wander freely.

Perhaps, he points out one day to a skeptical Clarus, there are other ways of reading than with the eye. Perhaps one does not need to interpret the words perfectly to know what it says in a book.

He has a particular book in mind: an outwardly unremarkable tome, printed in a slightly larger octavo format and bound in simple leather covers. The inside cover shows an image of a holy man of much advanced age, almost bald-headed but with a thick beard. He is wearing some sort of cloak or cowl on his body and in one hand is holding a bell and in the other a long staff with a cross at one end, shaped like the letter T.

The holy man's name is Antonius and the book recounts how he was born into a rich family but that his parents died when he was young and left him alone with a younger sister whom he loves above all else on earth. But because Antonius is tired of the world's wealth and idleness, he gives his full inheritance away to charity, leaves his sister in a convent to be raised by the nuns, then sets off for the desert. For twenty years he wanders the desert by foot and days pass without food, and when he does eat it is only bread and salt and water that he is given by good farmers and shepherds who clearly see the privations he is prepared to endure to seek the truth about himself and God.

Of course, a human being relinquishing what every other person aspires to in this way, and of his own free will, is not something the Devil can stand. So he besieges Antonius with visions and mirages, in his sleep but also in broad daylight. Women offer themselves up to him, gold is heaped in immense goblets, and when Antonius digs himself a grave to escape temptation, the earth itself turns against him, transforming into scorpions and snakes that coil around him and pursue him and do not balk at biting and squeezing into his body. The Evil One's harassment is such that when the disciples that have now begun to follow him finally roll away the rock he has crawled under to protect himself from the Devil's seed, at first they take him for dead.

But he is not dead.

In fact by descending to the realm of the dead he has finally managed to beat back his evil persecutors and when he emerges from the grave, Jesus appears to him as shining rays of light in the sky.

Now one could say, as Clarus does, that to see all that is evoked by the words in a book one must be literate. Looking at the pictures alone is not enough.

W. does not deny that he has always had a hard time deciphering written words in the order they follow each other on a book's page. Words become objects to him, often impossible to grasp with something like reason. But it was different with this book, Herr Hofrat understands. Several times he caught himself reading without moving his eyes. It was as though the words made themselves out the moment his gaze fell upon them. Or as if the book itself were a darkness. Sometimes when he glanced into this darkness there was nothing there but what the words usually stand for. Other times it was as if something were glinting behind them, not our Lord and Savior, as Antonius claimed to have seen behind the overturned stone, but a no-longer-young man in a threadbare uniform, rags wrapped around his hands and straw in his boots, struggling through a patch of dark wasteland. Again and again the carriages came rolling towards him, but it was not from them that the glow of light came, or from the wagon wheels casting their shadows on the gravel road, but from demons rising and sinking in the sky one by one.

When he realized this, he understood everything. What the book was describing, if but in a veiled form, was his own life.

True, the book was about a highborn man, that could not be denied, the highest of the high, but it was also about a soldier, the lowest and least of all. Many such connections united them both. The desert that the holy Antonius walked out into was like the War, the landscape devastated by inhumanity and greed, the harlots Antonius turned his back on. But the desert was also a place in which one could not linger without being beset by demons, for the Devil (this was written plain and clear in the book) could abide much of mankind without lifting a finger but what he could not abide was someone of their own free will choosing the path of virtue and truth, and when he understood this he also understood that what pained him so, what screamed inside him at night and stuck needles in his heart, was not an inner mania that he refused to acknowledge, but the demons who did not wish to set him free.

And as though to reinforce the veracity of this, again and again he relived events that had already happened, but as seen through the book's darkness, so to speak:

Once when he had just stopped reading, he couldn't even remember having set the book aside, he found himself back on the drill ground outside of Stralsund where he had first glimpsed the signs of light in the sky. Only now the ground is black, as though covered in ash and full of magnetic energy, and he is bidden to take a step, and then another step, and with each step he is weighed deeper to the earth, and beside him it is not the sergeant issuing orders who is laughing at him but the Devil himself, the same hollow-eyed goat-like head with a long chin like the Devil in the book as he whips his hosts onward.

And in another dream, which immediately follows this one, at least in the aftermath he can't account for any time having passed between the two dreams even though he is well aware that many days may have passed, several weeks even, between these two instances, he has buried himself in the earth to protect himself against the Devil's every guise and illusion and has had a stone rolled over him just like Antonius asked his disciples to do, and inside this darkness which belongs to the grave and the earth, voices can suddenly be heard speaking to him:

Oh, come on out, says one of them

—your time has come—

The voices sound very close, as though someone were lying alongside him, lips pressed to his ear, and right then it is as though a sharp object rasps his heart, right at the root where the muscle sits from which all the power in his body emanates but that also, if it is touched in a certain way, can paralyze his entire being, and for the first time he realizes that it isn't just the Freemasons and the staff sergeants and their lot but life itself, all that breathes and throbs inside him that must be overwon, and it is by summoning his full strength that he succeeds in rolling the stone out of the way, rising and staggering into the light, then making his way down the bending stairs to the inn where Frau Jordan is still drying glasses and tankards, whereupon he rushes out into the courtyard where Herr Warneck has just closed the gate and secured the crossbar. There he sits until Frau Warneck pays a visit to the privy and finds him curled up between the fence and the gatepost.

The brazier Rudolph Warneck and his wife were, upon the renewed interrogation of the detainee, to again corroborate these details. Frau Warneck also related to Clarus that W. had made a confused impression, flailing his arms in the air, and had in general behaved as though he were being pursued. He had been brought into the inn, and after being given sugared hot wine to drink, he sat a while in the corner by the stove and slowly regained his senses and then quietly and calmly spoke with his host and hostess, as he usually did, without showing any sign of a darkened mind.

AS FOR JOHANNA: PERHAPS SHE notices that something is not quite right with him. But if she does notice, then she doesn't have the patience to care.

He is too weak, that Woyzeck, is all she says. He allows himself to be too easily assailed.

Go on, pluck up some courage, Woyzeck—

Perhaps she is simply losing interest now that he spends his days in Volkmarsdorf. Her attention has always been of a more fleeting kind.

When he wants to get her up to the room, she who is hardly one to show restraint says that it isn't possible anymore. It's too noisy. Her mother who lives wall-to-wall has frail nerves, and Herr Warneck doesn't want any running on the stairs after the inn has closed. And if he dares make his way down, she turns her back to him and pretends to have her hands full. That wry smile is there as ever. But the smile is so large that it hardly fits on her face anymore, and something comes over her roving gaze, something impatient and cold, predatory.

Oddly enough it is when she most clearly demonstrates her disinterest in him that he desires her the most. When he sees her wagging between the tables with her emphatically sluggish gait something rises in him that he hadn't known was there. Like that time when through the crack in the stairwell he saw her bending over the washtub in the kitchen, hair tangled and wet across her shiny spine, the same searing stretch inside his pants now as then, this even though deep down he knows what those swaggerers who try to get her on their laps sometimes say out loud: that she is *ugly*, she is, that Johanna, with an ass as wide as a royal chaise.

But their words arouse him, their thick hands on her hips and thighs, their faces rubbing her chest with pretend intoxication each time she bends over the table with plates or tankards.

In their blotchy faces and fumbling hands he sees himself.

If it hadn't been for that large smile of hers, which isn't a smile so much as an opening in half of her face, as though something were missing there.

But he follows her too, as everyone else does, imitating her waddling gait, legs wide and ample rumped. As though he, as small in stature as he is, were also an instrument of the tavern's endless rut. And to a cacophony of laughter, he sneaks up on her from behind when she turns to the bar, grabs her by the waist with both hands and starts thrusting.

Only to recoil in fright when she slaps him sharply in the face.

What does the man think he's doing?

Does he think he owns me?

DAYS, SOMETIMES WEEKS, MAY PASS without her wanting to have anything to do with him. Then she'll be at his door again. And when she's with him it's like she can't get enough. Nothing can satisfy her hunger. She grabs hold of everything within reach, his hands, his knees, takes his sex in her mouth as if it were something to eat, turns him around and forces in the now slaggy, wet cock between her wide buttocks. He feels drained, turned inside out, a nothing, a scrap, something left behind, used up again. But she doesn't care, simply claws hold of his hands from behind and pulls him on like a backpack and then kneels on all fours on the bed with him on her back. And if he doesn't manage to stay inside her she collapses into an impotent heap, as though something had been stolen from her, something she had just been holding in her hands that suddenly isn't there anymore, and like a child she bursts into uncontrollable and helpless tears.

IT ALSO HAPPENS THAT SHE disappears and is gone for several days without anyone being able to say where she went.

Then he can often be found at the inn, sitting in a corner, despondent and alone, with a mug of beer or nothing in front of him.

Each night at brazier Warneck's table, where Warneck himself never sits (he says he can't sit down because he has too much to stand for), sit both of his assistants, Kloos and Binder, the tall one and the short one, who unlike their master seem to have all the time in the world. At the table is also the apothecary Thellman and the carter Potsch and sometimes the carter's cousin, a young slim man by the name of Filemon, who travels with him and takes care of the horses. The obvious center of the group however is constituted by the butcher's son Bon, his name pronounced in the French manner (*Bong*) because his mother is a Frenchwoman, from Alsace. According to one story his mother, after an unusually exhausting birth, is said to have propped herself up on one elbow and inquired after the sex of the baby. The midwife is said to have responded a boy, whereupon the mother leaned back with a sigh and said *C'est bon*. And so it was.

Even though he is already over twenty years old, Bon behaves like a fat overgrown boy. He spends his days in a cage his father had built to the right of the butcher shop entrance. Inside the cage his sensitive French mother has placed a small canapé, the smooth red velvet of which the boy wears down with the wide seat of his pants while abusing customers or counting money. The prison-like alcove in which he sits in fact also serves as a cashier's booth. The butcher or his wife gives him a handful of coins before they lock him in each morning and if no one is paying or requesting receipts he busies himself with the coins, rolling them between his palms until one or some slip through the grating and fall to the floor, where the father, gruff and silent of speech as ever, lets go of the piece of meat he is chopping to get down on all fours and look for the money between the floorboards while the big fatty presses his body with surprising litheness against the bars of the cage and screams in that loud piercing voice known to all in the neighborhood, far too coarse for such a young man:

Give me the money . . . ! Give me the money . . . !

He also yells like this at the customers, who have no choice but to stick in what they have been asked to pay for their sausages and trotters between the bars, and then receive their change from Bon's hand.

Bon always has loose coins on him. He rolls them slowly from palm to palm or stands them on edge and lets them roll around on the table, all the while staring over at W., his gaze equal parts arrogant horror and ill-natured curiosity.

That one over there hasn't made much of himself, he says at length.

(And amidst the laughter that always breaks out around the table when Bon is present comes a chuckle, embarrassed but inclined towards merriment.)

He came skulking home with his tail between his legs, that one did.

Or wherever that man keeps his tail.

If he has one at all . . . !

The group laughs, their faces turned away or hands covering their mouths. The apothecary stares down at the table. Though he too has cracked a smile.

Hush up, Bon, someone says, perhaps the driver Potsch who is brooding by nature and so is the only one around the table who stands for any form of measure.

But then something comes to life in W., who has been sitting there unmoving for hours. As the coins scatter and spin in every direction W. yanks Bon's chair out from under him and shoves him backwards into the room:

That's what he gets for puffing himself up and throwing his weight around!

The words are spoken in a voice that no one (not even he) recognizes. Booming, deep, somehow rugged. Then he raises the chair above his head and brings it down with such force that Bon falls to the floor and the chair breaks in two. He lifts up one half of the chair and goes after Bon again, who is flat on his back and trying to defend himself with his arms and legs.

As he beats Bon, W. sees Joost in front of him. As if the piece of chair were a doll made of wood and that doll were Joost: a fully realized figure with a long, slim, expressionless face and half-shut eyes. And the rage that precedes each blow (it is instantly clear to him) is Joost's *soul*, the one he had never before managed to catch sight of. Now Joost's soul has moved into him. As the blows hit Bon's back and shoulders, the Joost-doll emits a high-pitched whine that is only interrupted when Warneck, presumably called over by one of his two assistants, grabs W. from behind, pulls the beating arm upwards, and drags him away until W. slams into the floor by his own force, as it were.

Then it is as if the doll loses all its power, and now it is W.'s turn to cower in a corner, shielding his head with his arms. There he stays until Frau Jordan approaches with cautious, expectant steps only to put her arm around his shoulder.

Come now, Johann, she says, and as she helps him up to his room W.'s ceaseless whimpering can be heard:

That wasn't me, that wasn't me . . .

The next day Jordan will take Rudolph Warneck aside and set him straight: he can't have a lodger in the building who won't leave you in peace at night and drinks and makes trouble with the guests. Though it is unclear to which guests Jordan is referring. He could not have meant the shop assistant Bon, in any case, who recovers surprisingly quickly and doesn't seem to have been cowed at all by W.'s attack. While the others from the regular's table get down on their knees to rake up the coins he has dropped, Bon himself stands, legs wide, in the middle of the room smiling at the huddled W., as you do when you know you occupy the absolute center of the world and can never, no matter how many blows you're dealt, be removed from it.

SINCE HE HAS NO MONEY with which to pay, he goes without lodging for days until the innkeeper Jordan finally manages to convince his good old friend the newspaper seller Johann Haase to have mercy and give W. a roof over his head, temporarily at least. At Haase's, he is also given the attic room. By now summer has set in and under the roof ridge it is burning hot. Nighttime is no exception: there is neither a window nor the slightest opening through which the bad air can drift out.

During this time W. behaves as though he wants to atone for all the ways he has inconvenienced Jordan and Warneck and Widow Knobloch. Bare-chested because of the heat with only a candle beside him, he hunches over the cardboard work the bookbinder in Volkmarsdorf passed on to him so that he can at the very least earn a small income.

Unlike Rudolph Warneck, Johann Haase is gentle and conciliatory by nature. When he later is questioned by Councillor Clarus he will confirm that W. was a fundamentally peaceful soul, kindly in disposition towards all and sundry, even though he was given to drink and at times could make a confused impression. Yet even Haase understands that something is not right with his new lodger, who hoards masses of old newspapers and other inflammables. This worries him. As does the speed at which Woyzeck uses up candles. Day after day his guest finds new excuses to go down to the housekeeper and ask for more. Finally Haase loses his patience and explains that the cost of candles is greater than what his wretched cardboard work brings in and for this reason he cannot give him any more.

So W. goes about his business in the dark.

It is all the same to him. He knows the operation and has all the thumb and finger lengths in his head and can with a single notch, using his nail or the back of his hand, draw a line and then make a perfectly straight cut with a knife.

Long this way he lives, in a timeless space where all that exists is the heat surrounding him in the darkness and the rain that, when it pours in short showers, sounds like a pack of deranged animals trying to claw their way in through the roof.

Hardly does it ease the heat.

He imagines it is possible to clear the top of the darkness and cause a tree to emerge, like the tree in Warneck's courtyard emerged in winter from the film of window ice. This shadow tree reaches its boughs to the farthest corners of the attic room and sometimes he thinks he perceives a human figure behind the swaying branches. He even hears footsteps creaking on the floorboards. The figure, whether made of light or like Schwalbe's God is only another concentration of darkness within what is already dark, is accompanied by a gentle roaring and in this roaring someone is speaking with the same muffled, toneless rasping voice that came out of his own mouth when he attacked Bon in Jordan's inn, the voice of the Joost doll:

Come on then . . .

your time has come . . .

Right then the blind Russian peasant's daughter emerges from behind the branches: she who Dinkel killed. He only perceives her dimly because the shadow-tree's branches are now swaying violently back and forth, as though whipped by a mighty wind. She is barefoot and dressed in a smooth white garment, her hair loose and dark and in her hands she is carrying the remains of the excised fetus, as though they were a gift for him. Blood gushes from her nose and mouth, but her eyes are looking at him, large and pleading, and they don't stop their looking. And the roar intensifies and can't be distinguished from the tree, its branches whipping and beating the attic room's walls and roof as if the attic room has become a birthing cave, aching with all that is still inside it and bearing down and that wants out now, at any cost, out.

When he later tells Clarus about these events he describes it as pressure in one ear while hearing a roaring within. He also explains that someone had spoken to him in a very clear voice and that it sounded as if the voice said:

Come on then . . .

your time has come . . .

Of the gutted woman he says nothing.

Still he can't stop agonizing over her having appeared to him once more, and having spoken these words. Why would she do this if she were not an emissary, sent by a higher power to inform him that it is time for him to descend into the place in hell where evildoers like him belong, those whom God has cast off, and this is why she is carrying her unborn child in her hands. It's a sign.

But he does not dare heed the call. Where is he meant to go? Instead he sits unmoving in bed, body sweaty and eyes shut, as though this would be enough to dispel the visions and to dampen the roaring in his ears. When nothing happens, the roaring only grows even louder, he runs from his bed and down to Herr and Frau Haase's chamber, where it is either night or broad daylight: in retrospect he won't remember. But Haase remembers, how he sat with W.'s wet body in his arms, rocking him like a newborn, saying Johann, Johann, Johann, what plagues you so, getting only faint sobs and tears in response.

When questioned by Clarus, Haase had explained in his friendly, considered way that it had been as hot as an oven in the attic room that summer, which surely explained why W. broke a sweat and was having bad dreams. Moreover, as in every attic, it was full of mice gnawing at the floorboards and the straw mattress so anyone might believe there were ghosts flying about.

But the court councillor is not satisfied with this explanation.

Clarus. Was it the word of God to which he was listening or was he hearing demons?

(In the language of the voices the difference Clarus imagines is perhaps not as great. As with the difference between light and dark, which isn't as significant as is always asserted by judges and prelates.

Perhaps one should say, as Schwalbe the Jew did, darknesses are mani-
fold and the soul is not blind in each and every one. In fact day and
night, light and dark are but layers, across which the hours of the day
streak like pale shadows. Behind all that we know and what we think
we hear and see is an activity hidden to us and sometimes, but then it
is often the work of chance or incident, something of all the unheard
pushes through to us.

As signs.

We just don't see them.)

The more W. ruminates the surer he becomes that he is not suffering
from some temptation. On the whole it feels less as though someone or
something moved into him and more like he was moved, in relation to
that which is visible and perceptible in the world. Sometimes he feels
that God is very close by. There are moments when a great calm comes
over him, like that night on the road to Vilnius. He surely would have
dropped had not someone breathed upon his cheek and neck right then.
Sometimes he is transported far away, and then a sort of crack in time or
space appears through which other powers can emerge, like the woman
bearing her unborn child like a gift. Had not also the mighty roaring,
the tree's branches swaying back and forth, been signs of a rift arising
between this world and the other? It had been through this rift that the
great wind had blown.

Darkly he understands that on Earth there are those who are in
league with the other world and who know to interpret these signs: the
Freemasons, or certain officers, like that sergeant on the drill ground in
Stralsund. But neither do they have the power to direct and guide all
that happens there. Demons and the angels have their own heaven, they
rise and fall in their own order, it can never be decided under which sign
one will find oneself in a given moment. It is as though he is stuck in a
gigantic gearworks that moves him according to laws all its own, which
no human can predict, or even know.

All one can know is that one will constantly be transported.

He knows something else now, too. What is happening to him has
happened before. To others, before him. Such as this Antonius. Only what
was revealed to the ancient Egyptians looked different. It is inevitable

that the rift he saw open up between this world and the other one, the rift from which the cryptic rises, will continue to widen; and what will come to pass the day it can no longer be bridged will be frightful.

Something inside him girds itself. Something large and decisive, of which he knows no more than it has just been girded.

AND THEN ONE MORNING HE is unable to lift or stretch his arms or legs. And when he wants to roll onto his back he cannot bend his neck or move his head. He has a tingling, piercing sensation in each limb, and in his body a fever is rising, so high that even his eyes begin to sweat. Everything darkens and blurs as in a haze. He thinks someone is prodding him with the end of a long staff or cudgel. And likewise, as from a great distance he hears somebody whispering—

Heavens, let's hope it is not the plague he has caught

So he must truly be dead: if this is how they speak of him. And this must be how the dead perceive the voices of the living. As a faint murmur, muffled breaths, wind.

Strangely enough the thought lightens his mind. Perhaps he sleeps a while. When he comes to his senses again he still can't move his head or arms but the fever seems to have subsided and he can see clearly out of both eyes.

Johanna has come and is urging him to drink something watery from a wooden spoon, the edge of which knocks against his teeth.

He has been sick, Johann. Come come, she says.

He turns his head away but she comes after him with the spoon and does not relent until he has opened his mouth and swallowed. Like feeding a child. Then she begins, just as mechanically, to complain about a man, a soldier, whom she knows. It appears that she has been busy telling the story for quite a while, paying no mind to whether or not he was awake or listening.

Or perhaps he has been listening unawares?

Johanna keeps dipping the spoon in the soup bowl, wiping it off against the rim, then guiding it into his mouth.

Johanna should watch out for soldiers, he says curtly.

Again with the voice that came out of him at the inn that evening he almost beat Bon to death. *That's what he gets for puffing himself up and throwing his weight around.* Is what he said then. With the Joost-doll voice. Alien and rough.

And just as alien and rough is the voice coming from him now.

Johanna should watch out for soldiers.

It is as if he were dead and someone else were speaking through him. But how can he be lying here, seeing and hearing everything Johanna is saying if he is dead? He doesn't understand. Apparently neither does Johanna. She bends over as though to see if there is anyone or anything behind his eyes. Then she adopts a cheerful tone, though with her gaze half-averted, and says:

So says he, who was once a soldier himself?

It is more of a statement than a question.

And then he says:

I almost married a woman like you, who chased soldiers.

And again the words escape him without him knowing or being able to say from where they come or why. Never before has he said this to her and it would never have occurred to him to say such a thing had he not found himself in this unusual state. Johanna seems as puzzled. She keeps turning the wooden spoon over in her hand as though she no longer knows its purpose. Suddenly her eyes fill with tears. She turns away but can't hide her crying and she curls up and then her whole body starts shaking.

She had a child, says the voice that speaks from within.

She looks at him, tears streaming from her eyes.

So he is the father of a child? *He?* I never would have guessed!

She tries to laugh through the tears. Laughter is the only way to cope with this improbability, and so improbable it is that she can only laugh sincerely, try to muster one of those great, long, unfettered laughs from before and that would set her entire body rocking.

It wasn't my child, the voice then says.

And it is as though he stabbed her with a knife. Her eyes look fit
to burst.

Not fathered by me. I only took care of it.

It was a girl, says the voice.

Johanna stares at him, as though to say (and perhaps she says it too):
You? she says, full of misbelief.

And so she flies into a rage—*You . . . !* she says. You're all the same,
You talk and wish to be such great and decent men but when all is said
and done You are good for nothing. You only lie there, limp and dead.
Look at me! *Get up!* she screams.

And then she kicks him. She kicks him in the chest and side but
loses her balance and falls on top of him and starts punching his face.

Weakling! Good for nothing!

And then she stops punching and slumps over him, her whole heavy
body on top of his, howling:

Oh, why didn't you come, why did you never come . . . ?

He sees her hand clasp his. Only the rough outside of the hand he
sees, the hard red-chapped knuckles, the veins stretching and slackening
across the back of her hand.

Woost and I, she says. God didn't want to bless us with offspring.
Woost said it was because I wasn't fond enough of him and beat me so
senseless that even if I'd wanted to with him, how would it have gone?

She snuffles and looks away and when she turns back to him her
gaze is full of careless yet horror-struck lament.

Poor us, is all she says.

He wants to take her in his arms right then, but still can't move a
limb. Instead it is she who brings his lifeless hand to her face, as if to
kiss it. But an absentmindedness seizes her before she gets that far and
she merely runs the back of his lifeless hand awkwardly over her chin
as though to wipe away snot and tears. Then she stands up, gathers the
soup bowl and cutlery, and leaves the attic room without another word.

AND SO THEY ARE CLOSE to each other, and yet not. And oddly, it is in the very hours she allows him to be with her that he is most beleaguered by the thought that she is in fact somewhere else, with someone else. Nevertheless, the hours she isn't with him are even worse. Then there is no time. Not even emptiness exists. All that would have been her body and voice and face are torn from him and inside is but a large black wound and the pain is insufferable.

And never does she let him know in advance whether or not she's coming. If he asks, her gaze becomes flat and evasive. Or sharp and unwilling. And she says she doesn't know when she can come to him, and she has eyes on her now, Warneck is furious with her and Jordan won't give her a minute's rest.

But he makes his own promises of the little he gets out of her. As he lies in the attic dark at Haase's, a word that she tossed out in passing about some day or soon becomes a hunch or even a hope that she will come anyway. That she is perhaps already on her way. That she had only expressed herself vaguely and equivocally so that others wouldn't suspect a thing. That she may already be on the stairs, is only treading with particular care so that no one will hear her footsteps. And finally he is so sure that she is already on her way that he climbs out of bed, sneaks down the stairs, and opens the door that Haase has carefully locked, the last thing he does before he and his wife go to bed.

And if she still isn't there? He can't simply go back up to the attic and leave the front door unlocked. So he convinces himself that he is but going for a little walk down the street to have a look. And before he knows it he is standing outside of Frau Wognitz's house on Sandgasse, where he has promised a thousand times never to go.

But this restlessness makes it impossible for him to be patient. And like the Joost doll it is wild and unruly. It does not wish to be restrained. In the form of the doll he is equally another. Uncouth, strange, intemperate, he draws out his steps and does not fear being seen by anyone who might know that he should not be out at this hour. Still he retains enough of his old cunning to know which route to take so as to make his way to Sandgasse unseen.

The room she rents from Frau Wognitz, he has deduced, must be one of the rooms under the bending roof with a window to the street. He has seen light behind the curtain and sometimes he thinks he glimpses movement behind it that is more than fleeting shadows. But as long as the street is deserted it is only her shadow he thinks he sees, and he imagines that she is moving around in her room, undressing, and washing herself at the washstand, which she must have, along with a tub and water jug, as at his.

Until such a day it happens as has been happening all the while, only he had not been vigilant enough. A strange man appears at the gateway, stands a while, his legs splayed so he can fasten his trousers, whereafter he sets off towards Rossplatz. Up until then W. can't know for sure but after a few steps the man takes on Johanna's waddling gait; then he laughs and turns around and shouts something and immediately the shadow in the attic window acquires a contour and the window opens and out leans Johanna, swearing at him, telling him to toddle on off, and the man shouts *Shut up you damn whore . . . !* so that it echoes through the street.

Then he hears the sound of coins clinking against the cobblestones and when he turns around Bon is standing there, his porcine eyes peering out from inside the beardless face and with a smile so wide that all his fat cheek flesh seems to squish behind his ears.

And the coins jingling between his palms, which he lifts and turns over, once, twice; until one of them, as they are wont to do, falls to the street. As if the coin were being spurred on by a will of its own, it begins rolling slowly towards where he is standing on the street.

Go on, Woyzeck. No reason to be ashamed. Just pick it up.

He looks at the coin. Bon stays put, his smile as still as a disc of moon in the night mist. Actually it is incomprehensible that Bon would be here at all, since everyone knows he feels most comfortable in his cage, king of his canapé, and rarely is seen beyond Warneck's on Nikolaigasse and the regular's table at the Golden Goose. What is he doing here? Unless he too is one of the men who curries Johanna's favor at night.

Bon stands in the middle of the street, inviting and pompous, and at his feet lies the coin, small and shiny and desirable.

Come come. Take it, I know He will. He isn't ashamed of indulging in this pleasure, is He?

Go on, take it. Bon's treat.

The coin innocently lies in front of him. And at once everything in this illuminated night is innocent. Each object, each person, had been robbed of its shadow and everything is illuminated and unconditional. Bon stands there, generous and offering to treat him. And the coin lies there, bright and shiny. And Johanna is waiting for him upstairs in her apartment. In the room on Sandgasse to which he has never before been granted access. But the ban has been lifted now. No longer are there walls, hurdles, or bans.

But as he bends down to pick up the coin he sees Bon take a step forward as though to place his foot on it. And he shirks. He does it quickly. Without thinking. But also without straightening up. Which means that Bon's kick lands too high, only lightly grazing his shoulder. And as though the misdirected kick has furnished his movements with new strength, he is on his feet and running as fast as he can down the street.

Behind him Bon sticks two fingers in his mouth and whistles loudly, a signal directed at someone waiting a few blocks away. He glimpses a body leaning against a plank wall, a mere concentration of darkness inside what is already dark.

But this is enough to make him understand that there are several who are trying to tempt and trap him. He doesn't slow down to find out who the shadowy figures are, but keeps running as though the devil himself were at his heels. He runs until the breath wants to burst from his chest and the needles stabbing into his heart pierce all the way to the welt where his pulse heaves and throbs, heaves and throbs, and finally the pain overpowers him and he crashes to the ground like an animal.

HE KNOWS THAT THE PEOPLE who say she goes with others are correct, and yet he refuses to believe it. Or more rightly put: when he is by himself he believes it. But as soon as she is near him it becomes utterly unthinkable that she could have been with anyone else. Such is her presence. It does to man what madness does. It dissolves each boundary, each difference, each distance. She is the only one there is, everywhere she is just as close.

And while he wanted to ask, yes, has even prepared the question, went back and forth and twisted and turned it around so many times that it has been worn smooth and unusable, like a stone in hand, its purpose unclear, he could not bring himself to.

Is what they say true? Do you have another whom you hold dear?

The question is the easiest one to ask. He could simply let the words slip right out. Johanna will hardly notice, if she cares at all. Still he can't get the words to pass his lips. He twists and chews his tongue and parts his lips but nothing comes out.

She smiles at him, voice as soft as ever. Even though he can tell by her wandering gaze that she is on her way elsewhere, perhaps in her mind is already with another, only he is in her large, open, warm smile at this moment.

And how could he possibly believe such a thing about her?

She says.

And who could have said such vile a thing to him?

And: come to me, she says.

I am only kind to you, you do know that, don't you, Johann.

You're like a child, she says as she touches him.

She says that he has the smooth skin and downy hair of a child.

A pale, innocent child, frightened and kept awake for far too long.

Her hands are hard and calloused on the outside, but they are soft inside.

And when she touches him it is only with this inside part.

And it is only with the inside that he is close to her.

All is inside.

AND SO ONE DAY HE finds out the name of one of the men with whom she goes.

He is called Böttcher. A soldier in the City Guard.

ONE SUNDAY AFTERNOON IN MAY he encounters the two of them in Bosens Garten. He spots her from a distance, but even though her movements suggest that she is walking arm in arm with someone it is as though his eyes refuse to see anyone but her. Johanna walks with short, labored steps, elbow stiffly outstretched, and she keeps oscillating her head up to look at her cavalier, giving him an empty, artificial smile each time. The pair are walking straight towards him on the promenade path, but do not see him. As for him, he keeps walking, for what else can he do? If he were to promptly change course they would notice him at once, and this is the last thing he wants right now. But in the end, the inevitable happens. Johanna's short steps and oscillations are derailed. She stumbles, and when her cavalier grabs her by the arm she says something to him and looks at the ground. So, of course he, *this other man,* catches sight of *him,* too. Splendid is he in his blue full uniform, shoulders straight and chest proud, under the tall helmet his face is large and florid, smiling now from behind a thick tawny mustache. And even though this smile is in no way directed at him it seems to *include* him. As it includes all else in the world: the trees in bloom, the flickering sunlight and shadows flitting and reaching across the short stretch of the path that still lies between them. So large and potent is this all-encompassing smile that he can't help but stop and salute, as though the smile had been an order issued from somewhere deep inside. And so he stands at attention as the guardsman Böttcher prepares to glide by. As does she, Johanna, still looking at the ground, yes, she's dragging her gaze behind her until they are in line with him, and right then she turns her head and gives him the briefest of smiles, curt and stiff and somehow *gracious,* as though she were a distinguished noblewoman who had stepped out on her balcony in order to express her admiration of her subjects.

And despite the fact that he is there beside her, standing tall, back as straight as a broomstick, though of course unsightly in his dirty beggar's rags, not once does she turn around so as to indicate that this smile was meant for him.

AND HE WALKS.

He walks because he doesn't know what else to do.

He walks because the pressure from the world outside, all that is *not* her, would otherwise be unbearable. If he stood still for even a moment the pain would overpower him.

So he walks—

The long, hot summer limps towards its end. The light pales, and as the heat rises from the earth the clouds swell and blacken as if the sky were bruised.

He walks for hours under a thundering sky, along country roads whose surface of gravel and hardened mud shines bone-white in the afterglow, as the sky above so darkly forms a vault. Then coolth streaks through the humid heat and thunder delivers a few sharp claps. And as if a large trough up in the sky has been tipped over, masses of water wash down on him and run through his hair and down his face and seep under the collar of his shirt and coat sleeve and the ground beneath him becomes smooth and slick and his boots sink so deep into the mud that he can hardly lift his legs.

He seeks shelter under a bridge, crouching under the stone arch like an animal.

And so time walks on, the hours walk on, without anything happening but the rain continuing to surround him like a wall in the half-light on the other side of the bridge span.

Not knowing how it came to be, he finds himself in the stairwell at Sandgasse once more. Out on the street the rain lingers. It is the same rain. Its pattering on roofs and walls pushes like a dull echo into the narrow stairwell where Johanna's landlady, Frau Wognitz, is standing in a bedgown but no cap, her bald head bare. The glow of the lantern she is holding in her hand roves even more because of her bilious ire—

—*what do You permit Yourself, man, Frau Woost is not*—

He tears the lantern from her hand and watches as the shadow of his own body is slung against the whitewashed wall as though someone else were running ahead up the stairs. He opens a door at hazard and charges into a room filled with her scent. And Johanna is there, of course. The flickering lantern immediately lights up her angled eyes. Like an animal lazily rolling over, she turns on her side. A man's head flashes along with it, which she presses to her shoulder, half-hidden by her gray-streaked hair that is so vast it hangs over the edge of the bed halfway down to the floor. And deeper in the nest of the bed, two rough hands can be seen squeezing and kneading her bared buttocks. Atop, her body quivers and shakes from this patient kneading, shaking with that breathless laugh he knows so well. But the lupine smile, the look in those angled eyes, is directed at him now.

Go on and look, Woyzeck; look your fill,
it's all that he's good for . . . !

Then the hands stop their kneading and the man's head turns to him and he sees that it's the same guardsman he saluted in Bosens Garten. Böttcher. He recognizes the round pale blue eyes, the bristly red mustache, the straight nose; only the hair is a new sight for he is not wearing a helmet: bristled, it too. This is all he manages to see. Johanna has with surprising speed covered her legs with her chemise. She hides the man's body with her own and refuses to move even though W. tries to push her aside. Meanwhile Böttcher has grabbed his clothes and is out the door. W. runs after him, but his path is blocked by Frau Wognitz who is screaming something at him but he can't hear what because Johanna is standing right behind him, screaming in turn—

Get the intruder out, Frau Wognitz!
Get that feeble-minded wretch out—

He is trying to get back into the room, as though to hide, when he is dealt a hard blow to the head. It is so abrupt that he can't tell from where it came until he sees Frau Wognitz coming after him with a great broom in her tiny clenched fists. S*huffle on off now, whoremongerer*, she screams and again hits him on the head with the broom, again and again with powerful blows, as if trying to kill a rat or some other pest. He ducks out of the way and crawls backwards down the stairs. Then she turns the broomstick around and manages to get in a few mighty thrusts to his neck and chest. He runs through the echoing stairwell, out onto the street, out into the rain. It surrounds him again, pounding the tar- and board roofs, so hard the drops that meet the cobblestones spatter back up into the steaming air. From within the wetness a window is flung open, the same window he saw her in on the night he ran into Bon. But now she makes no attempt to cover herself, she leans her whole torso out and there is exultation in that rude voice:

You don't own me, Johann, she screams, laughing as only she can. Her peculiar laughter that begins in the pit of her stomach and little by little overwhelms her entire body.

Nobody owns me!

The window slams shut, but flies open again and as though her mirth had no end:

Go on home, Johann; farewell farewell . . . !

THAT NIGHT, THE FINAL ONE in Haase's attic, the now doubly scorned man drinks himself blind on cheap schnapps. He no longer drinks to dull something inside. He drinks to obliterate what remains of her inside him.

Finally he has had so much to drink that only his numb exterior remains upright, but barely.

He has a memory of falling down the attic stairs and of Haase and his wife trying to help him back to the attic. And that during this ascent parts of him came loose and fell off. Various body parts. Hands. Arms. Head. And that Haase and his wife had to keep turning around to collect the body parts left on the stairs. And even once they have gathered all of him up and continue removing him, a piece of him is still left behind twisting and writhing in agony and finally the otherwise calm Haase has had enough and says *it's high time he pull himself together, Johann, otherwise we'll have to call the police.*

Is this when he finally gives in, or does he continue to howl and whine the whole night through? He can't remember. All he knows is that on the next day he leaves the attic room with an outstanding debt of just over three months' food and lodging. He left us, Haase would explain to Clarus afterwards, of his own accord. He said he could not bear the shame.

SO WAS IT AT THIS time that he acquired the murder weapon? Clarus asks. Can the detainee account for when and in which way this occurred?

Woyzeck. My deepest regrets, Herr Hofrat. The only thing I remember clearly of the time after I left Haase was that I applied to be a soldier in the City Guard.

Clarus. A soldier in the City Guard? That's the most preposterous—

Woyzeck. It wasn't me, it was a former officer at the garrison by the name of Pfeiffer who suggested I apply. Once a soldier always a soldier.

Clarus. And when did this take place?

Yes, when? He can't be more specific, only that he returns to the bookbinder Wehner in Volkmarsdorf who takes pity and keeps him on at the bookbindery though work is scarce and he cannot make a living with it. Thereafter he made one or two half-hearted attempts at finding employment in his old professions, as a servant or barber. But of course he has nothing to show for it. The apprenticeship certificate he once had is long since lost. And his clothes do not make a favorable impression. He goes around dressed as a vagabond with a dirty shirtfront, a ragged overcoat and his old soldier's boots that have long since split at the seams. He does not have so much as a collar.

The latter is also pointed out to him by Lieutenant Pfeiffer:

If one wants to be a soldier, then one must learn to dress as a soldier!

They have ended up conversing in some tavern, W. can no longer remember which, and Pfeiffer has just told him about enlisting in the Saxon Army and marching with Napoleon on the Russians. They had gone south and been decimated down to the last man. *The last man.*

Does Woyzeck understand? Upon his return, he was given a job at the commissariat supply service. If there's one thing that teaches you, it's to care for your kit.

But W. isn't listening.

Since he is at the garrison might he know someone by the name of Böttcher? Perchance is that name familiar?

And Pfeiffer nods. Sure, he knows Böttcher well. He is in the City Guard, a pompous devil. He drops other names, too. He seems to know everybody, and holds them all in equal contempt. Then W. says that he wants to be a soldier in the City Guard.

Pfeiffer lowers his head to the table and looks at him from below, as it were, with a firm, intense gaze, and though they may have had a schnapps or two, Pfeiffer's voice is sure and clear when he says that if W. wants his opinion, well, the City Guard are *riffraff* the lot of them, drinking and thieving any chance they get, but if he insists by *tooth and nail* then he honestly can't see what would be standing in the way of obtaining one such post.

Seeing as how you've toiled and distinguished yourself in your lifetime . . . !

Yes, hearing Pfeiffer speak in this moment one might almost have thought it was the Evil One himself holding forth before the dismayed W., but in spite of the intoxication it seems that Pfeiffer both believes and means what he is saying.

You do still have Your military passbook? Pfeiffer asks.

W. does not, but Pfeiffer bats this away with an almost brusque gesture.

I'm on good terms with the officers, it'll work out, You'll see.

You can stay with me in the meantime.

As soon as the decision is made, a great clarity spreads through W. He doesn't tell Clarus this—how does one go about saying such a thing?—but more than any weapon, more than any intent to do harm or punish, it is this won *clarity* that contributes to what will happen later. Of course, there is no shame in having saluted a superior in Bosens

Garten. The shame comes from that awful *courtly smile* Johanna gave him afterwards. A smile saved for a person of lesser means. At once compassionate and condescending. If only he could have a rank, and walk around properly dressed, no one would be able to look down on him anymore.

SO HE CAN STAY WITH Pfeiffer for a time while arrangements are being made. And even though Pfeiffer treats W. as if he were his valet and expects to be attended to from morning until night, there is no shame in it. Neither is there in Pfeiffer's expectation of being constantly entertained. If W. doesn't have anything amusing to say, Pfeiffer yawns wearily and looks at him as though he were of lesser mind. But Pfeiffer is true to his word. He helps W. compose an application to the Office of the Commandant requesting that he be admitted into the City Guard and in anticipation of this application being examined W. assumes a highly provisional position as a magazine assistant at the commissariat supply service, or perhaps one should say as an assistant to the magazine assistant because, to be sure, Pfeiffer is the magazine assistant and only one person has that title.

Bogeschdorfer is the name of the man who supervises the commissariat supply service: a strapping fellow of whom it is said he once served as an officer in the cavalry and had brilliant prospects but was demoted to staff duty because of an offense so shameful not even Pfeiffer will name it. If it is because of this ignominy, or but because of the considerable body weight he has amassed over the years, Bogeschdorfer shows a certain phlegmatic nature, which means that he is not wont to remove himself from the desk in the middle of the magazine hall, at which he is sometimes seen sleeping so soundly he barely seems to be in this world.

But his sleep is only a thin veil behind which is an ever-watchful fish-eye gleaming white. It requires no more than someone trying to sneak by with an iron rod or a pair of manacles for *Wallentini . . . !* to be

shouted from the pulpit and then a thin corporal with a slender bloodless face appears by his side.

Corporal Wallentini is Bogeschdorfer's right hand and iron will who
spends his days keeping vigil over his superior officer's sleep. Each time
a drove of soldiers from the City Guard comes barging into the echoing
room he rushes out with a finger to his lips and *ssshhh ssshhh the sergeant
is sleeping* is whispered with such emphasis that it makes even the most
thoughtless pause mid-step.

The commissariat supply service is a strange world of long corridors
lined with whitewashed brick walls and tall solid wood doors furnished
with sturdy locks and iron fittings. A few of the doors lead into large
halls guarded by aging military men who are as reluctant to leave their
chairs as Bogeschdorfer is. Behind them in the long shadows of the
room hang uniforms and coats, racks of hats and casques rise towards
the ceiling, rifles and ramrods stand in long rows behind carefully barred
and bolted doors. Other rooms are as cramped as a spence. In one flags
and standards are stored, standing upright or meticulously folded away
in wide sliding drawers. These are the standards his bedmate Vitzthun
can be seen carrying in the military parades on Sundays. Vitzthun has
also showed him the instruments the band plays, the gleaming brass
trumpets and tubas and the large drum above the stretched leather of
which hang the municipal arms and seals.

Each room and chamber and compartment and drawer is equipped
with its own key, the smallest nickel-plated and with plate fittings.
Numbers and letters are stamped on the plates, corresponding to the
numbers and letters stamped on similar plates above the doorposts of
each and every room.

It is astonishing that W., though hardly literate and numerate,
so quickly finds his way in this carefully compartmentalized world of
alphanumerical designations. Perhaps it is because here a soldier's life,
which after all these years he knows as well as a hand knows the seams
of its glove, is freed from all that would otherwise cloud his mind, freed
from the stench, the mold, the crying hunger, and misery.

But it is the same world: the same rules and illusions.

W.'s duties include the processing of returned property, and in conjunction therewith locating the original requisition and checking off each
signed-for piece as well as those returned in a special ledger, noting time
and date in the column at the extreme margin. If an item is lost, a report
is to be written. And if anything is returned damaged or in an unusable
state, repairs shall be arranged, but only after a report has been written
detailing the damage and how it occurred (if this can be determined) and
this report is to be certified by Bogeschdorfer or an officer authorized by
him before the damaged object can be sent away for repair. And while
the pale Wallentini forces him to run this way and that with paperwork
and apparel (Pfeiffer, meanwhile, mostly stands around chatting with the
young recruits) it occurs to him that even if the Army is the outermost
outpost of divine order on earth and nothing gets past Bogeschdorfer's
staring fish-eye unnoticed, there will always be some small object that
goes astray, the odd spare garment, some tiny thing that no one can
remember what it once was for, and eventually W. rustles up the most
wonderful collection, consisting of a dented helmet and aigrette, a lapel
with sewn-on piping, a belt buckle, a bit of strap from a cartridge pouch,
and some surplus buttons in various shapes and colors. All of this he
keeps in a small box at the bottom of one of the magazine rooms. The box
could hold a pair of boots at most, but he has carefully furnished it with
a plate and a number that also seems to have gone astray somewhere. It
says *1.3.80* on the plate, which—it must be a sign!—happens to be the
date of his own birth. But where is the corresponding plate that com-
municates where the box with the treasures in fact belongs?

This is how he comes by the broken-off saber blade one day.
    It lies at the bottom of a box of rejected apparel that he has been
asked to process and itemize. It is only the upper part of the blade, broken
neatly off and about as long as his forearm.
    How does one go about repairing a broken saber blade?
    Under Wallentini's supervision, he spends some time going through
lists of returned saber hilts. But only apparently. In truth, he is already

figuring out how to add the blade to his treasures. It is far too long for the box.

But how is he to explain this to Clarus?

It would be tantamount to a confession of theft.

And how is he to explain that he spends his nights sitting at the head of the bed he shares with the garrison soldier Vitzthun sewing from the odd and ragged scraps of cloth he has come across at the commissariat supply service what was at first imagined as a holster for the broken-off saber blade but that increasingly resembles a scabbard or perhaps rather a pouch because he has to line the inside with leather scraps to keep the sharp point from pushing through the fabric?

And how is he to explain that from this day on he carries the broken-off saber blade with him, hanging in its sheath?

His bedmate Vitzthun also spends the lonely evenings sewing, and as they sit peacefully at each end of their bed Vitzthun talks about how he usually serves as a drummer in the guard company's band on holidays and parade days and he says that W. must come see the parade one day. It is splendid entertainment.

And how is he to explain to Clarus that one Sunday he is in fact standing there among hundreds of others on Marktplatz watching the band march by with flutes and brass and Vitzthun winks at him from his position at the end, the big drum hanging from his chest, *dunk-dunk-dunk*; but all eyes (including W.'s) are drawn to the drum major at the front who, knees high and with a strange lurching gait, swings the long drum major's mace between his fingers with playful ease as though it were no more than an unsightly stick.

And though the drum major does not resemble Böttcher in the least (he is significantly older and more stoutly built), W. nonetheless imagines that it must be Böttcher, at least Böttcher in some form, and later Vitzthun explains with the help of an ordinary wooden stick how the drum major signals to the musicians by holding the mace with the ball pointing up or straight ahead. If the ball is pointed straight ahead it indicates the direction of the march, and if it is pointing upwards then it is a signal to the musicians to follow the beat.

Strange, W. thinks, that the whole world can be kept in order with but a wave of this mace.

Of all that he is most fascinated by the parade sword the drum major carries in his baldric, and because Vitzthun is the keeper of the key to the band's magazine, one day W. asks if he can see it up close. Vitzthun says it shouldn't be a problem, as long as he is careful; so in one mighty gesture that engages his whole body (head, arms, shoulders) W. slowly draws the long sword out of the baldric and holds out the sharp gleaming blade so that it scintillates in the pale light still in the barrack window, and he repeats the gesture so many times that it feels like he is still holding the sword long after Vitzthun has returned it to the magazine, and then to Vitzthun he says that he knows he is destined for something, and Vitzthun with his weak voice asks what is he destined for, Woyzeck? And he: God has not yet made it clear to me, but it is something, of that I am sure, and so he lies at the foot of the bed and tells Vitzthun about all the strange signs he has seen, about the streaks in the celestial sphere that he previously had taken to be Masonic signs, but now he thinks that God up on high is holding a drum major's mace in his hand and beating it with full force until Heaven's floor begins to bleed, and that the light thus brought forth is God's blood, and when one day follows the next it is in fact God's own blood falling from the sky in the form of light.

And so the march continues: day after day God's sky-mace moves up and down, forward and to the side, and the rain of blood is unending. Until a few dull snores from one end of the bed attest that Vitzthun has fallen asleep.

AND HOW IS HE TO explain to Clarus that when the reply from the city commander finally arrives it's not a run-of-the-mill rejection? The second lieutenant who delivers the letter says it is a rejection by acclamation. Moreover he has personally arrived in the company of a couple of his men in order to see how W. takes it, and even though the letter has already been slit open, taken out, and read, perhaps more than once, he must stand before the grinning lot and pretend to open the already opened letter, take the page out and—

Well, go on, *read it*, urges the second lieutenant.

But that's just it: W. can't bring himself to read, not only because the words and sentences on the page blur before his roving gaze, but also because his hands are shaking so hard he can scarcely hold the sheet up to his face. The second lieutenant snatches it out of his hands, but instead of reading it aloud (which everyone in the magazine hall, including Bogeschdorfer's fish-eye, expects of him), he clicks his heels, leans in, and recites:

It has come to our attention that Woyzeck has applied for an appointment at the City Guard. It is said that he was in service of the Prussians and Mecklenburgers, but he has not been able to present, cannot present, a discharge from the Army because he has never been accorded one. Deserted, run away, and scarpered like a coward is all that he has done in his life. If he thought he would find final refuge here, he has been operating under a grave delusion.

I politely decline, the second lieutenant says, crumples up the letter and tosses it away as though it were sullied. W. has the day to gather up his belongings and toddle on off.

HE GOES TO VISIT JOHANNA wearing what he has left of his pilfered finery. On his head the dented plumed helmet, at his side the broken-off saber blade dangling in its sheath. Of course, he keeps this from Clarus, for how is he to say anything about the saber since it was not put to use on this occasion? *I was already carrying the blade with me then, but was not sure if I had it.*

How exceptionally foolish, Clarus would say.

Which is what he always says when W. does not give the obvious or expected answer to his questions.

It is at eventide. A strangely clear, shadowless light prevails, greenish, like bottle glass. Had he been wearing a coat of mail or a cuirass, his chest would have gleamed as if silvered. Now he is hardly visible in the shadow-less half-light by the entrance gate to Warneck's foundry. A pair of boys run by, oblivious to him, a cab grinds to a crunching halt at the neighboring gateway. A handful of men come stumbling out of the inn, but even though one or another surely recognizes him, no one stops to chat.

He stands still, like the sentry of fate he has chosen to be.

Then the noise inside the inn begins to wane, the din of voices is replaced by the monotone clank of dishes, and soon the doors to the courtyard are opened wide and Johanna comes out with a basket of plates and cutlery on her hip. She doesn't see him, but turns her wide back to him and shouts something into the restaurant in a gruff tone before setting off for the well under the broad ash tree.

Then she pauses. And it occurs to him that he must have the same effect on her as the shop assistant Bon did on him when he appeared in the middle of the street with his clinking coins. Like a mirage, or a phantom.

You . . . ? is all she says.

Then she starts laughing. Her laughter is full of misbelief at first, then becomes hollow and toneless.

Why are you standing there putting it on? Haven't I told you to go away?

And she stares at him with misbelief and derision. In order to banish that stare—or at least to escape its reach—he flings out an arm and happens to knock her shoulder. She takes two stumbling steps to the side, then falls backwards into the board wall that separates the courtyard from the latrines opposite the pigsty, the basket falls from her hands and the dishes crash to the ground and shatter. Regretfully he bends down to pick up the shards but suddenly she's standing over him, a mad stare embedded in that big head.

What are you doing here, you cretin . . . !

Didn't I tell you to go away . . . ?

As if he were a complete stranger. As if she didn't know why he had dressed up to see to her, why he would always return, day after day, for as long as he is able.

And yet he has power.

He knows it.

And the power is like intoxication, a boundless daze.

When he straightens up, his body is hard and cold inside his coat of mail. One of the shards has cut his palm. He feels the blood sticking between his fingers as he grasps the shard, and for the first time he can see fear in Johanna's narrow eyes.

Imagine, Woyzeck, a little soldier.

But she does not dare say this now. Once so sure of tongue she is silent of speech, palms and back pressed to the board wall as she shambles away. Like an insect, he thinks. Like an insect dragging what remains of its crushed body behind it in order to escape.

Only the stare lingers. It must go.

He aims the shard at her eyes and hears Johanna scream as she brings her hands to her face. Blood between her fingers: his or hers.

Then someone grabs his neck from behind and Warneck's hoarse voice is panting against his neck:

Don't I tell wretches like you to keep away.

At the same time something hard hits his crotch (a knee or an elbow), and Johanna is right in front of him. First she wraps her arms around his chest and waist, but he manages to get out of this embrace so she kicks his legs and genitals again.

And then he lies on the ground, Warneck atop him.

He remains inside his armor, but his helmet is too tight. And what's left of the sword is but a twig of a limb curling itself up in his groin for fear of the next kick.

HE WOULD HAVE BEEN ABLE to get away with a fine for harassment had there been no bloodshed, but he gets eight weeks in police custody instead. Which is just as well, for he has no other roof over his head.

Nevertheless, it is a time of great anguish.

Ceaselessly he ponders how the unfamiliar rage could inhabit him and blind him to the extent that all he saw was her eyes. Surely he would have cut them from her skull had it not been for Herr Warneck's timely intervention. As dour and grudging as the brazier may be, he owes him a great debt of gratitude. As he does everyone who always had his best in mind: Widow Knobloch, who rented her room to him, as well as the newspaper distributor Haase and his wife, and Lieutenant Pfeiffer. And he had behaved impossibly with each one of them. Is there no place on earth where he can escape the fearsome unrest that grabs and tears at him?

Then he is set free again. To his surprise he is allowed to collect all of his stolen goods. The helmet, the braiding, the aigrette, and the belt buckle, even the saber blade wrapped in rags. With these objects he wanders the city, the very image of a rattling beggar. Now and then he manages to nag his way to alms or a small loan. But lodging or a place to sleep is denied him at every turn and for the most part he must weather sleeping outside. Though one day providence is with him. His eyes fall on a notice for a bed for rent by one Frau Wittig on Ritterstrasse. He knocks and asks to be received. Unluckily it turns out that the landlady, Frau Wittig, is on her deathbed. The daughter is renting out the bed in the dying woman's room in order to scrape enough money together for the funeral. She cannot watch over her mother herself because she must

tend to her own house and home and now there is only one room and
if he wants a place to sleep he must well tolerate sharing a room with
the dying woman.

Frau Wittig lies as though she already were in her coffin: on her back in
a far too narrow bed with a tall bedstead. In the first days she does not
do much to make herself known, but one night he hears her speaking
with a booming voice that couldn't possibly be hers: *another* voice, of the
kind that rose out of him in newspaper distributor Haase's attic and left
him as good as paralyzed until Johanna finally came.

The dying woman's speech goes on for hours. The voice is plain and
clear, with properly formed words but their meaning escapes him, as if
she were speaking to him in an utterly foreign tongue. Near dawn when
he dares draw near the dying woman's bed he sees that her face is bathed
in sweat but otherwise she is still and her eyes are shut as though she
were in deep repose. Only her jaw and mouth are moving, as of their own
accord, in order to give way to the incomprehensible voice.

After several hours the speech stops. But as if something foreign
had in fact squeezed through, a foul odor hangs in the room. A smell of
corpse and something else: something rank, piercing, that spreads like
an itch in his throat. When the daughter comes to visit around noon he
tells her what happened during the night, and the daughter says that it
probably won't be long now. But when he says that he can't bring himself
to stay in the dying woman's room, the daughter demands payment for
the remaining days she says they agreed he would spend in the room,
and then he doesn't dare leave.

Two more days pass. An older man in a black coat appears, who W.
realizes after a while is a doctor summoned by the younger Frau Wittig.
The doctor briefly bends over the bedstead, then removes himself without
having opened his bag or saying a word to W., who again is left alone in
the room with the dying woman.

That night the woman is silent, but in return he has vivid dreams.
For the first time in a very long time he sees his sister in a dream. She
comes riding down the long grassy slope leading to the Memel River
and even though she is a little girl whose feet don't so much as reach

the stirrups she has already acquired a majestic head. It is the large and wise head of a queen's, her hair covered by a crown and a veil of the finest gauze. And: *The Horse*, she calls to him through the dream. It's like she doesn't think he can see clearly because he is sleeping. As though to show him the animal, she tugs at a rein and makes it turn around. And then he recognizes its round, glossy haunches. It is the Horse. The dead and resurrected, consumed and gnawed-to-the-bone but nonetheless resurrected whole and unharmed Horse. His sister lets go of the reins and the Horse lowers its head to the earth and grazes as the water flows by at such tremendous speed that it looks like the river might draw along not just the low banks overgrown with grass, but also the trees and crops and fields all around, it wants to drag along the sky as well and its dull sunshine, and he presses both hands to the mattress and labors to lift his body in the great roar made by all that is hurtling by.

Is it really true? he wonders.

Only when I am *outside myself* am I free.

When he wakes up, light is streaming through the window, its curtains pushed aside, and in the light he sees that young Frau Wittig is already in the room. As is the black-clad doctor and both turn to him and confirm what he already has understood. Old Frau Wittig is dead. Herr Woyzeck is free to go, the daughter says.

IT HAPPENS IN THE SPRING. Again he wanders, finding neither work nor lodging. The vile stench of death follows him wherever he goes. He can't get rid of it. Perhaps as he walks down a country road or in an open field, but directly he is locked in a room: the smell is there. As is the rough voice. Now he no longer knows whose voice it is or with which words it speaks to him: whether it originates with Frau Wittig, even though she's dead, or if it comes from within. In his despair he seeks out Haase anew, who is moved when he sees the pitiful state of him and allows him to spend another few nights in the attic room.

Then a miracle occurs: Johanna comes back to him.

Her smile is the same. As are the movements of her body, the touch of her hands. The only difference is that now this smell of death is in the room.

And inside Johanna is a kind of death as well. It is as if all the blood has drained from her face. All the roughness of her skin is gone too. She looks fresh-scrubbed and clean. Even her eyes have a certain clarity. Her gaze no longer flits or flees.

When she opens her mouth to speak to him her speech is pale, shadow-like, yet clear. She apologizes for treating him so poorly and says she would've done things differently had it not been for her mother, the widow Knobloch, and the ill-tempered Warneck and Jordan of course. Of course they all warned her about him. Now she knows that he never wished harm on anyone, even if he had on occasion acted out of anger. She says that she has often thought of the child that wasn't from his seed, but that he still kept as though it were his own.

He is a good man, Woyzeck.

When she says this he notices how against his will a snicker seems to rise from within him.

He shifts his torso quickly to the right, then to the left as if he can't decide which position to assume so as to make an impression on her, while appearing to be humble and worthy.

She touches him, and then she says that she heard he wanted to become a city guard at the garrison. He doesn't recognize her in the dead smile she is giving him. And then she says what he now realizes she must have had on her mind this whole time:

Is there any chance he may have bumped into a city guard by the name of Böttcher in the barracks?

A man with whom she once went with, but who now has begun to defame her and say malicious things.

He must tell her what this man may have said about her.

The feeling of wanting to prove himself worthy of her care is gone. She is suddenly much too close to him and he wants to push her away.

She does not allow herself to be pushed away, and keeps touching him and looking at him, smiling coldly. And there is something placid but also hard and ruthless in what her hands want. The rest of her body wants it too, once her hands have found their intended place. A lust, it too utterly cold because her fear endows it with a will and a face. She is impatient, cannot restrain herself or wait because then the fear would catch up with her. And perhaps this fear also gives him a body, stiff as armor at first. But her hands no longer have an interior, there is no gaze, no lips; only the panting breath of a great animal while that sour smell of sex envelops her, as tense and sharp as sweat. And finally all that is stiff bursts, she collapses on the floor and lies there with her bared eyewhites staring straight ahead, her face wet with tears.

He stays where he is, miserable and trapped in his incompetence.

Finally she gets up. She doesn't want to meet his gaze, but that cold smile has returned. And her words, equally cold:

If you still want to see me again, then we can make a date for Saturday.

If deceit had a tongue of its own, then it would have been speaking now.

HOW DOES ONE TELL THE story of a life? Like a movement of unknown origin heading for an evermore predictable and, little by little, more clearly discernible end? His life, however, cannot be recounted in this way. It has never run in a single direction. Rather it seems to have progressed one small uncertain stretch at a time, only to fold back in on itself, as when folding a piece of fabric: one length atop the other, edge to edge, seam to seam. And all that happened, and is happening now, is that he is repeating to Councillor Johann August Clarus what he has already said several times before. But Clarus is not interested in repetitions or patterns. He wants straight answers and the events presented in a clear and precise order, *if I may so request*. He must have procured the saber blade somewhere? And because the detainee, according to the selfsame man, didn't have a single groschen in his pocket he must have been given it or bartered his way to the blade somehow. Or did he steal it? In that case from whom or where, and when would this have taken place? Moreover the blade was broken, which is why he must have furnished it with a hilt of sorts, and how did all of this happen and how had he been able to afford it? W. hesitates. There was a woodturner he knew, but he was a distrustful fiend, and miserly to boot: he wouldn't have done it for free, not even if he had brought the hilt himself.—Could he have asked Warneck? Clarus suggests—And what would that have looked like? Imagine asking him!—But truth be told, on that day he hadn't given a single thought to the saber blade. Of that Herr Hofrat can be assured. His mind had been as light and peaceful as the wispy clouds in the sky. Yes, to be honest it had been one of the rare days that he had not thought of her at all. She had made him a promise, after all.

he thinks of nothing at all. Then it occurs to him that she might have set off for Funkenburg already. It's not too early to go there. The light is searing though the shadows are still long. The crown of his head burns, where the hair is thinnest. His down, his baby hair, as she calls it. It is also the outermost point of his soul, he imagines. Right at the scalp, at the parting line between the chaotic and quaking world outside of the brume of incomprehensible dreams and shadow images he carries within. He wonders if people in possession of a soul are by definition good, since the soul is a gift from God. As long as the person has not fallen into the hands of demonic beings. But Johanna has assured him that he is a good and honorable person. Surely she was thinking of the child he had with Frau Thiessen in Stralsund, the child who may not have been of his own flesh and blood but to whom he was nonetheless so attached. He thinks of how wet Johanna's eyes were as he disclosed this. Deep down you are a good and righteous man, Johann, she says to him again and no sooner are the words spoken than does the poor former foot soldier Johann Christian Woyzeck, with a too-tight helmet and a teeny tiny limb, transform into King Woyzeck the Noble, striding through the park at a leisurely pace with a smile to spare for everyone he meets. At swift speed he walks the long way to Funkenburg. Of course it is still too early in the day, no band has yet arrived, the chairs and tables are covered with a sticky coat of pollen that has blown down from the linden trees lining the avenue. But here and there, by the staging post outside the restaurant, and next to the stairs that lead up to the old brewery, men have begun to congregate. They are the timid, those unfit for work, who try to hide the fact that they have nothing to do by speaking as loudly as they can. He hears their voices resounding behind the bending film of sunlight, flickering leaves, and shadow. The brewer Gottschling is here, and come from the Golden Goose are both of brazier Warneck's two men, Kloos and Binder, and Bon, of course. His coins roll from palm to palm . . . *It looks like he's searching for one particular wench, that Woyzeck is . . .* hard laughter hangs in the air before yet another salvo of voices swells and bursts behind him . . . *Could it be Johanna he's pining for . . .* Yet another swell of laughter . . . *The strumpet isn't here, she's probably spreading herself around elsewhere . . .* and was it then that it occurred, what he would later tell both police constables (and Clarus), that it seemed a giant's hand had grabbed him by the chest and flung him straight up into the air. But perhaps this is not entirely correct, he says now. It was more like the ground disappeared and I was floating freely in something that I thought was thin air but was not air, it felt like a different substance. This lasted no longer than the blink of an eye, but it felt like an eternity. Does Herr Hofrat understand? And when I came to again, it was like nothing had happened. The flickering shadows cast by the slowly rocking treetops across the tables and the gravel-strewn paths between the inn and the brewery were the same, as was the quick flitter of birds in the foliage. Bon and the other men who had gathered in the penumbra by the brewery stairs have turned their backs on him, taking no further interest in the recently heckled man. There is only that spasmodic grip on his chest, the pull of dizziness as the ground disappeared beneath his feet and a voice that said (had it been now or was it later?): *this must end now*, and he (did he say it aloud or did he only think it?): *no*, and the voice again: *it can't go on like this*, and him: *no*, and the voice again: *stab them, just stab them, you know how*, and it was like a blood-rush, a feeling of urgency, he must find her, must find and *save* her before it is too late, before something happened that neither of them would be able to withstand. If anyone, then or later, asked if he knew what he was doing in that moment, he would not have been able to answer or he would only have said that he was driven to something that had long since been decided and that he could change as little as what has already come to pass. He has a vague memory of her saying around four o'clock. But when had she said that? Most likely she hadn't been specific. Most likely she hadn't even said that they *should* meet, but that they could meet, if he so wished. A vague half-promise, nonbinding in any case, that offers no clue as to where he should steer his steps. But now he must know. He must find his way to her. There is an urgency now that wasn't present earlier in the day, which he had spent in a sluggish and indolent mood, now incomprehensible to him. Everything around him has suddenly acquired hard rebuffing edges: buildings, people from whom he runs away like a dog afraid of being beaten before they even draw near. In this way he unintentionally steps out of the shadows cast by trees and walls and strides

into the burning midday sun. It is as though he had a bell around his
head, and inside this bell the light won't stop roaring. He wraps his hands
around his head to keep the light from pushing past the thin downy hair
on his scalp and slicing like a razor blade through his brainpan, baring
and bringing to light all that is raging inside him. But then his heating
head is as if doused by a cool scoop of water. The roaring stops. He stands
in the darkness of a stone archway that leads to turner Weprich's workshop. At least his steps have led him *here*. So, as he has already suggested
to Clarus, he was on his way to the woodturner all along. Only he hadn't
noticed the lateness of the hour until now. It is already afternoon, a
slackening, and as though self-contained time of day. The sunlight seems
to be slanting towards every object, long buttresses of light in which
swarms of small insects wrest and rove. The stubborn twitch of crickets
in the grass, bluish black in its lushness around the privy. The door to
the turner's workshop is an opening in the light that leads into nothing.
Somewhere nearby he hears a horse snorting but there is no horse or
wagon in the courtyard. In fact Weprich is eating in his kitchen. He
hears the clatter of plates, a thick buzzing of flies around the open window that stops as abruptly as it resumes; the scrape of chair legs being
pushed back, steps across a creaking floor. But no voices. A shaggy dog
rises from its shadowy lair and waggles over to him as he approaches the
entrance, then turns away as though seized by sudden malaise. He ends
up standing in the hall too scared to proceed until the woodturner can
be heard rising from his chair in the kitchen and shouting *Don't stand
there cowering, man—step forward!* But of course he cannot tell Clarus
any of this. Then it would sound like he had deliberately sought out the
turner. Bur it was the turner who snatched the cloth bag containing the
blade out of his hands himself, *what's this then . . . ?* as two children he
hadn't thus far noticed ran past him out into the courtyard, followed by
the woolly mongrel that has suddenly perked up, *aha you need a hilt*, and
so he and the turner follow the children into the courtyard. Weprich
ducks through the workshop door and rummages around in the darkness
for a hilt, finds one in a box, clamps the blade to a lathe and starts beating the blade with a wooden club to drive it into the wood, and as the
blows of the club resound dully but rhythmically across the yard and out

layer upon layer of paint until the entire wooden body began to glow. It had been in Barneck, when he was in the service of Councillor Hornig. The most beautiful bird the human eye has ever beheld, adorned with painted wooden feathers that he had inserted one at a time until they created a lifelike feathering, even the plumed train could be folded out if you pulled the loop of the attendant string. Then too the yard had been full of children; they had stood still, spread out, the tall black grass reaching the waists of the smallest. And in the shady linden avenue the servant folk stared wide-eyed, the women with their apron corners raised to their chests, all in tense anticipation of Fräulein Schindel appearing on the steps to wadding maker Richter's house to receive the much-discussed gift. And now she is standing there in the doorway, that slut Schindel, grinning at everyone but him and he says *take it, touch it, it's pretty*, and she (but before she has a chance to utter the words he tears them from her lips himself): *WHY, THAT'S NO BIRD*, he says with her voice and slams the back of his hand against the table, *I'LL GIVE YOU BIRD!* causing the older men sitting a few tables away to cower on their benches, startled, and the innkeeper behind the counter scowls at him. He has to come to his senses. He can't lose the plot. He is now in possession of something valuable, he must not let it slip from his hands. He chuckles at himself and grasps the hilt again, squeezes it, and releases; and when he is back out on the street the mild intoxication has become a sense of greater clarity. The space of afternoon is also greater, the shadows are deeper and people's voices, the blatter of hooves and wagon wheels against the cobblestones, all reach out in sweeping echoes. He too moves as though with great delay. He doesn't need to think about or feel where his feet are taking him. His steps run of their own accord, as if this path too were long since predetermined. First he passes by Warneck's again to see if she has returned to the inn. But in the yard in front of the forge all activity has ceased, only the hens on the other side of the latrine cackle persistently as though they were agreeing on something. Even on Sandgasse the gable window is shut and no movement is apparent behind the curtains. Only then does it strike him that she might not have come home at all during the night. Nor could she have been at her mother's, since he did not see her on the inn's stairs or in Warneck's yard. The gnawing unease in his body drives him back to Funkenburg. Many are on their way there now. Young festively dressed couples, packs of already drunken young men. He has already been here today. So he must greet a few people. His gesture is large and far too sweeping; as though to show that he is here to enjoy himself as well he even takes a seat at the edge of a long table and orders yet another half tankard of schnapps. Rowdy men pass by. Here and there groups of young women are pretending to have intent, intimate conversations with each other, while glancing over their shoulders to see who is coming and going. Then the evening deepens. The crowd and shadows surrounding him condense. The darkness seems to acquire a body, hot on the outside, soft inside. On the stage the musicians pick up their instruments. With her right hand around a clutch of beer flagons a portly barmaid squeezes sideways between the tables while waving with her free hand at someone across the restaurant. Then the music breaks out in full force, and couple after couple locked in sweaty embraces can be seen swaying on the dance floor. Crowding. Bared black and gray teeth, the whites of eyes. Right at the front, closest to the low wooden railing that separates the restaurant from the podium where his fellow musicians are standing, the violinist whips like a weathervane in all directions and works his bow arm as though he wished to wrench the world off its axel. Some part of him is greater than all of this, greater than the deepening night, the noise and all the condensing shadows. Some part of him scouts, gaze vigilant, for the slightest detail that could betray her presence: her unconscious but striking way of holding her head high yet slightly tilted back, the smile that always seems to come from below, as though she were trying to appear subservient or submissive, which then turns her whole face into a single great mouth; while the look from those angled eyes never changes, it remains ever watchful, evasive, anxious. But the longer the dance draws on, the clearer it becomes to him that she isn't coming or perhaps had never intended to. Otherwise, she would have long since arrived. Something must have delayed her, perhaps the same thing (the thought no longer allows itself to be batted away) that kept her from going home in the morning or making her way to the inn, where they had surely waited for her in vain. He feels how everything that had been idle and free earlier in the day, when any conceivable promise could have been fulfilled, is now hardening into determination. He must have a serious word with her. He must explain that she is taking this too far, that if it continues in this way one of them will irretrievably fall over the edge. Over which edge, he does not yet know. Only that there is an edge somewhere, a precipice that neither of them should draw near. Even though he doesn't feel the least bit drunk he is now careful where he treads, which has the natural consequence of him knocking right into people who, unlike him, are not exercising the least bit of caution. *Watch where you're going, fool!* one screams and tugs his arm. *It's him, it's Woyzeck!* This is Bon's voice. *A little dog sniffing around for snatch . . . !* Someone kicks his shin. At first he thinks he can continue walking upright but is pulled down in the scrum and falls headlong onto the dirty wooden floor. The sound of Bon's loose change clinking and jingling can be heard everywhere. Someone trips over him and follows up with an angry kick of the boot. Taking the utmost pains, shuffling on all fours, he finally manages to get to his feet and cut a path through the crowd. What's remarkable is that even though he could clearly feel the saber blade jammed between his legs, first when he fell and again when he stood up, it hasn't been in a single one of his thoughts. Which afterwards he takes great pains to explain to the two police constables who interrogated him first, then to Clarus. As though all thoughts of distinguishing himself for Johanna, getting her attention, or even punishing her are of the past. Now it is only a matter of saving them both. He sees Clarus scowl with a mixture of displeasure and aversion.—Saving them from what? he says. Do You think there is any salvation for You? You are a wretch, Woyzeck! A simple creature! Cowardly moreover, you only sidestep and procrastinate. And the fact that You yourself cannot find the words to describe the abhorrent act that You so meticulously planned to carry out is but further evidence of Your devious wiles.—But where and when did he ever give proof of wiles? Had he, before the constables who interrogated him or before Clarus, used words to describe his feelings at that moment, he would have said that something was about to slip away from him irrecoverably, from them both, from him and Johanna. Like when a look or a facial expression fades from the body of a dying person. He didn't

know what was gliding away, only that if it went on like this, then neither
of them would be able to grab hold of it again. It is then, right as he is
about to give up, that he catches sight of her. Like the most self-evident
thing in the world, she is walking in the midst of a crowd of people
making their way across Rossplatz from Nikolaigasse, as if they all had
the same goal in mind. She is walking with her head turned slightly to
the side, as if she were afraid of putting a foot wrong, now and then
reaching out an arm as if to steady or support herself on something. There
must be hundreds of people on the square this sultry Saturday night. But
when he catches sight of her it is as if she alone exists, as if the rest of
the crowd had already merged with the gray twilight. Everything about
her stands out with unreal clarity: her gray hair, what is left of an updo
long since come loose, her chest laboring after breath, her legs which
have a markedly difficult time keeping up with the rest of her body, and
the arm she has reached out as though to grab at or bat away invisible
hurdles, or is she just very drunk and must stabilize herself to keep upright
at all? But even though she steers her steps right to the spot across the
square where he is standing, she does not see him. Not even when she
is only a few strides away and already on her way past and he feels com-
pelled against his will to say her name out loud. *Johanna!* Not even then
does she stop. Or rather: she flinches mid-motion, presumably because
she heard her name being called. But she does not see him. Stepping
into her field of vision doesn't help. *We said four o'clock!* She gives him a
pop-eyed look from under her bangs, then keeps walking, her outstretched
arm wagging this way and that. He runs after her and grabs hold of it
as though it were a lost object he wants to return to her. She stiffens but
does not alter her stride or course, only walks in more clumsily now that
she has him and the loose arm to drag along. *But I waited, all day I waited,
at Funkenburg.* Now she does pause. Is it because she insists on fixing
her gaze on something over his head that he feels how small he is, half
a head shorter than she. How many times have I told you to stop nipping
at my heels, she says, and takes back her arm by prizing off his hand with
hers. He stops. Here something could have happened. He could have
called after her, or she could have turned around and perhaps laughed
at him, doing as she used to do: toy with him. But the space around them

is no longer large enough to hold such disarming games. She has made a fair bit of headway, others returning home have again come between him and her, and the weight of all the waiting he has already endured is such that he cannot stop without being annihilated. Then he wrenches himself from indecision and rushes to catch up with her. *At least let me escort you home,* he says in a voice eager to demonstrate greater decisiveness and again grabs hold of her dangling arm. This time, she puts up no resistance either. They have crossed the square and turned onto Sandgasse. Then she stops abruptly, as if something has caught up with her. *Let go of me, you ass, you limp beast, you . . .* she says her voice so shrill it echoes throughout the street. All he can do is beg. Johanna . . . ? But she is already going through the gateway and resists his attempts to catch hold of her again with sharp, jerking movements. Out on the street, people turn around. Some stop and stare. As though she sensed a sudden weakness in him, she attacks. With more than her fists, which he is now helplessly trying to catch in his own, with her elbows and head too, kicking his shins and kneeing his groin. And if he seized the saber blade then, it was because she was too close for him to be able to defend himself, even against her face, her mouth reeking of spirits and acrid spew. I assure You, Herr Clarus, it was only so she wouldn't get at the sword, or at most to defend myself from her blows, and I can assure You, there was also a moment when all of this noise almost stopped, when she turned to me, placed both hands on my shoulders and leaned her head into my chest, as though she wanted to hold me to her, I assure You, Herr Clarus, I was convinced she had changed her mind and was turning to me out of love, this was before all of that horrible hot blood spilled out of her mouth, spilled over my chest and my face and over the arm I was using to hold her up;

 I assure Herr Clarus that I never wanted
 that it was the last thing I wanted
 to kill the one I loved
 above all else
 loved

At the Inquest of the Detainee (3)
From a letter by Herr Hofrat Clarus to the publisher (conclusion):

In support of my conclusion that the perpetrator was fully accountable, albeit highly cold and callous, when he committed the crime, the following can be stated:

1. that in spite of more than three-year imprisonment, during which he a. continuously was under the strictest supervision of his confessor, the brother of his lawyer, b. had fallen prey to the most violent emotions, c. had endured an uncommonly hot summer and a winter at least as harsh, and finally d. that his imprisonment had a detrimental effect on his health (for example, his gums upon final examination proved to be severely deteriorated from scurvy), that during this time he did not once seem to have suffered from the visions and delusions from which he had hitherto claimed to suffer.

2. that up to the very last days he was apparently indifferent to his cardboard work; the distribution of the alms that had come to him during these days to his relatives, to his former sweetheart, to their shared child and its teachers; participated in the religious practices customary in these circumstances, not reluctantly but neither with any great fervor, he himself wrote the prayer he was to recite on to the scaffold, which on the morning of his execution day he continued to learn by heart; that on the same morning he once again ordered breakfast in the form of a goose leg, in which he partook with good appetite, though with the objection

that it was a bit too large for him, and then ascended the scaffold as if he were climbing into a horse-drawn carriage. The reason can in part be attributed to his conviction that after death the soul enters straight into paradise, of which he had a very material conception, in part due to his hope nurtured to the very last of a pardon, which explains why he deliberately tried to draw out his self-conceived prayer as long as possible, which he recited in a loud voice and with artificially expansive gestures. Thereto perhaps a certain *soldiership*, a contempt for death, as well disgust at his own way of behaving during this entire spectacle came to bear.

THE CELL: IT INCREASINGLY RESEMBLES the room he carries within. The riven walls, the worn, unwashed floor, the gray drab light that wanders from wall to wall, sometimes swelling to reach the bunk where he lies but still cannot reach into anything. Nothing more than an indifferent play of light: a dial of sun and darkness that measures not the hours of the day and the passing seasons, but the time through which his ruined life is slowly ebbing out, pulse by pulse. In his early days in the cell, when he examined each nick and scratch on the wall made by those who had sat in this cell before him, he thought the walls resembled a landscape: with valleys, hills, and fields. Now he realizes that they represent a face. But in order to see the face clearly one must step outside the cell. Which is an impossibility—at least for him. Sometimes he thinks it is his own face on the wall. Sometimes he thinks it is God looking at him from inside himself.

WHEN THEY ARRIVE ON THE afternoon of July 30th to inform him that his petition for clemency has been rejected, he is neither dismayed nor even particularly anxious. What is happening now has already happened. A thousand times they have stood in the cell reading or quoting something from some record, or told him to stand up and turn around or open his mouth wide or look to the right or to the left, and he has long since learned to recognize them by their footsteps and voices in the corridor. In addition to Prison Commandant Richter, the lawyer Mr. Hänsel, Pastor Oldrich, Doctor Stöhrer and his confessor Pastor Hänsel, the deacon from the St. Thomas Church, Pastor Goldhorn, who has also arrived to accompany him on his final journey. The assistant prosecutor nods to the court clerk who looks from one to the other before he, with a grand gesture that includes stretching his neck and taking his time to thoroughly clear his throat, unfolds the document in his hands and reads it aloud in a booming voice:

> *Decree of his Royal Highness King Friedrich August I, concerning the delinquent Woyzeck:*
>
> *Pillnitz, June 26, 1824*
>
> *The death sentence stands: ". . . with the decision of the highest court made after both appeals for clemency submitted to his Royal Majesty, dated August 10, 1822, and January 10, 1824, the matter shall rest here. It falls to the national government to take further action."*

After the court clerk has finished reading they look at him as though it is his turn to say or do something equally official. Unable to find big enough words, he flings out his arms and smiles wanly and with marked shame, the smile of one who has landed in a situation he does not know how to get out of. Those gathered seem disappointed, they had expected something else; the deacon and the prison commandant have already turned their backs on him, as the clerk is now doing. Their steps withdraw down the corridor once more, and even though it will take many hours for the cupping glass of the sun to complete its course along the wall, in that moment it is as if all light in the cell has been extinguished.

IT IS NO SMALL TASK to prepare someone whose soul is soon to be parted from its corporeal burden. Pastor Hänsel has a large official briefcase with him, from which he takes a stack of documents, the contents of which he presents in a loud, monotonous voice.

Pastor Hänsel. When Your hour has come, after you have been granted Your last request, You will be led to the courtroom where the charges against You will be read out anew. These charges shall be heard without interruption by You or any other party. Afterwards, You will admit your guilt with a firm and clear but also humble voice, after which the judge will break the staff over his head and announce to the court that the sentence shall be carried out.

Do You understand, Woyzeck?

(He says that he understands what Pastor Hänsel has told him.)

Pastor Hänsel. Thereafter You will be taken to a separate room where You will be dressed in a white robe and a scarf will be tied around Your neck. You shall divest yourself of this scarf once You are upon the scaffold, so take good note of how the scarf is knotted so that You can later untie it without incident. After these final preparations You will be escorted to the scaffold with me on Your left and the deacon on Your right, and when you are at its foot, You shall take leave of us both. You will do this with poise and dignity. You will kneel and receive the blessing. Then You will follow the three executioners onto the scaffold. One of them will be holding the sword behind his back. Do You understand, Woyzeck?

(He says that this too he has understood.)

Pastor Hänsel. When You ascend the scaffold it's important You do so with dignity, as well. Remember, it is that last time Your eyes will rest on the people whose judgement has fallen upon You. It is also the last chance they have to form an opinion of You. You must make a determined yet humble impression. Ascend the scaffold with firm steps, but not so quickly as to suggest arrogance. Believe me, Woyzeck. Many have failed in this. They believed themselves to be strong in this hour of need and had a spring in their step, only to make a rash and defiant impression. It is a difficult balance to strike, Woyzeck. Only the most skilled can master it. And when You are standing up there You shall recite Your final prayer with a firm and loud voice, but also in such a way that makes clear Your remorse. In all this, nothing may go wrong. To assure You of this, I will now help You find Your last words. It is important that they in truth come from the heart.

The priest digs around in his briefcase, takes out a pen, ink and ink pot, puts it all on the desk.

Pastor Hänsel. There is now time for You to write Your last will and testament, along with any other confessions You would like to make before the court, Your confessor, and the citizens of the town. Choose these words wisely, Woyzeck. Never has so heavy a burden rested upon a man's shoulders as when he is called upon to author his own legacy, a legacy that will live on far longer than the memory of his deeds. But it can also be a balm to a soul in need who, in genuine pursuit of penance, faces God and humbly asks to be freed from his burden.

HE DOES NOT KNOW WHAT to do with all the blank pages. To whom should he write? To Johanna? To the dead Woost? He looks at his hand. He remembers the time in Vilnius when he tried to grab hold of the glass but his hand would not obey. How is it possible that in one moment a person can be in full possession of their faculties and in the next not be able to sense anything at all, how the blood now streaming in his veins will be shed like that of a slaughtered animal when the executioner strikes his head from his body. Perhaps in the rain of blood that seeps into the scaffold's planks it will be possible to read God's script.

At random, he begins to fold a couple sheets of paper at their corners, then without quite knowing what his hand is doing, he has folded another few, and soon the sheets of paper have become a scaffold.

Or possibly a theater?

Perhaps it is all the same. In any case, there is a gallery, at least, in the form of three interlinked sheets in front of a stage with a cyclorama and backdrop curtains on either side. There are figures who can step upon the stage. A king or a bishop also plays the role of a hangman, the miter he wears on his head could just as well be an executioner's hood. Here is a slightly smaller figure that resembles an angel, wings fixed to a slit on its back. By moving the paper flap on the figure's back up and down he can make the angel wings rise and fall.

What light there was in the cell has long since vanished. But ever since newspaper distributor Haase forbade him to work by candlelight while sitting up in the attic with his paperwork, he works as easily in darkness. Now he doesn't even have to do so in secrecy. In the darkness the riven walls are gone and his hands reach into all of space, to the outermost stars and planets in their orbits. He folds angel shoes for Little Heart. They must be soft and light if she is to rise up to heaven by the strength of her small, springing steps alone.

HE RECEIVES A LETTER FROM Marie Thiessen, now Wienberger by marriage, in Stralsund. In the letter she no longer calls him Johann, or even Wutzig. Not Woyzeck either. But Wutzek. *Dear Herr Wutzek*, she writes. It sounds alien. As though she were addressing some third party with but a similar name.

For this *Wutzek* she recounts that in February she was visited by the police who had questions to ask about how he comported himself in her company, as well as his other activities in the city at the time of his stay there. The visit has greatly upset her. Not least because she is an honorable and respected woman and a visit of this kind could damage her and her family's reputation. But also because it gradually dawned on her what a terrible position he had put himself in. Then, and on several occasions thereafter, she had told herself that this was an end she could have foreseen, that she had seen the evil within him. If he must now suffer the worst punishment for his actions, may God nonetheless have mercy on him when his final hour is come and at least ensure that his suffering be brief.

She would also like to add a few words about her daughter, who is now at school, a privilege she herself was never granted and for which she has her husband, the good Wienberger, to thank. Since she knows that Wutzek is fond of the girl, the little he has been able to see of her, she only wants to say that if any spare funds are left behind by him, she would appreciate it if he would keep the girl in mind.

Perhaps then God will look more mildly upon his many iniquities. And so she adds the address where she wants the money to be sent.

PRAYERS OF INTERCESSION ARE OFFERED up to him in the city's every church. Each night he sits on the empty bunk and listens to the bells' heavy iron clang slowly fading along with the last daylight. Then the corridor falls silent, too, as do the other detention rooms. Only the heavy, close August heat is still in the cell as though it came from the very walls and a heavy, disturbingly oppressive silence reigns, as though the entire prison were holding its breath.

One evening, long after darkness has already engulfed the cell, he is roused from a troubling dream by the sound of light footsteps in the corridor. The cell hatch is slid aside, but where once Conrad's face would appear illuminated by a hand lantern is now nothing. No face, no darkness. He gets up, shouts in alarm: who goes there? Then the key is heard scraping in the lock and the door is pushed open.

Then at once, he knows who it is.

Through the massive walls comes a fresh roar from the Memel River, the air is filled with the sound of water masses traveling at a speed that defies human comprehension.

Pastor Oldrich has aged. When he takes off his hat he sees that his once coal-black hair is now almost completely white.

Could it be that death is visiting him in the guise of a prison chaplain? But the hand that reaches out in the darkness to touch his neck and head is soft and warm, as if it wanted nothing more than to draw him out of darkness and confusion. And the voice when it finally speaks is the same: as if it only wanted to listen to his breathing, the beating of his heart, to make sure he is still alive, and without Pastor Oldrich requesting it, they kneel together beside the bunk.

At the prematurely aging priest's side, W. lowers his forehead to his clasped fingers and recites the words to the only prayer he knows.

> *A sinner, poor and wretched, I am.*
> *To Thee my heartfelt thanks and praise are due.*
> *O Merciful one.*

The darkness has deepened now. As he kneels in the dark cell he can barely make out the body of the priest beside him, knows only that he is there, like the sound of the river still flowing and rushing as if following its course right behind the notched cell wall.

Pastor Oldrich. Do you know, Woyzeck, since we last saw each other I have given much thought to the vision you said you had while in military service. You said that you saw your rival's hand blacken into a crucifix before you on the battlefield. Do you remember this?

Woyzeck. Yes.

Pastor Oldrich. And do you also remember that you confessed your anguish over no longer being able to clearly differentiate between the work of demons and the Lord's blessed wonders?

Woyzeck. Yes!

Pastor Oldrich. Come closer, and I will tell you a story.

It is said of none lesser than the archbishop of the country of Mexico that before entering the sacristy each morning, he would kneel as you and I are doing now before the body of Christ and kiss his feet. These were uncertain times in the country and the bishop had many enemies. One of them snuck into the church before the bishop arrived and covered Christ's feet with poison, and the bishop would surely have been dead had he, upon his arrival a few hours later, not seen that Christ's body and aspect had blackened with the poison.

This took place many years ago, and the story has been told many times and each time it is told it has been emphasized that Christ, in order to spare the bishop from certain death had he on this morning as every other kissed his feet, absorbed the poison himself. The bishop then went on to live and serve for many more decades. In this way Christ secured the reigning order with a miracle.

Perhaps the story is not as it has always been told. Perhaps Christ absorbed the poison in the first instance not to save the bishop but to prevent the murderer from committing his deed.

The person Christ saw was the *murderer*.

You know, Woyzeck. The importance of doing good deeds and so be blessed for them is much discussed among priests and the learned, as though our salvation were assured only if we did right and acted justly according to God's law. Forgiveness, however, is little discussed, and do you know why, Woyzeck? Because it's not possible to put a lien on the future with forgiveness. He who is prepared to forgive must also be prepared to risk everything. He who forgives does not only take on another's debt, he also takes on their misdeed. It was this that Christ showed the bishop and the whole congregation, but no one understood.

Nevertheless, forgiveness is all that is true.

At the same time—and this is the story I mean to arrive at, Woyzeck—there lived in far-flung Mexico two brothers, both children of God, equal to each other, as you and I are, Woyzeck, as we are all equal before our Creator.

With these two brothers it was such that one of them had committed a horrible deed. No one knows why or what the purpose of this deed was, only that it had been committed and it could not be undone and he had to carry it with him for all eternity. And with each passing day the burden of this deed only grew heavier, ultimately weighing him down so deep into the ground that he would no longer be able to move and only the burden would exist, not the man who had borne it.

But then, right as this is about to happen, something comes to light.

It comes to light that a mistake had been made.

In fact, it was the *other* brother who committed the gruesome deed, the one who had borne the burden had suffered unjustly.

Let us now say, Woyzeck, that you were the one who had unjustly been forced to bear this burden, would you be prepared to forgive the brother who should have borne it instead?

Such is God's forgiveness, Woyzeck. God looks after the burden and not the bearer of it, and before him we are all brothers, and no burden we bear is ever too heavy for him to bear it in our stead.

Be sure of this, Woyzeck:

The moment you are ready to forgive all, all shall in turn be forgiven.

ON THE LAST NIGHT HE dreams that he is walking through a vast alien landscape. Everywhere are stones and boulders, and it is bright as midday even though there is no sun in the sky, or even a sky. The boulders, taller than men, stand close together and are all of wildly irregular shape with hard, sharp edges, so they can't be climbed or squeezed between. He does not know how long he has been here. In the dream there is no time. He puts his hand on one of the boulders and notices that the rock is both damp and warm. He leans in to see what is making the stones sweat but the light that surrounds him is at once too hazy and too sharp for him to discern anything. It strikes him that the landscape is not something through which he is fleeing, but the landscape is *flight* itself, all that he has fled and left behind. This is how God sees his life. He wakes up despondent, tormented, and with a great pressure on his heart.

A FEW HOURS LATER, WHEN they come to pick him up, the cell is no longer a cell and all that exists is a great passel and the sound of voices shouting and objects incessantly being moved around. But he only has to shut his eyes to see the walls dripping with moisture like the stones in the dream and it occurs to him that the moisture is the sweat that ran down the face of God when He saw his life lying there so misspent and derelict and desolate.

Sweat is also running down Pastor Hänsel's face as he leans forward and whispers, his breath thick and piercing with acetone.

You do remember everything You've learned, don't You, Woyzeck. The prayer! Remember it word for word! And that You have the sense to comport Yourself now that You've come to Your end?

Consider Your legacy.

Pastor Hänsel places a firm hand on his shoulder, palm closed and knuckles out, as if to inspirit courage and strength. But the gesture only exacerbates the need to urinate, which he is already struggling to contain. Conrad, the wooden mask who does not for a moment let W. out of his sight, clearly perceives his distress and hurries over with the latrine bucket, which has recently been emptied for the sake of decency.

Don't I get any food? he says so as to divert all these gazes that continue to stare unremittingly even as he stands astride the bucket with his trouser flap down.

It is clearly a winning line. Everyone laughs.

We've prepared a big breakfast for You, Woyzeck. And into the cell strides a third person, a waiter by the look of his attire, bearing a goose leg on a wide platter. A table is set out, a napkin, cutlery, and beer.

This is your last meal, Woyzeck. Bon appétit.

He knows, and his onlookers know, that he has a mouth full of rotting teeth, so he can't possibly consume this food. Therefore he says: my, what a big, fat goose thigh, what, you couldn't have found a bigger one?

Which is appreciated even more. This laughter is almost gay.

Platter and cloth and plate are removed and Doctor Stöhrer steps forward. He is ordered to bare his torso. But his hands are not up to the task. He tries to make it look like the shaking has moved into his shoulders and is in fact resounding laughter and says that he can't unbutton his shirt because the goose thigh made his hands greasy. He shows them his hands. Again appreciation is shown through laughter.

What a buffoon! someone is heard saying.

But by then Conrad, ever at the ready, is underway unbuttoning his shirt. It is quickly pulled over his head, and Doctor Stöhrer steps forward with an auscultation horn and listens to his heart and pulse and pronounces loudly and clearly to the clerk, who has slunk to the front, that the delinquent is in good health. Fresh clothing brought out. These are the white garments, the pants and shirt with black side stripes that Pastor Hänsel told him about earlier.

Now there is no question of him doing anything for himself. Helping hands are everywhere, threading his legs into pants and arms into sleeves and tying the band at the waist. From behind someone wraps a scarf around his neck and knots it.

Then he is given a shove in the back and is driven in the middle of the crowd out of the cell where he has spent the last few years, down the long corridor through which he has thus far only heard footsteps echoing, the floor of which he can no longer recall ever having set foot upon. He can no longer remember anything. It is as though he were treading backwards through his own life out into something entirely foreign to him.

THERE IS A FEBRILE DIN in the courtroom that morning. People are scrambling to get as close to the delinquent as possible, ideally close enough to brush up against his body or face, as though touching this man who has done evil will by some magic protects against the very same evil, or might the touch fill another function: to lay a never-so-fragile bridge between the living and the one who before long (yes, the time is nigh) will be among the dead.

And so it was said even afterwards, by those who managed to come into contact with the condemned as he entered the courtroom or who had witnessed the final hours of his life from a seat farther back in the hall, that the impression he made was not dispirited nor resigned but deeply confused. He had to be led into the room. And each time the guards, because of the considerable crush on all sides, for a second were forced to release his arms, he stood there dumbly, as though he hadn't the faintest idea where he was or what he was expected to do next. Even in the dock, to where he was finally led, he sat speechless, his lawyer on his left and his confessor on his right. Then the court was called to order and Judge Deutrich entered the room in full regalia. Without hesitation, he asked one of the bailiffs to bring the delinquent to the bar.

W. is led forward and stands before his judge. In the room every splinter of word has fallen to the floor and a great echoing silence has arisen, greater than the great hall in which they are and where the verdict shall now be pronounced.

Judge Deutrich. Johann Christian Woyzeck! Before this court I ask you: Do you confess that on June 2, 1821, you, by your own hand using a dagger-like instrument which you carried on your person, you killed Frau Johanna Christiana Woost with several stabs to the chest?

W. [after the bailiff elbows W. hard in the side] Yes!

Judge Deutrich. Do you confess to having committed this act?

W. Yes!

Judge Deutrich. Then hear your sentence:

Since you, Johann Christian Woyzeck, have confessed before this court that on June 2, 1821, you, using a dagger-like instrument which you carried on your person and with several stabs to the chest, killed Frau Johanna Christiana Woost, I, Doctor Christian Adolph Deutrich, in my capacity as acting criminal judge of the city of Leipzig, declare this sentence to be lawful and in accordance with the law and that for the murder of Johanna Christiana Woost, to which you have now confessed, you shall be sentenced to death by sword.

Deutrich rises, lifts the judicial mace over his head, and breaks it in two.

The mace is broken!

Apparitor, summon the executioner!

A bailiff rushes over to the tall doors, opens one a crack, and whispers something to someone outside, and at once, as though they had only been waiting for this thin whisper, church bells fill the hall anew with their heavy iron clang.

They ring for the third time that morning.

crowd is screaming curses and the cuirassiers take one threatening step forward, and without him noticing two men have fallen in alongside him: to his left walks the prosecutor and to his right a serious gentleman in full canonicals. This must be Deacon Goldhorn. He wonders where the prison chaplain is. If the man is farther back in the procession. But he is not allowed so much as a turn or a twist of the head, the nudges to his back and shoulders intensify, and the spectator's cheers rise higher and higher, finally reaching all the way up to where the unending thunder of church bells has fitted the sky with an iron lid. Or has something been stuffed in his ears? Once again he does not understand why everything has to be so visible. The scaffold: the steps he will climb to heaven. And the cobblestones all around and under him bestrewn with fine sand, as though to catch the blood before it has even begun to flow. And all of these voiceless, faceless people screaming and crying out even though he is not yet dead. Even though it is not yet clear if he will die at all. At the last second someone might reach out a hand and save him. Hänsel, or someone else. Little Heart. Now he is standing at the foot of the scaffold and the cuirassiers have taken a few steps back. He wills his knees to buckle so that he may lie on the ground, but instead he notices that he, by his own power, is walking up the scaffold steps and the crowd notices that he is walking unaided and cheers erupt. He glimpses the faces around the scaffold, as though scores of gaping mouths and staring eyes have been tossed at random atop of the crush of bodies. Following one step behind are the three executioners. Their footfall is so heavy it sets the scaffold asway. But he cannot walk any faster, neither can he lift his eyes. He gestures boldly with one hand, as if about to speak, but only loses his balance and so must be supported again. And this is not the audience's will or desire. He senses the crowd's rising impatience. People are squirming. He kneels before the chair and prays the prayer as Pastor Hänsel instructed. He tries to emphasize certain words so that their meaning won't be misunderstood. The wave of discontent threatens to surge, but subsides as soon as he stands back up. Firm hands are placed on his shoulder and guide him onto his seat. In the high hollow of the sky, birds of prey are already circling. It is silent. He sees that there is a hatch under the chair. Is he really meant to fall right through it? The same firm hands that led him to the chair untie the scarf and place a blindfold over his eyes. Behind the blindfold his naked eyes stare straight up at the sky. Up there it is crystal clear, an icy clear light that he does not recognize. Inside that light the birds draw ever tighter circles. *Lord, help me!* They plunge.

Woyzeck's last words
[prayer, conceived of and recited by he himself, in devotion]

I am coming, Father! Yes, heavenly Father, Thou callest me, Thy gracious will be done, I praise Thee with all my heart, glorify Thy name and honor Thee, O Thou most Merciful, that in spite of my great guilt Thou dost look upon me with steadfast love and Thou dost allow me a dwelling place in Thine house forevermore, I thank thee for after all the suffering I have endured Thou dost wipe away the tears I so often shed for Thee. Father! Into Thy hands I entrust my spirit! For Thee I live, for Thee I die, and for Thee I rise again to life. Amen!

O Lord, save me! Lord, send now prosperity!

COUNCILLOR CLARUS HAS SECURED A place where he can stand unobscured so he can clearly see what is taking place on the scaffold, just as later in the day once the corpse has been transported to the anatomical theater, he will secure a seat close enough to follow the removal of each and every one of the delinquent's organs. It is a sunny day, Clarus feels hot in his thick coat and hat. Thank God it all transpires without delay. At exactly 11 o'clock the mace is broken over the delinquent's head and the bells of the city's every church begin to chime. Mr. Hänsel and Deacon Goldhorn emerge from between the cuirassiers, between two guards the delinquent follows in the row behind. At the sight of the condemned man an ever-louder murmur rises from the crowd. He looks out over the sea of spectators, they are everywhere, in windows, on roofs, on balconies. And of course he regards this with satisfaction, because this is in no small part his own doing. But his satisfaction is shadowed by a vague unease. His demonstration of the delinquent's guilt may be an indisputable fact, but perhaps one of little value as seen from the perspective of the onrushing crowd. The mob craves justice, not necessarily clarity. And although the court councillor would never admit it, not even to himself, he is aware that the two concepts cannot always be reconciled. Now the retinue has reached its destination and the prisoner is climbing the scaffold. Deacon Goldhorn and Pastor Hänsel remain at the foot of the stairs, as does Mr. Hänsel and his assistant. Up there, the chair has already been set out, and behind it the three executioners take their place. The prisoner hardly seems to know where he is but nevertheless performs the actions expected of him, if but with the slowness that even after years of conversation Clarus has not yet learned to endure. At last the scarf is untied and one of the three executioners steps forward. He raises the sword and severs the head with a single swing. A surprisingly quick procedure. A faint murmur of surprise, or is it dismay, moves through the crowd, which may have expected more. The headless body stays seated for a brief moment, as though it too were surprised by the speed at which everything has transpired; then the trapdoor opens and chair and body fall from view.

Immediately thereafter the cuirassiers march off, the crowd disperses, and the dismantling of the scaffold begins.

At the Inquest of the Detainee (4)
From a letter to the editor by Herr Hofrat Clarus (conclusion):

At the autopsy, performed under the direction of Doctor Bock, all organs in the head, chest, and abdominal cavities were found to be in *perfect condition*, with the exception of *the heart* which revealed itself to be surrounded by an unusually large amount of fat. When the head was separated from the body only a weak stream of blood rose from the carotid artery, possibly a consequence of the heart's reduced propulsive force due to its position during the fall. I recall the newspapers reporting a similar occurrence at the execution of *Sand*, who was reported to have suffered from empyema.

THE HEART REMOVED FROM THE delinquent's body is considered quite remarkable. So remarkable in fact that after it has been placed in a dish, it is passed around for viewing among the medical and legal experts gathered in the autopsy room. Years later the image of that heart beset by fat would still not leave Clarus in peace. Had the embedding occurred as a result of the years-long stay in prison and the poor fare there offered? Or was this condition already present in the delinquent from the beginning and the heart, after embarking upon his miscreant path, embedded itself more deeply, only to then, when its beating no longer resounded, force him into these shameful final acts of violence? Might the fat embedding the heart, then, be the sole and simple explanation for the delinquent's state of mind, an explanation he had so long sought, apparently in vain? Clarus preferred not to delve further into this thought. He was of the opinion that the assessment he made and the attendant punishment were nonetheless correct. It is reasonable to think that the blood which flowed from the carotid artery constituted a relief, as it finally freed this heart of the unbearable burden that rested upon it.

Sources

The Holy Bible: Standard King James Version (kingjamesbibleonline.org: May 24, 2021).

Büchner, Georg. *Woyzeck.* Trans. John Mackendrick (London: Methuen Drama, 2020).

The quote "Så lad bare nat vaere nat, der er alligevel dagslys alle vegne." is taken from Christensen, Inger. "Nattens skygge." *Essays: Del af labyrinten, Hemlighedstilstanden.* Trans. Translator's own (Copenhagen: Gyldendal, 1999).

Heinroth, Johann Christian August. *Textbook of Disturbances of Mental Life or Disturbances of the Soul and Their Treatment,* volumes 1 and 2. Trans. J. Schmorak (Baltimore: Johns Hopkins University Press, 1975).

Herder, Johann Gottfried. *Johann Gottfried von Herder's sämmtliche Werke zur Philosophie und Geschichte,* volume 8 (Tübingen: J. G. Cotta'sche Buchhandlung, 1808).

Luther, Martin. "A Mighty Fortress Is Our God." Lutheran Book of Worship (Augsburg Publishing House/Board of Publication, Lutheran Church in America: Minneapolis/Philadelphia, 1978).